To Anne

CW01020435

REJUVENATION 2

The Rejuvenation Trilogy, book 2

Byddi Lee

To many more
writing meet ups.....
Byddi Lee

Cover designed by The Gilded Quill

Byddi Lee
Visit my website www.byddilee.com

Published in the United Kingdom

First Printing: Aug 2020
Castrum Press

For my wee sis

CONTENTS

CHAPTER 1

"We need to tie Granny down," Bobbie said, leaning forward, then slumping back. The gunshot wound to her upper left arm made every movement agony now that the adrenaline and painkillers had worn off, but Bobbie was in the seat closest to the bed at the back of the hovervan, where Granny lay. Joy, Bobbie's sister sat in one of the two front seats, preparing to manually fly the hovercraft through the next stage of their journey. Bobbie's best friend Ryan Hicks sat in the other front seat. Behind Hicks, Jimmy, an old friend of Granny's, sat in the seat to Bobbie's right. Jimmy shifted forward. Bobbie placed her hand on his forearm. Jimmy was in his nineties and, though relatively fit for his age, he was unsteady on his feet. There was no need for him to get up.

"I'll do it," Hicks said, getting up from the seat in front and moving to the back of the hovervan. Bobbie mouthed a thank-you to Hicks as he passed her. Hicks patted her good shoulder, the warmth from his hand radiating across Bobbie's back, easing her pain a fraction.

"Should have secured her on take-off," Joy said, stabbing a finger at the touch screen. "What the fuck was I thinking?" She massaged between her eyebrows with index and middle finger.

"Go easy on yourself, girl," Jimmy said from the seat beside Bobbie. "It's been a tough day, and about to get tougher." The old man's words landed brisk and matter-of-fact. Tough didn't begin to cover it.

Jimmy had insisted on helping them find and rescue Granny from the research center where they'd discovered Bobbie's boyfriend, Davitt, worked for Belus Corps, experimenting on the ultra-elderly with age-reversing nano-technology. Belus planned to release a virus to deliver the nanobots to an unsuspecting population. The virus would inject the nanobots into the elderly, and the nanobots would rejuvenate them, making them younger, turning their eyes bright orange, and making them psychotic at the same time.

Bobbie had stolen that virus but had been shot in the arm and had dropped the vials inside the hovervan, releasing the virus and exposing them to it. Now the bright orange of Jimmy's irises told Bobbie that the nanobots were at work in his body too. How long before his white hair and matching white mustache began to show the pigmentation of his youth?

They had escaped in the hovervan and were en route to a safe place Joy knew of – safe once they had crossed the super-heated dustbowl of California's Central Valley. Terrified, Bobbie stared out of the hovervan's windows, appalled at the magnitude of the giant dust devils springing up at random across the floor of the valley, a malignant forest of whirling tubes.

Bobbie closed her eyes to block out the terror but was haunted by the image of Granny's contorted face as she had died at Bobbie's hand less than twenty-four hours earlier. Granny had been out of her mind from the effects of the rejuvenation nanobots and had attacked Joy. In a split-second decision, Bobbie had used the taser on Granny, not realizing that the electric current would destroy the nanobots that supported Granny's youthful cells.

Granny had aged from her thirties to her nineties in a matter of seconds, as Bobbie had looked on horrified. But it didn't end there. Without the nanobots to support the cells, the cells had disintegrated completely – every single cell in Granny's body broke down at the same time.

Bobbie opened her eyes, gulped in a lungful of air, but couldn't shift her grief or her guilt. She had killed her beloved Granny, and the thought crushed her. Nothing could tear her mind away from those moments. Even this view of hell from the passenger window of the van could not dislodge those harrowing last memories of her beloved Granny. Now they flew twenty-five meters above a swirling mass of sand and dirt that made up the Central Valley of California. Beyond the dust-laden whirlwinds, the mountains shimmered from the heat, or was it moving sand? Bobbie couldn't tell for sure.

It was only an hour after dawn, with the air conditioning on full, but sweat dripped down Bobbie's face, dampened the hair on her scalp, and puddled in the creases of her limbs. The salt from the sweat stung her eyes, making her blink rapidly to clear her vision. Former patches of sweat on Hicks' shirt had now joined, making his entire tunic damp, the wicking sensorfabric not able to keep pace with the production of moisture and only drying out along the bottom edges. Jimmy had sloughed off the tweed jacket he always sported in the tropics of Ireland.

They were only halfway across the Central Valley of California. Joy flew the craft manually to take them around the dust storms.

"The dust storms shift so erratically that the computer system controlling the self-drive can't recalculate a new route quickly enough to avoid them," Joy had explained. Ironically, she had to drive slower than the self-drive would to gauge the storms' direction.

How much hotter would it get before they reached the camp in the Sierras Joy had told them about? Bobbie hadn't wanted to go there. She hadn't wanted to leave behind her work, her home, and everything she knew, but now that the four of them were wanted criminals, there wasn't any choice. And Davitt, her ex, what was he now? Their prisoner?

Davitt lay on the floor behind Bobbie: drugged, bound, and tied to the leg of the bed. Yes, Davitt was definitely their prisoner. Bobbie would never forgive him for the way he had developed the Rejuvenation technology with no regard for the people he was supposed to be helping. Of course, he had needed people to trial the application of the nanobots, but Davitt hadn't asked the ultra-elderly their permission. Granny had never given her consent, nor would she have, Bobbie knew, because Granny had been accepting of the fact that she had lived a good life and her time was near. Granny had spoken of being prepared to join her daughter, Bobbie and Joy's mother, in the afterlife. Bobbie's grief was too raw to follow that train of thought. She needed to close off her mother's recent death, deal with it after this craziness was over. Being a doctor had trained Bobbie to compartmentalize her feelings, but with so much to process in so short a time, Bobbie wondered if she would break under the strain of it. She looked around her at the people in the hovervan: her sister, her best friend, and darling old Jimmy. Bobbie would find the strength for them, the people she had left in this world, the ones she loved the most.

Hicks returned to his seat and buckled in again. He hauled in a deep breath, rubbing his hands up over his face and through brown hair that stuck straight up, damp with perspiration. His fingers traveled down the back of his head to cradle the nape of his neck. Swinging the seat around on its pedestal, he peered at Bobbie with gray eyes beneath furrowed brows. "Your arm any better?"

"I'll live." Bobbie flexed her elbow. Her upper left arm stung where the bullet had ripped through the flesh. The wound-glue had healed the skin quickly, but the muscles inside would take longer. "How's your side?"

"Not so bad." Hicks looked down at a spot on his sensorfabric tunic, rusty from the dried blood that had oozed through the bandage covering where a laser bullet had carved a slice of skin from under his ribs. He was lucky to be alive.

"Don't worry, I just need to go around these bad boys," Joy said, steering the hovervan wide of the nearest spinning columns of dust.

Everyone leaned as the hovercraft banked with the turn. Bobbie's arm throbbed. Joy set the van on a straight course, and Bobbie felt the pain ease.

"'Bad boys'? Looks like a bloody tornado to me!" Jimmy held tight to his armrests, his arthritis-swollen knuckles whitening.

"Totally different things." Joy kept her eyes on the way ahead as she went on. "Dust devils are caused by dry heat and go up. Tornados start at the top and go down." Joy looked back at them quickly and threw them a grin before facing forward again. "But don't worry, I've run this route plenty of times. It's just a bit twisty. Might want to keep a sick bag handy, big sis."

"Great!" Bobbie grunted, feeling her stomach lift, right on cue.

"Oh shit! Where did that come from?" Joy punched at keys on the console in front of her.

Hicks rotated back to face out the front window just in time to lock in his seat.

The hovervan veered to one side.

Bobbie's sensorfabric clothing couldn't wick her sweat away fast enough and left her sliding in her chair. Fighting against the centrifugal force, Bobbie's belt felt too flimsy as she rattled in her seat, pain searing through her left arm and shoulder. The van changed direction again, flinging them the other way.

"What the fuck!" Davitt's words accompanied a loud bang, followed by a groan from behind Bobbie. The floor offered little traction. He was only secured by the wrists, not that she would any sympathy for him. Bobbie considered giving him another sedative. They couldn't risk him knowing their location, but when she twisted in her seat to look at him, she realized the knock to the head had left him unconscious. No point wasting the sedatives.

In front, a half a mile out, a gigantic dust devil – bigger than the others – swirled a hundred meters into the sky, a spinning beige tube twisting towards them. Bobbie could hardly believe the size of this beast.

Joy swung them left, out of its path, tipping the van so that the downward thruster lost effect, and they dropped five meters before she had the thrusters righted.

Davitt slammed back down onto the floor behind Bobbie with another grunt.

"No, no, no-no-no!" Joy's alarm blasted adrenaline through Bobbie.

A second dust devil of similar size slipped into view from behind the first, and skittered across to their left, about a mile from them.

"Can't you just go higher and avoid them?" Hicks asked.

"No, this hovervan can't go higher than twenty-five meters above the surface, less on steep terrain," Joy answered.

Bobbie could see that most of the dust devils were as high as that. They had to fly between these monsters to get to the safety of the Sierra Nevada mountains. Saliva thickened in Bobbie's throat as she swallowed back fear and nausea.

"Girl, you weren't kidding when you said the dust devils got pretty big here," Jimmy said. "I thought you were exaggerating."

"I wish I had been," Joy said. "But that's not all. That powdery sand is so fine that it barely settles. If we go down here, we'll suffocate in the dust, if we could bear the heat."

"Then let's not go down here," Hicks said.

"If that dust overwhelms the cooling system for the engines, we'll have no choice." Joy tweaked the control stick, and they glided equidistant from the revolving pillars on either side of them. Despite her terror, Bobbie marveled at Joy's skillful flying, at how she kept her cool and seemed so in control.

Bobbie had only ever witnessed Joy as the drama queen – her crazy kid sister, fourteen years younger, who never took responsibility – yet here was Joy, with their lives in her hands. Who was this woman, twenty-one and totally in command of her world? Why had Bobbie never seen this side to her before?

"How far have we to go?" Jimmy asked.

"Forty miles as the crow flies, but longer as we wriggle through this lot." Joy pointed at a small cone rising from the ground in the distance.

The land beneath them was mostly flat, with a rippling sheen over the surface – an ocean of sand, ruffled by the wind. Bobbie watched the newly emerging cone grow up from the valley floor into an elongated peak, wobbly and flaccid. The tip of the cone flopped over, and the entire structure collapsed down on itself.

"It's cooler over there," Joy said. "Hot temperatures build the dust devils up, but there must be a pocket of cooler air sliding down from the mountains just there, keeping them down. Looks like a safer route."

The engine revved up a notch, and the hovervan pushed forward. Outside, a high-pitched whistling grew louder. The dust devil to their right shifted closer.

Bobbie gripped her armrests. "Joy, watch out for that."

"I see it."

The van shifted course, but along with the whistling wind, a percussion of tiny pings played off the back-left panels.

Bobbie twisted in her seat and wished she hadn't looked. The devil to the left had crept up on the van, flaying it with its outer tendrils. The world darkened as its shadow fell over them.

"Oh, shit!" Joy furiously worked the panels in front of her. The tube to their left kinked and bent closer to them, flinging dust and debris into their path, and rattling with fury down the van's flank. They cleared the dust just as a crack in the side passenger window next to Hicks blossomed into a silvery spider web across the pane. The window bulged for a fraction of a second, then gave way in a blast of glass cubes, each one slicing anything it connected with. Hicks tucked his head to his chest and covered his face with his arms and hands. Hot wind blasted through the broken side window, hurling dust and glass. Hicks' body shielded Bobbie and Jimmy from the worst of the glass fragments. Beside Hicks, out of the main gust from the broken window, Joy kept her eyes on the scene ahead, steering their hovercraft through the snaking forms on either side. A kick from behind tossed the van forward, nose down. It dropped and righted as the gyroscope controls fought to keep them level.

Fire blossomed in Bobbie's left arm. Swallowing back another wave of nausea, she hoped Hicks had covered Granny's body. The glass couldn't hurt her grandmother now, but the thought of Granny suffering further damage was unbearable. Bobbie twisted around in her seat, pain snatching her breath. The small bed was littered in debris, but the blanket was intact. Davitt, face down on the floor, seemed to have escaped damage from the glass too. Heart pounding, Bobbie looked out the front window.

The van climbed. Below them, sand swirled and pocked. Wisps joined the main funnel, while above them, sand and debris released from the monster's pull rained down in staccato on the roof of the van.

The engine sputtered, then revved again.

"Just clearing its throat," Joy shouted above the combined roar of the swirling winds and the whirr of the engines, but her white face and wild eyes belied her brave words.

The dust devils pulled in different directions, now about a half-mile apart, and the world brightened.

"There's the mountains!" Jimmy yelled.

Rolling hills appeared from the low dust clouds of the valley floor, giving way to the steep flanks of the Sierra Nevada mountains about twenty miles off.

In a spurt of movement, the swirling pipe to their left swung towards them, closing the distance between the two dust devils to a sliver of sky. The one on the right bounced away from its brother; then the apex toppled left, and they joined together at the top in a fury of wind and dust.

Bobbie's stomach pitched to the base of her throat as Joy aimed the van at the gap between the twisters lower down and charged towards it. G-force plastered Bobbie against her seat, her lungs laboring to pull in air, her heart slamming against her ribcage.

Above them, one monster sucked in the other. The fallout hammered the roof of the van.

Bobbie covered her face with her hands. The skin on the backs of her hands shredded as incoming dust and debris sandblasted her. Adrenaline kept the pain at bay, but she'd feel it later, if she survived that long.

The van juddered. The engines fell silent. They plummeted. Joy screamed but hung on to her controls, head down against the wind, hair streaming out behind her like a flag. Engines silent, the only noise was the roaring wind behind them and the clatter of loose objects rattling through the van. Bobbie lifted her head long enough to see the impending swirling sand below. She squeezed her eyes shut and braced herself for impact. Perhaps she'd die straight away, avoid the pain of horrific injury and death by suffocation. Ironic to die at thirty-five when she'd spent her life caring for geriatrics and the ultra-elderly.

The engines coughed into life. Joy worked the control stick, lifting the craft out of its dive.

Hicks' whoop was the most joyful sound Bobbie had ever heard.

Behind them, one dust devil remained, moving away from them as it too frayed and fell apart.

"Holy shit!" Hicks said. His face was nicked, and blood trickled from a few different places, accentuating the whites of his eyes.

"Everyone alright?" Bobbie asked, panting hard. She checked the bed, Granny's body still secured and covered.

"I think Davitt's unconscious," Hicks said.

"Leave him till we land," Joy said. "Should be smoother, but no need to risk it for him."

"Well, your in-flight entertainment certainly leaves a lot to be desired, my dear," Jimmy said. He reached over and patted Joy's arm. "Nice flying, though. Your father would have been proud. Damn fine pilot himself."

Joy turned to him and smiled, tears shivering in her eyes.

Bobbie hiccupped back the sob that crested a rush of emotion.

"Not too far now," Joy said. "And at least you didn't throw up, Bobbie."

"Let's not use abject fear as a tactic to avoid motion sickness in the future, though." Bobbie failed to see Joy's source of humor. "Is there somewhere to land other than your settlement?" she asked. "We can't risk infecting them with the virus."

"There's a place." Joy looked ahead as the van lifted up into the hills.

CHAPTER 2

As the hovervan climbed into the foothills, Bobbie's relief was swiftly replaced by foreboding. The first steep mountainous slopes they flew over were barren rock-fields. Ten meters below them, patches of loose scree appeared to ripple as it slid downhill. The peaks rose around them, jagged and stark against a cerulean sky. As the van crested the first series of high ridges, Bobbie pointed at flashes of green in the creases of the deeper canyons. "There's vegetation down there?"

"The highest elevations get precipitation coming in from the north," Joy said. "The water flows through those old riverbeds, but eventually, the heat dries them out at lower altitudes."

"How high are the mountains here?" Bobbie asked.

Joy swung her chair around to face Bobbie. "About twenty-five-hundred meters, but we'll be climbing another thousand."

"Shouldn't you, you know..." Bobbie pointed out the front window.

"Nah, we're in self-drive now. The van calculates the terrain faster than I can, giving us a smoother ride. At least this terrain does jump up to bite us. I'll take over when we get to Lake Helen. It's a tricky approach, and I need to steer us in. It'll be a bumpy landing." She added, "If I can find the place."

Death Valley, Joy had said before. After the flight across the Central Valley, drained of adrenaline and numbed by the stress of the last few weeks, Bobbie's mind whizzed in a flurry of questions. Were they infected by the virus? Were Davitt's nanobots swarming their body tissues at this very moment? And Jimmy? Bobbie glanced over at his profile, where he sat in the back passenger seat beside her, eyes forward, white eyebrows furrowed in concentration, matching white mustache twitching. Would Jimmy turn crazy too? If necessary, would Bobbie have the guts to administer the electric shock to deactivate the nanobots and risk killing him? Christ almighty, she needed a whiskey!

Bobbie tried to check her blink messages, but her Optic Nerve Intercept Visualization was offline.

"Bobbie, stop trying to use ONIV." Joy sounded irritated.

"Sorry," Bobbie mumbled. "I just wondered." How the hell did Joy know Bobbie had tried to access her blinks?

"I know it's hard to get used to being offline." Joy softened. "I was the same at first, but I need to block everyone's ONIV. As far as Belus Corp knows, there's no-one here. If a blink gets traced to this location, we're busted."

"So how do you communicate?" Hicks asked, his face reflected in the windscreen in front of him, giving Bobbie a clear view of his face as she sat behind him. She wondered if he could see her, if he knew she was quietly watching him, soaking him in visually.

"The old-fashioned way." Joy flashed him a smile. "We talk."

"Ha, very funny. You know what I mean." Hicks' smile was warmer than his tone.

"We stay offline. Messengers like me, coming in and out, carry the information for the group in Yosemite," Joy said. "Other than that, it's a total disconnect."

Bobbie had sat alone by her mother's deathbed for weeks, trying to contact Joy. Their mother's last words had been about Joy, but their mother never asked where Joy was. A realization pierced Bobbie. "Mum knew, didn't she?"

Hicks' reflection looked straight at Bobbie, heavy with sympathy.

"I had to tell her, in case I couldn't be there ... and I wasn't." Joy looked down at her hands in her lap, her black hair falling like a veil hiding her face. "But she understood."

"And you didn't trust me to understand?" Bobbie asked.

Hicks frowned, his lips pressed together; he dropped eye contact and busied himself with opening a tube of wound glue. Bobbie felt a chill of aloneness.

"No." Joy looked up. "You had too much faith in the system. You'd never have seen it my way until you actually experienced something like this. You still have too much faith in Lisette Fox, but at least now you know that Belus Corp has a rotten element too." Joy's eyes pleaded for understanding. "We can't afford to lose the site in Yosemite now that we have water and crops."

Bobbie sat mute, her words and emotions an impossible tangle.

"How high is the camp at Yosemite?" Hicks asked, looked up from dabbing wound glue on the cuts covering his arms. "I thought it was much lower. Won't it be too hot?"

So Bobbie wasn't the only one with questions. Joy glanced back at Davitt, and Bobbie followed her gaze – Davitt was still unconscious. That seemed to satisfy Joy.

"It is lower," she said. "Just over one thousand two hundred meters. Luckily, those north-facing canyons cooled quicker than Belus Corp had projected, the east end of Yosemite Valley more so. We can grow crops there now."

"Really? But didn't Half Dome suffer a direct hit?" Hicks asked.

"Yeah, it sure did! That melted granite in Half Dome became rock-form that loses heat more quickly than most rock types," Joy said. "It's pretty amazing, actually."

"And I thought I'd seen it all," Jimmy said, nodding.

The rocks below didn't seem any different to Bobbie – gray, barren, and harsh. She couldn't imagine living here for any length of time. Already she missed the tropical lushness of Ireland.

"Why hasn't Belus Corp moved in?" Hicks asked.

"We've intercepted their heat monitors and are sending them false data." Joy smirked. "Belus Corp thinks it's still too hot."

"It's pretty amazing when you consider how hot and dry the Central Valley is," Jimmy said.

Bobbie admired his sense of wonder; she was too exhausted to dredge up her own.

"The weather patterns here have always been weird, even before the Melters War annihilated Silicon Valley," Joy said. "Here's the kicker. If the state hadn't built a seawall at the Carquinez Strait, the Central Valley would have been underwater, and the people living in the Sierra foothills might have survived the latent heat."

"Were there any survivors?" Bobbie needed some hope.

"A few," Jimmy said. "But not many. Canada accepted them in their refugee program."

"Some made it to Yosemite and formed the Candels," Joy said.

"Candels?" Bobbie asked.

"It's now the collective name for the groups of rebels who joined together after the war," Joy said.

"Rebels." Bobbie sighed. "Because history needs another war?"

"We're trying our best to be peaceful. We're not trying to make war."

"Right."

"Look, enough of the judging." Joy scooped in a deep breath, exhaled with a long sigh, and continued, "Our group is named after Candelifera, a Roman god of childbirth. She carried a candle to light the way for each baby to come into this world. This light wards off the demons who steal children away. The founders liked the name – it accurately describes what we do. Our prime directive is to facilitate the birth of children who would otherwise be terminated because of the Dependency Law. We live under the radar, slipping in and out of Belus Land as we need to," she said.

"And that's all you do? Birth babies?" Bobbie asked.

"You know it's not as simple as that. Belus is very powerful, and as you've seen from what they do with the elderly, their motives are suspect. What drives those? Who knows, but trust me, Bobbie, the Candels are good people. You'll understand when you meet them."

Bobbie felt a rush of impatience. "When?"

“Soon.” Joy turned back to look out the window as the hovervan followed the contours of the mountains. “Their camp is about twenty kilometers due south of us right now. We could be with them in mere minutes, but...”

“We can’t risk infecting them.” Bobbie struggled to believe Joy, but for now, there were more urgent issues. “We need to quarantine ourselves. When Davitt comes round, we can try to get some information out of him.”

“I hope he knows the incubation time for the virus.” Hicks put the wound glue back into the medical case and snapped the lid closed before stowing it in the nearest locker.

“I hope he knows a lot more than that,” Bobbie said. “Bastard!” She looked back at Davitt’s form as he lay on his side on the floor. She couldn’t see his face, but the rise and fall of his ribcage told her he was breathing. Since he was already on his side, there was less danger of him choking. Despite the hatred she felt for him, she hoped his concussion wasn’t serious. They needed his expertise.

When Bobbie had smashed the virus vials, releasing their contents into the van exposing everyone, Jimmy’s irises had turned bright orange almost immediately, a sign he had been infected. Davitt had assured them that since they were younger, with more robust immune systems, they could fight the virus. If so – and it was a big if – Bobbie would be able to extract the antibodies to the virus from their bloodstreams, develop a vaccine, and stop the spread of the virus to anyone else.

But Bobbie still worried that the virus would do what it had been designed to do: deliver a dose of nanobots to their systems that would turn back the effects of aging at the molecular DNA level. Davitt hadn’t run tests on the effects of the nanobots on anyone younger than ninety, and so no-one knew what they would do to people already quite young; and then there was the psychiatric problem. So far, the nanobots had affected brain chemistry and turned the rejuvenated into raving psychopaths.

Granny had been one of them.

Granny’s face, youthful and beautiful, flashed into Bobbie’s mind. With horror, she replayed its transformation into mottled skin and melted features in a matter of seconds. That had been nearly two days ago, given that the journey from Ireland to California had taken almost thirty hours in the hovervan. Those were hours they had needed to catch up on sleep, but the nightmares of the past few days had played in her dreams instead.

Bobbie shook her head and sat up straighter, clambering back to the present.

Below them, a road came into view, snaking along the mountain ledges. In places, massive landslides had wiped it away, leaving plunging gaps.

“Wow,” Jimmy said. “The Tioga Pass. Some of it’s still there.”

“Just about! Look.” Bobbie pointed to a huge boulder higher up, which had been dislodged and was tumbling down the slope. The rock smashed off the mountainside just above the road and cut a path right through the hardtop. It bounced haphazardly, and where it landed, more scree and rubble dislodged, traveling various distances down the slope. Some areas came to a halt, while other sections kept charging downhill. The entire slope looked like a strange creature coming to life, stretching and slithering.

"With no vegetation to stabilize it, the land's particularly susceptible to sliding," Joy said, as if thinking aloud.

"It's always been like that up here," Jimmy said.

"It's worse under the hovercraft's down-thrust." Joy shrugged it off. "There's Tioga Peak, the highest point. We turn north here. Not far now."

The land to the east fell away in a series of bleak valleys and rocky canyons plummeting into a short section of hills. Beyond that, the land smoothed out into a wide valley with a strange shallow, vaguely circular depression – possibly a dried-up lake or salt pan. This wide expanse terminated at another steep wall of rising rocky peaks in the distance. More dust devils danced through this valley, sending a shudder up Bobbie's spine. She really didn't want to go down there. Her head pulsed with pain, and her heart raced. Altitude, she figured. She'd never been this high up, and the thinner air made her body work harder for its oxygen. At least the pain in her shoulder had eased.

Hicks pointed out the western side of the van. "There's a lake!"

Bobbie followed his line of sight. Two joined lobes of bright green water in the shape of a figure eight appeared.

"Saddle Bag Lake." Jimmy's voice held a wistful tone. "I camped here as a very young man."

"You've been here before?" Joy asked. "Why didn't you say?"

"I'm saying now." Jimmy craned his neck to see out the window. "So many things have changed on our planet, and yet these old mountains are still here. That lake, God, I have great memories of that lake." His voice wavered.

"Why not stop here, Joy?" Hicks asked.

"That water's stagnant. The algae's poisonous. Lake Helen's better."

"And completely steep-sided all round," Jimmy added.

"I think I can land it okay."

"You think?" Bobbie asked.

"Well, I'll know for sure in about five minutes." Joy pushed some buttons before taking the control stick. "Switching to manual in three, two, one..."

The van swooped. Bobbie's stomach lurched into her throat, then plummeted. The van soared, rose, dropped again, but stopped short of the rocky terrain beneath them. Ahead the horizon swung and tipped. Bobbie closed her eyes, fighting nausea and fear in equal measure.

"Yes, yes, yes!" The triumph in Joy's voice made Bobbie open her eyes to a cascade of floating black spots, which slowly cleared.

"I found it!" Joy said, leaning forward as far as her seatbelt would allow.

A flat circle of blue lay in the inverted cone made by the mountainsides surrounding Lake Helen. On the southern side, along their approach, a small canyon – more like a gully – delivered a stream to the lake.

"I can't land too close to the stream or the lake, in case of a flash flood." Joy worked the control stick, and the noise notched up a pitch as they hovered within five meters of the surface.

Bobbie gasped at the gradient. It certainly looked like more than a forty-five-degree incline. They had already rolled this van only last week in Ireland on a less steep gradient when they'd been escaping gunmen on their way to rescue Granny.

About twenty meters upslope from the lake, ten meters from the stream, Joy brought the van to land, aligning the van downhill, facing the lake. This way, Bobbie guessed, it was less likely to topple and roll.

"Nice landing, Joy." Relief flushed through Bobbie. "After all your dire warnings, you had us worried."

Joy flicked back her black hair, tipped with blue. "Well, you know, under-promise and over-deliver!" Her laugh sounded like music to Bobbie.

Bobbie was about to undo her seatbelt when a large crack came from somewhere above. The noise echoed off the opposite slopes and merged with a low rumble that grew louder and more terrifying by the second. A sharp thud rang off the roof. A large rock, half the van's size, rolled past them, careening downhill and splashing into the lake.

"Shit! Landslide," Joy yelled. "Tuck in." She rolled up in her seat and covered her head with her hands.

Bobbie mimicked her sister. Her heart hammered. In the small space between her face, her chest, and her forearms, her breath felt hot and damp as she exhaled. A sudden jolt started the van sliding with the rocks, which caught up with them – overtook them in a bumpy percussion of pings, thumps, and bangs. The van skewed left. Bobbie felt her direction of momentum change. A rock smashed through the side windows on the right and ricocheted through the van. Bobbie glanced up in time to see the rock – the size of a fist – smack off Jimmy's back, making him cry out.

"Jimmy!" Bobbie screamed.

"I'm okay!" Jimmy said, but the fit of coughing that ensued did little to reassure her.

The van changed direction, resuming its headlong charge by mercifully staying upright, just surfing along on the surge of the landslide. Bobbie lifted her head, horrified to see how fast they were traveling towards the lake. Davitt was tied in. If they went underwater, he'd drown. And Hicks! Dear God! How could she manage him if he freaked out in the confines of the van underwater – Hicks couldn't swim and had a phobia of small spaces.

Before Bobbie could find any solutions, the van hit the lake nose-first. Water rose in a wave up the front windshield, splashing in through the side window.

The van smashed hard into something solid and stopped, but the momentum flung the van's occupants against their restraints. Pain exploded through Bobbie's injured arm, shoulder, and neck. Her head slammed against the headrest so hard she saw flashes of light interspersed with the black spots. The ache scorched her brain, but a numbing grayness drifted in Bobbie's vision. Heaviness in her limbs beckoned to a soft place without cares. If she just unclasped from reality, Bobbie could float away.

Cold water around her feet made Bobbie jump. She had to get everyone out.

Joy lay slumped over the control panel, her face turned towards Bobbie. Joy's eyes were closed, and blood dripped from a gash on her forehead. Bobbie fumbled with her seatbelt but couldn't find the release.

Get free, get out of this seat, out of this van, out of this lake!

But Bobbie's fingers, still heavy, didn't respond. She pulled at the belt. Nothing. A moment to breathe. Her fingers searched for the release mechanism.

Jimmy sprang from his seat and, in one movement, had reached and unbelted Joy. She slumped against him, but her eyes fluttered, then opened wide.

"Everyone out," Jimmy yelled, but no-one needed to be told.

Hicks was out of his seat and turning to Bobbie, still fumbling with her belt. Suddenly her shaking fingers found the button and the belt released.

"Go, go, I'm right behind you," Bobbie said, the world spinning as she stood up.

Hicks pulled the side door open. They were only in about four feet of water at the deepest point, the back wheels of the van still on dry land, but rocks still shifted on the slopes around them. Hicks stepped back, allowing Joy, supported by Jimmy, to exit.

"Hicks, go now," Bobbie shouted from inside the van behind Hicks. "The van might slide." The wheels didn't turn. They were for show, since the van was a hovercraft. The van's exterior was a shell modeled on the old-style Volkswagen campers.

"I can't leave them," Hicks said, nodding at Davitt and letting his gaze rest on Granny's body for a second before he bent over Davitt and untied him. Davitt groaned and turned over, easing up onto a crawling position. He vomited. Hicks grabbed Davitt by the collar as he gagged and shoved him out of the van.

"Go now, Bobbie." Hicks grabbed her right hand and pushed her to the door. "I'll get Granny." He shoved Bobbie out after Davitt.

"No, wait, you..." The cold water made Bobbie catch her breath. She stumbled. Her head went under. She got her feet under her, felt the bottom, and pushed towards the bank. Surging forward with a few short steps, Bobbie was out of the lake and standing dripping by the back of the van. A random loose rock hurtled by, feet from where they stood, and then splashed into the lake. Other than that, the sliding had stopped. Bobbie scanned the mountain slope, looking for more solid ground, but everything was scree-covered. She didn't want to start another slide by moving too much.

Ahead of Bobbie, Davitt staggered up the beach a few steps past where Joy was sitting, cradling her head in her hands. He sagged to his knees and then onto all fours, retching. The combination of sedative and possible concussion made for a hefty hangover, but Bobbie had no room for compassion for Davitt. She swung towards the lake, looking past Jimmy stumbling on the rocks at the lake edge, and worried the hovervan might sink further.

Hicks appeared in the doorway with a blanket-wrapped body in his arms. The van slid a couple of feet. Joy squealed where she sat on the scree slope, further up behind Bobbie. Hicks fell backward into the van and landed on his butt, still holding onto Granny. He scooted forward, got his feet out the door, and was lowering himself into the water just as Jimmy reached him. The old man hooked his arm under Hicks,' and together they dragged Granny's body to shore, landing on their backs with their feet in the water, their torsos pinned beneath the blanketed bundle.

With a metallic creak, the van shifted but didn't slide.

"It's pinned against a boulder." Joy pointed. "I don't think it will go any further. But I don't think I'm going to be able to get it working again."

Bobbie's dread added to the pressure in her skull. "We're stuck here?"

"Not if I can help it," Jimmy said. "Good job we didn't land too close to the stream, though." He peered at Joy dolefully before adding, "Or the lake!"

"Well, do you want the good news or the bad news first?" Joy asked, unfolding her legs and standing slowly.

"Give us the good news." Jimmy's orange eyes scanned the peaks of the mountains.

"We won't die from the heat or suffocation in Death Valley." Joy rubbed her head with finger and thumb and twisted around, as if taking in the view.

"And the bad news?" Bobbie asked.

"All our matter streamer stock is in the forward compartment, and I don't know if the matter streamer will work." Joy sat down back on the ground, hugged her arms around her shins, and rested her forehead against her knees.

"So, we might starve." Jimmy cast a hand over the lake. "But at least we have plenty of water."

CHAPTER 3

The five rested on the shore of the lake, catching their breath, lined up in a row with Granny's body at the end – rolled in a sheet, reduced to a bundle, so much smaller than she had been in life. At first, Bobbie didn't dare move, fearful that she would dislodge more rocks and start another landslide. Eventually, the pain in her injured arm settled into a dull throb. She was exhausted, but there was too much to do before she or the others could rest.

"We need to get that van onshore," Bobbie said. "Any ideas?"

"Will the slope hold if we shift the van?" Hicks held his hand to shade the sun from his eyes as he scanned the mountainside.

"It's likely the down-thrust from the hovervan caused the slide." Joy shrugged. "But we've no way of knowing anything for sure."

"Doesn't matter either way." Bobbie stood with deliberate care. "We need the matter streamer, or we'll starve. There's a solid patch over there." She pointed to a beach of bare rock. "If we can push the van that far, we stand a chance. I think we can move it between the five of us."

"I'm not pushing anything!" Davitt growled.

"You don't help, you don't eat, shithead," Bobbie said. "Do you know how long it takes a person to die of starvation? And how unpleasant it is when they've been sedated so many times that they go cold turkey when the sedation is withdrawn?"

"Fuck you!" Davitt glared at her.

"Seems like we're going to find out, then." Bobbie took a sedation jet from her pocket. "Let's hope no more vials of the virus broke in the storage case. We're going to need them to figure out the vaccine, especially if this arsehole doesn't co-operate."

"Don't waste that sedative just yet." Jimmy clambered to his feet and walked over to Davitt. "Oh, he'll co-operate. I'll guarantee it." Jimmy brought his face right up to Davitt's and said in a low, cold voice, "Get on your feet now and help."

Davitt gave him a sour look but stood up, head down, shoulders slumped.

"I'll get the cargo straps from the van." Bobbie placed her foot on a rock and tried to jiggle it, stepping up onto it when she was confident it wouldn't move.

"No, you won't." Jimmy stepped more confidently towards the van. "I'm the most expendable member of this team right now. I'll do it after I check that the damn van will work again." He walked into the lake. "No point dragging it out if it's past fixing."

Bobbie took stock of the old man's straight-backed posture and easy gait. Jimmy was rejuvenating already. If he turned sociopathic, she'd have to act quickly. Bobbie's gaze lingered on her dear old family friend as fear ripped at her heart.

Hicks followed Jimmy into the water, his face ashen, lips tight. Little muscles flickered at the jaw-hinge just in front of Hicks' ear. He seemed so weary in comparison to Jimmy. Bobbie felt Hicks' fear, but stopping him from entering the water, emasculating him, would be worse. Hicks had a shitload of courage to face his fears head-on. Bobbie's heart ached for him. She pressed her lips together —no way would Bobbie let her feelings for Hicks get in the way of the love she saw blossoming between him and Joy.

Jimmy, thigh-deep in the water, duck-dove and disappeared around the front of the van. Hicks glanced back to shore.

"Wait and see what Jimmy thinks," Bobbie said from the edge.

They listened to a series of snorts and splashes, interspersed with a couple of sharp coughs.

"Oi, arsehole," Joy interrupted in a loud voice. "Stop that now!"

From the corner of her eye, Bobbie saw Davitt jump back as a fist-sized rock bounced off his upper arm and landed with a clatter on the rocks.

"He was trying to blink!" Joy yelled.

"I was just trying to get us help," Davitt said, rubbing his arm. "I can still put in a good word for you with Slade. We can explain that you were worried about Granny. You only did what any granddaughter would do."

"Shut up!" Bobbie growled, and raised the sedation jet so he could see it.

"I'm trying to help." His words petered out, and Bobbie thought she heard him mumble, "You idiot."

Bobbie ignored Davitt, more concerned about Jimmy, who had just reappeared swimming back, a bodiless head sailing around the corner of the van. He swam a couple more strokes back towards the shore, then stood up in knee-deep water at the back of the van. Jimmy's sensorfabric tunic clung to his narrow shoulders. Bobbie saw dark patches of his chest hair fading into opacity again as the sensorfabric dried. She held her breath, awaiting his verdict.

Jimmy shook his head slowly as he wrung out the ends of his tunic, saying, "The front of the van is shattered. There's nothing but crushed cylinders, and a jumble of wires 'n' circuitry hangin' outta a gaping hole, and it's leaking coolant." He pointed at iridescent blue liquid spreading onto the surface of the water. "We'll have to take our drinking water from the other side until I can figure out how to clear up that mess."

"I heard the fans for the hover components crushing as we slid," Joy said wearily. "The fucking fucker's fucked." She sat down with her head in her hands.

Bobbie's heart sank. Joy looked so beaten. What the hell would they do, stuck in the middle of nowhere with no resources? Bobbie had to focus on them saving themselves before she could even consider how she'd tackle fixing the Rejuvenation fiasco.

"I think I can get the matter streamer working," Jimmy said, poking at a bundle of wires and fiber optic cable that hung out through the dislodged back panel. A shower of sparks made him jump back. "I can do it, I can," he said, more to himself than to anyone in particular.

"We'll strip everything we can out of the van and set up camp here for the duration of our quarantine," Bobbie said. It wasn't much of a plan, but it was a start.

Everyone, bar Davitt, nodded.

"I can get us help," Davitt insisted. "If you tell me exactly where we are."

"Oh, shut up!" Joy said. "Bobbie, if you don't knock him out, I will." She lifted a larger rock.

"Settle down, Joy," Hicks said. "And Davitt, knock it off, or I won't be able to stop her."

"Davitt, get your arse down to the lake." Jimmy's voice held a razor edge, and Davitt followed him into the lake. "Hicks, stop there. We need you to relay these straps to Davitt for securing the van. We'll start with passing the virus case to Joy, so each of us walks as little as possible. We'll take that out of the van first, in case the rocks slide again."

Hicks gave a single nod and stood knee-deep, rubbing his hands together.

Jimmy waded in waist-deep water to the side door of the hovervan and hoisted himself inside it. There was no more rumble from the rocks. The only sounds were the splashing of the men in the water, and the gentle suck and gurgle of water through rocks at the lake-edge.

The van creaked and groaned while Jimmy clambered around inside. Bobbie heard several locker doors open and close, and then the sharp snap of metallic clips, before Jimmy appeared at the door of the van.

"Good news. We've still got the three intact vials of the virus." His teeth flashed white with his grin, and he gave a big thumbs-up. "I checked it out in the van just to be sure. No point risking infecting you – if indeed you aren't infected already. We live in hope."

Bobbie surprised herself with a croaked laugh, not sure if she was more tickled with Jimmy's optimism or his idea of "good news."

Jimmy eased out of the van and handed the case of vials to Hicks, who, in turn, took a few steps to Joy and handed the case to her. Joy brought the case to where Bobbie stood and held it out for her.

"I dropped it before," Bobbie whispered.

"Yay, big sis, 'cos someone shot you in the arm. That hardly counts." Joy took Bobbie's hand and placed it on the handle of the case. "You've got this. I know you do."

"Thank you." But Bobbie wondered if she would really get through this. Her head pumped, and her stomach felt raw. Altitude sickness could be fatal if it caused pulmonary edema. Hopefully, they weren't high enough for that. Fatigue and stress were taking their toll on all of them.

Except on Jimmy. He had tied one end of a pair of cargo straps to the back of the van and given the other ends to Hicks, who walked a few steps towards the shore and threw them to Davitt.

Davitt fumbled the catch and had to bend to pick them up. Joy rolled her eyes, shook her head and went over to help him tie the long strap around a huge boulder that hadn't shifted in the landslide. Bobbie kept her distance; afraid she might be tempted to punch Davitt when no-one was looking.

After a few hours, the beach resembled a yard sale as they stripped out the van. A jumble of assorted cushions piled up beside angular chair frames. The bed had floated, much to Jimmy's delight, and they had transported the matter streamer and the van's batteries on it in several runs. Now it lay drying against a boulder.

The virus vials were secure in the medical case, which Bobbie watched closely as she sat on a cushion on the ground a few meters away from Davitt. He might do anything to gain the upper hand, and Bobbie couldn't bear that. Talking to him was a hateful chore, but she needed information.

"Davitt," Bobbie shouted over to where he lay spread-eagled on a large boulder. "How long is the incubation period for the virus?"

"Not long. A few days."

Bobbie curbed the urge to go over and kick him. "How many, exactly?"

"Seven, eight max."

Bobbie looked at her feet. She still wore the hiking boots she had put on to cross the Burren in Ireland. How long ago? Only two days, but it felt like a lifetime. Bobbie wanted to sleep for a year. Instead, she turned to her sister. "Joy, how long will it take us to walk to the camp?"

"I don't know," Joy said. "It's thirty miles away as the crow flies, but I've never actually walked in these mountains."

"I have." Jimmy came beside Joy. "Long time ago, but there are trails all the way from here to where I think your camp is. It's a two-day hard hike, three at a more comfortable pace." His gaze lingered on Bobbie's injured arm.

"Let's prepare for three days, then," Bobbie said, picking up the case. "We'll quarantine here for four days. It's two days since we were exposed, and three, maybe two, give us our eight days plus some." Bobbie opened the medical case and checked to see if they had sample containers – enough for the autopsy, which couldn't be put off any longer, if it wasn't already too late.

Hicks joined her as she carried the case to where Granny's body lay. Together they stood staring at the small bundle. Bobbie swallowed back a rush of hot tears, tipping her head back and blinking rapidly. Granny's body lay wrapped in Sensorfabric, her face covered. But the image of her grandmother's death throes was scorched into Bobbie's mind.

Granny had aged from thirty to a hundred in mere seconds, and then continued to deteriorate as the nanobots disintegrated within her cells. Her flesh had melted beneath her skin, distorting her beautiful features into a gruesome mask. The mere memory of it hurled pain through Bobbie's heart and threatened to split open her chest. If her grandmother had died a natural death in her old age, perhaps her corpse would now look peaceful. But Bobbie would never see in Granny's features the relaxed expression she'd witnessed in so many of her geriatric patients as pain and life had simultaneously let them go.

"I'll do the autopsy," Hicks said.

Joy hiccupped in a sharp gasp, cupping her hand over her mouth.

"No, I can do it," Bobbie said more smoothly than she felt, and turned to Joy. "Don't look. Go sort out the matter streamer with Jimmy. You know we wouldn't do this if she'd had an ordinary death."

"I know," Joy said softly.

But Granny had died an extraordinary death. She had tried to kill Joy, her own granddaughter. Bobbie had jumped in to save her sister, but now carried the burden of having killed Granny. They needed this autopsy to see more clearly how the nanobots had worked to rejuvenate Granny and eventually contribute to her death, especially now that Davitt had developed a vaccine to carry the nanobots to everyone else. So far, only one of them had shown the telltale signature of nanobot infestation – Jimmy, Granny's oldest friend.

Soon he'd start to look younger. His wrinkled skin was already smoothing, his folded body already straightening. Color would return to his hair, and fluidity to his movement. He'd feel better than he'd felt in years, but Bobbie dreaded seeing any signs of him developing the psychosis that had taken over Granny and the other eleven original rejuvenated patients.

Bobbie bent down and pulled back the sheet. A mass of golden-red hair, the same color as her own, lay in a pile below Granny's bald head. Mottled gray-mauve skin sagged over the bones of the face and skull as though it had been thrown carelessly over facial features, now skewed and misshapen. Creamy-gray fluid oozed from the mouth, ears, eyes, and nose, as if Granny had been liquefied inside her own skin. Sour sweetness hummed from the body, like overripe fruit but more acerbic. Granny's dead body didn't smell like a normal corpse. Bobbie touched her grandmother's hand, but her fingers sank as if she were touching dough.

Bobbie tried to remember Granny, searching for an image of her laughing or smiling, but all that came was the rejuvenated Granny, that beautiful but insane version, shoving a garden fork into a man's guts and pushing him over a cliff.

Bobbie bent double. Bright stars flashed in her vision, interspersed with floating black patches. She panted. Sweat trickled down her back, the wick-away properties of the sensorfabric degraded from the abuse her clothing had received in the past few days.

"Bobbie, it's okay," Hicks said softly.

Bobbie felt Hicks rub her back, and she unfolded, drawing in a long breath and allowing her eyes to focus on the body again.

"I'm here," he said softly. "Whatever you need me to do, just ask."

Bobbie clutched his arm, steadied herself. "I can do this. It's not her anymore."

"Let's grab a drink of water and start again in five," Hicks suggested, his breath brushing past her ear as he turned Bobbie gently around.

"Okay." Bobbie nodded and walked past Davitt, who was sitting on a pile of cushions.

Davitt rounded on her as she drew near.

"Where have you taken me?" he snarled. His curly black hair, a tatted mop, framed his pale face. Bobbie reckoned Davitt would survive the smack to the head that had knocked him out, but he did look worse for wear. Gray smudges stained the skin beneath his dark blue eyes. Blood had dried on his lip where he'd bitten it at some stage.

She walked on.

"So, you're just gonna ignore me?" Davitt rose to his feet, stumbled backward, and promptly sat down again. "Slade will find me, you know. Belus Corp will send you all to the PARC."

"Yeah, yeah," Joy mocked, leaning up on one elbow as she lay on the bed. "I'm so afraid of the PARC!"

Maybe you should be! Bobbie had seen the Personality Augmentation and Rehabilitation Center up close as a student doctor, and their correction procedure for the most extreme criminals still gave her nightmares.

"You bitch," Davitt hissed. "You were always trying to turn Bobbie against me."

"Turns out, you were perfectly equipped to do that yourself." Joy lay back down again and stretched out.

"You won't get away with this," Davitt stood up, his legs working to keep his balance on the loose scree. "Kidnapping is a serious offense."

Bobbie snapped around to face him. Rage out-strode her sorrow and left behind the searing agony in her arm.

"Are you fucking kidding me?" Bobbie roared at Davitt, triggering her headache again. Pain fueled her fury. "Kidnapping? You hypocrite!" Bobbie pointed at Granny's corpse lying on the far side of Hicks. "First, you experiment on my grandmother against her will. You inject, inject, her with nanobots. Jesus, who uses hypodermics these days? But you..." Bobbie punched her finger in Davitt's direction and strode one step closer to him. "...You secretly inject a defenseless old woman in the middle of the night and fill her system with nanobots which A, you can't control and B, you have no idea really how they'll affect her. You turned her into a psychopathic killer."

Davitt shook his head, looking confused. "A killer?"

Bobbie held up her hand. Fuck! She'd said too much. Davitt didn't know that Granny had fatally stabbed a man with a garden fork. Bobbie had to distract him from that detail.

"Don't try to deny it," Bobbie hissed through gritted teeth. "You kidnapped her. You fucked her."

"What?" Jimmy jumped to his feet.

"He slept with Granny?" Joy asked. "No!" Suddenly she looked so young, so vulnerable, so hurt.

Bobbie was making everything worse. She jammed her mouth closed and raised her hands to press over her lips.

"Yes, we found them in bed together just before you met us in the research lab," Hicks said, going to Joy and putting his arm around her shoulder. "We didn't get a chance to tell you all the details before things got" – Hicks glanced over at Granny's body – "out of hand."

"She was ninety-fucking-four!" The sass slammed back into Joy's voice as her hurt turned to rage.

"You sick bastard!" Jimmy said.

"You saw her? She didn't look ninety-four." Davitt took a step back. "She didn't act like it either."

Bobbie found her voice again. "My God! You were my boyfriend. Her age was immaterial. This isn't about your taste in women! It's about you being a rotten human being. You got her hooked on narcotics to control her so that you could continue to experiment on her, and eleven other victims who are still at the mercy of your team. As. We. Speak. You created a vaccine to deliver this..." She waved her hand. "... this..." She searched for the words.

"But..." Davitt began.

"Dammit, no, you do not get to speak, fucker." Bobbie heaved in a breath. "You intend to infect everyone with these nanobots. To do what? Turn them into psychopaths too? Get them hooked on drugs too? Traffic them off as slaves. What?"

Davitt tried to speak again.

"No!" Bobbie screamed. "No, no, no!"

"Bobbie." Joy placed a gentle hand on hers.

"No," Bobbie yelled. "Because of him, Granny's dead, and he has the audacity to sit there and complain! He's the one that should be dead, not her."

"I made her young again. All of them. Me. I gave them back their youth," Davitt spat. "You killed Granny when you fried her nanobots with a taser – that was keeping her young, alive for all we know. She was nearly a hundred; of course she turned to mush without them!"

"You bastard!" Bobbie launched at him, her pulse pounding in her ears. Before he could get a hand up to protect himself, she clawed her nails down his face. Someone's arms pinned her hands to her sides. Bobbie struggled, but didn't have the strength to break free.

Hicks' voice penetrated her white-hot anger. "It's okay, Bobbie, shush now."

She stopped struggling and sank to her knees. Hicks knelt with her. Succumbing to his gentle rocking, Bobbie heard Hicks whisper, "Nobody blames you."

Like a wall of glass shattering, her defenses fell apart. Sobs tore from her lungs, rang across the lake, and rebounded back to her. Joy embraced Bobbie in a flurry of black and blue hair. The three of them rocked together, the sisters sobbing and Hicks murmuring, "It's okay. It wasn't your fault. You had to save Joy."

Save Joy. Bobbie had done what her mother had asked on her deathbed.

Joy pulled away. "Bobbie. If you hadn't used the taser, Granny would have strangled me. You saved me. You... you saved me." Her words melted into a garble of crying and "thank you" as Joy hugged Bobbie to her.

Bobbie's entire body trembled. Exhaustion dragged at her. When she looked up, Bobbie saw Jimmy standing guard over Davitt. Bobbie was gratified to see fear on Davitt's blood-stained face, skin pale against the three red scratch marks down his left cheek. Instead of being horrified at what she'd done, at what she was becoming, she sensed an awakening.

Bobbie had had enough of wrestling her emotions from the public domain back into the hidden part of her soul that she never accessed. She was done with being stoic, hiding her feelings behind her professional mask. No more. A fat lot of use holding back her tears had been.

Yet she hadn't the courage to bare her heart just yet.

Heat from where Hicks' hand rested on her arm spread throughout her entire body. No, she had to keep some secrets, had to preserve her friendship with Hicks. Hiding love was one thing, but grief was a totally different boil to lance.

Joy was the best gift Bobbie's parents could ever have given her as a wretched teen, devastated by the loss of a twin to a horrifying disease that caused premature aging and death. But Bobbie's anguish at losing Gracie had affected her bonding with Joy, the "replacement" child under the Dependency Law.

Joy had been too young to get to know her father or her grandfather before they were killed fighting the Melters. At least Bobbie had her memories, if she'd been able to bear playing them over in her broken heart. Poor Joy must have been so lonely, growing up with such an angry, introverted sister. Bobbie took her sister's hand. Small, warm, Joy's hand gripped Bobbie's back fiercely.

With Joy and Hicks by her side, Bobbie might just be able to face her new existence. The trembling in her limbs had stopped, and she felt stronger again. Bobbie disentangled herself from Joy's embrace, giving her sister a kiss on the crown of her head as she stood up.

"It's okay," Bobbie whispered. "Thank you. I love you, little sister."

Bobbie straightened her back, held her head high, and strode to the medical case beside Granny's body. Slowly and deliberately, Bobbie picked up the scalpel and held it up as the sun flashed off the blade. It was time to do the autopsy. And now she was ready.

CHAPTER 4

The matter streamer gurgled. A splatter of gray goop landed on the plastic tray Bobbie was using as a plate. She sat down beside Joy on one of the chairs they'd salvaged from the van.

"Bloody hell, what did you order?" Joy looked from Bobbie's plate to her own, which held a similar gelatinous blob.

"Beef casserole," Bobbie said. "You?"

"Satay chicken," Joy said. She nodded up the slope to where Davitt stacked plastic containers of water from their temporary camp. "Maybe I'll feed it to him and try one more time."

Three crusty lines of scabs ran down Davitt's cheek into thick black stubble. He had kept his distance since Bobbie had clawed him, but he'd carried out every task Jimmy had demanded of him with silent, sullen compliance. He'd filled a dozen gallon containers already and lugged them up from the lake to where they were gathering a pile of resources for their departure. An equally big pile of sour mood gathered around Davitt. Bobbie wondered how it would be long before it exploded.

Davitt cowered, swearing as a shower of fist-sized rocks from higher up bounced down the slope ten meters from him. Bobbie's gaze followed the rocks as they splashed into the lake. How long before one of them was injured or worse in these shifting mountainsides?

"No point getting fancy with this here machine," Jimmy said, coming up behind them, making them both jump. "It's grand for producing the non-organic plastics for the water carriers and such. It's just the food formulas that are screwed up."

Joy sniffed at her plate and pulled a face. "Oh, gross!"

"Ah, don't worry. It's safe. I've been chowing on it for twenty-four hours, and it hasn't poisoned me, though it's not filling me at all." Jimmy patted his stomach. "I'm still ravenous, can't imagine how hungry the rest of you must be after waiting a day to see if I'd croak."

Joy raised an eyebrow. "We appreciate your sacrifice."

Jimmy shoved his plastic bowl into the matter streamer, pressed a few buttons, and received another bowl of gray sludge.

"What's that supposed to be?" Joy asked, scrunching up her nose.

"Porridge. Bon appétit!" Jimmy flashed them a wry smile, walked to a large boulder, and sat down to eat.

"So, we just gonna eat this until we get to the camp?" Joy called after him.

"Ah, give him a break. He's doing his best," Bobbie said.

"I'm sorry," Joy answered. "But I'm hungry, and my head hurts. When am I going to get acclimatized to the altitude?" She stretched and lay back against a rock, then abruptly sat up again. "Oh my God, maybe it's not altitude. I mean, we are only fifteen hundred meters higher than the camp. Can it really make such a difference? What if it's the virus? How do you feel?"

"Headachey, dizzy–" Bobbie also worried that it might be the virus, but if so, wouldn't they have orange eyes like Jimmy? "Altitude affects everyone differently," she said. "I'm sure it's perfectly normal."

Bobbie clicked the electrodes in her fingers before remembering ONIV was offline. She'd relied so heavily on quickly referencing her blinks that she wondered if she really actually knew as much information as she thought she did.

"A few days, maybe up to a couple of weeks. But we'll be leaving for lower altitudes soon, so it will get better," Bobbie said, hoping she was right. Her arm ached, her head hurt, her stomach was all over the place. And the goop from the matter streamer didn't help. "Are there fewer landslides in the valley?"

"Better than here, but there's still the odd rockfall. You're safer inside the caves, of course." Joy shoveled up a mouthful of gruel and grimaced. "And no altitude sickness down there. God, it's like having a damn hangover without the fun of the party!"

"Hangover?" Bobbie said, thinking of the biosensors monitoring every aspect of their biochemistry. She'd never been drunk. Belus Corp wouldn't permit the consumption of poison.

Joy's cheeks flushed, and she looked hard at the ground. "I told you I went off-grid a long time ago. Rerouted the data through some idiot I went to school with. She's a model citizen."

"Can you... Is it easy? You know, to reroute the biometrics for someone else?" Bobbie asked.

"Big sis!" Joy's smile split her face. "You wanna live a little now?"

It was Bobbie's turn to blush. "At some point, maybe," she admitted.

"Already done," Joy said. "I took everyone off-grid on our way to the research center. As far as Belus Corp is concerned, you don't exist."

Joy's words spooned out a hollow space behind Bobbie's sternum. Sure she existed; she knew that much because Slade knew to look for her, knew she'd taken Granny and Davitt, knew Hicks was with them. But did Slade still represent Belus Corp? Bobbie found that hard to believe. Belus Corp and their leader Lisette Fox were the good guys, the people who had saved them from the Melters. Until Bobbie could reach Lisette Fox and expose Slade, then Bobbie's career was over. As an exile from the world, cast adrift on a bizarre ocean of upheaval, Bobbie had a heavy feeling that she truly did not exist anymore. She felt lost.

"Do you think this matter streamer could still make alcohol?" Joy said, grinning, oblivious to the avalanche of emotions she'd triggered in her sister.

Bobbie dragged her thoughts from her wounded places and fixed Joy with a stare.

"No way, Joy," she said, "the matter streamer's having a hard-enough time making food, and anyway alcohol's not a good idea at this altitude. Besides, we've far too much to do without thinking about ... about ..." Her eyes flicked to the mound of rocks they'd used to bury Granny, right where the last rays of the setting sun winked out each evening.

"Granny would have partied," Joy said softly, following Bobbie's gaze. "She should have had a big wake, a huge funeral with all the fanfare."

"I know." Bobbie's gaze drifted from the mound out across the lake and settled on Hicks and Jimmy, packing the rucksacks. Jimmy must have a flip-top head to have downed his meal so quickly, she thought. The two men chatted and laughed at something, their voices sailing up to where the two sisters sat. Bobbie shifted her focus to Joy's face and held her eye. "There'll be a time to party again."

"I know," Joy said. "But I suppose we better help those eejits prepare for the hike out of here."

Joy's smile sparked a contagious hope. Bobbie felt her lips turn up to mirror Joy's.

* * *

The effects of high altitude made it difficult for Bobbie to sleep, though she was exhausted. Frustrated, Bobbie longed to get up but didn't want to wake everyone else. Scree was impossible to tiptoe across, so instead, she lay on the bed salvaged from the van, letting her mind race in a million different directions. Joy slept beside her, snoring so gently it sounded more like a purr.

Bobbie stared at the clusters of stars pinpricking the black sky above her and wondered what enemies lurked in the recesses of the galaxy. People had stopped writing poetry about the stars after the Melters War. Anything could slide from the blackness between the dots of light – something had – and vanish as quickly into the vastness of space.

Seventeen years old and terrified of the sky, whether it was black or blue, she'd still had to take her turn as a cadet at the Observatory in Armagh, scanning the skies and beyond, into the exosphere, for the enemy. Hicks had managed to be partnered up with her, and that had been the only thing that had made their four-hour-long sky-watching shifts in any way bearable.

One evening in May, as the oncoming summer delayed the dipping of the sun and prolonged the dance of colors flaming along the horizon, Bobbie had nearly finished a shift. A flash of mauve in the lower quadrant of her search zone caught her eye. This was the first time she'd actually spotted a live craft. The protocol had been drilled into her so many times that her training kicked in immediately, even as her heart jolted against her ribs. She copied the coordinates to central comms with a few keystrokes, judging it to be in the mesosphere, about eighty miles above them.

"Incoming craft," she had said into her microphone, her voice remarkably steady. The on-screen data stated that the lozenge-shaped craft was about three feet long and two feet wide. She saw a cylinder hanging from the belly of the craft.

Hicks, following protocol, had already seconded the sighting when central comms clipped back, "Not ours."

Bobbie's mouth went dry as she tracked the craft, trying to zoom in as close as she could. She'd never had a chance to see one before, and curiosity clashed with fear. If this Melter got through, it could zap the entire island of Ireland. She glanced quickly at Hicks. Perspiration sparkled on his face. Bobbie glued her eyes back onto her own screen.

"Intercept drone on its way." The person at central comms spoke with a Swiss accent.

"Can you see into it?" Bobbie asked Hicks. She pushed her viewer to its maximum magnification, lost sight, and zoomed out again to re-find it. She needed to see a Melter, confront what scared her, but they were usually blown to pieces in the defensive strike. There were no confirmed "in the flesh" sightings after nearly a year at war, though a woman in Arizona, USA, claimed she had seen one crawl out of a crashed craft – said it looked like an oversized gecko.

"No, but it is getting closer, perhaps in a few – shit!" Hicks jumped back from the viewer.

"They got it?" Bobbie held her breath.

"Yep." Hicks rubbed his eyes. "Damn, that's bright."

Bobbie exhaled and scanned the skies for more, her muscles quivering, her body itching to move. Another thirty minutes left on their shift. "I wish we could capture it," she said.

"I'm just glad we stopped that one." Hicks studied his screen, his feet tapping, fingers drumming the desk. "It was packing some energy, judging by the blast. Good job, it was in the mesosphere."

"I know, but if we knew more about them, we would stand a better chance. I want to know what our enemy looks like." Bobbie had never met her enemy or learned what it looked like.

As she lay awake beneath the stars, mulling over her memories, Bobbie realized that was what bugged her so much about Rejuvenation. She still didn't know who was behind it. Sure, Davitt had engineered the mechanics of it, but who had commissioned it, and why? Who was the enemy?

Perhaps when they finally got to Yosemite, they'd find out. Joy had said very little about who was actually there, only that they'd meet everyone when they arrived.

Bobbie mentally repacked her rucksack and the provisions for the trip. A chill shivered up her spine as she remembered the samples from Granny's autopsy in her pack.

They had enough water for four days, though Jimmy reckoned three days maximum would do it, two if conditions stayed favorable. Water was the heaviest thing they had to carry, next to the gray sludge they had made in the matter streamer. They'd been converting the matter streamer stock into what was, in theory, edible. The goop was more sweet than savory, with an aftertaste that reminded Bobbie of horseradish. They'd spent the last four days preparing for the thirty-five-mile hike to Yosemite Valley. "Downhill all the way," Jimmy kept saying, though the climb up from Helen Lake looked daunting.

Bobbie woke everyone an hour before sunrise. "Let's get the uphill section finished before the sun gets too hot," she said.

They were ready to go in fifteen minutes. Bobbie looked over the campsite that had been their home for the last four days, nettled to be leaving it looking as though the van had vomited its contents on the shore. She'd tried to tidy the sprawl of the belongings they couldn't bring, but the pile of mattresses, chair cushions, and angular metal frames would never look the part here in this wilderness of rocky peaks.

Humans – so messy, Bobbie thought as she hefted her rucksack onto her back. She staggered back a few steps, recovered her balance, and lurched forward to follow the others as they scuttled over the scree in single file: first Jimmy, who claimed to know the way, then Joy, Davitt, and Hicks, who wanted to keep an eye on Davitt.

Though Hicks hadn't said much about his injured side, Bobbie noticed him grimace when he'd hoisted his rucksack. They'd been escaping gunmen at The Buckets in Belfast when he'd been nicked in the side, just a scratch, and fortunately not deep enough to damage underlying muscles and organs. Wound glue had amazing healing properties, but if her arm was anything to go by, his injury would still ache. They both could do with a week of rest and good food – not a thirty-mile hike and goop.

For the first half-mile, they scrambled up a gully alongside a river. It was steep enough to have them panting, but Bobbie put that down to the altitude as much as the gradient. Near the top, scree shifted beneath their feet, tipping them prostrate and dispatching them a body length down the slope before coming to a halt. The clunky clatter of rocks rolling on other rocks sent spikes of adrenaline through Bobbie. She froze, awaiting the last swarms of pebbles to settle, feeling the pulse of pain in her shoulder and registering a chorus of smarts and stings from the new grazes and bruises this fall had inflicted.

"Anyone hurt?" Bobbie asked, sitting up when the courage to move returned.

Thankfully, no-one had suffered serious injuries. They picked themselves up and carried on up the gully, finding a trail and more stable ground underfoot. But each time Bobbie's ears picked out the distance clack-clack of other rock-falls, a fresh squirt of adrenaline sent her heart racing.

The trail flattened out along a ledge, with the land sloping down to their left into what had once been a larger lake. Now a murky pond remained. The landscape was devoid of trees, shrubs, grass, even moss. Scattered in the hollows, piles of black charcoal told a story of fiery devastation. The trail broke into patches of rubble in places, which took more time to pick their way across, while Bobbie worried about twisted ankles.

The eastern horizon glowed pink through orange, then blazed red as the sun broke onto the landscape. Bobbie felt heartened by the early morning light. Moving at this brisk pace got her endorphins pumping. She felt herself smile, an odd sensation after the sorrow she carried. Bobbie's arm felt better, despite having a pack on her shoulders. She walked, scanning the higher elevations for signs of movement. On two occasions, Bobbie spotted boulders the size of vans thundering down the valley, thankfully far from them – far from them this time.

They'd been walking for two hours when they met Highway 120, the route over Tioga Pass. They turned right onto the road.

"Wow, the road's in good shape!" Hicks said, stamping his feet.

"The vegetation up here wouldn't have sustained very hot fires when they burnt. But look here." Jimmy kicked the stones loose at the road's edge. "The tar melted here. Enjoy it – this stretch might be the only hardtop still intact."

"It'll be faster than the trail," Bobbie said, smiling. "And maybe more stable."

"Don't get your hopes up yet. Remember, we saw the road wiped out in places with landslides," Joy said. "Let's hope we can climb over those patches easily."

"I know." Bobbie's smile stayed where it was. "But we're making progress. How are you feeling, Jimmy?" she called ahead.

"Grand so." Jimmy didn't break stride but lifted his hand as he answered.

Joy skipped a few steps to catch up with him.

Bobbie matched her pace with Hicks, keeping Davitt between them and Joy and Jimmy, upfront. There was nowhere for Davitt to run except barren mountains, dotted with black twisted branches and the charred remains of trees that had yet to crumble to ash. He carried his own provisions; Bobbie didn't trust him with anything else. Her supply of sedatives was running low, but Davitt didn't know that. He did know that if he was given too many, he'd suffer withdrawal when they ran out. So for now, he was behaving himself, and in a way, it worried her. Davitt was too smart and too quiet.

They walked on, the only soundtrack the beat of their footfalls on the asphalt, leaving behind a sad dried-up lake that Jimmy identified as Tioga Lake. She could hear Hicks' breathing beside her own, steadily feeding his lungs and muscles with oxygen, an efficient engine chugging away. Hicks, too, seemed to be in good form. For the first time in a while, he had a glow in his cheeks above dark stubble. Tiny muscles in his face pulled the corners of his lips up towards his calm gray eyes, etching dimples into his cheeks. Hicks wore his content face – a look Bobbie knew well – a look that echoed the ten-year-old sitting beside her in school, contentedly working on his sums.

As though sensing her scrutiny, he flicked his eyes to her and smiled.

Bobbie held Hicks' gaze for a heartbeat, smiled back slowly, then broke the connection and looked ahead again. He was by her side, and she felt good.

Further along, the road split around a tumble of stones, flanked on the right-hand side of the road by the blackened ruin of a stone house. Jimmy stopped and let everyone catch up. He stood taller now – the oldest-looking thing about him was his tweed jacket. His skin had lost the translucent look of the elderly, a fuzz of sable hair on his chin contrasted with the bushy white mustache, and his orange eyes glittered.

"The entrance to the park," Jimmy said with a catch in his voice. "This was a magnificent place once upon a time. Full of life."

"It still is magnificent," Joy said, taking his hand and giving it a pat before dropping it again. "The mountains are still here, and things are starting to grow back. Nature hasn't given up, and nor should we."

Jimmy wiped his face, nodding. "Yer right, girl, yer right."

"Let's stop for a rest and some food." Bobbie took off her pack with great care; her arm had started a slow burn – so much for the wound glue – and her legs, not used to such long distances, felt tired. The slopes here had a gentler gradient, and less chance of land movement.

"How far do you think we've come?" Davitt asked.

Bobbie considered not letting Jimmy answer but decided it didn't make a difference. Short of blindfolding Davitt, or sedating and carrying him, he'd always figure out where they were to some extent. Why did it matter if he knew their location? He had no way to escape.

"'Bout seven or eight miles." Jimmy looked past Bobbie and Hicks along the road they had just walked, and then turned to the road ahead. "D'you think you can do the same again today?"

"I can," Hicks said, but looked at Bobbie, concern shadowing his eyes. "What about you? You lost a lot of blood when you got shot. How are you holding up?"

"I'm good," Bobbie said, despite her aching limbs and her worry of falling rocks. The walking gave her body a release for the built-up adrenaline, and despite the desolation and the danger in the mountains, it was beautiful. The low humidity was a treat after a lifetime of dampness, and then the tropical humidity that had enveloped much of the planet after the icecaps had been destroyed. When they dropped to a lower altitude, they would feel the benefits of the richer air.

"Jimmy, where do you reckon the halfway point is?" Bobbie asked.

"Tuolumne Meadows, give or take." Jimmy packed away his empty goop bag and slugged back a draught of water. "It's hard to get my bearings. The last time I was here was about sixty years ago. There was vegetation, trees, meadows. It looks a lot different. I'm just banking on Highway 120 staying intact as far as Olmstead Point. In my day, that landmark was hard to miss. Big granite dome, but –" He scanned the bare rocky slopes around him. "It stuck up out of the trees that used to cover this place. I'm afraid I might not recognize it now."

"Great!" Davitt slapped his thigh. "So, we're lost?"

"Shut up, shit face," Joy snapped. "Jimmy, I know the dome. The camp is southwest of there. But I don't know of any trails. I've never walked in this area – only hovered."

"Well," said Bobbie as she stood up, her muscles aching, "there's only one way to find out. Let's hit the road."

The afternoon sun made Bobbie sweat, though her pack got lighter as she replaced the lost fluids. Their little group had fallen into formation again – Joy and Jimmy up ahead, Davitt on his own in the middle, and Hicks and Bobbie keeping pace at the back.

Once, Jimmy stopped, stood with his hands out wide, and turned around slowly, shouting, "I remember when this was huge trees." Then he walked on again.

All Bobbie could see was the odd blackened tree stump, and drifts of ash among rocks.

They came upon a rounded granite dome shoved up through the rocks on their right.

"Lembert Dome – I climbed that as a boy," Jimmy shouted back to Bobbie and Hicks from his lead position. He turned and said something to Joy, walking beside him.

Joy's laughter floated back to Bobbie, who nudged Hicks and smiled.

"They seem to be getting on well," Bobbie said.

"Too well," Hicks said. "And he keeps telling Davitt the names of the landmarks. I wish he'd shut up."

"Davitt's never been here, never been to the USA before the war, so how's he going to connect a few place names and figure out some foreign spot that was destroyed by the Melters?" Bobbie said. "And if he did, who's he going to tell? There're no blinks, there's no way he can fly out of here by himself. His sense of direction is crap even when he has full navigation on."

"You're too trusting, Bobbie," Hicks said, barely loud enough for her to hear him.

"What that supposed to mean?" Bobbie looked at him, trying to read the space behind his eyes. Poor Hicks was probably hungry, sore, and tired. His bad humor puddled around them.

"Look, I'm just saying that we need to keep an eye on Jimmy." Hicks stopped, sloughed off his pack, and set it down. He hunkered down and fiddled with the straps, looking up the road as the others moved farther away from them before he began again. "Bobbie, please, you know I have great respect for you as a professional. You are the smartest, bravest woman I know..."

"But," she said, stiffening at the snap in her tone as she fought it back. How quickly her good mood had seeped away. Bobbie looked down at her fingers as they folded the end of her waist strap into a roll, then let it cascade out again, only to roll it up again.

"You don't exactly have a great track record for reading people. I know what Davitt did was terrible, and he hid the facts from you." Hicks stood up, but she didn't look up as he cleared his throat and continued. "And Joy kept her secret about the camp in Yosemite from you for years, so you could be forgiven for not figuring that out. She had us fooled."

Bobbie couldn't speak past the lump of tears aching in her throat. Hicks was right. She'd missed it completely; two people so close to her had lied so effectively for years. Bobbie felt warmth upon her shoulder where Hicks rested his hand, soothing the muscle, easing her tension.

"But Jimmy is more self-aware than Granny was. He might be able to cover up his craziness for longer."

"I know what you're saying about Jimmy," Bobbie began.

"Do you? Because you seem extremely comfortable with him."

"He's been faultless, Hicks. What has he done wrong so far?"

"Nothing, yet. But here we are, blindly following him."

"Yes, because he's the only one who's been here before and who remotely knows the way."

"He could get us lost, for Christ's sakes."

"Why would he do that? What's in it for him? Besides, Joy concurs with the general direction."

"General direction? Out here?" Hicks looked up the road as the others walked further away, and back the way they'd just come, where it looked the same: parched, bleak, and barren.

"Have you a better idea?" Bobbie asked, irritated with Hicks for asking the hard questions and tired of not having answers.

"No. This isn't an idea competition." Hicks' gray eyes turned flinty.

"Well, what is it then?" Bobbie recognized this Hicks: hungry, frustrated, itching to argue if only just to release his stinking mood. This was like their first years in medicine – shitty working conditions, long hours, no sleep – all over again, but worse.

"Look, if he is changing mentally, like I said, he'd be smart enough to hide it from us, and I just want you to be aware. We can't trust him," Hicks said, casting sideways glances up the road at Joy and Jimmy walking away.

"I'm aware, okay?" Bobbie snapped. Hunger made her tetchy, but on top of that, she couldn't get away from the idea that they were here because of her, because she had insisted on rescuing Granny, and she'd failed them at every turn. "Jimmy's contamination is down to me. I dropped the vials, I let him come with us. So, yes, I will be watching him, but I can't just... just taser him because ... what? You're jealous that he's getting on with Joy?"

"No! Jesus Christ! Now you're being ridiculous."

"So why throw these things at me now? Yes, Joy fooled me for... I don't know how many years. That tears me apart, and what Davitt did to Granny... Where do I start with that? But sure, thanks for reminding me. As if I'd forget!"

Hicks winced. "But you've also failed to see the truth in people not hiding it from you, too."

"What?" She pulled away from him, stung.

"You've missed so many signals, Bobbie, and now I'm terrified."

"Of what?" Bobbie said, confused. Hicks was the bravest person she'd ever met. What new devastating revelation was he going to dump upon her? She looked up at him, his features hidden, backlit by the sun. Her stomach tumbled with fear, and she braced her heart as she waited for the ax to drop.

His lips moved, but a loud rumble drowned out his words as the ground beneath their feet shuddered, forcing them to crouch down like surfers on a wave. Several boulders thundered down the slopes around them. Bobbie froze, afraid to run into the path of one and terrified she was already in their fall-line. The shaking below her feet stopped after a few seconds, but her body continued to tremble. Her knees buckled. Bobbie summoned as much control over her limbs as she could muster, stood up, and ran past Davitt, who had rolled up into a ball on the ground, to where Joy clung to Jimmy, her eyes like saucers. Hicks arrived beside her.

"Earthquake?" Bobbie asked.

"Yes." Jimmy disentangled himself from Joy. "You're alright, it's over now."

A thunderous roar echoed off the mountainsides, ripping through the crags a thousand feet above them. Everyone whipped their heads around, trying to locate the source of the din, but the percussion of the clamor made it impossible. The sound bounced off the slopes surrounding them until all Bobbie could hear was the heaving breaths of her companions.

"Jesus Christ!" Bobbie said.

"And yet, it's about the most natural thing we've encountered in the last couple of weeks." Hicks combed his fingers through his brown hair, making it stand in tufts.

"I hope the tunnels at the camp haven't caved in," Joy said, her face white, her brows pinched together. "We haven't felt one this big before."

"So, you've felt earthquakes here before?" Bobbie asked.

"Sure." Joy shrugged. "It's California. Shakes happen."

Fatigue swamped Bobbie, suddenly making her want to sit down and cry. In the western sky, the sun, a ball of molten light, began its plunge for the horizon.

"Jimmy, are we far from Tuolumne Meadows?" Bobbie asked.

"Just round the next corner," he replied. "A good night's rest, and we might make it to the camp tomorrow evening. If," he added, "it's still there."

CHAPTER 5

Bobbie's feet felt leaden after walking all morning, on top of yesterday's hike.

"I think we might make it to the camp tonight," Jimmy said. He lifted his hand to shield his eyes and looked up at a bald granite dome to their right. "Yep, I'd bet everything in my granny's shoebox that that is Olmstead Point. The trail's off to the left. We'll be able to see Half Dome just round thon corner." He pressed forward, his pace increasing.

Bobbie sped up. There might be something approaching food at the camp. She couldn't bear to eat any more gray goop. Walking got harder by the minute. Hicks had hardly spoken to her since their argument, and she still smarted from his accusations of naiveté. Her shoulder hurt. Her legs hurt. Her soul hurt. Bobbie missed the chirp of birdsong, the rustle of wind wafting through leaves, the snap of twigs beneath her feet, the scent of flowers. Here there were only rocks, stones, and dust. She tried to distract herself with the rare sight of thin green blades of grass growing where water had seeped into the hollows of former meadows and stream beds. Returning the planet to what it had once been might never happen, but nature didn't stop trying.

Their shoes beat rhythmically off the hardtop, harmonized by the soft swipe-swipe of their trouser legs rubbing with each step. A slight breeze skimmed across the bare slopes, lifting Bobbie's hair over her shoulders and cooling the sweat on her face. Even with the sun-visor, the sun dazzled off minerals in the rocks that had congregated to form shiny specks. The granite rose up in a rounded block to their right. To their left, rocks and boulders scattered down the slope beyond view. Ahead, the road climbed in a gentle gradient, disappearing on the near horizon, wedged between boulders and slabs.

They followed the road as it hugged the contour of the dome. A wider area – once a parking lot – provided a platform with a view over a huge valley.

"Jesus Christ!" Jimmy stopped. "It's gone."

Joy put her hand on his arm. "It's still there, Jimmy," she said softly. "It's just different."

"What's wrong?" Bobbie asked.

Jimmy pressed his lips together. His chin wobbled. It scared the shit out of Bobbie to see Jimmy's face flooded with emotion.

"Half Dome." Jimmy's voice caught, but he went on. "Look, right up the valley, it looks like a pile of rubble. Jesus! It used to be a landmark before. It was so beautiful..."

"It suffered a direct hit," Joy explained. "It melted. Up close, it's actually quite stunning, but in a different way. You'll see."

"I need a minute," Jimmy mumbled as he walked to a low stone wall that bordered the parking area. He sat down, his back to everyone, and knitted himself together—his shoulders pulled to his ears, elbows at his sides, and his face in his hands. He groaned out loud.

Something in Bobbie's chest broken open as Jimmy succumbed to quiet sobs, reminding her that the Melters had taken more from them than she could ever fathom. You may never miss what you had not experienced, but Jimmy had known this place in its full glory. Bobbie felt his grief rolling off him, understanding too well what loss ripped out of a person.

Bobbie squinted into the distance, tipping her head back to keep her own tears in check. One protrusion along the horizon looked as though it had a bite taken out of it. There were random stripes down its flanks, ridges that spread into a series of circles, like a melted candle with wax running down its sides and pooling at the base.

"Bastarding Melters!" Jimmy spat as he stood up again. "I thought I was past being shocked by what they did." Fire burned in the wet orange glint of his eyes.

Bobbie blinked away the shiny film across her own eyes and shoved her voice back into her throat. "We have to keep moving. Which way?"

Joy pointed at the melted dome. "Down there."

Hicks looked at the sun. "That's southwest, alright, so yep, we go that way."

Bobbie looked, but could see no trail. The day already felt heavy and difficult, though they'd been walking on a paved road, albeit burnt and destroyed in places. Joy's pinched face and drooped shoulders told Bobbie she wasn't alone in her suffering.

"It's too early to stop for the night, but maybe we should rest?" Bobbie suggested.

"I don't think that's wise," Hicks said, sizing her up. "I'm sorry. I know you need a break, but we're going to have a problem with water soon."

"What do you mean?" Bobbie asked.

"I think the plastic containers are breaking down, degrading somehow. Mine's leaking." He turned his back to them. The rucksack was soaked and dripping. Droplets of water beaded on the outside of the quarter-full plastic container hooked to the outside of his pack.

"Shit!" Bobbie said. "Is that all you have left?"

"No, there's still a full gallon in the pack, but I think UV light is breaking down the plastic. Your container's dripping too." Hicks pointed at damp spots on the ground near Bobbie's feet.

"Damn matter streamer," Jimmy grumbled.

Bobbie took off her pack, wincing as the straps slid down her arms. "Crap!" There was a third of a container left, but it had been full only a half-hour ago when she had taken it out of her pack and strapped it to the outside for handiness. It was her last container.

"I kept both of mine in my pack, and they're okay," Joy said.

They collected everyone's water carriers and placed them in the shade of a boulder while they took stock.

"We have to push on," Hicks said. "We've lost at least a day's worth of water, and who knows when the rest of the containers might fail."

"Let's pack the water into the intact containers and keep those in our packs," Bobbie said. "We can carry the food –"

Joy snorted. "Well, what passes for food."

"On the outside, if we're short on space," Bobbie continued. "Do we have any means to boil any water that we find?"

"I've still got the flare gun from the van," Jimmy said.

Joy shuddered.

A burning man, screaming in agony, on the rooftop of the research center, leaped into Bobbie's mind. Joy had shot him with the flare gun after he'd shot Bobbie. Bobbie put her arm around Joy's waist, and Joy rested her head on Bobbie's shoulder with a sigh.

"But there's no fuel, no wood, nothing to maintain a fire long enough to boil water," Hicks said. "If we had water to boil."

"You know, while you're standing around gabbing, we could be walking," Davitt said. "You're a fucking disaster waiting to happen! Does anything you do ever go right?"

"Yeah, fuck-face, seeing you die a slow death from dehydration," Joy spat.

Davitt hugged his pack and walked off down the hill towards the valley.

"We should go." Bobbie lifted her pack, which felt ten times heavier despite the lack of water. She gritted her teeth past the pain in her shoulder and walked. A blister brewing on her heel stung. The muscles in her legs had tightened with the brief stop and walking down the slope made them scream in protest. Bobbie wondered how long her knees would hold up. Downhill all the way sounded less appealing now.

Sometimes they'd find a trail, and though never sure if it was made by animals or humans, if it went southwest, they took it. Everyone wore their moods like heavy, clinging cloaks. Hicks was withdrawn, and passively hostile to any suggestions Jimmy made. Davitt snarled questions and bickered with Joy, who at this point seemed to relish verbally abusing anyone who crossed her path. Jimmy appeared the least irritable, as though his earlier emotional outburst had given him a release of sorts, but he remained quietly contemplative.

Bobbie felt despondent. Would this hike ever end? She ached all over. Though her headache wasn't as bad as it had been the day before, she was weary to the core. As the afternoon wore on, they walked straight into the sun. Bedazzled, Bobbie's retinas felt scorched, her face muscles tired from squinting. The heat made her thirstier and thirstier. The terrain became steeper and steeper.

"I can carry your pack," Hicks said without looking at Bobbie. "If it helps you keep up."

"I'm fine," she lied, stung. Sure, she was lagging, but after her spat with Hicks, Bobbie didn't want to show any weakness. She willed her legs to walk faster, her feet to ignore the smart of the blisters and her arm to stop throbbing.

Eventually, they picked up a solid trail that hair-pinned back and forth. Joy, leading the way, attempted a shortcut down the mountain's side from one section of the trail to another, cutting out the bend.

Three steps off the trail, the ground below Joy's feet crumbled, whipping her feet out from under her. Joy screamed, stretched out her arms behind her, and landed heavily on her butt, sliding a couple of meters downhill in a cloud of dust and a rattle of rocks and stones, stopping just above the next loop of the trail.

"Joy," Bobbie yelled. She dropped her pack and ran along the trail to where Joy lay motionless. "Joy! Can you hear me?"

Joy blinked, then groaned.

"Don't move," Bobbie said. "Just tell me where it hurts." Bobbie ran her fingers gently over Joy's skull.

Joy held up her left arm. "My wrist."

Bobbie swallowed her reaction. A swollen lump along the line of Joy's arm set her hand off at a deformed angle.

"That's the only pain? You didn't bang your head?" Bobbie asked in confident doctor-mode.

"No." Joy pursed her lips and blew out on her exhalations, sucking her in-breaths through clamped teeth. Sweat popped on her top lip.

"Neck, back, okay?" Bobbie asked as she felt down the length of Joy's legs and other arm. "Just the wrist, then?"

"Do you think it's broken?" Joy whimpered.

"Maybe or dislocated at the very least. Either way, it requires the same treatment. Hicks?" Bobbie felt more than saw him at her side. "She'll need a closed reduction."

"Agreed. That's definitely a dorsal angulation. You want to hold or pull?" Hicks asked.

"Wait. What?" Joy squeaked.

"We need to set the joint," Bobbie said, keeping her voice calm. "We've done a load of these. Geriatric patients are great at breaking wrists, and we've become pretty good at fixing them. Right, Hicks?" she added brightly. Joy didn't need to know just how brutal this procedure was going to be – not yet.

"Yep." Hicks nodded but kept his eyes on the injury.

"Think now, Joy," Bobbie went on. "You said you had a hospital of sorts at the camp, does it have an Intescan or any kind of internal structure scanner?"

"No," Joy said through gritted teeth.

"Anything? Even something as archaic as an MRI?"

"There's nothing like that," Joy snapped.

"Okay, that's fine. It would just be good as a back-up. It would let us know we've got a perfect fix," Bobbie soothed. "That's all. There's no advantage in splinting and waiting to do the reduction then. It's always better to reset the bone as soon as possible."

Bobbie looked around for Jimmy. His face was furrowed, orange eyes downcast beneath heavy white eyebrows.

"Jimmy, any idea how far now?" Bobbie asked while pulling a piece of foam she'd brought for her own comfort at night from her pack and placing it beneath Joy's upper arm. Hicks was rifling in his pack too. He carried the medical case.

"Well, judging by the switchbacks, I'd say we've picked up Cloud's Rest Trail." Jimmy shaded his eyes and looked down the slope. "These aren't as bad as I remember them. See, the trail straightens out again there, then turns again." He pointed to where it went out of sight around the curve of the mountainside. "My guess is the switchbacks start proper a little ways further on from here. It gets really steep, but if you stick to the switchbacks –" He flicked a glance at Joy. "It should be plain sailing."

"Please, would you take Davitt and scout it out for us? You could leave your packs here." Bobbie didn't want Davitt to witness any more of Joy's agony while they reset the bone, nor did he need to know they would probably use the last of the sedative on her.

"No bothers." Jimmy dropped his pack. "You're with me, Davitt. Lucky me," he added, casting his eyes skywards.

Davitt stared Bobbie down. "I'm not leaving my pack here for you to drink my water."

"Whatever, Davitt, you can fucking drown in it for all I care." Bobbie gave a dismissive wave.

Hicks and Bobbie busied themselves, unpacking the medical case until the two men disappeared.

"Okay, Joy," Bobbie said, sitting down beside her sister. "I have to be honest with you. This is going to hurt like hell."

Joy swallowed. "Okay."

"We have sedatives for you," Hicks added.

"But we can't knock you out fully," Bobbie continued. "We need you to be able to walk down to the camp. There's not enough water for us to spend the night up here, and we can't carry you. It's too dangerous if we dropped you..."

"I get it," Joy said. "I trust you, big sis." She gave a wan smile.

"I'll talk you through what I'm doing–"

"Do you have to?" Joy asked.

"Well, Hicks and I need to co-ordinate, so you'll hear us anyway." Bobbie applied the sedative jet. Joy relaxed after a few seconds.

"I'll pull, you hold," Bobbie said to Hicks.

"You sure?" he asked, glancing at Bobbie's injured arm.

For a moment, Bobbie was annoyed at him for questioning her in front of a patient, even if it was her sister. Then she realized Hicks was afraid that she wouldn't – or couldn't, with her gunshot wound – apply the brute force needed for the reduction.

"Okay, switch." Bobbie moved back, stroked Joy's face, and noted her lolling eyes and lopsided grin.

Hicks gripped Joy's hand as though giving her a handshake. With his other hand, he felt the fracture. He nodded at Bobbie, and she applied her weight on Joy's upper arm. Hicks bent Joy's wrist back.

Joy yelped.

Bobbie's emotions skittered between sympathetic sister and down-to-earth doctor. She snatched practical and pressed her weight into her hands, holding Joy's shoulders. In her head, the voice of the professor in medical school: "...first recreate the injury, the patient won't like it..."

Hicks continued to pull the hand back, feeling with his other hand for the projection of bone on the other side. Joy squealed, kicked her feet, and sobbed, her hand back now at more than ninety degrees. Bobbie was glad that she'd switched places with Hicks.

He lifted Joy's arm with all his might. Joy's curdling scream tore through Bobbie and echoed off the far valley. Hicks slid his thumb up her arm towards the hand. Bobbie watched the wrist smooth out as the bone clicked into place. Then Hicks pulled the hand back over, palm down. His cool gray eyes met Bobbie's, and with a nod, confirmed the job done. Bobbie exhaled a breath she hadn't until then realized she'd be holding.

Joy settled into a quiet moan as Bobbie wrapped the Set-a-strap from Joy's fingers to her shoulder, keeping her elbow bent and her hand in line with the lower arm until the Set-a-strap hardened.

Joy looked pale. Her dark almond eyes – so like their father's – were large with suffering but losing the spaced-out effects of the sedative. She had a crust of dried blood on her lower lip where Bobbie guessed she'd bitten it either in the fall or during the reduction. Poor Joy – the chain of khaki bruises around her neck from where Granny had throttled Joy broke open Bobbie's heart. Her little sister looked so fragile.

"Any tingling in your fingers or thumb?" Bobbie asked, her voice professional, as though they sat in a clinic with intepanels and trolleys.

"No," Joy answered in a feeble voice.

"Think you can wiggle those fingers for me, li'l sis?" Bobbie let warmth come to her tone, and she pushed back the sweat-dampened hair from Joy's forehead, pitch-black in contrast with Bobbie's ginger locks.

Joy's fingers moved.

"Good," Bobbie said, and Hicks sighed. Bobbie wanted to hug him, to rest her head on his shoulder, breathe him in, but she simply said, "Thank you."

"My pleasure," he said.

"Oi," Joy exclaimed, then smiled. "Thank you, both of you."

"I'll make a sling from the straps of your rucksack – gotta keep it elevated," Hicks said.

"Do you think you can walk? How do you feel?" Bobbie asked.

"Like I've been flung down a mountain," Joy said. "But I suppose we better make tracks."

They divided the contents of Joy's rucksack between Bobbie and Hicks, who then each grabbed a strap of Jimmy's pack and slung it between them. Joy had just taken her first tentative steps along the trail when Jimmy appeared jogging up the trail towards them, slathered in sweat.

"What's wrong? Where's Davitt?" Hicks asked.

"Oh, he won't get far," Jimmy said, panting. He bent over, hands on knees, and heaved a few deep breaths before standing up again. "It's bad news. The trail's gone."

"Oh, crap!" Bobbie said, annoyed that Jimmy had wasted his energy running back just to tell them about the trail. And he'd left Davitt alone, too.

"I'm not making myself clear," Jimmy said, gulping in a couple more breaths. "It's not just the trail that's gone. The entire mountainside is gone. The whole thing collapsed, there's nothing but a cliff there now. Three hundred meters, I reckon, straight down."

"The earthquake we heard last night," Joy said.

"So how do we get to the camp now?" Bobbie asked, starting off down the trail. "Can we go around?"

"Nope, doesn't look like it." Jimmy shook his head slowly. "I'm sorry, Joy, but there's no sign of a camp down there at all."

CHAPTER 6

Joy sank to her knees a couple of paces from the edge of the cliff. "No! Oh, God, no!"

"Careful," Bobbie said, terrified that any closer might cause more crumbling to the cliff face. "What is it, Joy?" Bobbie, Jimmy, and Hicks stood in a row, hands on hips, surveying the view. Davitt stayed back, off to one side, and Bobbie kept him in her line of sight.

Joy pointed with her good hand, white-faced and trembling. "Jimmy couldn't recognize any camp because we live inside those mounds."

"Jesus!" Bobbie said, looking down at the valley floor. Chunks of the cliff, earth, and boulders lay strewn in piles, as if some giant child had stomped on its sandcastle. The rubble stretched across to a dozen bulbous mounds of rock radiating out from the base of the mountain Jimmy had referred to as Half Dome. One mound had been within range of the rockfall and looked like a crushed egg, its shell poking up in jagged angles. Bobbie didn't think anyone inside it could have survived. Dread pressed heavily on her.

"How many people would usually be in there?" Hicks asked.

"Two families lived in that one." Joy swiped her cheek and gave a hiccup. "About twelve people."

"We need to get down there fast," Hicks said. "We might be able to help the injured."

"How do you suggest we get down that?" Davitt said, standing well back from the edge.

"I'd be happy to throw you over," Jimmy said.

"If only," Bobbie said dryly.

Davitt backed-up.

Hicks whistled through his teeth. "I'm guessing that's three hundred meters straight down." He shook his head. The sounds of rocks hitting the valley floor still tinkled up from below, sounding innocent in their distance.

"If we signal somehow, they might send a hovercar up to investigate," Joy said. "They know we're on our way. I got through to comms before we left Belfast. There's usually someone on lookout, but with the cave-in –" She put her face in her hands.

"The flare gun!" Bobbie said. "It will be dark soon. We could send up a flare." The thought of getting a ride down the mountain gave her a burst of energy, but would the noise set off more rock slides? It was a risk they had to take.

"But it burns up quick," Hicks said. "If there's no watch, they'd miss it."

"How many cartridges are left?" Bobbie asked.

Hicks fished the gun out of his pack. "Two."

"So, we send one up. If no-one arrives, we light a beacon fire with the other." Bobbie looked around for sources of fuel. She'd passed a couple of scraggy lumps of charred wood, all that remained of once-giant trees – there wasn't much lying nearby.

Jimmy started emptying his pack. "This will burn." He held up the empty plastic water carriers. "I'd say it will give off black smoke."

"So, we light the fire now, while it's still daylight, and send up the black smoke," Bobbie said. "By the time the sun sets, the fire should be glowing, and then we'll use the second flare. Davitt, strip."

"What?"

"You heard me. Take off your clothes," Bobbie said. "We'll burn yours first."

"No way." Davitt pointed down to the valley. "What if there's no-one coming for us? What if they're dead? Or maybe they just packed up and left. I'd need my clothes more then."

"If there's... if there's no one down there," Joy said quietly, "we're dead."

Davitt rounded on her. "I'm not taking off my clothes!"

"Really, shithead?" Jimmy stomped towards him. Bobbie noticed Jimmy was actually taller than Davitt now, his old bones strengthening, his joints straightening out, cartilage regrowing.

Davitt shrank back.

Jimmy's lips shimmered around a smile, as if pleased with Davitt's reaction. "You first. Then I'll go next, if needed. Age before beauty and all that." Jimmy winked at Joy. Bobbie felt a chill rattle up her spine. Granny and the other rejuvenees had been lewd and promiscuous. Was this the first sign of it in Jimmy?

"No chance," Joy said, managing a weak smile. "You'd no luck turning my sensorfabric invisible either!"

Bobbie relaxed. Maybe Jimmy was just being Jimmy, but Hicks scowled behind him, seemingly unconvinced.

"Clothes, Davitt," Bobbie demanded. "Now!"

Davitt swore as he took off his tunic and trousers.

"You can keep the underpants. There are some things I'm no longer prepared to suffer," Bobbie said.

"Bitch," Davitt hissed.

"Don't tempt me," Jimmy snarled, and raised his hand, sniggering as Davitt flinched.

Davitt glared at Jimmy, then slunk off to sit on a rock, his arms wrapped around his torso, the knuckles of his spine punching out against the skin of his back. Once, the lost little boy that simmered below the boasting man had stirred Bobbie to something approaching love. Pity poked at her sternum briefly, before rage and grief flapped their wings like quarreling birds.

Joy had upended her pack with one hand, picked out the full water and food containers, and packed them away again, leaving a jumble of electronic gadgets and a small pile of empty wrappers. "You can have these." She handed Jimmy her trash. "I gotta think about these." Joy poked through the electronics, placing them back in the pack one by one until none were left.

With great care, Bobbie lifted her empty wrappers and a pair of mud-encrusted socks from her pack. There was no need to dig deeper. The bottom half of her pack was chill-packs filled with samples from Granny's autopsy – all she had left of her grandmother.

The pile of fuel remained disappointingly small. The shadows had pushed further into the evening, stretching, claiming territory for the oncoming nightfall. Coolness had uncoiled the clench of the afternoon heat.

"We should get the smoke signals going," Joy said.

Hicks stood a couple of meters from the pile and aimed the flare gun. The pop made everyone jump. The fire sizzled to life. A black pall of smoke chugged straight up into the air. The reek of burning plastic, odious and aberrant, made Bobbie cover her mouth. She coughed and moved back.

"They should see that," Joy said. "I'd give them an hour or so to debate what it means, decide what to do, then actually get a hovercar to us." She stood closer to the edge than Bobbie was comfortable with and waved her good hand in an arc above her head. "Hey!" Her shout echoed off the valley walls, an obscene taunt: yes, we can hear you, but can they?

"We're too far away, and if they're inside, or –" Joy's shoulders drooped.

"Where's the food stores, the vehicles?" Davitt said. "How do you know that the rest of the mounds didn't cave in from the inside?"

In one movement, Jimmy was there, open-palmed, striking the side of Davitt's head. The force knocked Davitt flat. Hicks jumped up, but Bobbie was faster. She stood in front of Jimmy, hands out, and spoke as if talking to one of her dementia patients. "Okay, let's stay calm. Let's sit down." Behind her, Davitt swore.

Jimmy bristled.

"Leave him, Jimmy." Bobbie kept her tone tranquil. "We can't afford to waste medical supplies on him if you really hurt him. And I'm certainly not carrying him."

"He has a point, though," Hicks said, his voice unnervingly calm. "We need to think about what's next if there's no-one down there."

Jimmy frowned and tipped his head towards Joy, who had her back to him, staring down into the valley. He pulled a blank expression as Joy swung around to face them.

"We could go back to the van and try to get it going again," Joy said.

"Not gonna happen, love," Jimmy said. "It's banjaxed. The matter streamer's pretty low on stock, though we'd have water. I could try and get comms to Radar Net going."

Joy sucked in a breath.

Jimmy spoke again quickly. "If the camp's gone, we don't need to protect them."

"But we need to protect us," Bobbie said. "If we connect to Radar Net and they come to get us – which they may not do – Belus Corp will send us to the PARC." The thought made her sick, especially after what they'd come through.

"Better than dying of starvation," Hicks said. "And while we're alive, you never know what other opportunities might present themselves."

"Well, aren't we the fucking glass-half-full guy!" Davitt said, rubbing his jaw. "I'm not a candidate for the PARC. Might put a good word in for you."

Jimmy launched towards him, stopping short as Bobbie yelled, "Stop! Stop it now. No more violence."

Davitt cowered, his hands over his head. Jimmy stamped a foot close to him and laughed as Davitt flinched. Bobbie felt angry at both of them – acting like children when they all needed to pull together and cooperate.

Hicks drew himself to his full height. "We may still need him, Jimmy."

"Aye, and if I get really hungry, I'm sure I'd find him very useful." Jimmy moved around to the other side of the fire from Bobbie and sat down. Hicks sat opposite her, between Davitt and Jimmy.

"Joy, maybe you can tell us a bit about the camp," Bobbie said, sitting down again beside Joy, closing the circle between Jimmy and Davitt. "What are those mounds?"

Joy gave her sister a sad smile, and Bobbie reckoned Joy was wise to her distracting everyone more than pumping for information.

"We think that when the rock melted, it behaved like lava, cooling on the outside and staying molten on the inside," Joy said. "It wasn't exactly the same consistency as lava, and bulged out into those mounds, but in most cases when the mound reached a certain size, a weak area in the wall gave way and the inner chamber emptied, leaving huge caverns accessible via tunnels from where the molten rock flowed out."

Bobbie remembered seeing tubes snaking from the base of the mounds. "So, you just dug into those?"

"Yes, they're huge and interconnected," Joy said. "And the walls are quite thin, less than twenty centimeters thick, so if they cave in, you will see from the outside. So, Davitt, I'm pretty sure the other mounds are intact on the inside."

Davitt, brows knit tight over downcast eyes, gave a half-shrug in a fucked-if-I-care manner.

"But who knows how many people were in the dome that was crushed." Joy bit her lip, her gaze drifting to the valley.

Bobbie couldn't bear to think they'd come this far to find the colony destroyed. Surely everyone wouldn't have been in the same small cave? She put her arm around her sister's waist. "You okay?"

"Yeah." Joy rested her head on Bobbie's shoulder. "I'm worried about them. And for us, too. I brought us here, it would be my fault if –"

"Shush, now. You've done your best. I'm proud of you," Bobbie whispered, but her words didn't placate the unease she felt. The thought of contacting Belus Corps horrified her. What were their options if the colony had fled like Davitt had suggested? They had no food, next to no water. Davitt had no clothes. They couldn't walk to any other settlements. There was no point discussing it, especially with everyone so tense. Her tongue felt glued to the roof of her mouth.

Joy seemed to disappear into her thoughts as Bobbie held her close, understanding her fear.

The fire settled down to a lick of orange flames, intermittently mingling with green and blue as the rubbish and clothing melted, combusted, and melted some more. Soon the liquefying carcass collapsed in on itself in a crackle of sparks.

After thirty minutes, the billowing black smoke thinned to a gray wisp, the embers an orange glow that dimmed and brightened as evening breezes stirred. Night settled around them. Bobbie could no longer see the valley floor. Thirst, hunger, and fatigue hung off her like tree ornaments, each one heavy on its branch.

They needed the next flare to work. Bobbie couldn't face another day of walking, and they didn't know how far they'd have to go to find a safe route to the bottom.

"Fire the flare right across the valley," Joy said to Hicks.

Another crack. Fire flashed from the stubby gun in Hicks' hand, illuminating their faces for a split second before the flare soared high, ripping the blackness apart with its ball of flame. The orange disc pulsed, expanded, shrank, the brightness sucked from it until the night arranged itself around them again.

Nothing happened.

"Shit, shit, shit," Joy said, on the brink of tears.

"Give it a minute," Hicks said. "We should rest." He didn't say that they'd have a long walk tomorrow, but Bobbie knew he was thinking it.

The firelight disappeared. Then the flames resurged, giving Bobbie enough light to see Jimmy standing by the fire, naked from the waist up and pulling his trousers down too. He dropped those on the flames and stood wearing his saggy old-man's boxers, his body firm, his leg, torso, and arm muscles defined. A trick of the light, or was he that young already?

Hicks stood up. "We should keep a signal fire burning as long as we can," he said, and stripped too, setting his clothes to the side for when the fire got hungry. The white bandage covering his wounded side picked up the light of the fire and stood out against his tanned skin, reminding Bobbie of how close she had come to losing him. He stood taller than Jimmy, broader too, more heft in his muscles, and Bobbie couldn't help but admire the primordial specimens they presented in the golden flicker of the blaze.

Bobbie wished she'd had the courage years ago to tell Hicks that she loved him. Maybe it would have screwed up their friendship, and he wouldn't be here now, waiting to be rescued. Maybe they'd be sitting somewhere safe now, surrounded by their children – unlikely, as the Dependency Law would have put a stop to that until her mother's death just a few weeks ago. Still, the fantasy felt like a good place for Bobbie to hang out as fate selected the next scenario: the colony would come to save them – though that looked less and less likely. Or they would manage to turn themselves in to Belus Corp and get sent to the PARC for a lobotomy. Or die – dehydration would kill them first, shrinking the cells in their bodies. Her kidneys would fail, her brain cells would shrink, and delirium would set in. So no point in mulling over regrets; if this was the end for her, for all of them, Bobbie could at least try to direct her thoughts someplace happy, fulfilling, while she went insane from thirst.

Jimmy stuck his head forward. Slowly he stood up, lifted his hand, and pointed. "There." He stepped closer to the edge, disappearing into the darkness lurking outside the dancing circle cast by the flames. "Lights! Moving upwards!"

Hicks threw the rest of the clothes on the fire and fanned the flames. Ribbons of amber, yellow, and ocher climbed and twisted, laced with turquoise. Bobbie and Joy jumped up, waving, hollering, and dancing in the firelight.

CHAPTER 7

A beam of light slashed the night sky, coming closer and closer. Bobbie felt giddy with relief. Food, water, and some rest. Then they'd find a vaccine for the virus and bring it to Belus Corp, and this nightmare would be over.

The rising hovercar landed in a flat area near the campfire, and two men wearing neat tunic suits got out. They were clean-shaven, with short, tidy haircuts. Bobbie's stomach turned cold. Wasn't Joy's group a bunch of renegade misfits? Bobbie turned to her sister, but Joy had already started moving, cradling her broken wrist as she ran.

"Jacob! Mo! Am I glad to see you!" Joy hugged them with her good arm. "The rock-fall? Is everyone okay?"

"Not everyone. Get in quick. We'll tell you on the way. What the hell happened to you guys?" asked Jacob – or maybe Mo – in the dim light of the fire, and backlit from the headlights of the hovercar, the two were homogenous silhouettes. The men looked from the three near-naked men to Joy, and back to the guys. "Last we heard; you were on your way from Belfast. We expected you a week ago."

"I'll explain later, Mo. First, tell me – is he back yet?" Joy said. "Just a yes or no. I... they" – she nodded towards Bobbie – "haven't been fully briefed yet."

"No," Mo answered. "Nothing yet."

Bobbie felt Joy tense up. Who was she worried about? Had she a boyfriend here? She'd denied any romantic attachment to the guy she'd brought to their mother's wake, but Joy had been hiding more than that from Bobbie back then.

"You okay?" Bobbie asked.

Joy shrugged her off and climbed awkwardly into the car using her good hand. "We need to get going."

Bobbie and the underpants-clad Hicks, Jimmy, and Davitt piled in, followed by Jacob and Mo. Under the interior lights of the car, the two men did look different. Jacob was pale with short black hair, and thin black eyebrows over close-set eyes that crowded a long narrow nose. He looked pointy and sharp. Mo, by comparison, had darker skin, a broader face, bushy eyebrows, and wide-set eyes. A dimple indented his chin.

"Tell me about the rock-fall," Joy said when everyone was seated. "Did anyone... were there casualties?"

Jacob worked the controls, his face drawn, his eyebrows pinched.

Mo nodded and sighed. "Howard and Matthew were killed outright."

Joy put her hand over her face.

"Ten badly injured, but most are stable. We need qualified doctors." Mo looked at Bobbie and Hicks.

"You don't have a doctor?" Davitt asked.

"We have an obstetrician and midwives," Mo said. "But they aren't equipped to deal with this."

"Get us down there, and we can start right away," Bobbie said. So much for rest.

"How are you fixed for supplies?" Hicks asked. "Pain relief, antibiotics, anesthesia?"

"We have some, and hopefully more on the way," Mo said. "We're waiting on Joy's–"

"There's enough," Joy cut in. "We're landing. Work with what you have, and Mo, grab some clothes for Hicks. We're bringing them straight to the medical center."

They glided into a black cavern in the side of the largest of the rocky mounds. Headlights bounced off the walls and ceiling in a chaos of twinkles and flickers. Deeper into the cave, the light around them steadied to a buttery gleam from lighting outside the car. Bobbie hardly noticed the car land and climbed out, dazzled by what she saw. The roof sparkled in hues of yellow, gold, and peach, ten meters above her head. The walls had been polished to a smooth, glassy finish because otherwise, the crystals would be too sharp. The thing that really took Bobbie's breath away was the hoard of children milling around, some bickering and squabbling, others quietly holding hands, some clutching bedraggled soft toys. A group of six peeled off and skipped towards the entrance to the cave with cries of, "Joy's back!"

"Alright, alright!" Joy raised her hand in the air, and the older kids stopped at the signal and helped rein in the younger ones. A slim girl with a head full of braids picked up a nearby toddler, perched her on a hip, and shushed the little one. Bobbie estimated about forty children, ranging from toddlers to pre-teens, pressing forward to see the new arrivals.

"Introductions later." Joy's voice was loud but friendly. "We have two doctors with us; they are dehydrated and hungry but in general good health. We need to help them as they help the wounded. So, everyone scoot and make yourselves useful, putting the wanes to bed, and you wanes..." Joy wagged a finger. "Do as your olders tell you. See you in the morning in the sun cave."

The children scuttled off amid a babble of complaints, while Bobbie and her companions watched slack-jawed. Hicks, Davitt, and Jimmy stood with hands held together over the front of their underpants, shoulders hunched around their ears, each looking like they wished the ground would swallow them.

"The medical center is through here," Joy said. "Jacob, please take Jimmy and Davitt to the intake quarters and give them clothes. Protocol A1.3, please."

Jacob nodded. "This way."

Jimmy and Davitt filed after him.

"Jacob knows Davitt is dangerous?" Bobbie asked, watching the three disappear into the bowels of the cave, impressed by the clout her little sister seemed to have in this community.

"He needs to watch Jimmy too," Hicks added gruffly.

"Yes, we have protocols for every class of arrival." A dark look passed over Joy's eyes. "Except for this case, where I need to set you to work right away."

"Of course, show us where." Bursting with unasked questions, Bobbie welcomed the thrum of nervous energy that always preceded her workday, the tug of sadness for people who were hurting against the surge of hope that she could help them. Work was a safe mental space for Bobbie, and she welcomed the respite it would give her.

Mo reappeared, and Bobbie realized she hadn't noticed him slip off. He passed a bundle of clothes to Hicks, who dressed quickly.

"Where are the other adults?" Bobbie asked.

"Fixing the cave-in," Mo said.

Joy opened her mouth to speak, then hesitated.

"Or off on a mission," Mo said.

Joy's shoulders dropped, and she seemed to relax.

Then they were off, following Joy down a twisty tunnel. The colors of the walls swirled and bled into each other like a crazed rainbow, nature experimenting with art. Joy's words to Jimmy when he'd first seen the devastation of Half Dome drifted back to Bobbie.

It's still there... It's just different.

Joy had chosen to see the new creation rather than mourn the loss. Like Granny had always said, death was necessary for the next stage. Bobbie had spent her lifetime trying to beat back death. And yet, could destruction be a rebirth? It seemed so in these caves and tunnels beneath the demolished Half Dome.

Around the next corner, cries of pain rushed out of the cavern, crashing off the walls. Bobbie and Hicks hurried, arriving at a bed-filled cave. The tang of blood hung in the stuffy air with the sour odor of sweat.

Bobbie looked for the medic in charge, but saw no-one, apart from an elderly man and a kid who looked to be in her late teens. They approached, relief dripping from their faces.

"Hello, I'm Bobbie. This is Hicks."

"I'm Yoon," said the slender girl with black hair cut in a bob, the crooked fringe too high above her eyebrows.

"Henry." The man was tall, though stooped with age, his skin deep-bronzed, his bald head burnished. Wrinkles creased around his eyes, along his forehead, and set grooves on either side of his mouth, which deepened as his smile flashed white teeth – a smile gone too quickly. "I was an obstetrician in Belus-land before I left. I'm the best they have, I'm afraid, and my experience is wider now than just delivering babies, but I'm not ready for this type of disaster. I'm glad you're here. I set up a triage." He handed them a bottle of Kwik-san.

So they had electricity for lights, but not Electro-san sterilization. Bobbie cleaned her hands and passed the Kwik-san to Hicks. She'd have preferred soap and water but didn't want to waste any more time. The acrid smell of the sanitizer cut through the soggy stink from the patients.

Henry spoke while they scrubbed. "Jenna is the worst. Head injury. She's been so quiet, just staring."

"I'll see to Jenna," Hicks said.

"Who's next?" Bobbie asked.

"Nero, over there." Henry nodded to a small bundle on a bed. "Five years old. He was completely buried; breathing is shallow, pulse thready, in and out of consciousness." He shook his head.

Yoon cleared her throat. "He's my brother."

"I'll do my best," Bobbie said.

The child whimpered when Bobbie approached, but didn't wake up. He was covered in so much dust that Bobbie couldn't be sure she was reading his skin tones accurately. Muddy tear tracks ran down each cheek.

"I need water and cloths," she said, feeling the air move behind her as Yoon left.

Bobbie checked Nero's breathing and heart rate, relieved to see his pupils react normally when she tested them with light. His skin was hot. Hard to see bruising under the grime, but the right leg was badly swollen. No pulse in the ankle.

Yoon brought the water, and Bobbie quickly cleaned the right foot. His toes stayed black, and his skin crackled at her touch. Anguish squeezed her heart, but she knew what she had to do. Bobbie kept her face and voice calm as she turned to the little boy's anxious sister.

"Yoon, please get Doctor Hicks," Bobbie said. "Bring me any antibiotics and anesthesia you have, bandages, scalpels, scissors, and a saw. Then boil water. Lots of water."

Yoon scurried away, her hand over her mouth.

Hicks and Henry arrived together.

"Yoon said you wanted a saw?" Henry said, his eyebrows pulled tightly together.

"I'm sorry," Bobbie said. "The blood supply to the foot has been compromised. There's gangrene in his toes. It's causing sepsis. We have to remove the dead tissue." The clinical words and her matter-of-fact delivery didn't stop Bobbie's stomach from twisting.

Hicks nodded. "Maggot therapy?"

"The pharmacy probably doesn't have maggots," Henry said.

"So, there is a pharmacy here?" Bobbie was impressed, despite her disappointment at there being no maggots.

"Yes, and it's well-stocked, too," Henry said. "Just not with maggots, right now. We can order anything we need, and people like Joy bring it in."

"Even if we had the maggots, it would take too long to make the site wet enough." She patted the little boy's face with a cool cloth. His eyes fluttered, and he moaned.

"We have to take the foot," Bobbie said softly, cringing deep-down for the child.

Yoon shook her head, then tilted her head back so her chin jutted forward. She pressed her lips closed as she struggled not to cry.

"It's his foot or his life. This infection will kill him if we can't stop it." Bobbie placed her hand on the girl's shoulder and looked into her face. "Go get your parents."

"We have no parents."

Yoon's simple words nearly broke Bobbie. She inhaled, counted to three, and exhaled slowly before asking, "How old are you?"

"Sixteen."

Legally, Bobbie didn't need Yoon's permission. Legally, both children should be wards of Belus Corp. But then, legally, Bobbie should be in a hospital ward in a subscraper in Belfast, surrounded by ultra-elderly and looking out at the ocean depths.

"If you don't let me operate, he'll die for certain," Bobbie said, gently but firmly.

Yoon swallowed hard. Tears spilled down her cheeks.

"Okay." Yoon wiped her face and took a deep breath. "Tell me how I can help."

The operation took four hours, both doctors, and nearly all the supply of anesthesia. It would be another few hours before Bobbie could see if the antibiotics were helping, but the wound was clean. The flap of skin she'd sewn over the stump just below the knee should heal. She thought of Joy's hand. What if they hadn't been there to help her? People were so easily broken, life so fragile. Bobbie had a purpose. The idea, the responsibility, filled and emptied her at the same time.

Mo appeared just as Bobbie and Hicks had finished a quick recap assessment of the remaining patients – sixteen in total, ranging in age from a two-month-old baby, who was simply dehydrated and hungry, to an ultra-elderly woman with a head injury who would probably not see dawn – no, dawn was only a matter of minutes away. Bobbie changed her assessment to dusk. It had been a long night, a long week. Her injured arm throbbed, her thigh muscles ached, and the blisters on her feet buzzed. Woozy-headed, Bobbie looked forward to a good sleep.

"I'll bring you to your quarters," Mo said, as if reading her mind. He led them down another tunnel. Bobbie wondered how many times she'd get lost in the coming weeks. The tunnel opened into a large cave. The fresher air made Bobbie think it probably led outside.

"Well," Hicks said, walking ahead of Bobbie, "I for one am looking forward to a shave, shower and –" He stopped so abruptly Bobbie nearly walked into him.

"Sh-it!" Hicks hissed. "Luke!"

"Hicks!" Bobbie said, exasperated as she backed up. "Look at what?" She nudged him to the side. Hicks placed his hand on her shoulder as he looked from Bobbie to a man standing beside a dusty hovercar – an older man, not much taller than Bobbie, with a thick head of short hair that tufted on top, flashed through with silver.

Bobbie stared at his almond eyes in disbelief – eyes so dark the irises appeared the same color as the pupils, just like Joy's.

How could it be? Bobbie's lungs worked as though she'd been winded by a blow to the solar plexus. The world around her paled out. Her entire awareness collapsed onto the man standing in front of her, whose beautiful eyes she'd missed for so long – eyes she was sure she would never look into again. In utter confusion, Bobbie sucked in enough breath to utter one word:

"Dad?"

CHAPTER 8

Bobbie stood mute. Words clogged her throat, trying to escape. Her father stepped towards her. Bobbie backed up.

"No," Bobbie whispered, unable to believe her eyes.

Silver frosted her father's hair. He was all angles and elbows. His skin folded more at the corners of his eyes and mouth, hung looser at the jowls. Nineteen years had taken their toll.

Bobbie squeezed her eyes tight shut and opened them. Her father was still there.

"Hicks, can you see him too?" Bobbie whispered.

"A-huh," Hicks said, taking her hand. His warmth spread to Bobbie, real, solid. She gripped him tighter.

Bobbie reached with her other hand and felt her arm quiver as she took her father's hand. She felt the patches of dry, hardened skin on his palm below each finger, like he always got when he'd been using a hammer or a shovel for too long. Both hands she held were real.

"It's me, Bobbie. I've waited so long to see you." Her father took a step toward her. Like a spring released, Bobbie flew to him, her arms out. He scooped her up. She buried her face in his chest, inhaling his smell, the same spiced musk, the scent of protection, of comfort, of home. That fragrance peeled away the decades as though they were husky scales, exposing the tender sixteen-year-old he'd left behind.

"Oh, Dad." A sob shuddered up from Bobbie's ribcage as she tried to control its release. It turned into a laugh-cry. Tears bubbled from her eyes. Crying, laughing, hugging her father, pushing him away to look at him, tugging him close, Bobbie rode out the wave of jubilation as she sobbed.

"Shhh," her father rubbed Bobbie's back. "It's okay."

Bobbie felt like a child again, as if her father's words could make the world's hurts go away and she didn't have to worry about anything. She wiped her hand over her face, felt the wetness there. The tears were real.

"Look at you." Luke lifted a strand of her hair, holding it up so the copper tones glinted in the lights. "My beautiful Bobbie. I missed you so much."

"But..." Bobbie's voice rasped. "They said you'd died. And Grandad?" She quivered, jangly-boned, as if unable to tighten her joints and hold herself together. "How?" she asked. "How are you alive? Belus Corp told us your plane was vaporized. No-one could survive that."

"Grandad didn't make it. Heart failure. He died quickly," her dad said softly.

Bobbie nodded, chewing the insides of her lips, not trusting herself to speak. Grandad had died at the barracks, just as the army had told them. Hot tears spilled down her cheeks.

"Joy!" Bobbie spun around to Hicks. "We have to tell her that Dad's alive."

Hicks opened his mouth, closed it, and nodded without taking his eyes off Luke.

"You must be exhausted," her father was saying. "You should get some rest, and we'll talk in the morning."

"How can I sleep now?" Bobbie said, her voice shrill in her own ears.

"You've waited this long," Luke said. "What's a few more hours?"

"No!" Bobbie said. "I never waited. They said you were dead. There's no waiting for the dead. But you're alive. I'm not waiting. Tell me. How did you survive? Why didn't you come home? Where were you?"

"Shhh, you're getting too upset," Luke said. "You're overtired and overwrought. I can't bear to see you this way. I'm so sorry. I was trying to get to my quarters before you came this way. I told Joy we would talk after you'd gotten some rest."

"Joy knows?" Bobbie said, hearing the bewilderment in her tone before it hit her – Joy knew her father was alive. The heat of envy licked through her puzzlement.

Her father nodded without meeting Bobbie's eyes.

"What? How?" Confusion swamped Bobbie again. How could Joy not tell her right away? Maybe she hadn't wanted to interrupt the surgery. "Is Joy okay? Where is she?"

"She has work to do," Luke said.

"But –"

"Come sit down," Luke said. "I'll see you in the morning, Mo."

"Kay, boss." Mo left.

Bobbie let her father lead her to an alcove nearby with seats and a table, her movements robotic and clumsy as she sat down.

Hicks stood by the table. "Do you still want me to stay?"

"Please." Bobbie needed Hicks more than ever.

Hicks sat down.

Bobbie turned her gaze to her father, folded her arms to quell their shaking, and said, "Tell me everything."

Her dad shifted his weight forward to lean his elbows on the table.

"We were stationed in Whitehorse. The allied government had commandeered the airport there, you know? Good position. Close to the coast but far enough inland; high enough, too. I was sent over to Alaska with a search party, looking for a grounded cruise ship. The ocean off that coast was crazy. Freak giant waves as the glaciers melted and released tonnes of water into the bays and channels."

He shifted back in his seat and placed his hands flat on the table, staring at them for a couple of seconds before continuing. "I was flying the amphibiplane, grid pattern, looking for the ship, but when we found it, a wave had turned it over, and the ship was smashed to pieces. It was incredible. This giant cruise ship – like a broken toy. It had about four thousand people on board, and there were thousands in the water, drowning, dying of hypothermia, terribly injured. God, the injuries..."

Luke stopped. Muscles around his eyebrows flexed. A vein bulged at his temple, his mind far away.

"Dad?" Bobbie connected to his pain, and it hurt her to think of him back then, in that situation. Was she being cruel, forcing him to explain? But she had to know what had happened; she needed to make sense of it.

He pulled his focus back to Bobbie and continued. "I set the plane down, but our mission had only been to locate the ship – we had no facility to rescue. There was nothing we could do. The cries for help, the desperation, the hands grabbing at the plane... We only had room for three of them. We had to beat back the others—we had to—they would have overtaken us. We pulled in three people. Raj, my co-pilot, was with me on that. But we left the others behind. We dropped the rescued off in Whitehorse and went back to take three more, when we saw a flash of light from the nearby observation tower and an explosion above us. Belus had hit a big Melter craft. You know those ones with the pulsers? Big, real big. That bird careened towards us. We'd no chance. It clipped our tail – forced us to make an emergency landing on a lake, only a click from the Melters' crash site. We knew we were in the termination zone –"

"The termination zone?" Hicks asked, looking sideways at Bobbie. She shook her head, not familiar with the term either.

Luke answered, "When Belus took over military operations, they introduced a protocol to wipe out a Melter crash site with incendiary bombs, regardless of personnel in the area."

"No!" Bobbie was appalled. "How could they kill their own people?"

"Ha, now there's a funny question." Luke didn't look like he was laughing, though. "Belus said they didn't want any kind of extra-terrestrial virus or organic life that may have hitched a ride in the Melters' crafts transferring to humans."

Bobbie nodded. "I can see why they'd do that, if there was a real threat of infection."

"If..."

Bobbie sat forward. "You don't think there was?"

Luke placed two fingers against his pursed lips, appearing to search for the words before he inhaled sharply and sat back, drumming his fingers on the table. "I knew it wasn't going to end well for us."

He reached for Bobbie's hand. "Raj stayed with our amphibiplane, waiting for the wipeout, but I had to see what those bastards looked like, and this was my chance. I had nothing to lose."

"I understand," Bobbie said past the sandpaper in her throat. "What did you see?"

"I didn't make it to the craft."

"So, you didn't see anything?" Bobbie asked, swamped with disappointment. Like her father, she craved to know what these bastards looked like.

"No, and believe me, I spent the weeks that followed kicking myself for giving up the opportunity of a quick and easy death," Luke said.

"Oh, Dad, no."

"I was swimming to shore when an Alliance fighter jet flew over. The weird thing was, they dropped two bombs on our plane first. Didn't make sense to me – still doesn't. Then they doubled back and hovered over the Melter craft. Far too close for the bogus excuse they were basing their protocol on. Then they dropped another bomb on the Melter craft."

"But that doesn't make sense," Hicks said. "Surely they'd try to save the humans? Or at least, not risk exposing themselves to these space viruses..."

Luke raised an eyebrow. "You'd think."

"What were they looking for?" Bobbie said. "To see the Melters for themselves? Maybe the pilot was curious, like you."

"It's possible." But the slow shake of Luke's head told Bobbie that he was no more convinced of that than she was.

"So, they didn't see you? How did you survive the fires?" Bobbie asked.

"The only thing that saved me was being in the water. I lay at the edge of the lake for days," Luke went on, "choking on the smoke from the forest fires that followed and wondering if the fire would use up all the breathable air. I'd nothing to eat and no-where to go, even if I'd known which way to go. I was hoping that eventually I could make it back to base, but the air was so thick with smoke, I couldn't tell which direction the sun lay in. The light was strange – night-time with the glow of burning on the hills, and by day, the smoke cloud filtered the sun's light to a surreal orange hue. I was becoming delirious and spent some time... don't know how long... hours, maybe, searching for you, Bobbie."

"Me?"

"Remember our green tent, and how the world looked first thing in the morning when you got out of the tent?"

“Yes, tinted with pink,” Bobbie said, her heart aching at the thought of her poor Dad out in the wilderness, searching for her.

“Well, that’s what the place looked like with the smoke, and I suppose it confused me or fed into the delirium.”

Bobbie knew what he meant. As soon as she’d come out of the tent the first morning to a world tinted with a rosy blush, she’d looked up online to find out what had caused it. She’d been fascinated at how the cells in the retina detecting the green light were so saturated that her eyes only picked up the other colors in the light spectrum for a while. She’d read out her finding from the handheld phone they’d used back in those days as her parents and Gracie sat eating breakfast around the campfire. The memory was clear and sharp-edged with nostalgia.

“You were so interested in how the eye works, how the human body works, I knew then you’d be a doctor,” Luke said. “Especially after how you’d looked after Gracie.”

That brought another ball of thorns to her throat, but Bobbie sad-smiled and squeezed Luke’s hand.

His brow wrinkled as Luke fought off his own memories. He cleared his throat and continued, “After the fires died back, I wandered aimlessly, trying to figure out which way would bring me home. Eventually I came across this guy, Mac. Well, he came across me, actually. I’d passed out from lack of food. I would’ve died if Mac hadn’t found me. He was a survivalist and had been ‘waiting for the end of the world’ since he’d left Australia after the bush fires of 2020. He and a bunch of like-minds had stockpiled food, water, guns, everything we needed in a system of caves. When I told them my story, they told me of soldiers lost in battle who, when they turned up, were sent straight to the PARC and never seen again.”

“They were treating them for PTSD.” Bobbie had never believed that the Personality Augmentation and Rehabilitation Center willfully intended for lobotomies to be the result of their correction treatment, but she had seen procedures accidentally go wrong.

“I believe there’s more to it than that, pet.” Her dad squeezed her hand, just as he had years ago when giving her bad news about Gracie’s health. “In the beginning,” he continued, “there were only six of us. That was okay with me. I was afraid I might have some virus or other contamination from the Melters, but after six months, I was getting stronger, and I reckoned I was in the clear. I wanted to try to contact home, but Mac was worried about Belus sending me to the PARC. Good job he stopped me, because as the war ended, we began to hear stories on the radio comms about Belus outright killing soldiers that turned up, other guys like me – anyone who had been anywhere near a Melter craft.”

“Belus Corp would never purposefully do that,” Bobbie protested, but in her mind’s eye, she saw the vacant faces of the patients who had been on the receiving end of botched PARC treatments.

"Hear him out," Hicks said calmly.

"It doesn't make sense to create more inpatients; why would they damage anyone on purpose?" Bobbie asked.

"Damage? Bobbie, they killed those soldiers," her father said.

Sour bile rose in her throat. "Did Lisette Fox sanction this? Do you have any proof?"

"Proof? Bobbie, I saw them bomb my plane with my copilot still in it, and if Mac could believe me after how crazy I must have sounded, then I can believe his guys. Why would anyone make this up? We wanted to go home, but..." Luke shook his head and pulled the tone of his voice down a notch. "As for Fox... We don't know if she sanctioned this. But someone at Belus did."

Just like the Rejuvenation Project, Bobbie thought. Hicks had been right about her naiveté. She stared at her fingers, still interlocked with her father's. "That's why you couldn't come home. Belus Corp would have killed you."

"Belus is bad news, Bobbie," her father said. "We still haven't gotten to the bottom of why they shot their own soldiers. There's a theory that they didn't defeat the Melters..."

"What?" Bobbie and Hicks said together.

"Perhaps they surrendered or struck a deal with them. Let's face it – once Belus became involved, the war ended pretty darn quickly. It was too easy, too good to be true, and when something is too good to be true–"

"Sounds like a stretch," Hicks murmured.

"Perhaps," Luke said. "But some believe that Belus might have struck a deal. A trade deal."

"There's only one thing to trade that they couldn't easily take," Hicks said slowly.

Icy horror washed over Bobbie. "Us!"

"We think they're harvesting humans for the Melters."

"Slaves?" Hicks asked. "That's a bit last-millennium B-movie, don't you think?"

"Look, I know." Bobbie's father spread his fingers wide. "It's one of many conspiracy theories floating around. But when Joy told us about rejuvenation and Granny–"

Grief pierced Bobbie again. She thought of the rejuvenees she'd left behind in Ireland, how malleable they were, how young and fit, yet controlled by drugs.

"Belus did this to Granny... on purpose?" Bobbie whispered.

"I'm sorry, love. That must have torn you to pieces."

Torn. That was exactly how Bobbie felt – ripped open. She nodded but whispered, "Please, finish telling us what happened to you."

"For five years, we had no contact with anyone. We lived in the wilds of Alaska, eating game, fish, vegetables when we could get them. Sometimes other people would join us, after a strict vetting process. We..." Luke pulled in a long breath, then gritted his teeth. "We vetted your mother and you, but –"

Bobbie put her hands to her face and pressed, unafraid of the dark behind her eyes as random ghost colors sparked her retinas. She knew what was coming, just knew.

"I didn't pass," she managed to say before giving in to a strangled sob.

"No," Luke's voice was damp with decades of unshed tears. "You were on the brink of going to college. I could see you had a promising career as a doctor, and the Belus-land society needed you. We needed you too, to get that training, but by the time you qualified, you believed so strongly in the system that the other Candel members thought you wouldn't be suitable."

"Suitable?" Bobbie asked. "And now I am?" She heard the bitterness in her voice. "What changed?"

"You were willing to walk away from Belus-land when it came down to choosing between them and Granny. Hell, you were willing to run before you had somewhere to go. Our operatives saw that. They backed me up when I asked them to let you come."

"But you hadn't asked for me before?" The ache of betrayal singed Bobbie's thoughts. She clasped her hands to her chest.

Luke fixed his gaze to the table and rubbed a finger over a mark in the wood. "It wasn't up to me, love. There were too many lives at risk."

"My job is to save lives! I would never have –" Bobbie stopped herself. She knew what he meant, and fighting him now wasn't going to change the fact that she had only ever looked at the surface of the world. Sure, she had demonstrated against legislation she didn't like, such as the Dependency Law, but she had conformed to the will of the government, trusting that Belus Corp knew best.

"What about Mum?" Bobbie asked, leaning her elbows on the table and folding one forearm over the other.

"She wouldn't – couldn't leave you," Luke said.

Bobbie felt like she'd been punched in the gut. Her mother had known her father was alive and had kept this from her – on her death bed! How could they have let her grieve for years? Yet despite her anger, Bobbie knew and understood. She, gullible fool that she was, had only herself to blame.

Luke, Bobbie, and Hicks sat in heavy silence for a while as time grew shapeless, stretching the minutes into years, the years into decades and the decades into centuries of loss, yet contracting those same decades into angry minutes, laden with *what ifs* and *why nots*.

Bobbie took in her father's deep frown and sagging posture. Had those years been harder on him than on her? Her mother had lost her father because of Bobbie trusting the government and being too willing to put her faith into the good they appeared to be doing. But Joy? Envy cut through Bobbie's sorrow.

"Joy passed the test." Bobbie's mouth fouled with a sour bitterness she couldn't swallow.

"Yes."

Bobbie slammed her open palms on the table and screamed from the bottom of her belly, shattering the quietude until she grew hoarse.

When she stopped, Hicks took her hand gently. Bobbie let him. "Better?" he said, his eyes locked to hers.

"No," Bobbie whispered.

Luke sat with his head bowed.

He has patience that I'll never have, Bobbie thought. "Please, tell me about Joy," she whispered.

"Our group grew. We had women who were pregnant and refused to obey the Dependency Law. So when elective passing for an elder was ruled out, and they still wanted to have their baby, they came to us. Thank God for Henry. You've met him?" Luke stared up the hallway they had just walked down, as if Henry might appear at any moment.

Bobbie and Hicks nodded, mute.

"He left Belus-land when the Dependency Law required him to perform too many abortions. When he was able to utilize technology for safe embryo transplantation, those women remained as host mothers, allowing other women to return to society, visiting their children here when they can. We have layers of security for this, but you'd be surprised whose children we have here."

"Very little would surprise me now," Bobbie muttered.

"Yeah, I guess." Luke crinkled his eyes, a hint of a smile. "We had an influx of teens when the biometric chip became compulsory."

"But Joy," Hicks interrupted. "She has a chip, right?"

"Yes, she does." Luke cast a guarded look at Bobbie before going on. "We'd been watching her and her tech capabilities. Her skill at hacking and keeping herself off Radar Net was the first sign that she might be a good fit. She developed 'ghosting' – mimicking and transposing biosensors' outputs. This allows our members with major health issues to go back to Belus-land for medical care, undetected by Radar Net. Ori helps massage the protocols on the Belus-land side, so Joy didn't have to be a full exile – she could live in both worlds, like Ori."

"Ori?" Hicks asked.

"Our leader. That's for another time. But Joy, Joy is special –"

Joy, Bobbie thought bitterly, had had two parents, yet the teenage Joy had caused so much worry, had enjoyed two worlds, while Bobbie's had shrunk to almost nothing as she watched her mother die. Joy had missed her mother's death while hanging out with their father, whose absence had worn a hollow in Bobbie's heart.

"When the children come of age, Joy will hack the Belus system, and that will allow them to enter 'society' in Belus-land." Luke continued talking through Bobbie's mental angst. "It will be a trickle, but over time, there will be a large enough influx to the population that we'll be able to demand elections, overthrow Belus."

"How have you avoided Belus?" Resentment crimped the edges of Bobbie's voice.

"Radar Net only covers the parts of the planet that are habitable," Luke said. "Our communities found tiny pockets of habitable land along the fringes. We kept in touch with long-wave radio. Really outdated technology, but reliable, if you have the basic equipment. Some communities still had a Cessna or two, so I'd scout out and see what we could find. Then we acquired hovercrafts, and our exploration became a lot easier. We got to the valley here and noticed it was cooling very quickly. Joy set up the decoy thermosensors, and we've been here for five years now."

Five years. Joy had kept this from Bobbie for five years. Joy had been only sixteen when she'd set up the decoys. It seemed so young to entrust her with such a task, yet, Bobbie reasoned, she'd been the same age during the war, searching the skies for Melters.

Bobbie's father looked past her, and as Bobbie turned to follow his gaze, Luke said, "Ah, Joy, perfect timing. I was just talking about you."

"Bobbie," Joy said softly. "I've wanted to tell you so many times, but –" She looked down at her hands. Her hair fell forward, a black silk sheet hiding her face.

Questions and accusations dammed up in Bobbie's throat. She wanted to launch herself at Joy, tear her nails down her face, rip her hair out by the roots, but the image of Granny attacking Joy rushed her brain, and a confusing collision of fury and compassion made her head spin.

"How's Nero?" Joy asked.

Bobbie had almost forgotten about the little boy whose foot she'd amputated only hours ago. Those had been long, long hours – decades had passed since.

"We'll know more in the morning," Hicks said. "How's your wrist?"

"Okay," Joy said, holding up the bandaged arm. She looked at her father. "Does Hang know you're back?"

"Hang?" Bobbie said. Hang was her father's father – her other grandfather, who had died when Bobbie was only three, or so she'd thought. "Is Yeh Yeh still alive too?"

"No, Bobbie, no. I just hadn't gotten to that part yet," Luke said.

Joy backed away. "Sorry. Bad timing?"

"There's probably no good time," Luke said. He paused and gave Bobbie an apologetic grimace, saying, "Hang is my son. Your half-brother."

"No, no, no more!" Bobbie shouted as she stood up. She tore past Joy, down a corridor with flickering yellow lights, and into a large dim cavern. Three dark tunnels led outward. Not caring which black hole she plunged into, she ran.

The tunnel was short and dumped her outside. Fresh air tightened tear-soaked skin. The sky, moonless and star-pocked, gave little light as Bobbie hurtled over hard-packed earth. Her toe caught a rut. Her feet tangled. She splayed forward.

Inertia replaced her frenzy, gluing Bobbie face-down in the dirt. Forehead to knees, breast to thighs, hands to feet, she scrunched herself into a ball and cried. The world faded out around her as Bobbie gave herself up to her exhaustion.

CHAPTER 9

"Please talk to me, Bobbie." Joy squinted and held a hand to shade her face as she looked up.

"I've nothing to say," Bobbie said. Nothing nice – nothing that wouldn't burn Joy and shred their relationship beyond redemption.

Bobbie hadn't spoken directly to Joy since the reunion with her father the day before last. Since then, Bobbie had concentrated on catching up on sleep. When awake, she kept herself busy tending to Nero and the other injured people. Bobbie took stock of the lab facilities and ordered the equipment she needed to be brought in on the next hovercraft so she could start developing the vaccine. When there was down-time, Bobbie wandered the mists of the past, playing out parallel universes between her life and her father's. Each time she thought of what her mother had lost, a band tightened around Bobbie's temples. Hang was thirteen, the same age that Gracie had been when she had died. So far, Bobbie had avoided meeting her half-brother. Before her father had flown out on his next mission, he'd met with her again and implored her to meet Hang, telling her that his mother had died when he was only seven and that the child was eager to get to know his big sister.

"I don't know if this makes up for any of your hurt and feeling of betrayal," her father had said. "But Hang reminds me so much of Gracie. I know you'll love him if you can give him a chance."

Bobbie couldn't imagine a time when she'd embrace her half-brother without thinking of her own dead mother. With her father away again, the only reality Bobbie had was her work.

Today the community had gathered further down the valley, where the earth was softer, to bury those who had died in the landslide. Through three long days and two nights, family and friends had visited their dead — touching their loved ones' hands and faces, bidding them farewell, crying, remembering, trading stories, and even laughing. Bobbie felt like an intruder, watching their pain but not partaking. Instead, she wallowed in her own agony, torn between euphoria at having her father back from the dead and guilty anger at the years she'd mourned for him.

Thirty adults and twice as many children milled around the clearing. Dust coated their clothes: simple tunics and trousers in default black, without the coding chips for the color and patterns the fabric could otherwise display. Their voices rose in a soft burble following the silent moments after Mo's few words. Bobbie found it hard to concentrate as he talked about how Matthew and Howard had loved each other and their six children, how their family had been everything to them. Love, children, family. The words seared Bobbie, scorching her ears.

Mo didn't mention the added pressure on the rest of the adults now that two had died. Bobbie wondered who would take care of the orphaned children. Every adult in the community seemed to be fostering several children already. She understood that many of these children had been born to surrogate mothers, transplanted as embryos when their genetic parents were unwilling to have an abortion or see an elder euthanized in Belus-land to make room for the new child. Why Belus Corp hadn't repealed the Dependency Law years ago was a mystery to Bobbie, and she sided with the rebels – no, she corrected herself, the Candels – on this point. But did she believe her father's claims that Belus Corp was rotten? His conspiracy theories about them being in cahoots with the Melters seemed outlandish, but Bobbie worried that the terrifying nature of his speculation had sent her off in a spiral of denial.

At the end of the service, Bobbie sat alone, reluctant to engage in conversation, yet finding solace in the chatter spreading through the dispersing crowd. On the periphery of a group of about a dozen kids, two small boys' playful wrestling escalated into a more serious ruckus. One pushed the other, who landed face-down in the dust and squealed. Bobbie was about to rush over when she saw Jimmy approach. The older kids dropped their heads and shuffled off before he'd spoken to the child on the ground, who had already snapped the volume off and lay with wide, fear-filled eyes, staring up at Jimmy.

"That's enough squealing, do you hear me?" Jimmy said, his voice loaded with menace.

The child nodded, whimpering as his wrestling mate pulled him to his feet.

Jimmy stepped one foot in their direction. The two boys scuttled off sideways like frightened crabs. Jimmy laughed and turned towards Bobbie, his orange eyes glittering. Those orange eyes would frighten most people, never mind little kids, but the enjoyment that danced there raised the hairs on the back of Bobbie's neck.

Joy joined them, dabbing her eyes, and Jimmy focused his attention on her. Bobbie watched Jimmy put his arm around Joy's shoulder and give her a squeeze. Was there more to the embrace, or was he simply comforting a friend? Bobbie couldn't trust her own judgment anymore, not after finding out how badly she'd used it in the past.

People drifted off – some in couples or by themselves, the younger ones in larger groups, clouds of youthful energy. Two girls, about seven or eight years old, wandered past Bobbie, just within earshot.

"Do you think they'll be all smooshed up in heaven?" the smaller child asked, swiping wisps of her brown hair off her forehead only for it to fall back into her eyes.

"No, silly, they'll leave their bodies behind. Like taking off your clothes at night." The taller one nodded, pleased with her explanation.

"So, is everyone, like, naked-er than naked in heaven?" The small one held her hands out palm up, incredulous.

"I guess, but Ori says it's just our spirits..."

The kids wandered away, leaving nostalgia in their wake, phosphorescence on a black sea. Bobbie and Gracie had pondered heaven at great length. Gracie, the older by four minutes, the wiser by a hundred years, had woven her theories with legends, convinced she would be going to the land of the forever young, Tír na nÓg, to make up for dying of rapid aging. Gracie's short life had filled so much of Bobbie's whole life. Bobbie hadn't been able to prevent losing Gracie, but her envy of Joy was every bit as dangerous as a disease. Bobbie knew that she had to push aside her resentment of Joy yet again, that she needed the only sister she had left, that she loved and needed Joy as much as she had loved and needed Gracie.

Joy and Jimmy joined Bobbie.

"Let's go, girls, the theatre beckons," Jimmy said.

Bobbie watched the tips of Jimmy's fingers sink a fraction into Joy's flesh, just above her hip, as he steered her away. Wasn't it too low down? More like a lover's touch than that of an old family friend.

Joy pulled away from Jimmy and gave him a look– a warning frown blended with a coy smile that dropped too late as Joy turned to Bobbie and put out her hand. "Will you come with us? We gather when we have blink footage to view. It's a way of briefing everyone, and a chance to catch up on Belus-land."

Instinctively, Bobbie reached for her sister's hand, her protective instinct kicking in. But almost as quickly, Bobbie pushed the warm feeling away and pulled her hand up short of Joy's. Hurt flickered in Joy's frown, glancing off Bobbie's anger like a bug off a windshield. Bobbie couldn't dislodge her acrimony, didn't want to. Bitterness was easier to embrace than the hollow void of loss and self-mistrust. Bobbie had spent so much energy trying to protect Joy in the past when there had been no need. How could Bobbie trust her senses now? Yet her thoughts shifted to Jimmy – had he purposefully scared those children? And had he touched Joy too familiarly?

Bobbie took stock of the tall, handsome man Jimmy had become in the eleven days since his exposure to the virus. His white hair thickened with supplementary brown at the roots and flopped about his ears and neckline in a parody of a sun-bleached surfer. He'd cut back his bushy white mustache, so all that remained was a skim of sable stubble over his lower face. His flashing orange eyes, strangely appealing, danced with humor, matching the ever-ready smile at his lips. His torso, once concave and bent, flanked by spindly arms with outgrown elbows, now filled in with meaty pectoral muscles, framed by biceps and triceps that strained against the tunic he wore. Jimmy had become a fine specimen. Bobbie could see the lights come on when Joy looked at him.

How would Hicks feel? It would hurt him. Bobbie fretted about that. Then again, her track record for seeing things as they really were was so skewed that maybe she was wrong. What did she know anymore? She felt lost inside her own skin.

Bobbie fell in beside Joy and Jimmy as they walked back to the cave system. They passed plants growing in orderly rows, lined up like soldiers on parade.

"How come Belus Corp doesn't see this from the air?" Bobbie asked, pushing civility into her tone.

"They might if they flew over here, but they rarely do," Joy said. "They have no reason to. Their heat sensors tell them it's too hot for habitation. But if they did, we have screens to pull over them so they can't see the greenery." She pointed at huge rolls, half a meter in diameter, at one end of the field. Bobbie spotted posts scattered throughout the area that would support the fabric without it lying on the plants and breaking them.

"I'm surprised we didn't notice them from the cliff-top," Jimmy said.

"We were at the wrong angle to see this part of the valley." Joy smiled at him and her dark eyes aglow.

"That's a lot of work. All that gardening," Bobbie said, taking in the different shades of green.

"It is hard work. The kids help as soon as they can. Sadly, this generation will have a very short childhood," Joy said. "They work hard."

"They seem happy." Bobbie thought of the little girls who had passed earlier, but her heart grew heavy as she thought of little Nero with only one foot.

"Needs must," Joy said.

"What are you growing?" Jimmy asked.

"Potatoes, beans, broccoli, kale, tomatoes," Joy said, pointing at different rows.

"We could use potato plants as bioreactors for vaccine production," Bobbie said, thinking aloud.

"Cool – whatever it takes. We tried peas, but it's still too hot. There's an herb garden in that far corner, and we have garlic too. What else?" she asked herself, scrunching her face in thought, "There's other stuff." Joy waved her hand. "But I can't think of it."

"I bet if I asked you to list the gadgets in the comms room, you'd not miss a thing," Bobbie said.

"You know me too well, big sis!" Joy smiled.

Bobbie peered at her. "Do I?"

Joy's shoulders sagged. She stared at her feet as they walked the rest of the way to the cave. Bobbie regretted crimping their conversation so abruptly. Containing her resentment took so much effort. If she released any pressure, something toxic would leak out.

The theatre was in the huge cavern where Bobbie had met her father two nights ago. Now it was transformed, with a large rectangular screen of shimmering silver material several meters high, wider than it was long. A narrow aisle ran from front to back, bisecting the rows of benches that filled the space.

Hicks already had seats halfway up. Joy indicated to Bobbie to sit next to him. His face lit up when he saw them.

"Hi," Hicks said, smiling. "How's the wrist, Joy?"

"Same." Joy held up her hand. Her fingers wiggled daintily out of the clunky bandage. She nodded at the bench. "I need to sit on the end in case they have tech issues." She shrugged a what-can-ya-do.

Bobbie hadn't seen much of Hicks since she'd woken up to find him sleeping on the floor by her bed some hours after she'd run away from her father. Hicks had found her passed out from exhaustion and had carried her to her quarters. He'd told Bobbie he had been worried about her, but also exhausted, so he'd laid down on the floor beside her bed and slept there.

"Wanna talk about it?" Hicks had asked when Bobbie woke and sat up dazed.

"It's going to take a while for this cow pat to dry out enough play Frisbee with," Bobbie said sadly.

Hicks nodded, a hint of a smile brightening his eyes. They often compared emotion to cow manure – soft and goopy when it first lands and totally unmanageable, but given time to dry out, could easily be picked up and thrown away.

"You know where I am," Hicks said, "when you feel like flinging your shit."

Bobbie nodded, her words jammed.

"You know I knew nothing about your father being alive either, Bobbie," Hicks said.

His concern threatened to unravel her. Bobbie nodded again and let her ginger locks fall over her face. She kept her head bowed as he left the room.

They split up the doctor tasks. Bobbie took on the younger patients, usually more surgical cases, whereas Hicks had concentrated on medical cases with chronic conditions and elderly patients. They'd taken on Yoon and Henry as "apprentices," to share as much of their medical knowledge in as short a time as possible. The days had been busy, and Bobbie was grateful for the distraction.

As the lights in the cave dimmed, a hush settled over the people sitting on the rows of benches in front of the screen. A cone of light beamed from the darkness behind them and cast a white square, filling the screen. Bobbie hadn't seen an antique projector working in real life.

"Pass the popcorn," Jimmy's voice said behind them.

"Shush!" from somewhere in the darkness.

The footage began with an ultra-elderly lady who kept touching her hair and adjusting her tunic.

"Go ahead, you can talk now," a voice off-screen said.

"Hi, Jacob, it's Mimi. We miss you, but things are going well. I'm feeling so much better after they gave me my new medicine. I sent you a blink, but I don't know if you were able to download it."

A ripple of laughter ran through the audience. Bobbie smiled at the elderly woman's old-school terminology. Blinks were opened, not downloaded, though Bobbie wasn't sure how it worked without an ONIV up and running. She was struggling with the lack of tech, and sorely missed blinking. She had been taken aback when Mo had given her chalk and a slate to write her list of things for the lab.

"Don't you at least have a pencil and paper?" she'd asked.

"Be grateful I'm not handing you a chisel," Mo had replied.

More people appeared on screen, with messages for loved ones. Bobbie was bored, feeling guilty about wasting time when she could be working. The transmission ended, and a hubbub arose as people shuffled and took advantage of the break to move around.

"Not much privacy in these messages, is there?" Hicks said to Joy.

"I know, but it's kind of a tradition, and it helps everyone feel connected, I guess." Joy shrugged. "I think it's nice. Ori set it up when she started the colony."

"Who is Ori?" Bobbie asked. She'd heard the name several times.

"She's one of the main undercover operatives in Belus-land," Joy said, lowering her voice. "I've never met her face-to-face. She keeps her image off everything, as much for our protection as hers, but I heard rumors that she may be visiting soon. People are quite excited, but then again, these rumors do the rounds every so often, and when she does drop in, it's always unannounced and brief. Dad knows her well."

Bobbie stiffened at the mention of her father.

"He'll be back in few days, Bobbie," Joy said gently. "You'll have time to reconnect then."

Shushing hissed around the cave as the break ended, and footage started up again.

Bobbie felt the warmth of Hicks' hand on her shoulder. "Look. There's Lisette Fox."

Bobbie studied Lisette's face. As glamorous as ever, the woman's low forehead was crowned with a mane of rich brown hair, her high cheekbones like shelves supporting hazel eyes more cat-like than usual as she smiled into the camera. Lisette raised a slender hand to stall the applause from the crowd.

"Thank you, thank you." Lisette half-bowed, and the camera pulled back. She was thin to the point of being androgynous, flat-chested and formless. Her blue sensorfabric tunic fluttered with moving images of butterflies at the hems and sleeves.

"Today," Lisette began, beaming a high voltage-smile, "brings phenomenal change for humanity. Today, we change our lives and those of the generations to come. Today, we are on the brink of a lifestyle of leisure and longevity that has never before been witnessed by humanity. Everyone behind me on the podium..."

The camera panned back more to show a stage with a hundred or so people standing side by side.

"...is a centenarian."

Bobbie felt the burn of bile in the back of her throat as the camera zoomed in on a woman on the stage, then moved to the face of the man next to her, panning slowly from one face to the next. Each had smooth, glowing skin, thick heads of hair, and eyes blazing bright orange. They looked straight at the camera, waved, and smiled. Each one could pass for a twenty- or thirty-year-old. In the background, thunderous applause told Bobbie that a massive crowd of civilians attended the spectacle. Bobbie froze in horror. Had Belus released the virus, and if so, how many more would be infected by the virus? Was this driven by the Melters? Were Lisette Fox and Belus Corps really in cahoots with the Melters?

A buzz hummed through the cave as people nudged each other and turned in their seats to look back in Bobbie's direction, and it took a second for her to realize they were staring at Jimmy. Beads of sweat popped on his brow as he dipped his forehead and stared at his own hands. An eerie hush fell, punctuated by the creaking of benches as everyone turned back to the screen. Bobbie's heart thumped so hard, she was sure everyone around her could hear it.

The camera came back to Lisette, who waited for the crowd in front of her to settle down. She glanced around as quiet resumed, then with outstretched arms, proclaimed, "Today, Belus Corps brings you Rejuvenation!"

CHAPTER 10

So, Lisette Fox knew about rejuvenation. The realization completely crushed what was left of Bobbie's confidence in her worldview. How could she trust her instincts when they had been so badly wrong? Bobbie sought sanctuary in what she could trust – medical science. In the week that followed the broadcast, Hicks had taken over more of the daily doctor rounds, and Bobbie had thrown herself into the development of the vaccine, a standard protocol once she'd received the right equipment. The vaccine was nearly ready.

Bobbie wanted to believe, needed to believe, that Lisette Fox was ignorant of the danger of its side effects, but she remembered her father's account of the people killed at Belus Corp's hand, for the greater good. If Lisette Fox and Belus Corp were willing to kill soldiers to prevent the spread of deadly Melter viruses, it made no sense for them to release the rejuvenation nanobots, especially through a vector they would find difficult to control. Her naivety and stubborn willingness to trust the government haunted Bobbie. It had resulted in exclusion from her father's life for so many years. Bobbie had to accept that Lisette Fox would hardly endorse rejuvenation without knowing the details. Could it be that Lisette Fox and Belus Corp weren't the benevolent entities she had believed in? The thought left Bobbie bereaved like she'd lost something precious, something solid. Her sense of floating adrift intensified.

Bobbie sat apart from everyone else in the sun cave. Outside, dawn had just broken, sending rays of the rising sun through a series of openings high on the cavern's walls. Golden light reflected around the interior, lighting the cave. Beams of sunshine refracted through the prisms, throwing rainbows across the walls and floor, moving with the sun.

Bobbie savored the quiet, despite having people close by. Mo entered the cave. He looked around, spotted her, and strode towards her with purpose. So much for contemplation – life was like that for doctors. Bobbie stood as Mo approached.

"Sorry to interrupt," he whispered. "Can I have a quick word?"

Bobbie followed Mo outside. In the distance, the rattle of rocks down slopes made her shiver despite the warm morning air.

"Davitt wants to see you," Mo said.

"So, he's heard Belus released his virus?" Bobbie wasn't surprised. Davitt would be pissed about Lisette Fox presenting his project to the world without him there to take the credit. "Take me to him."

Mo led Bobbie to a section of smaller caves, stooping at the low ceilings. These were dark, dimly lit, and smelled of urine. The walls, barely visible in the gloomy light, glistened as the shards of unpolished crystals reflected what little light there was, like the eyes of beasts waiting to pounce from the shadows. The interiors were sectioned into cubicles using parts of old hover-vehicles. A side of a Mercedes F-class reminded Bobbie of her own car, docked back at her apartment in Armagh.

Davitt looked terrible. Black and yellow bruising began at his temple and spread down into his bristly black beard. His curly hair had matted into tufts and stuck out from his head. He wore a dusty black tunic, and trousers that were too short in the arms and legs. His face looked thinner, and he smelled of body odor, his breath heavy with the stink of stomach issues.

Bobbie tried not to care, turning down her empathy gauge as much as she could. His actions had led to Granny's death. She must remember that.

As Bobbie entered his cell, Davitt clambered to his feet and said, "You have to let me help you with the vaccine."

"I can manage." Bobbie kept her tone crisp and detached, though her stomach roiled.

"My invention was nowhere near ready to be released. You know what the nanobots do. I have to stop the virus from spreading."

Bobbie gave him a dirty look. "So conscientious all of a sudden?"

"I know how these things go. I'll be vilified, my work panned when these old people turn evil. My work will be for nothing," Davitt said, pacing.

"How do you know it's your work?" Bobbie stayed in the doorway, one eye on Mo, waiting further down the hall. "Maybe someone else was working on the nanobots and produced a better version? Something Lisette Fox believes is safe?"

Davitt ran his fingers through his hair. He tilted his head back, blew air out his mouth, making his lips vibrate. He stood, looking at the ceiling, his hands clasped at the nape of his neck. "Nope," he finally said. He dropped his arms to his sides and shook his head. "I was the only one who had the working prototype. The others..." He turned away from Bobbie.

"What about the others?" Bobbie asked, her scalp prickling.

"Their prototypes caused... they weren't successful."

"They didn't make people younger?"

"No; the nanobots had an adverse effect on the subject." Davitt turned slowly to face her. Shadows lurked in his dark eyes.

"By *adverse effect* you mean killed, and by *subject* you mean people?" Bile burned the back of her throat. Bobbie swallowed it back and curled her lip, channeling her disgust for Davitt through her stare.

Davitt raised his hands. "I didn't intend for this thing to happen the way it did. The people running the program had no patience. They kept pushing us for more and more results, which meant using more and more subjects."

"Enough of the subject shit, Davitt. Call them people, human beings." Bobbie clenched her fists. "How many?"

Davitt backed away, shaking his head.

"Answer me, admit it! How many?"

"Thousands," Davitt whispered. "Thousands before I hit on a design that worked. The other scientists working on the project… they… I never saw them after that."

"What do you mean?"

"They disappeared, and their resources were handed to me." Davitt stepped forward from the bowels of his cell. "I tried to make it more humane. I begged them to stop using PARC inmates, to keep it at the ultra-elderly. They were going to die anyway."

Bobbie stumbled back and leaned against the door jamb. Mo moved down the hall towards her. She held up her hand. "I'm okay."

Mo stopped, but stood his ground.

"You're a monster," Bobbie said to Davitt through gritted teeth.

Davitt sucked in a breath as if Bobbie had physically struck him.

"No." He projected the word on an exhale. "I wanted to develop a cure for aging to help people, for fuck's sake! You of all people should understand that."

"There are protocols for experimentation, Davitt. Procedures you decided didn't apply to you." Rage rattled her limbs, made her voice quiver.

"I had no choice. Slade threatened to shut down my research. I needed results quickly. I had to take risks."

"Risks?" Bobbie said. "Risks?"

"I'm sorry about Gloria. Really, I am. Please, get me out of here. Let me help. If we make an airborne vaccine, we can stop the spread of the virus. The virus is the vector for the rejuvenation nanobots. Its only purpose is to deliver the nanobots into the cells. Without a working virus, the nanobots would need to be injected into one sub… patient at a time."

Davitt was right, but Bobbie wasn't sure she could trust him. Hell, she wasn't sure she could trust herself anymore. Making her vaccine airborne would take a bit more work. Maybe Davitt could help with that.

"Let me talk to Hicks," Bobbie said quietly.

"Make it quick. We need to move fast."

Bobbie turned to leave.

"One more thing," Davitt said. "I've been thinking about the sociopathic tendencies that the nanobots induce. I think it's inherent in the spliced DNA blueprint, and that the donor may have had it."

Bobbie swung around to face him. "Who was the donor? The people running the program? Was Slade acting alone?"

"I don't know."

"Oh, fuck you, Davitt," Bobbie said. "I've had enough of your games."

"I'm not playing games. The people in charge blinked us anonymously. We were threatened with the PARC if we talked about it."

She nodded. "What about Slade?"

"Slade didn't know who the donor was."

"What? How do you know?"

"Because she asked me who the donors were on several occasions."

Bobbie was sure that Slade had been behind it all. "I find that hard to believe."

"I tell you, I was given the samples and told to use those and only those–"

"But you spliced them with your own, didn't you?" Bobbie said.

Davitt flushed red. "Yes, because the sample I was given for the male chromosome had degraded. It had been frozen, and the defrosting process damaged some of the bases and the hydrogen bonding."

"How could that happen with the technology we have for freezing samples?" Bobbie asked. This was easy science.

Davitt paced again. "It could happen if you used older technology to freeze the sample."

"But that makes no sense."

"I know." Davitt stopped and turned towards Bobbie, his face more animated than she'd seen since she'd found him in bed with Granny. "Why use an old donor? I've been stuck on that question for almost five years."

Five years! Davitt had been secretly working on rejuvenation for five years – almost as long as they'd been together, and Bobbie hadn't suspected a thing.

"There are plenty of donors, fresh, unfrozen samples," Davitt continued. "Why risk using a damaged sample?"

"Unless," Bobbie said, "there was something special about that sample, that person. Something the person behind the project wanted to pass on to the nanobots, or recreate. Where is the sample now?"

"Back in the lab, frozen," Davit said. "But we couldn't use it. That's why..."

"You used your own," Bobbie finished for him.

"Yes," he said, hanging his head.

"So how can we be sure the psychotic genes aren't from you?" Bobbie asked.

"Do you have to be such a bitch?" Davitt said, looking up with narrowed eyes.

"I suppose that's two trick questions in a row." Bobbie moved out the door of the cell and turned back.

Davitt glared.

"We'll never know. Because if you were psychopathic, you'd hide it." She swung the door closed behind her.

"Fuck you!" Davitt shouted as Bobbie walked away, his anger somehow soothing her.

"I hate him, but I'll work with him," Hicks said, putting his hands on the metal table-top and leaning forward in his rickety seat.

"Me too." Joy nodded, cradling her injured arm against her chest. She looked pale, with smudges of mauve in the skin beneath her eyes. Bobbie worried that Joy's wrist wasn't healing well, but anytime she examined Joy, the fracture site seemed fine. Perhaps Joy was upset that Bobbie had turned away from her again.

That, Bobbie decided, was just too bad. She couldn't help her feelings of bitterness and anger, though on the surface, she remained as civil as possible towards Joy. Inside, Bobbie harbored a dark and spiteful resentment.

"Nope," Jimmy said. "Not gonna happen. I can't be in the same room as that slimeball. When I think of what he did to my Gloria, I just wanna rip his head off."

My Gloria? Bobbie remembered gently teasing Granny about 'Old Jimmy.' Granny had scoffed it off, and Bobbie was certain that Granny had never reciprocated Jimmy's feelings for her. Bobbie let it go. If Jimmy wanted to believe now that he and Granny had something going on, what good would it do to dissuade him?

"You don't have to be in the same room as him, Jimmy," Bobbie said. "We just need some of your cells to test the vaccine."

"Fine, whatever." He pushed back from the table and stood up. "Will that be all?"

"Yes, thanks, Jimmy," Bobbie said.

No-one else spoke as Jimmy left.

Hicks drummed his fingers on the table.

"What?" Joy asked.

"I don't like his attitude," Hicks said. "He's not the same old Jimmy we knew before."

"Of course, he's not," Joy answered. "Are any of us? For a start, he's not exactly old anymore."

"Do you think he's developing the psychosis?" Bobbie didn't relish the idea of tasering him. It seemed ridiculous, here in the relative normality of a group setting with a loosely-defined social structure. She thought of the makeshift prison where they held Davitt.

"I do," Hicks said.

"Oh, come on!" Joy said, jumping to her feet. "You've had a thing about him all along."

Jealousy, Bobbie thought, with a fresh lick of her own.

Joy swayed and put her hand to her head, as the color drained from her face.

Hicks stood up just in time to catch her. Her eyes rolled, her knees unlocked, and Joy crumpled against him. She came round immediately, her eyes focusing as Hicks guided her back to her seat.

"Put your head forward, between your knees," he said.

"I'm okay now, really, I am." Joy's hands trembled. "I just stood up too quickly."

"You're shaking," Hicks said and put his hand on her forehead. "And clammy."

"I–I think I might have a bug," Joy said.

"In that case, you need to stay in your bed," Bobbie said. "We don't want to risk you spreading it. Go on. I'll bring you something to eat later." She wondered if the virus that Davitt had used to transmit the nanobots had a pathology of its own. She was asymptomatic so far. Bobbie made a mental note to ask Davitt which virus he'd used to begin with. They needed to know more. After all, they'd brought Davitt so they could use his knowledge. Or had that just been a way to delay serving out their own justice?

"Maybe I'll lie down for a while." Joy stood slowly. Hicks stayed by her side.

"So, it's settled. We need Davitt's help." Bobbie stood up. "Whether we like it or not. We went to the trouble of bringing him with us, so I'm going to have him work in the lab with us. And at least he volunteered. That makes it easier."

"Unless he's up to something?" Joy said.

"We'll keep a close eye on him," Hicks said. "Now, let's get you to your quarters."

* * *

Shipments had arrived the night before. The cave designated to Bobbie and Hicks for a lab was full of boxes of different shapes and sizes. The sooner Bobbie got everything unpacked, the sooner she could have a look at the samples she had taken from Granny.

The perimeter of the cave was a rough oblong about four meters long, and three at its widest spot. A large workbench took up the space in the center. Bobbie began by opening the boxes, setting up microscopes, data loggers, and analysis machines as she found them. She uncovered a glove box and stood back to admire its antique lines. She had used one in science class. The sealed clear acrylic box had two holes, each filled with a one-piece Hypalon glove. It would be the perfect place to develop the virus.

Behind her, Bobbie heard someone clear their throat. She swung around to see her father with a boy by his side. The boy hung back with his head bowed, and fidgeted with something in his hands.

"Bobbie, I've only got a couple of days before I take off again," Luke began. "I just wanted you to meet Hang. Say 'Hello' to your big sister." Her father turned sideways and put a hand on the thirteen-year-old boy's shoulder, gently pushing him forward.

"Dad, I'm really busy here..." Bobbie began, but stopped as Hang lifted his head, causing her heartbeat to skip. Bobbie had always known that face. Hang could have been Gracie without the disease. A sense of needing to protect him welled in her. How vulnerable he looked standing by Luke, shifting his weight from foot to foot. Hang smiled shyly and held out a figurine of a girl with wings instead of arms, carved from wood.

"This is for you. I made it." Hang's cheeks dimpled with his smile.

Bobbie turned it over, admiring the detail, melting inside. "It's beautiful. An angel. Thank you."

The boy's face flushed. "Act-actually, it's a girl changing into a swan." His brow furrowed, and he seemed worried that he'd offended Bobbie.

"From the Children of Lir?" Bobbie asked.

Hang nodded.

"Dad said that our sister, uhh," Hang stammered, "the one who died, I mean, uh..." He looked to his dad for support.

Luke smiled and nodded. Bobbie recognized the look of love and support. It was like a balm. Her heart swelled. There was a time Bobbie thought she'd never see that again.

"Well, Dad said that she loved the old Irish legends. So I looked them up. The Children of Lir was my favorite." Hang's beseeching smile tugged at Bobbie.

"That was my favorite too," she said, admiring the detail in the figurine. "What do you like about that legend?"

"It's like Dad. He had to fly away, and now we live in exile until the Evil Queen is dead," Hang said.

"I see." Bobbie couldn't help smiling at the child's earnest expression. He was every bit as invested in the stories as Gracie had been. "Gracie's favorite was the one where Oisin went to the land of the forever young," she said.

"Tír na nÓg." Hang tapped his mouth with his forefinger, looking so earnest Bobbie had to press her lips tight together to not appear to laugh. She looked over his head and locked eyes with her father. Luke beamed with pride that warmed Bobbie too. Hang was her blood too.

"You know your legends alright," Bobbie said, shifting her gaze to Hang again. The child's shoulders released, and he cocked his head to one side.

"I do, but they have such sad endings," Hang said.

"Only because we don't know what comes next in each person's story," Bobbie said.

"But everyone dies in the end," Hang said. "The Children of Lir grow to three hundred years old and die. Oisin gets off the horse, touches the ground, and gets old and dies."

"But maybe…" Hairs stood on Bobbie's neck. Granny could be here right now saying this to comfort the lad. "Death is the beginning of a whole new story. We all have to grow old. Then we die. Just because we don't know what life after death looks like, doesn't mean it won't be amazing. Think of how a butterfly feels when it changes from a wormy old caterpillar. I bet it doesn't want to go back to being a caterpillar, right?"

"I suppose so." Hang shrugged, then his face flooded with animation. "I saw a butterfly once. It was beautiful. I made a carving of it too. Would you like to see it?"

"Not right now, young man," Luke interrupted, his eyes aglow. "I'm sure Bobbie is really busy."

"Later," Bobbie said.

Luke smiled and glanced from Bobbie to the boy. Luke steered him away, then looked back at Bobbie and said in a voice graveled with emotion, "I'm so proud of you, Bobbie."

"Oh, Dad." Bobbie strode forward and gave him a hug, whispering in his ear, "Thank you."

He patted her back before they pulled apart, and he followed Hang down the corridor, leaving her alone in the lab.

Bobbie looked around, and a sense of belonging, of family, of contributing to some great plan reached tendrils out to her. Her envy and mistrust of Joy may have been unfair. Bobbie loved Joy, though she was seared by envy and raging with anger towards her. Joy had only been doing what their father had asked her to do to keep everyone safe. Poor Joy; she'd had very little choice about telling Bobbie her secrets.

After fetching a bowl of stew and some bread from the canteen, Bobbie made her way to Joy's quarters. At the door, Bobbie managed to balance both plates in her left hand while she turned the handle – quietly, lest she disturbed Joy taking a nap.

The room was dimly light, but a creak in the bed and a rustle of material helped Bobbie to orientate towards the bed. She tiptoed forward. Dark lumpy masses around the room materialized into possible places to set the tray as Bobbie's eyes slowly adjusted to the dusky light.

Then Bobbie saw Joy naked on the bed, sleeping, her legs still wrapped around those of the man half lying face down upon her, bare butt up.

Bobbie dropped the soup and swore as the hot liquid splattered on her legs and feet.

"Sorry, sorry." Bobbie bent down, trying to contain the spillage. Cringing, she talked without looking at the bed. Who the hell was Joy with? Was it Hicks? But Bobbie didn't want to look, didn't want to know. "I'll just go get something to clean this up if you two want to make yourselves more–"

"Shit!" Joy said.

A dull thud made Bobbie turn back to the source of the noise beside the bed. Jimmy lay sprawled on the floor naked as Joy pulled the sheet around herself.

"Jimmy!" Bobbie exclaimed. It was supposed to be Hicks. Didn't Joy love him? Bobbie was certain he loved Joy. Right now, that was the least of her worries, but she felt heartsore for Hicks.

"Bobbie, I can explain," Joy said, reaching a hand out to her.

Jimmy laughed. "Why does everyone say that at times like these? Especially when they don't have to."

"What the fuck are you doing, Jimmy?" Bobbie said.

"Exactly what it looks like." Jimmy stood up and placed his hands on his hips, showing no shame at his nudity. "You're really making a habit of catching members of your family playing hide the sausage, aren't you, dear?"

"Joy, what the fuck are you thinking?" Bobbie's angered exploded. "He's infected with nanobots!"

"Calm down, calm down." Jimmy spread his hands, fingers wide in front of him as if pushing down Bobbie's concerns. "We've taken precautions. We aren't stupid."

"None of us know how the nanobots spread." Bobbie grabbed a tunic and flung it at Jimmy. "And cover yourself up!"

He caught it in one hand, then hung it around his neck like a scarf, folded his arms and cocked his head to one side. "Look at me. I feel great and have never looked better. If I spread a little of this inadvertently your sister's way, what's the harm?"

"You know the dangers, Jimmy. How can you be so selfish?" Bobbie felt like ripping his head off.

"There's no danger." Jimmy pointed to himself. "I'm one hundred percent."

Bobbie glared at Joy.

Joy shrugged. "He does seem okay." She shuffled towards Bobbie, still wrapped in the sheet. "And you and Davitt told us that I'm immune to the virus. So, I can't catch rejuvenation, right?"

"Unless the nanobots infect you by themselves," Bobbie said. "Through bodily fluids."

Joy looked sick. She swallowed and looked over at Jimmy, who shrugged, still naked.

"Christ, Joy, you know how this works," Bobbie said, hearing the panic in her own voice. "You both heard Davitt explain this back at the lab!"

"Actually," Jimmy said, picking up his pants and stepping into them, "we weren't in the lab, remember? We were busy saving your ass."

"But you were patched in – oh shit!" Bobbie felt sick. Their blinks had been blocked, and Jimmy had coordinated with Joy by using facility camera footage that he'd hacked into. Neither Joy nor Jimmy had heard the conversation in the lab.

Bobbie sat on the edge of Joy's bed, panting, trying to bring her heart rate down – trying not to throw up.

"The virus, by itself, only delivers the nanobots. That's not the problem." Bobbie heard the quiver in her voice and worked to steady it. "The nanobots can still infect you if they're injected into you or –" Bobbie felt weak with fear. Joy was presenting as ill already. Was it too late?

"Through bodily fluids?" Joy asked.

"We don't know... but," Bobbie said. "You two... this" – Bobbie waved a hand – "has to stop."

"No," Joy said. "You can't tell me to do that. If I'm going to catch the nanobots, then it's probably too late. Jimmy and I... it's... special. Please try to understand."

"You're impossible, Joy!" Bobbie said. "You both are." She slammed the door hard behind her as she left.

CHAPTER 11

Each night since Bobbie had arrived at the Yosemite camp, she had collapsed onto her cot, fatigue winning the battle with her whirring brain, and had slept the night through; but tonight, Bobbie couldn't sleep. Silence crackled around her, and darkness shimmered too bright as she lay worrying about Joy's risk of exposure to the nanobots Jimmy had in his system. On top of that, Bobbie dreaded telling Hicks that the woman he loved was sleeping with another man and might be in mortal danger because of it. But Bobbie had to tell Hicks for a multitude of reasons, not least because she needed another doctor to help her figure out how these nanobots might affect young tissue.

The sooner Bobbie finished setting up the lab and examined Granny's samples, the sooner she would be able to get a picture of what she was dealing with. Bobbie swung her legs out of bed and scooped her mop of red hair into a knot on the top of her head. She downed half of the container of water by her bed and splashed the rest in her face. Once dressed, she quickly left her room, trying to remember the most direct way to the lab.

Bobbie chose the wrong tunnel and found herself in a dorm room that housed the boys. A gentle chorus of deep breathing, snuffling snores, and the odd whimper came from a row of ten bunk beds arranged in a semicircle. The air stank of sweaty bodies and cheesy feet.

"Can I help you, Doctor Chan?" asked a female voice in hushed tones. An old lady appeared from the shadows, wearing an old-fashioned brushed-cotton pink nightdress.

"Sorry," Bobbie whispered. "I'm trying to get to the lab."

"Having no blink-nav takes some getting used to," the woman said, her voice warm and soothing. "It's straight through the boys' dorm, that way." The woman lifted her hand and pointed a swollen-knuckled finger to another exit. "The lab is in the biggest dome. You'll be able to pick it out. Just follow the wall to the left until you come to a door. It's got motion sensors for the lighting, so you'll be able to see once you get there."

"Thanks," Bobbie said.

"I'll see you out." The old lady hobbled past the sleeping children. Bobbie matched her pace and followed her.

After the stale air of the dorm, the night air felt fresh on Bobbie's sweat-damp skin. The full moon lit the landscape with brittle white light, coating the world in a fine silver sheen. Bobbie looked up. The domes of the caves humped together, towering over her, and immediately Bobbie saw the one she was headed for. A little tension released between her shoulders. Soon she'd be back at work, doing something productive to help answer her questions and stop the worry she felt for Joy.

"Do you know where you're going now?" wheezed the old lady as she dropped back and shuffled alongside Bobbie.

"I do. Thanks." Bobbie turned to her. "Perhaps you should rest? Must you sit up with the children?"

"With so many little uns, it's necessary," the woman answered. "They would get up to too many shenanigans if we didn't have someone posted. These are either orphans, or their parents live in Belus-land. Kids will be kids, especially when they think they can get away with it. It's not ideal to lump them together like this, but at least they're getting a chance at life." The woman's words drifted off on a raspy cough.

With their Dependency Law, Belus-land had decreed that those precious, snoring children should not exist. Would the sterile, tech-enhanced, orderly world that Bobbie had so blindly believed in snuff out their existence if they found them? Or instead, would Belus demand the life of their carer, the old lady, and others like her?

"Come see me in the morning," Bobbie said gently. "Let me check out that cough."

"No need. I've had this cough for the last twenty-five years, sounds worse than it is." The woman turned and limped back the way they'd come. She stopped at the door, framed by a soft orange glow from the low lights, and said, "I'm sure you have much more important things to be dealing with than an old doll like me. But I appreciate your concern. Have a good night now." She closed the door behind her.

Bobbie smiled. The woman's accent was different, but her humor was so like that of Bobbie's patients in Armagh, back in her former life. Were those patients rejuvenating right now? Getting younger? Madder?

It took a second for Bobbie's eyes to adjust to the moonlight. The stars arranged themselves as if floating up from the edges of the peaks around her, too bright, the black spaces between them too ominous. Bobbie walked to the largest dome and found the door. Inside, she groped in the dark for a second before the lights flashed on. She recognized the lab.

The microscope she'd unpacked was as Bobbie had left it. She found the cold packs where she had stored samples of Granny's tissue. Bobbie's chest tightened as she stared at what was left of her grandmother.

"It's just samples. I can do this," Bobbie said out loud. She expelled a noisy breath and lifted out a sample bag – brain tissue – as good a place to begin as any. The cell structure had been shredded, the nuclear membrane ruptured in many places, and its contents demolished. The resolution wasn't high enough to pick individual nanobots. Bobbie needed the nanoptric viewer for that. It had only arrived that afternoon and wasn't set up yet. But the nanobots clumped together, visible at full magnification in shiny masses, reflecting the light from the microscope in sparkles. Already it was clear, from using the light microscope and Lugol's iodine, that the nanobots had inserted themselves right into the genetic material of the nucleus. Taking them out safely might be impossible. What would their impact be on someone young and strong like Joy? Bobbie worked steadily through the samples, recording her findings, struggling to remain objective, but she couldn't stop her mind straying.

Ashamed, Bobbie thought of the times she'd shunned Joy throughout her life, and of the times Hicks had quietly stood by both of her sisters, often bridging the divide between Bobbie's hurt and one or the other sister. Often Bobbie had been too weak, too fragile, too broken, and Hicks had carried all three of the Chan girls one way or another.

Another slide processed. Bobbie moved to the next, compiling data as she worked. Her hands, eyes, and brain worked away, while her mind tumbled with memories.

Before Gracie had become too ill to attend school, she'd had to use a wheelchair. Each day, Hicks had walked home with them. Bobbie wheeled her sister out of the schoolyard and over the old stone bridge that crossed the river at the bottom of the school property. Once out of sight of the school, Hicks would lift Gracie out of her chair. At first, she was still strong enough to sit on his shoulders.

"Be careful, Gracie," Bobbie would fret.

"I have her," Hicks would say. "She's as light as a feather." He'd bounce Gracie gently, but enough to make her whoop with glee.

Gracie, her face radiant with smiles, would laugh and say, "He can handle it. Our Ryan can handle anything."

In the drag of days when Gracie weakened more, she would beg Hicks to lift her out of her chair, as she winced with pain. Thirteen years old and new to his muscles, Hicks had handled Gracie like crystal. She'd settle in his arms, a delicate little doll, having barely grown since she was six. Sometimes she'd fall asleep before they got home.

Bobbie's mother never admonished Hicks for carrying Gracie. She'd smile, lift her daughter from his arms, and thank him.

When Gracie passed, Bobbie found solace in those same arms. Hicks had held Bobbie as she cried, emptying herself to the universe, and he'd promised he'd always be there.

"Gracie said I could handle anything, Bobbie," Hicks said as he had rocked her back and forth, brushing her hair back from where it stuck to the tears on her cheeks. "But this is the hardest yet."

The datasheet filled with digits and notes. Bobbie couldn't yet pick out any patterns. Nothing obvious jumped out at her; just ruptured cells leaking cytoplasm and organelles. She stretched her neck and wriggled on her stool to flex her spine, then went back to it, working steadily, one sample after another.

After Gracie's funeral, Hicks had continued to walk Bobbie home from school.

The day baby Joy arrived from the hospital, Bobbie and Hicks heard her squawking from the street as they approached the garden gate. Bobbie turned on her heel and ran away. Hicks caught up with Bobbie and grabbed her hand, pulling her to a stop.

"What's wrong with you?" he'd asked.

"I-I can't go in there," Bobbie had stammered.

"She's only a baby." Hicks gave Bobbie's hand a gentle tug back towards the house. "Give her a chance."

Bobbie stood her ground, saying nothing as she swallowed her envy.

"Please, Bobbie," Hicks persisted. "Try? I know she's not... she's not –"

Hicks' eyes softened, moistened. He turned away and tracked back towards the house. Not only was Bobbie envious of the baby, but she was also jealous of Hicks for having room in his heart for both Gracie and Joy. With heavy footfalls, she'd trailed after him.

Granny and Bobbie's mother were in the living room, changing the baby, who protested all the way. Granny picked up Joy, who mewled like a strangled cat.

"Shush now, baba, shush." Granny rocked her. Joy stuck her fists in the air, opened her mouth, and launched a stream of undigested milk down Granny's front. Joy's howls subsided as Granny passed Joy to her mother and ran to the bathroom to clean up.

Joy settled in her mother's arms.

"Can I hold the baby?" Hicks asked shyly, kicking his heel off his toe.

Astonished, Bobbie watched her mother hand over her infant daughter.

"Don't drop her!" Bobbie warned.

"He can handle it," Granny said, arriving back in the kitchen, blot-drying her blouse.

Hicks held baby Joy between his hands. Then he cuddled her into his chest and looked down, smiling at her the way he'd often smiled at Gracie, a soft light in his gray eyes.

Bobbie had another surge of envy. That smile should have been for Gracie.

Back then, Bobbie hadn't wanted Joy in her life, but now it was a different matter.

"I'm sorry. Please be okay, Joy," Bobbie whispered now into the empty lab. Tiredness, the back door to despair, gave Bobbie a dull ache between her temples. She switched from scanning the microscope slides to looking through the data she had collected. The numbers and pictures told her what had happened to Granny's tissues once the nanobots were no longer supporting the cell structure. Bobbie hypothesized that the nanobots' insertion into the cell was in itself a process that damaged the cells so that they became dependent on the nanobots. Destroying the nanobots meant destroying the cells.

Bobbie needed cells from Jimmy and Joy to view under the nanoptric viewer. She groaned, exasperated to her core. Only Davitt knew how to set that machine up. Nanotechnology wasn't something a geriatrician needed to study. She hated having to rely on Davitt.

It was nearly six in the morning. The night had slipped away as Bobbie worked, but she hadn't come any closer to easing the concern lying like lead in her gut. Nothing she had learned could help Joy. Bobbie put her forehead on the metal worktop, relishing its coolness, watching condensation from her breath cloud its shine.

In the first months of Joy's life, Bobbie had carried Gracie's absence as though it were a rock tied to her heart. For the next three years, that glug-glug of sorrow had formed part of Bobbie's identity. She was the girl who mourned; the kid whose twin had died a slow, unusual death. No one could compete with such bereavement. Bobbie had been the winner of a horrible status – until the Melters attacked.

The war, the great leveler, brought everyone on par with Bobbie's grief. During the first wave, Bobbie had watched the devastation in foreign countries and worried about her father and grandfather, but the floods and fires were mere extensions of the disaster movies she had watched. The people and places seemed unreal and far, far away.

The water level crept slowly up the skirts of Ireland. Dublin and Belfast both battled the rising tides and storm surges, but as all children building sandcastles knew, the unstoppable sea always won. People from coastal cities moved inland, to live in tattered tent cities on higher ground. Still, Bobbie was safe with her mother, baby Joy, and Granny in the rolling drumlin country of Armagh.

When the war department delivered the double-barreled bad news that her father and grandfather were killed in the war, Bobbie vowed that never again would she allow herself to love someone so much. She would never again endure that kind of pain. At sixteen, she nipped her crush on Hicks in the bud. By eighteen, she had convinced herself that their friendship was more important than any failed romance could ever be. Better to never try. Bobbie thought she had quashed her love for Hicks, but it was horribly obvious now that she hadn't. All she had done was hide it from herself. No wonder she'd never really loved Davitt.

Was it too early to wake up Davitt? Bobbie should just drag him down here and demand he set up the nanoptric viewer, but that would give him leverage.

"Bastard," Bobbie muttered under her breath. Though she wasn't in love with Davitt, his betrayal had stung. She didn't want Hicks to feel that way when he heard about Joy. Technically, Joy wasn't betraying Hicks. They had made no promise to each other. Nevertheless, Bobbie knew how Hicks would feel when she delivered the news to him about Jimmy and Joy.

Joy. Oh God, Joy could die – like Granny – going crazy, her cells turned to gunk.

"Stupid, stupid girl," Bobbie muttered as she lowered her face into her hands. But who was the stupid girl?

Joy - who should've known the risk - yet chose to sleep with Jimmy? She didn't really understand the risks, though. Yet, how could she have thought of Jimmy when Hicks was there for the taking?

Or Bobbie? She should have debriefed Joy and Jimmy properly after they'd returned, but Bobbie had been too angry to look at her sister, much less talk with her. Yes, she was angry and sorry, but above all, scared. Bobbie cried, rocking herself back and forth, letting the tears flow.

Footsteps scuffled behind her. A hand touched her shoulder.

Bobbie tried to stop crying, but only ended up hiccupping. Wiping her hands across her cheeks, she curled into herself.

"Bobbie, it's just me." Hicks rubbed his hand in a circle between her shoulder blades.

Her weeping calmed to soft snuffling. Bobbie wanted him to go away, but she also wanted him here. Loneliness and self-doubt battered her.

"Granny's samples," Hicks said, his gaze falling on the microscope slides. "Oh God, Bobbie, no wonder you're upset."

Bobbie could just leave it at that, but she had to tell him about Joy. She opened her mouth but couldn't find the words.

"How long have you been here?" Hicks asked, pulling a stool up beside her.

"All night," Bobbie said.

"All night! You must be wrecked." Hicks gave her a sideways hug. "Bobbie, you need your sleep more than ever."

Tell him...

"Joy's sleeping with Jimmy," Bobbie whispered.

"Fuck," Hicks said under his breath. "Did she tell you?"

Bobbie pressed her lips tight together and shook her head. "I caught them at it."

"Oh, Bobbie." Hicks wiped his hand down his face, tugging at his chin. "Jesus."

Bobbie tried to think of something comforting to say. That he was worth ten Jimmys; that Joy would see the error of her ways; that she, Bobbie, loved him, and he didn't need that stupid sister of hers anyway. But Bobbie needed Joy. She couldn't bear to lose another sister.

"Fuck," Hicks said again. "What were they thinking?" He stood up and gave Bobbie's shoulder a squeeze. "That must have been awful for you."

Bobbie burst into another flood of tears. Typical of Hicks to worry about everyone else when his own heart must be breaking.

Hicks rubbed her back. "Cry it out. That'll do you the world of good." As his arms went around Bobbie, she stood up and leaned her head against his chest, threading her arms around his waist. After she had stopped crying, they stood locked together as he rocked her gently back and forth.

"This is bad," Hicks said, breaking the reverie. "How could Jimmy put Joy at risk like this? We have to do a full panel on her as soon as possible. Even if the virus is dead in his system, the nanobots will be in his semen."

Bobbie kept her ear to his chest, using the thud-dump of his heart to ground her as she spoke. "I don't know if they're using any kind of contraception, but if they are, intercourse is still a risk."

"She's probably infected," Hicks said in a clipped tone.

Bobbie couldn't meet his eyes, didn't want to read the hurt she was sure she'd find there. Hicks was being realistic like she ought to be too, so she said, "Yeah. We don't know how these nanobots might transfer between individuals. His saliva, never mind his semen, would be full of nanobots. Could they get through the lining of her mouth, intestines, uterus? Fuck! I thought she was smart, but this? This is as stupid as it gets. It's reckless. It's irresponsible. It's –"

"It's Joy," Hicks interrupted. His hand between Bobbie's shoulder blades worked on her clenched muscles. She instantly felt calmer.

"She's always been like this," Hicks said. "And at least now you can agree with me that Jimmy is different. We need to decide what to do about him."

"True, but the thought of tasering him! God, I hate it." Bobbie pulled out of the embrace.

"We could contain him in a holding cell," Hicks suggested.

"Like the one Davitt's in?" Bobbie looked up. "It would buy us some time."

"Jeez, could you imagine those two holed up beside one another?" Hicks chuckled.

"I'm sorry I had to tell you like this," Bobbie said, stepping back, the space between them becoming an abyss.

"Like what?" Hicks reached forward and wiped a tear from her cheek with his thumb.

"I mean... you're taking this really well, considering..." Bobbie faltered and looked at the floor between their feet.

"Considering what?"

"Oh, come on. Don't act coy." Bobbie looked into Hicks' face but saw confusion cloud his gray eyes. "I know you're in love with her."

Hicks' eyes widened. "What?"

"You don't have to deny it," Bobbie said.

"How could you think that?" Hicks demanded.

"Last year, I overheard you talking to her friend... that guy from her class... at her twenty-first birthday party." Bobby backed up, shaken. She hadn't expected anger, not from Hicks.

"What are you talking about?"

Bobbie took a breath, steadied herself. "You asked him if he'd asked Joy out yet, and he said there was no point. That she prefers older guys."

Hicks gave a brittle laugh, like shattering glass. "He got that right!"

"He said that you were in with a chance." Bobbie's chest constricted at the memory of how heartsick she'd been. Her blood pounded in her head as she stood stock, still trying not to let Hicks see her tremble. "And you ... you said, 'I should be so lucky.'"

"Oh, fuck sake, Bobbie." Hicks ran his fingers through his hair. It stuck up in angles, giving him a crazed look. "She's like a sister to me. A sister." He tipped his head to the side, looking so sad it nearly broke Bobbie's heart.

"You love her. You as much as said so when she asked you to come to Yosemite. You said she was everything to you, or something to that effect. I mean, you did give up your life to come here."

Hicks turned his back to her, shaking his head and saying, "Oh my God, Bobbie Chan – you are such an idiot!"

"Hey, what the –" Bobbie began, but Hicks didn't let her finish.

"How can such an intelligent woman be so blind? So stupid?" Hicks turned back to her, staring with such intensity it made a bubble in her chest expand.

In two steps, he stood right in front of her. He put his hands on her shoulders. "I came here for you, Bobbie, you!"

Bobbie stared at Hicks. No matter how much she'd vowed to never let him in, he was a part of her. She needed him.

"No! I can't do this," Hicks said, and rushed towards the door, knocking over a stool that rolled into his way. He kicked it aside, but it gave Bobbie time to catch up with him and grab his hand.

"Wait," she said. "You came here for me?"

"Yes," Hicks whispered, reaching his hand forward, stroking her cheek. She nuzzled into it, her eyes glued to his. "Yes, I couldn't bear to lose you," he said.

"Lose? Me?"

"Good God, Bobbie!" Irritation edged his softened tone. "You're my whole world. You're what I get up for every day. Your happiness is my happiness. Your misery is my heartbreak."

"Why didn't you tell me?" Hope unfurled within her but was so alien it scared her.

"I tried to. Remember?" Hicks' eyes bore into hers, pleading for understanding.

Bobbie couldn't speak.

Hicks rested his hand along her cheek gently, as though handling delicate crystal, and said, "I asked you to our school dance, and you told me you'd never go out with me. We could only ever be friends. I listened to you. I believed you." He lowered his hand.

Bobbie's face felt cold in its absence. She still couldn't speak, couldn't believe her ears, yet the truth was arranging itself as the years scrolled back in her head, and she felt defensive. Hicks didn't understand how hard it was for her to let anyone in. She'd lost so much – too much.

"Later, when we were older, I was too shit scared – you left a trail of destroyed relationships and broken men in your wake." Hicks rubbed his chin. "I hated Davitt the most, but I was jealous of the whole fucking string of men who crawled into your bed, the only place in the world I wanted to be. And I rejoiced every time you dumped them."

"Jesus, you make me sound like a right bitch!" Bobbie snapped. "Your love life was no success story either, you know."

"At least I tried. Believe me, I tried to let you go, to make a go of it with other women, but the problem was always the same – they were never you." A muscle flexed in his jaw.

Bobbie opened her mouth, then shut it. Time stopped. Every moment they'd spent together flashed through her head. She had wasted so much time, squandered so many moments, but what if she lost Hicks? How could she bear it? Bobbie couldn't keep him out when she didn't know how he felt; when she'd tried her hardest to push him away. How could she keep him out now?

As if starting the clock again, Hicks lifted her hand and kissed her open palm. "I'm here for you. If Joy gets sick, we'll fix it together."

"But what if she–" Bobbie began, but couldn't bear to think about Joy dying, much less say it.

"For one second, stop thinking about her. You can't make her behave any better. She's a grown woman. She can make her own decisions. Has made her own decisions." Hicks put his forehead on Bobbie's. "You are not responsible for Joy. I know you're terrified of losing her, of losing anyone. Who isn't? But you don't have to do this alone. You've never needed to." Hicks brushed a soft kiss past her ear to whisper, "I'm with you every step of the way."

Every hair on her body bolted to attention, every nerve alight. She tilted her head back and leaned into him. Their lips met, yielding and delicate. A frisson of energy arced right to her groin, making her groan. He sighed, low and resonating. Fever broke inside her, releasing a storm of sensation – his hands in her hair, her hands on the muscles of his back, pulling him to her, her to him, kissing harder, their tongues exploring, tasting each other.

Hicks pulled back, like water dousing flames.

"What's wrong?" Bobbie asked.

"Nothing's wrong." He laughed deep and throaty. "I love you, and I've waited all my life for the right moment to tell you that I love you," he said. "I'm pretty sure this is not the right moment, but I wish I'd told you years ago."

"Oh, Ryan, me too! We've been such idiots!" Bobbie pulled him to her in a joyous bear hug. "I love you too, Ryan Hicks, with my heart and soul." Her heart raced with joy and fear. She had everything she had ever wanted in the whole world, had always had it, but now, Bobbie realized with a fresh slice of terror, she had so much more to lose.

CHAPTER 12

Everything felt easier, and Bobbie knew why. Beside her, Hicks hummed to himself as he prepped samples for the nanoptric viewer further along the workbench. Bobbie adjusted the settings on the viewer. An image appeared on the intepanel on the desk between them. Hicks frowned and went silent.

"Need help with that?" Bobbie asked, glancing at the brightly-colored bobbles in bulging clusters – body cells in nano-detail.

"I got it," Hicks murmured.

Bobbie stepped aside so Hicks could see the screen better. He moved wordlessly into position but trailed his hand around her waist, giving her an absent-minded rub as it passed the small of her back. The contact filled her heart. As he studied the image, Bobbie studied him, reveling in the thrill of drinking him with her eyes, not worrying about being caught looking at him.

"Stop it, will ya?" he said, his lips parting in a wide smile. "I know you're looking at me."

"I've got a lot of catching up to do," Bobbie said. "But you're right, I shouldn't be distracting you." She stepped away from him, curbing her desire to touch him, hug him to her, pull his face level with hers and sink into his cool gray eyes.

He loved her – her! The idea made her fizzle with happiness, despite everything that was happening. Her deep contentment came from knowing that she no longer had to hide her love for him.

"So, have you decided what you're going to say to Joy?" Hicks asked.

"Not exactly," Bobbie said. "I don't understand her. I never have, but then again, I wasn't privy to all the information. I've been such a dope, Ryan. I wasted so much time worrying about the wrong things."

"You also spent a fair bit of time worrying about the right things," Hicks said. "You were on to the serious side effects of rejuvenation right away. You risked everything to rescue Granny. You've pretty much gotten a vaccine to work against the virus."

"Making the vaccine is the easy part, especially with that medical matter streamer they have here, but it feels so pointless. Even with the vaccine, there are hundreds of people already infected with the nanobots. The vaccine just prevents the spread of the nanobots via the virus. Nanobots can still be injected, or..." Bobbie stopped talking, squeezed her eyes closed and massaged the spot between her eyebrows.

"I'll ask Joy for those tissue samples," Hicks said.

"Why do you need tissue samples from Joy?" Davitt asked from the door.

Hicks and Bobbie, snapping to attention, turned to face him. He stood with Mo behind him, untying his wrists. He'd had a shower, a shave, and been changed into a fresh set of clothes, but the side of his face still had the yellow hue of old bruising, and gray-tinged skin circled his eyes.

"He's to stay in this room until you don't need him anymore," Mo said, giving Davitt a shove forward. "Jacob or I will guard him."

"So, are we at risk?" Davitt asked, frowning. "Did the virus deliver nanobots to Joy? I was sure we had gotten through the incubation period without contracting the virus."

"She may have picked up the nanobots without the virus," Bobbie said.

"Impossible," Davitt said. "The nanobots aren't airborne. They need a vector like a virus to penetrate the skin, or maybe an exchange of body fluids –" Davitt slapped his hands together with a harsh laugh. "That dirty old bastard!"

"We keep this information in the lab," Bobbie said through gritted teeth, but the thought hammered in her skull – You slept with Granny, you hypocritical fucker!

Mo nodded.

"I might need some incentive," Davitt said, looking at Mo, "such as nicer quarters and less of the bondage." He held up the red welts on his wrists.

"Or solitary confinement," Mo hissed back.

Davitt dropped his hands. "You fucker."

"On that subject," Hicks said, folding his arms and leaning against the workbench, looking as if he was settling down for a good old chat. "How did you manage to not get contaminated when you screwed the subjects?"

The last word burned like acid in Bobbie's ears, but she knew where Hicks was going. Davitt could have infected her too, and in turn, she had put Hicks at risk. She was mortified that she'd not considered this.

Davitt flushed red, and he cleared his throat. "I programmed my medical matter streamer to make..." He cleared his throat again. "A fabric that's nonporous to nanoparticles, and..." He wiped his hand over his mouth. Bobbie read the shame in his eyes. "... We never kissed."

Think about something else – don't think about how he treated Granny like a whore...

"So, what do you know about nanobots in young cells?" Bobbie asked.

"Not a lot," Davitt said, leaning against the counter. "Once the nanobot gets into a cell, it integrates with the cell structure where it's needed. If it's not needed, it doesn't insert itself."

"So, Joy might not have cellular damage?" Hicks asked.

"Except in cells where senescence has begun," Bobbie said.

"True," Davitt said, "But in someone as young as Joy, it might be a while before the nanobots would insert themselves. I could engineer an anti-nanobot that would dismantle the rejuvenation nanobots like Jinko–" Davitt interrupted himself and tapped his finger off his chin, lost in thought.

"Your colleague?" Bobbie asked. "What about him?"

"Yeah," Davitt shook his head. "Never mind him – he's a loser."

Bobbie sneaked a glance at Hicks. He raised an eyebrow. She'd explain to Hicks later that Davitt was paranoid about Jinko stealing his work.

Davitt was saying, "You need to get Joy into the lab. And Jimmy – I need tissue samples from him. There's no time to waste."

"And your incentives?" Hicks growled.

"Despite what you think," Davitt said, "I'm not a monster. I wanted rejuvenation to work properly. It's pretty obvious it's not ready yet, though Fox has released it to the population. Do you think I want to live in a world full of psychopaths? Jimmy was enough for me." Davitt pointed to his bruised face.

Hicks bristled.

"Let's just get started," Bobbie said. "We'll run a full biosensor work-up on Joy." She turned to Mo. "You have an offline Succor Tech reader, I presume?"

Mo nodded. "It's in the medical wing."

"Okay, let's get Joy down there ASAP," Hicks said.

* * *

Anger rolled off Jimmy in waves as he stood over Joy, lying on the bed in the medical wing. They had been screened off from the other patients, but sounds reached through: a hacking cough followed by the sound of a moist spit, a low murmur of conversation – the words a blur, and every so often a child cried out, its squeal hushed by unseen carers.

Bobbie felt sorry for Joy. She looked frightened and tired, and Jimmy's attitude seemed to cause her distress.

"I'm not giving you my samples," Jimmy said, his voice clotted with rage.

"We need to see what's happening in your cells, Jimmy," Bobbie said, struggling to remain reasonable with him. "We need that information to help Joy."

"Joy's fine," Jimmy said, taking her hand. "Aren't you, honey?"

His term of endearment turned Bobbie's stomach sour.

Joy squeezed his hand. "Yeah, but it won't do any harm, will it?"

"No harm? That bastard got us into this mess to begin with – fucking around with nanobots!" Jimmy said.

"Excuse me." Hicks moved between Jimmy and Joy, forcing them to uncouple their hands, and began applying electrodes to her skin.

"Davitt doesn't need to come anywhere near you. I'll take your samples," Bobbie said, clamping down on her anger, working hard to keep her tone professional. "It will only take an hour. Please, Jimmy?"

"The coward," Jimmy spat. "I'm not leaving my samples alone with him. I want to know everything he's doing."

"He's confined to working in the lab," Bobbie said.

"Fine, I'll go there," Jimmy said, then turned to Joy. "Will you be okay here until I get back?"

"Please, just go do it," Joy said. "I'm fine." But her voice quivered in a way that made Bobbie's skin goosebump.

"Watch out for that slimy shit face," Jimmy said.

"Don't worry, I won't see him. Like Bobbie said, he's under lock and key at all times." Joy patted Jimmy's hand as he gave her a peck on the cheek, making Bobbie cringe inside. Jimmy stormed off.

Hicks finished hooking Joy up to the Succor Tech diagnostics and handed her a glass of thick creamy liquid. "Drink up, kid."

Joy grimaced at the taste. "What is it?"

"You need to ingest a sensor. This does some of what your medulla biosensor would be doing if it were online. Unfortunately, the old-fashioned way takes quite a bit longer. We won't have a full panel of results for twenty-four hours." Hicks set the machine going. It made a soft hum, and lights flicked on as it clicked through each new test.

Bobbie moved away from the table. "I'd better go do the same with Jimmy."

"Wait," Joy said.

Bobbie stopped, but didn't turn around.

"Please, don't blame Jimmy for this," Joy said. "I love him. Perhaps I've made a mistake, with the nanobots, you know, but... but we ... we're just–" Joy gave a loud sigh. "I don't know how to explain it."

Bobbie pivoted slowly as she selected her words. "You shouldn't need to explain anything." It came out too sterile, and she tried to inject a gentler tone. "But consider this. Would the man who truly loved you put your life at risk?"

"We thought that if I didn't have the virus and he wasn't contagious anymore, well," Joy said. "Look at him. He's fitter than he's ever been in his whole life. It's amazing. So, what if he passes that on to me?"

"You don't know how it will affect you, Joy." Emotion pressed on Bobbie's vocal cords. She inhaled, exhaled, steadied her voice. "We still don't know how it's affected him...mentally, I mean." The children's reaction to Jimmy at the funeral sprang to her mind, but Bobbie couldn't put her finger on what she found so unsettling about it. Maybe his orange eyes had freaked them out.

"He's kind and loving," Joy said. "What's wrong with that?"

"Nothing, but there may be another side to him–"

"No! We'd have seen it by now. I'd have seen it," Joy said, propping herself up on one elbow.

"Not if he didn't want you to," Hicks said. "Sociopaths are good at hiding these things."

"I'm telling you, Jimmy's not a sociopath," Joy said. "He's fine."

"That remains to be seen," Bobbie said.

* * *

Bobbie was surprised to find Jimmy chatting to Davitt when she arrived in the lab. Davitt seemed wary of Jimmy, keeping the workbench between them. Davitt's bruises had faded, but his memory of the whack Jimmy had given him obviously hadn't.

Jimmy sat relaxed on a stool, leaning one elbow on the bench and swiping through images of nanostructures on the desk intepanel.

"So, these nano-robot things could hunt each other down and wage war against each other?" Jimmy was saying.

"The first nanomedical techniques were used to fight cancer cells," Davitt said. "We've cured ninety-five percent of the known types of cancer." He looked up, making eye contact with Bobbie entering the room. He pressed his lips together and scrunched up his face in an expression of regret.

"My mother had one of the five percent." Bobbie's mother had died only a couple of months ago – it felt like a lifetime, yet it hurt as though Bobbie had lost her yesterday.

Davitt nodded. "It's all about the tracking system. Nanobots need to seek out a signature. In the early days, it was oxygen-depleted tumor areas, known as hypoxic zones, and they'd target these to deliver the drug – basically a parcel of poison that kills the cancer cell."

"Yeah, I know that, but how do you propose to use nanobots to combat rejuvenation?" Jimmy asked. "What's your tracking system based on?"

"The nanobots I engineered for rejuvenation give out a distinctive magnetic pulse. It's similar to the pulse your biosensors give off, but different enough so that the anti-nanobots don't attack those devices." Davitt pulled up an image on the intepanel that reminded Bobbie of an ECG, but with more frequent peaks and troughs. He overlaid it with another, and she saw how the pattern differed. "Finding the rejuvenation nanobots is the easy part."

"And the hard part?" Jimmy asked. His voice seemed pleasant, but the micro-muscles in his cheeks supporting his smile appeared taut, as if he had to concentrate to hang his lips from them.

Davitt kept his attention on the slides in front of him. "Well, we can find the rejuvenation nanobots, but what should we do when we find them? We need to dismantle them without the cells collapsing."

Jimmy's frozen smile twitched. "Would aging recommence?"

"Probably." Davitt looked up. "But at a measured pace. Not the way Gloria–"

He looked at Bobbie, but she kept her face impassive. If Jimmy flattered Davitt's ego enough, Davitt would tell them what he knew. This Jimmy wore a mask too. Gone was the aggression and hatred he'd displayed in the medical center. He'd shifted his attitude too quickly for her liking. Bobbie was used to observing her patients' behavior swings, especially those confused by dementia, or haunted by hallucinations triggered by any of a host of aging disorders and medications. She had her eye on both these men, but each one was doing her work for her right now, drawing the other out with their preening and boasting, two peacocks flashing their tails.

"And if that doesn't fix the sociopathy?" Jimmy said, dropping his smile completely. "We all just get old, but stay crazy?"

"So, you admit you're crazy," Davitt said, triumph glinting in his eyes.

"Fuck you, shithead." Jimmy slammed the counter with open palms, making Bobbie jump and Davitt hop back from the bench. The screen on the desk flashed a warning message and shut down. Somewhere between a snarl and a grin, Jimmy hacked out a cruel chuckle. Another character switch, Bobbie noted: docile to violent in a millisecond.

"You think you're smart, don't ya?" Jimmy moved along the table towards Davitt like a cat stalking a bird.

"Jimmy!" Bobbie said, hearing the high-pitched alarm in her own voice, wishing she didn't sound so desperate.

Jimmy stopped abruptly. In one heartbeat, his countenance completely changed again. His eyes softened. He looked at Bobbie, saying as he rolled up his sleeves and sat down in a reclining chair, "Take your samples quickly, I need to get back to Joy."

Bobbie wondered how wise it was to discuss their progress with Jimmy. He was smart. He might be able to help, but would he help if it meant he'd go back to getting old?

She administered anesthetic patches to Jimmy's skin in various parts of his body. She needed only tiny amounts of tissue, but from as diverse a selection of types as was safe for Jimmy. She wouldn't be able to access the brain tissue, since that was too dangerous. How much would that have told her about his psychosis? She couldn't risk using techniques that utilized magnetic fields, in case she disrupted the delicate electronics of the nanobots. She'd longed to "cure" Granny of her psychosis. If Jimmy was changing, and Bobbie was pretty sure he was, then she wanted to restore him too, back to his lovable old self. Maybe she could try something else?

"Jimmy," Bobbie began, keeping her tone even. "Could I do an EROS scan of your brain to assess what, if any, impact the nanobots might have on it?"

Jimmy raised one eyebrow; the orange irises more startling with the expression.

"If we can rule out any change in your brain chemistry, then we wouldn't need to stop your rejuvenation." She held her breath.

"And if you find changes?" he asked in a low voice.

"It would really help us with factoring in risk with regard to Joy," Bobbie said. "But you seem fine, isn't that right?" She went on quickly, "It's non-invasive and can only detect brain activity to a few centimeters' depth, but it might help us –"

"Let's see how you get on with these samples first," Jimmy said.

Bobbie knew she'd been sidestepped. She finished taking the last sample as Jacob arrived in the lab, breathless.

"We're not due for a shift change yet," Mo said.

Jacob leaned forward, hands on knees, panting. "I know..." He hauled in a breath. "But your mother... just arrived."

Mo jumped up. "I have to go."

"No need." Jacob stood tall, hands at waist, and flexed his back. "She's on her way here."

"Here?"

Jacob nodded. "Ori wants to meet with Bobbie and Hicks," he said, then turned to Bobbie. "She says you know her."

Bobbie shrugged. "Do I?"

"Oh, I think you do," said a nasally voice from the hallway.

Bobbie dropped the tray of samples in a clatter onto the workbench. She knew that voice, hated that voice. Fear twisted through her chest as Bobbie faced the woman who had taken Granny away – the woman who had been the frontline to the Rejuvenation project. There she stood, framed in the doorway, her black bob swinging around her ears. Her close-set dark eyes crowded against her thin nose above a wry smile.

"Slade?" Bobbie said.

CHAPTER 13

Bobbie snatched the only weapon to hand, a needle-sharp dissection probe, and lunged towards Slade. Jacob grabbed Bobbie around the waist. Luke appeared and seized her hands, prying the probe from her grip.

"Enough, Bobbie," her father said. "This is Orinda Slade. Ori. She's on our side."

Confused, Bobby looked around for Hicks before remembering he was in the medical wing with Joy, both of them away from Slade, and hopefully safe – for the time being. What the hell was Slade doing here?

"She wasn't on our side when her men shot us." Bobbie wriggled out of Jacob's hold, but he stayed between her and Slade. Bobbie sucked in air and panted, her heart ricocheting against her sternum. Slade stood unflinching, her gaze fixed, her expression neutral, her hands clasped and held comfortably in front of her abdomen.

"She took Granny away. She's behind rejuvenation, in on it with Fox. They're friends, for God's sake – you know that. Everyone knows that," Bobbie said, looking wildly from her father to Slade. "How could you be friends with her?"

"She... you... they..." Davitt's mouth continued to move, but no more words came out.

"For Heaven's sake, catch a hold of yourselves. I don't have time for this. Your actions nearly derailed our entire organization," Slade said, touching the intedesk and turning on a screen.

"Thank God, you're here," Davitt said, sounding winded. "I've been taken against my will. They forced me–"

"Shut up, arsehole!" Jimmy elbowed Davitt aside. "Luke, get her the fuck out of here, then explain."

"Ah, Jimmy, you really are a great advertisement for rejuvenation, aren't you?" Slade said. "Joy told me you were infected... in the line of duty."

"Joy?" Jimmy said, shaking his shaggy blond hair. Bobbie could see how someone seeing him for the first time would admire the youthful glow of his skin, tanned and taut over his strong features, rugged, yet fresh and healthy.

"Let's calm down," Luke said. "Joy only knows her as Ori. Not her full identity." He cast Slade a firm look. "Go easy on Bobbie, like we've discussed. She's my daughter – just like Joy."

Go easy on Bobbie. Wasn't it a bit late for that? Bobbie tried to piece together what was happening, but the details shifted and changed so quickly she was at a loss. What the fuck was going on?

"Christ Almighty! Always the peacemaker, Luke." Slade regarded Luke with what seemed like wary respect. "I don't need her to like me. I just need her to play her part. Davitt, too. If they refuse to play their parts, then they're a liability, and you know what that means."

"Fuck you," Bobbie spat.

"Hear her out," Luke said. "Ori wasn't responsible for those men who shot you. She was trying to stop them."

Bobbie shook her head. "I don't believe you." She turned from her father to Slade.

Mo had stepped over to Slade and gave her a one-armed hug, lightly kissing the top of her head.

"We'll chat later, son, when we've got this cleared up." Slade ushered him out the door.

Cleared up? What the fuck did Slade think this was? Spilled milk?

"She tried to kill us!" Bobbie said.

"No, I did not," Slade said, sighing with exasperation.

"I saw you on the camera..." Bobbie spluttered, "... in the room at the hospital trying to get Hicks to break his non-disclosure agreement. Then you sent your men after us."

"They were not my men," Slade said with deliberation. "I was trying to find out where Lisette had put your grandmother. I only made you sign the NDA so that she wouldn't send you to the PARC too." She stretched out her arms, submission laced with irony. "Think about it. What did I say to Hicks back at the hospital?"

"You wanted him to tell you if we'd found Granny," Bobbie said, trying to recall the details.

"And if you hadn't set those carebots on me, I could have explained," Slade said.

Jimmy laughed. "You wouldn't have told us diddly squat. That hospital was covered in cameras. If what you say is true, you wouldn't have risked being caught."

"Jesus, Luke, how long have we got for this little show and tell?" Slade asked.

"Just tell them," Luke said. "We need Bobbie, and it's important to me that she understands."

We need Bobbie.

Bobbie glared at her father, hurt infused with her rage. Was that all she was to him – a necessity to the cause?

Slade blew out an aggravated sigh before going on, "Joy has never met me in person as Ori. We have a code word to let operatives recognize each other so that covers don't get blown during an op. I could have used it at the hospital and told her I was Ori if things got dicey. I knew she was listening in on ONIV."

"So why not just tell her?" Bobbie said.

"Need-to-know basis," Slade said. "You know what those drugs in the PARC can do. No matter how strong a person is, they'll talk, but if they don't have the information, they can't impart it."

"Why did you conduct unauthorized experiments on our patients? On my grandmother?" Bobbie asked.

Slade's face softened. The anxiety seemed to ebb from Luke's features as Slade said in a softer tone, "Belus took them away, not me."

"No! You–" Bobbie jumped in.

"Shut up and listen to me!" Slade roared, stunning Bobbie into silence. "I had to make you fight back, Bobbie," she said more gently. "That's why I threw you out, prevented you from being on the research team. I couldn't let you become a pawn. I knew you'd fight for your granny, for the rights of the elderly. You always have done."

"You could have just told me."

"No, I had to know which side you'd choose. I have too much to lose – we" – Slade waved her hand expansively – "had too much to lose. You were a conformist, but I knew you'd kick back, given the right pressure."

"You played me?"

"Get over yourself, Bobbie. We're up against a huge force here. We can't make mistakes, and we can't risk... traitors."

"I would never –" Bobbie started.

"If we don't vet every single person," Slade said, talking over her, "and get it right, we are all at risk."

Bobbie tried to process what she was hearing, to figure out what exactly she was dealing with. There was more to Slade than Bobbie had given her credit for. She acknowledged a grudging admiration for Slade, evidently an accomplished undercover agent. But what were Slade's motives? Glory? Could it be that she was truly humanitarian?

"You stood by and let people die," Bobbie said. "I could have saved Ayushi, but you wouldn't let me resuscitate her. You shut me down at the board meeting. I could have saved her."

"Saved her for what, to become insane? Younger? Yes, but that beautiful woman didn't deserve that–" Slade began.

"Nor did she deserve to be experimented on," Bobbie roared.

Slade's face dropped. "I was powerless to stop the experimentation," she said softly, looking over at Luke.

"I know," Luke said before directing his next comment to Bobbie. "If Ori had interfered too much, she could have been caught. There's too much at stake to lose her."

"What's at stake? Explain," Bobbie said through gritted teeth. "And don't leave anything out."

"The lives of everyone here, the future of humanity," said Slade, her face grim.

"The future of humanity?" Jimmy gave a fractured laugh, devoid of mirth.

"For a start," Luke said, "there's the unborn. Either they die or their great-grandparents have to. With Ori in place, we can safely get women to where they can get an embryo transplant. She was one of the first to do it and went on to save nearly all the children here. They were scheduled for termination when their mothers "lost" the babies unexpectedly, thanks to Ori's embryo transplant program. She's committed to the cause."

"The cause?" Jimmy said.

"Replacing Belus Corp. There's not been an election since the war, because the general population in Belus-land thinks that the world works just fine." Luke caught Bobbie's eye. "You thought Belus worked fine, Bobbie; I suspect you still think that, deep down. But it doesn't. There is no freedom." Slade sounded just like Joy.

Bobbie snorted. "Freedom to what? Starve? Kill? Freedom is a false god. We're slaves to our biological needs, food, shelter, our diseases, each other's greed. The freedom you describe is anarchy. No-one in charge. Communism didn't work because people at the top were too greedy. Capitalism's just another form of Darwinism. Democracy became a popularity contest, with those with the most money or fame being voted in over those who were decent and honest and who could have done so much better for everyone. At least with Belus Corp, there's order. Society needs rules. Lisette Fox is fair, and she saved us from the Melters."

Bobbie's father whistled through his teeth.

"What?" Bobbie hissed.

Luke shook his head and massaged his forehead.

"I get it," Bobbie said. "I know Belus is the bad guy now. Lisette Fox stood on that stage and presented rejuvenation. Someone commissioned Davitt to work on people without their knowledge and consent. Hell, yeah, I do want to help. But I'm a doctor, not a soldier. I preserve life, not destroy it. I've been through a war, and I don't want any more. Life is too precious. I stepped in against rejuvenation. I sure as hell didn't sign up for a revolution. That would be... would be... Chaos!" Bobbie threw her hands up. "Rules," she stammered. "We need rules..."

"Society needs the right rules," Slade said. "I understand what you see in Belus Corp. I did at one time, too. But there's something rotten at the core. I know you think that the Dependency Law is wrong."

Bobbie swallowed and nodded. Slade had her there.

"What about the PARC?" Slade asked. "You've seen what goes on there."

"The alternative is equally cruel," Bobbie said. "Locking up offenders, or worse, capital punishment. At least with the PARC, offenders are rehabilitated."

"Some are, but fewer and fewer. The statistics are alarmingly thin on the ground, and there's a lot more corrective surgery going wrong these days." Slade sat down on the stool Luke brought over.

"May as well get comfortable," Luke said, nodding at more stools under the bench.

"And rejuvenation?" Slade asked Bobbie.

"Rejuvenation has a lot of potential." Bobbie sat. She thought of the ultra-elderly trapped in the pain of their wasting bodies. "But the development of rejuvenation was ethically wrong."

"Two things seem to tally well, though. The Dependency Law only allows a child to be born if an elder dies, and rejuvenation would keep the population young." Slade folded her arms and leaned back against the bench.

Bobbie fitted the ideas together like puzzle pieces in her head. "A static society. The same people here forever."

"No more children, no more evolution, no more life as we know it," said Slade.

"And don't forget the Melters," Luke said. "It's possible that Belus is working with them."

Bobbie gave an impatient sign. "I still think that's a stretch. No human would risk trusting an alien."

"It's happened throughout history," Luke said. "Native peoples welcoming the Europeans – remember how that turned out?"

"But they were human," Bobbie countered.

"Or inhuman, more to the point," Luke said. "And if you think about the differences in culture, technology, even how different the people looked to each other, is it really that far of a stretch to imagine that Belus made a pact with the Melters?"

Bobbie's puzzle pieces fell apart, and she grappled for them as something important slipped away.

"But you came to the research center," Bobbie said to Slade. "You knew where Granny was. You brought your men and gunned us down."

"That's not what happened," Slade said, unfolding her arms and gesturing with her hands.

"I saw it!"

"For fucks sake! This had better be worth it, Luke – only for you and me coming through so much together..." Slade got to her feet and paced. "Yes, you saw me at the facility because I followed you. The van, well, it wasn't that hard to find."

"She's right," Jimmy said from the far side of the bench. It made Bobbie start. He'd been sitting so quietly, listening and watching. "I wasn't able to hide the van's electro-signals all the time. Joy's firewall had been damaged with our hard landing."

"The men were Belus Corp staff. I fooled them into thinking I was part of the team. Same for Ellis," Slade said.

Davitt looked startled at hearing his surname.

"I'd been taking updates from him for months," Slade continued. "But I hadn't been able to pin down exactly where the facility was."

"Oh, fuck!" Davitt said, his face flushed.

"Oh, fuck, indeed, Ellis." Slade nodded slowly, staring him down. "You thought you were so smart and that you'd been kidnapped by a bunch of fools. Right?"

Davitt shook his head and exhaled a slow hiss of defeat.

"Bobbie, you left a right mess." Slade's gaze swung to Bobbie. "I had a lot to explain away. I said I'd follow you after meeting Hicks in the hospital, and that you'd gotten away from the research center, but we couldn't follow because Joy shot out the engine in our hovercraft."

"When did Joy do that?" Jimmy asked.

"She didn't." Slade sighed. "I did, when no-one was looking. I didn't need to follow you; I already knew you'd be coming here."

"But if you knew that, why not just let us get on with it? Why follow us at all?" Bobbie asked.

"Belus had an arrest warrant out on you. I saw it and said that I'd take care of it. I botched the so-called arrest on purpose. Took a heap of shit for that too." Slade folded her arms again and sat back down. "My dear friend Lisette threw quite the hissy fit that evening."

"Lisette knew about rejuvenation all along?" Bobbie asked, queasy to the pit of her stomach.

"Yep. And I need you to discredit rejuvenation so we can topple her." Slade looked at Luke. "Which is why I'm going through this rigmarole," she added under her breath. Luke nodded his encouragement, and Slade continued, "Bobbie, I know you're well respected in medical circles... for a geriatrician."

"What the fuck is that supposed to mean?" Bobbie hissed.

"Please! Cut it out, the pair of you!" Luke bellowed. "Ori, just tell her what you need."

Slade cast her eyes and sighed. "I believe that Belus is building an elite force of rejuvenees. Do you understand?" she said. "Young, fit, psychopathic killers."

"Why?" Bobbie asked. "That doesn't make sense. How would they control them?"

"Narcotics," Slade said, "same as they did in the research center."

"Fuck!" Davitt said. "Who are they fighting against?"

"Us, to start with –" Slade began.

Bobbie closed her eyes, bracing against the shot of liquid fear that made her scalp tingle and her throat constrict. An image flared in her mind – a man's eyes bulging in agony after Granny had speared him in the guts with a pitchfork. Bobbie understood exactly what the rejuvenees were capable of. She counted to three, opened her eyes. "Go on."

"We need you to make a presentation to the medical board to convince them that rejuvenation is hazardous to humanity, highlight the dangers–"

"But it could be great," Davitt said. "Just let me finish my–"

Slade held up her hand to him. "No," she said. "It's not great. It's a fucking disaster. Stop justifying it."

"But you threatened to close me down if I didn't get results," Davitt said.

"I was trying to close you down," Slade said, putting her hand to her forehead. "But your ego misinterpreted me." Slade dropped her jaw and threw him a piercing glare that made him flinch. "You used your own DNA, didn't you?" Under her breath, she added, "Idiot."

"But... but... but... you weren't the one sending me the samples?" Davitt said, squinting his confusion.

"No – that wasn't me. I'm still trying to find out who it was," Slade said.

"So why don't you push it out on the media channels, ONIV, the news? Why make us present to the medical board?" Bobbie asked.

"We need an encryption key to access the media broadcasting system. Lisette Fox is the only one with access to it," Slade said. "Joy is brilliant, but this password has been her biggest challenge. She hasn't been successful, but she hasn't given up yet."

"Can't you use blinks? Go p-to-p?" Bobbie was aware that person-to-person wasn't as regulated, but it was slower and more prone to interruption and dropped connection.

Slade shook her head. "Tried that. It doesn't work; doesn't scale up."

"If we could prove to groups like the medical board that someone from Belus Corp was behind it all along," Luke said, "perhaps we'd gain some traction without going through the usual channels."

"Belus media would wipe it out," Davitt countered.

"Maybe, but we have to try," Luke said. "If we could trigger a revamp of the government, give people their say again..."

"Oh, preserve us from democracy!" Davitt snorted. "Uneducated masses calling the shots. No thanks – look where that got us before the Melters War."

"What we really need is a better democracy," Bobbie said.

"Exactly. It wasn't democracy that was at fault then," Luke said. "It was education, the delivery of information. Social media was governing, and we were collectively too immature to utilize it properly. But with the connectivity we have now–"

"That Belus Corp has put in place," Bobbie said. "And you've upheld that for decades." She stared at Slade.

Slade shrugged. "Sure. We're not saying everything about the regime is bad."

We're – the collective term jarred Bobbie. It included her father.

Luke spoke up again. "Something was wrong from the beginning, like the needless killing of our own soldiers. I believe it began there, and then the rot spread. The continuation of the Dependency Law, though the population is far lower than it was pre-war –is that really necessary? We've survived a high population of children at this colony and others. It may not be easy, but it can be done."

Luke had a point; Bobbie could give him that. "But what do you suggest in its place?"

"Human rights, elections, accountability, transparency," Luke said.

"And justice," Slade added.

"That's rich coming from you!" Bobbie said, thinking back to the time she'd butted heads with Slade in her student days, when Bobbie had been holding protest rallies against the DNR Law that prevented resuscitation past the age of one hundred. "You supported the DNR law."

"I was doing my job," Slade said.

"Yes, that's been said many times throughout history." Bobbie stood up. "For the record, I don't trust you, Slade. You may be an important person here, but I'm not doing anything here because you tell me to."

Slade peered down her nose at Bobbie. "Oh, really?"

"My mission here is clear," Bobbie said. "Make the vaccine. Stop rejuvenation. Do not expect to embroil me in your plans to bring down the government."

Slade stared Bobbie down with narrowed eyes. "You need to present your findings on rejuvenation to a medical convention in Switzerland in three months' time. You need to have enough evidence to be irrefutable. To that end, we have to get you back to Belus Land and connect to your ONIV. It has recorded data that documents rejuvenation and its side effects. We need to get that information to the medical board," Slade said. "We'll have measures in place to ensure your safe escape afterward. That's the only reason why you and Davitt are both still here, despite..." Slade looked at Bobbie's father. "...What Luke would like to think."

The blood drained from Davitt's face. Speechless, he stared at his feet.

"I don't need an answer right now," Slade said. "You have twenty-four hours, but there is only one answer."

"So much for justice and freedom. Now, if you don't mind," Bobbie said, turning away from Slade and clenching her fists to stop her hands from trembling, "I have work to do."

Hang appeared at the door, out of breath. His eyes lit up when he saw Slade.

"Ori!" He flung himself at her, and she caught him in a bear hug, her face melting into a warm smile, transforming before Bobbie's eyes.

"Hello, little man," Slade said, popping a kiss on his forehead. "Whatcha up to?"

Hang looked from Slade to Luke, then to Bobbie. "I have a note for Bobbie from Hicks."

Slade put out her hand.

Hang pulled away from her and shook his head. "Hicks said it was only for Bobbie, and she has to read it right away, in private."

Bobbie caught her breath. Joy! Something was wrong with Joy.

"Thank you, Hang," Bobbie said, tousling the boy's hair with one hand and taking the slip of cardboard with the other.

"We have to go anyway," Slade said, stepping towards the exit.

"We'll chat later," Luke said, giving Bobbie a peck on the cheek before taking Hang by the hand and following Slade out.

Fear crept through Bobbie as she clutched the message.

"Excuse me," she said to Jimmy and Davitt, and moved past them towards the door.

As much as Bobbie wanted to, she didn't trust her legs to run – they felt as wobbly as a newborn colt's as she followed the tunnels to the exit. Once outside, she strode to a large boulder and sat down, hardly able to breathe.

Written on thin cardboard, folded, the edges of the note were sealed with wound-glue. Hicks hadn't trusted Hang not to read it. But why hadn't Hicks come himself? Bobbie's insides turned to ice – whatever he'd found, Joy was too upset for him to leave her alone.

Bobbie worked a finger between the edges of the thin card and carefully pried open the note. She stared in horror at Hicks' scrawl as she read, "Nanobots +ve, hGC 60,000 mIU/mL."

Bobbie dropped her face into her hands and wrestled back a howl of anguish. Not only was Joy infected with nanobots, Joy was pregnant.

CHAPTER 14

The smell of bacon cooking flooded the dining hall.

"Ori always brings us bacon," Hang said. "Yum!" He inhaled deeply through his nose and sat down beside Bobbie, across the table from Joy. Hicks and Jimmy arrived with platters of bacon and eggs, setting them down in the middle of the table before climbing into their seats.

"What's wrong, big sis?" Hang asked.

"Nothing," Bobbie said, then noticed Hang was looking not at her but at Joy. Bobbie followed Hang's gaze, trying to get her head around the notion of Joy as someone's big sister.

Joy held her nose, looking queasy.

Jimmy stabbed the yolk of his egg, oozing yellow over his bacon. Joy jumped up, clambered out of the bench, and ran.

Bobbie caught up to find Joy dry-heaving by a pile of rocks. She put her hand on Joy's forehead and rubbed her back. Joy's back muscles strained as she choked out another gut-wrenching cough.

"It's okay," Bobbie soothed, fighting her own nausea at the sound of Joy's retching. "Deep breaths in through your nose and out through your mouth."

Eventually, the muscles in Joy's back relaxed beneath Bobbie's palm. Joy stood up slowly and wiped tears from her cheeks.

"It sucks," Bobbie said. "But sickness like this is perfectly normal."

"Even this early?"

"Yes." Bobbie didn't hold Joy's gaze. If Joy was telling the truth – that her affair with Jimmy began the night of the burial of the rock-fall victims – then she was no more than four weeks pregnant, by gestational age, but the hCG count was abnormally high. In fact, it was a thousand times higher than Bobbie would expect it to be.

Hicks had run the tests twice. The results were unusual, but not impossible. Bobbie was concerned about how unwell Joy already felt. As her pregnancy hormone levels rose, the chances were she'd feel worse.

"Henry scheduled you in for a scan this afternoon. Maybe we should get him to have a look sooner?" Bobbie said.

"No!" Joy said. "There's too many women already needing his help. I don't need special treatment."

Oh, yes, you do.

"Have you told Dad yet?" Bobbie asked instead.

"I'm seeing him later," Joy said, beginning to walk back towards the compound.

"Do you want me to be there?"

"No."

"Is Jimmy going with you?" Bobbie wasn't sure what way she wanted Joy to answer this.

"No. Just me," Joy said in a quiet voice.

Bobbie didn't press it. She was meeting this morning with Slade, Davitt, and Hicks to discuss the anti-bot. But Joy's pale face and sad, dark eyes ran a bolt of worry through her.

"Why don't you go have a rest before you go to the appointment?" Bobbie suggested. "Let me take you to your room."

"I can do it." After a beat, Joy added, "But thanks."

"No probs." Bobbie tried to sound normal, not miffed at the brush-off. "And try to drink some water, okay?"

"Okay." Joy took the nearest opening, and Bobbie watched her sister walk, head bowed, as the cave system ingested her.

* * *

Slade was already at the lab when Hicks and Bobbie entered. Hatred pressed behind Bobbie's eyes, as if trying to get out at Slade. Accepting the woman wouldn't happen overnight, but Bobbie knew she had to work with Slade, despite the differences they had held in the past, in a world that didn't exist for either of them now. Bobbie had been angry at Slade for such a long time, it seemed unnatural to disarm that. Yet Bobbie could see clearly that her dad and Slade were a team – bonded in a camaraderie born out of surviving horrific experiences.

"Mind if I join you?" Luke asked, coming in behind Bobbie.

She turned to welcome him, but Luke's gaze was directed at Slade. It was obvious who he thought was in charge.

"If you like." Slade pulled up a stool and sat at the workbench, folding her hands in front of her. "Do you have an answer for me yet, Bobbie?"

"If I say no?" Bobbie glanced around and saw in her father's face a measure of real fear. Like a contagion, it spread beneath her skin.

"This conversation is over, for all of you." Slade stood up.

"Wait," Bobbie said. "Hicks and Joy, they stay here..."

"No way." Hicks pushed his chair back. "If you go, I go."

Bobbie hadn't discussed this with Hicks, because she knew he'd want to come and felt bad for dropping him into the conversation blindsided. But Hicks was too precious to Bobbie to risk. Her life would be unbearable if she lost him, especially now that she had truly found him.

Luke cleared his throat loudly before he spoke. "We're here for one thing only today, and that's the briefing on the anti-nanobots. Your answer can wait."

Slade flung him a scathing look that jolted satisfaction through Bobbie. Luke didn't seem to notice.

Jacob brought Davitt into the lab. No-one spoke as Davitt settled himself at the workbench. Jacob stood back framed in the doorway, a silent sentry.

Slade began proceedings by inviting Davitt to describe how his anti-nanobots would work. He repeated the same thing he'd told Bobbie in his cell, outlining how he could design them to target the rejuvenation nanobots but not be able to prevent cellular collapse in the affected ultra-elderly. Slade gave her full attention to his explanation, but Bobbie revisited Granny's death all over again. Granny's flesh as it turned to mush beneath her skin. The agony in Granny's eyes as her personality returned along with the pain. These anti-nanobots would kill the rejuvenees the same way.

"The vaccine is the priority," Bobbie said. "We have to stop Fox from using the virus to deliver the nanobots to the elderly in the first place. We need to cut down on the number of rejuvenees that are created."

"I agree," Slade said. "But we still need to take care of the rejuvenees that currently exist."

"Is there any way to round them up and keep them until we find a more humane way to fix them?" Hicks asked.

First, do no harm...

Bobbie nodded as he spoke, but she knew the answer before Slade voiced it, and it broke her heart.

"We don't have the resources," Slade said. "I know this goes against the grain, Bobbie, but you have to understand–"

"I understand," Bobbie said, "but I don't have to like it. Do you plan to weaponize the anti-nanobots?"

"Can we release them into the air?" Slade asked.

"Yes. Airborne, it will be inhaled. We can spray the areas affected, along with the airborne vaccine Bobbie is working on. We can also put it in the water supply," Davitt said.

Bobbie whistled through her teeth. "That's hard to control."

"The anti-nanobots will be harmless to humans. They only attack rejuvenation nanobots, and I'll put a timestamp in them, so they break down into harmless organic molecules in, say, a year's time," Davitt said.

"Good," Slade said. "How long will it take you to have these anti-nanobots ready to deploy?"

"I have the schematics drawn, and the blueprints are ready for the matter streamers." Davitt scratched his head, shuffling his black curls. "I can have the first ones ready to test in a week."

"How will you test them?" Slade asked.

"I can culture cells and do it in a Petri dish. I have samples of Jimmy's tissues," Davitt said.

"And what about Jimmy?" Bobbie asked.

Everyone fell silent, Hicks the only one who could meet her eye.

"We, em, won't be deploying the anti-nanobots here, right," Davitt said. "So, he'll be okay, I guess."

"Guess?" Bobbie said.

"Look, he's not right in the head," Davitt said, looking around and shrugging.

"I'll deal with Jimmy," Luke said quietly. "When the time comes."

The time would come sooner than her father counted on, Bobbie thought, especially when he found out about Joy's pregnancy.

"Good." Slade stood up and narrowed her eyes on Bobbie. "I'll get your answer tonight."

Bobbie folded her arms and looked away.

Slade left, her footfalls echoing up the corridor like fading heartbeats.

"Bobbie, you haven't much choice here, you know," Luke said.

"I can't believe a father would put his daughter in so much danger," Hicks said, standing up and placing a hand on Bobbie's shoulder. "If Bobbie gets caught, she'll be sent to the PARC or worse..."

"Believe me, I will be taking every precaution to keep her as safe as possible," Luke said, his jaw set as he faced Hicks. "And if she doesn't do it, Fox might release the virus into the air over a major city. Or people might be lining up to volunteer to take the stuff. People need to know the risks as soon as possible."

"Why can't you tell them?" Hicks said.

"I will, dammit, but a doctor has to present the findings to the medical board. I'm not equipped to. I'm just an old soldier – but keeping my daughter safe? That, I am equipped to do," Luke said, thumping the table with his fist.

"Ryan, Dad, stop," Bobbie said. She glanced at Davitt.

"Don't mind me." Davitt held up both hands. "I just work here."

"Give us a minute," Bobbie said to Hicks. He held her gaze; the look shot straight to her heart, then his eyelids closed in a slow blink.

"Meet you later in Obs," Hicks said. "For the scan?"

Bobbie nodded.

"You too, Dad, I need a minute with Davitt." She directed her next words to Jacob. "Alone?"

"I have to stay at the door. He's under guard." Jacob moved to the outside of the doorway but kept the door open.

"Don't forget, you said you'd spend some time with your brother," Luke said. "Hang is expecting us after lunch."

"I know," Bobbie said. "Go. I'll find you guys outside."

Jacob stepped back to allow Hicks and Luke to pass, then followed them a little way down the corridor, before positioning himself with his back to the wall, eyes in their direction, probably out of earshot. It was the best she was going to get.

"We may have no choice in the matter of this presentation," Bobbie said, slouching low over the workbench across from him, keeping her voice down.

"I know," Davitt whispered, bending forward. "We should work on the basis that our answer is yes. But why don't you want to do it? I thought whistleblowing would be right up your street."

"I still don't trust Slade, but I do think the medical world needs to know about the dangers of rejuvenation. I know we have to go. I just need time to make sure we do it right." Bobbie didn't want to tell Davitt that the real reason she didn't want to leave right away was that she was worried about Joy, not to mention scared shitless about crossing that damn desert full of monstrous dust devils. In the few weeks she'd been kicking around Yosemite, Bobbie had gotten used to the freedom and security of living in the colony. It was selfish of her, Bobbie knew that. Fox was certainly moving forward, and they needed to act. And so she would – as soon as Bobbie knew Joy didn't need her doctoring skills, dust devils or no dust devils.

"I'm surprised you want to go," she said. "Or are you still trying to take credit for rejuvenation?"

"No. Not that. Not anymore. I'll do it to try to make up for the things I've done wrong. I'm not the evil villain you think I am, Bobbie," Davitt added softly. "Rejuvenation was... me doing my best. I know how you felt about your patients and their pain. I know the toll Gracie's death has taken on you. There was a time I would have given you anything you'd wanted, but..." Davitt shook his head slowly. "The light in your eyes was never for me."

He stopped talking. Bobbie felt sorry for him. Davitt was right. She'd never shared her heart with him.

"I know." She stopped short of saying sorry, because she wasn't, and there was, after all, what he'd done to Granny, with Granny. Bobbie cleared her throat. "So, anti-nanobots in a week?"

"Maybe less." Davitt winked. "Under-promise and over-deliver."

Same old Davitt, Bobbie thought, full of himself. She left him working in the lab to go do her rounds.

* * *

After a working lunch, Bobbie found Hang and Luke outside the children's play area in the shade of the vertical valley walls. As she approached, Bobbie saw they were crouched over a tiny model village made out of materials that Hang had scavenged from around the complex. Most of the people were carved from wood, like the swan-girl Hang had presented to Bobbie when they first met. The buildings, mostly hewn from twisted and deformed plastic, imitated the rocks they stood amongst now – liquefied and misshapen.

"Where's the shopkeeper?" Luke asked.

"I re-carved it," Hang said. "He got broken in the rock-fall, and I used the wood to make the hover ball boy."

"Oh, that's clever," Bobbie said to announce her presence.

"Bobbie!" Hang gave her a quick hug, but her dad was frowning.

"And where did you get the wood for the rest of the team?" Luke asked.

"Old pieces," Hang said. "They were getting too old, and some were broken. I made them better, younger – like Jimmy."

They stood looking at his creation with their perfect figurines – recarved, reshaped, rejuvenated.

"Jimmy is still old," Bobbie said. "He just doesn't look old anymore."

"He's lucky," Hang said, and pulled a face. "Getting old looks like it hurts."

Bobbie wanted to hug the child and shake him at the same time. Yes, Hang was scared of old age; the young always were. Too often, Bobbie had tried to explain to people that aging wasn't the problem, that with age came experience and appreciation and wisdom. But her father got to the crux of the matter first.

"Getting old is not the worst thing that can happen, son," Luke said gently. "I saw so many people who never reached old age."

"Like Gracie," Bobbie said, before she realized she'd spoken.

"But Gracie got old," Hang said, his eyebrows knitted in confusion.

"No, she didn't," Luke said, staring skywards, his dark eyes shining. "Not really. She never had her life, lived out her dreams, fulfilled her purpose."

Bobbie cradled her sorrow but didn't entirely agree with him.

"Oh, Gracie had a purpose," she said, her voice over-bright. "She inspired me my whole life, showed me what it was I wanted to be." Her tone softened. "She's with me all the time, and it's good."

"I know what you mean," Hang said, grinning at his father. "My dad inspires me."

Luke's Adam's apple bobbed beneath his wordless smile.

"And my mum is always with me." Hang tapped his chest. "Here."

Luke's lips pressed tight together. The toe of his shoe kicked a trough in the sand.

Bobbie wasn't ready to discuss Hang's mother yet, either. She stared at the model village and thought, instead, of Gracie with her vivid imagination and how she loved to make up plays.

"Do you make up stories for the wooden people?" she asked.

"I do," Hang said. "I had bad guys and robbers and everything, but then I decided it was a better place without them, so I killed the bad ones and cleaned the world up."

"Understandable," Bobbie nodded, but brushed her hand over her forearms, patting down the tiny hairs that suddenly stood on end for reasons she couldn't fathom. "I have to go. I'll see you two at supper, okay?"

Father and son hugged her. Bobbie walked off to the backdrop of their voices chattering, her shadow trailing beside her, its length reminding her that it was time for Joy's scan.

* * *

Bobbie arrived at the antenatal clinic – a room off the main medical center – at the same time as Hicks and Joy.

"Perfect timing," Hicks said. Joy forced a wan smile.

Henry stared at numbers on a screen by the examination table. Yoon worked with her back to them. The *tink tink* of metal on metal sounded grossly cheerful as Yoon tidied instruments away. Bobbie hadn't seen Yoon since the day after Nero's amputation. Henry had usually stayed with the boy during Bobbie's follow-up examinations. Bobbie wondered if Yoon had blamed her for her five-year-old brother losing a foot.

"Hello, Yoon," Bobbie said tentatively.

One tink turned into a clatter. Yoon turned her head only. "Hello, Doctor Chan."

The tink tink resumed.

"How's Nero?" Bobbie asked.

No more tinks.

Yoon turned around, her face crimson. "He's doing well, thank you. He's hopping about on crutches. I..." She blinked hard and bowed her head, her black hair falling over her eyes. Lifting her head with a jerk, she swung her fringe back and said, "I never got a chance to thank you. You saved his life."

"No need to thank me," Bobbie said. "I'm glad he's feeling better."

Yoon gave a stiff little smile. "Better get these in the sterilizer." She walked out with the tray of instruments.

In the dimly lit area, the screen beside the exam table blazed white light over Joy as she lay waiting. The walls twinkled around them as Henry geared up the scanner for his examination. The glow bounced off Hicks' face, his gray eyes still and focused on Joy.

"Hello. How are you feeling, Joy?" Henry said.

"Nervous," Joy said in a tremulous voice. "And sick. Nauseous."

"That's the hormone human chorionic gonadotropin, better known as hCG. It's produced during pregnancy by cells formed in the placenta," Henry said. "Your levels are reading very high. It could indicate that your pregnancy is further along than you realized. Is that possible?"

"No." It came out in a croak. Joy cleared her throat and repeated, "No."

"Well, it can indicate twins," Henry said.

Joy sucked in a sharp breath.

Or a mole pregnancy or a tumor, Bobbie thought, clicking through what she could remember from med school. How she yearned to dredge through ONIV now and have more immediate answers.

"It's early, but we might be able to pick up two gestational sacs with the scan." The grainy image flashed, and the screen showed what looked like foam. "Here we go," Henry said, pointing to a black circle. "This looks like a sac. I'll change the setting, and we'll have a look inside. The data will be coming through from the micro-cameras you ingested earlier, too. If you've been able to keep them down?"

"Only just," Joy said.

"Good. The software will take a sec." Henry swung the screen out of Joy's and Bobbie's view, but Hicks still had a line of sight. Henry's brows furrowed. Dread slithered in the pit of Bobbie's stomach. Hicks flicked a glance her way, allowing Bobbie to read his concern too. She couldn't demand to know what they saw. Henry was trying to protect Joy, and so must Bobbie. She stood hardly daring to breathe.

Joy turned her head to find Bobbie. Terror lurked in her dark eyes. Bobbie reached for her hand. Joy held on tight as if something were pulling her down, drowning her.

"I'm sorry, Joy," Henry began.

Joy's grip on Bobbie tightened.

"There's no viable embryo here. This imaging technique is the most advanced we have. Usually we can see a zygote a week after conception. In your case, the cells have divided, but each time, it seems that the cells are behaving as if it was the first division.

If this happens once, it leads to identical twins, but in this case, it hasn't stopped at once." Henry held Joy's gaze, his forehead wrinkled above kind, sad eyes.

Joy blew a breath through pursed lips and nodded.

Bobbie squeezed Joy's hand. "Could the nanobots have interfered with cellular differentiation?" she asked.

"That's a good guess," Henry said. "The cells have continued to grow and divide, but haven't differentiated into viable tissues –"

"Like a tumor?" Joy interrupted, wide-eyed.

"In some ways, yes." Henry looked sideways at Bobbie, then continued. "Of bigger concern is how they've dispersed and spread, inserting themselves into tissue beyond the uterus and into the fallopian tubes. If they each continued to grow into a zygote, it would cause a lot of damage."

"Damage?" Joy's lip trembled.

Bobbie jiggled Joy's hand gently. "Henry won't let that happen." She sounded more confident than she felt. Terror lurked at the edges of what Bobbie understood to be happening in Joy's body.

Henry took a deep breath. "Joy, I'm sorry to have to tell you this, but the best option would be immediate surgery."

"Of course, if you think that's best," Joy said in a whisper.

"It's clear that we'll have to remove the growth," Henry said, staring at Joy intently. Bobbie could tell Henry was masking his own reactions as he said, "You should know too that there's a risk we may have to remove the uterus."

"Oh God," Joy breathed, ashen.

Bobbie bit down on the inside of her cheeks, working to keep her expression placid, her heartbeat slamming against her sternum.

"We'll save what we can. I'll look into scheduling the surgery as soon as we can determine your fasting period. Yoon will prep you," Henry said.

"I'll scrub in," Bobbie said.

"Doctor Chan," Henry said sternly. "Our obstetrics team is highly qualified. You are too closely related to the patient. I can't allow it."

"But–" Bobbie began. She felt Hicks' hand on her forearm.

"He's right," Hicks said.

"I'll be fine," Joy said, her voice watery. Her smile wobbled.

"You will." Bobbie nodded. "Of course you'll be fine. Henry knows what he's doing, and we'll be right outside waiting." Bobbie kissed her dry lips to Joy's hot, damp forehead. "I love you, li'l sis."

Joy swallowed. Tears welled and spilled down the sides of Joy's face from the corners of the dark pools of her eyes. She tried to speak but stopped, sniffed, nodded. "I know," she managed to whisper.

Bobbie let Hicks guide her to the waiting area of the medical center. Someone had provided cushions for the seats, and cheerful non-recyclable mugs sat by the matter streamer that had a sign saying, "coffee only."

Hicks tipped his head towards the sign, raising an eyebrow.

Bobbie shook her head. She didn't want coffee, or anything other than for this to be over and for Joy to be well and happy. Anger at Bobbie's own helplessness fired up like flames beneath her skin, untamed and frenzied. She stood up and paced.

Hicks sat with his head in his hands, then stood as well. "We should go eat something," he said. "You know this could take hours."

Bobbie knew this was the advice she would give to waiting relatives.

"Okay." Bobbie hugged Hicks to her and whispered, "Thank you."

Shouting drifted through the hallway.

Bobbie and Hicks froze to listen.

"Hicks, Bobbie, come quick." Hang's voice was frantic. He burst into the waiting room. "Jimmy and Davitt are fighting – you have to stop them."

"Where's Dad?" Bobbie sprang into action, moving towards the direction he'd come from, passing Hicks, who had stopped to lift a medical kit from the shelf by the exit door.

"I don't know." Hang panted the words as he led the way. "Just hurry! Jimmy was shouting and saying bad words."

"Christ almighty!" Bobbie said, remembering Granny attacking Joy, and Jimmy's recent mood swings. Jimmy might really lose it and do something he – no, all of them might regret. Bobbie notched up her stride to a trot.

Hang ran ahead. He looked back at Bobbie with round, frightened eyes. "Jimmy said he was going to kill Davitt."

"Hang, go quick, and find Dad," Bobbie said as she broke into a run.

CHAPTER 15

Bobbie charged into the lab, the sound of Hicks' footfalls still echoing in the tunnel behind her.

Pinned against the far wall, Davitt cowered with arm up, elbows cocked, trembling.

Jimmy, red-faced, veins popping at his temples, hands held out from his sides like an attacking bear, towered over him.

"You fucking son of a whore." Spit flew from Jimmy's lips, his screams raking his vocal cords. "You killed my Gloria. You sneaky bastard, after you fucked her too. And now your stinking nanobots are in my Joy. I'll rip your fucking balls off and shove them down your throat."

Davitt, inches from Jimmy, eyes scrunched closed, tried to turn his face. Jimmy grabbed Davitt's chin and yanked him forward.

"Look at me." Jimmy's nails bit into Davitt's skin.

"Jimmy!" Bobbie yelled.

Jimmy turned.

Davitt twisted away and ran two steps.

Metal flashed in Jimmy's hand as he raised his arm and swung a hammer.

Bobbie's scream jammed in her throat. She heard the sickening crunch of the back of Davitt's skull splintering.

Davitt took one wobbly step, his knees buckled, and he dropped. The lab bench blocked his fall. He ricocheted backward, and momentum carried him over – a sack of unconscious flesh – to land on his back. Davitt's eyes fluttered. A stain darkened his crotch as his bladder let go.

Bobbie took a step toward Davitt, but froze as Jimmy turned toward her, hammer raised again.

Detachment lingered in Jimmy's eyes.

"Jimmy, put the hammer down." Hicks' voice came from behind Bobbie. He walked past her, raising his open hands, positioning himself between Bobbie and Jimmy. "Let's calm down. Set the hammer down, and we can talk through everything that happened."

Bobbie heaved in breaths, pulse throbbing in her head.

"Talking solves nothing," Jimmy said, the venom now leached from his tone.

"I understand how angry you are with Davitt," Hicks said. "We all are. I know you don't want to hurt anyone else."

A flicker passed through Jimmy's eyes. Compassion softened his glare for a moment before his eyes narrowed. Jimmy focused on Hicks, his grip tightening on the hammer. "The fuck you understand."

Move back! Bobbie wanted to scream but was mute with horror. Torn between her alarm for Hicks and her professional instinct, she looked at Davitt, motionless on the floor. Nausea swelled. A glossy red pool haloed from the back of Davitt's head onto the polished stone floor.

Mo appeared at the door and aimed a taser at Jimmy. Fizzles of blue jangled between the prongs.

Jimmy looked from the taser to Bobbie with a haunted expression. Mo kept his attention on Jimmy.

"One zap from that will kill you, Jimmy," Bobbie said, finding her voice, keeping it steady. Hicks moved closer, between Bobbie and Jimmy.

"I was defending myself," Jimmy said. The hammer clunked to the ground. He raised his hands in submission.

Hicks kicked the hammer out of Jimmy's reach.

Bobbie ran to Davitt and knelt beside him.

"He attacked me first," Jimmy said. "He was trying to escape, but I won't let him escape justice. He deserves to die, after the evil he's done. You know it, you said as much."

Blood spread outwards, widening the pool beneath Davitt's head. His eyes were partially closed, and his breathing uneven.

"Davitt? Can you hear me?" Bobbie said, tuning out Jimmy's rants. She found a weak pulse in Davitt's neck. Blood trickled from his nose, across his pale cheek, and then dripped to the ground, where it pooled into the blood already lost from his wound.

"Davitt," Bobbie continued, "you're going to be okay now. I'm going to examine your head. If you can talk or indicate if I hurt you, that would help."

Gently pressing with her fingertips, Bobbie felt over Davitt's skull, starting at the crown of his head. She supported his neck so she could slip her fingers beneath his skull, cringing as she felt the back of the skull, the occipital bone, grating.

"I had to do it," Jimmy started again. "Bobbie wanted me to do it. Everyone did."

Hicks, still between Jimmy and Bobbie, balanced on the balls of his feet, ready to pounce.

Bobbie couldn't stand the sight of Jimmy. "Mo, get him out of here. Lock him in a cell. Full guard."

"I'm not the one needing to be locked up, I tell you! It was self-defense."

The taser sparked again. Jimmy jumped, placing his hands on his head.

"Be careful with that thing, Mo. One touch will kill Jimmy," Bobbie said, glancing up at him for a second. She wasn't sure why she cared, but inside that cruel Jimmy was the old Jimmy, the family friend who'd been with them through so much – and she needed his cells for research; there was always that.

"Walk on," Mo barked.

"Alright, alright! Keep your taser in your pants, big man!" Jimmy said.

Bobbie heard them leaving, heard the rattle of the handle as Hicks grabbed the medical kit from where he'd dropped it at the door. Bobbie had to stop Davitt's bleeding. She pressed the wound gently despite the fracture. The bone moved again beneath her hand.

"What have we got?" Hicks said, kneeling beside her, pulling on gloves.

"Head wound, suspected compound depressed fracture. Pulse steady but weak. Breathing abnormal," Bobbie said, sliding into doctor mode but feeling in unfamiliar territory.

Hicks opened the medical kit beside her and pulled out a wad of absorbent padding. Bobbie held it against the wound while Hicks placed a collar around Davitt's neck, immobilizing any possible fractures to the cervical spine.

Hicks handed Bobbie a penlight. She pulled back Davitt's eyelids. "Pupils uneven and not responding to light."

It was bad, but they both kept what they knew off their faces and out of their voices. Davitt might still be able to hear them.

"We're going to take you to the medical wing now, Davitt. We'll be able to help you better there," Hicks said as he assembled a stretcher, and Bobbie finished dressing the head wound.

"Would you give us a hand here? Please," Hicks said to a gathered crowd of passersby, workers from nearby rooms. "You and you, please." Hicks nodded at two men, both of a similar height and sturdy build.

They knelt down beside Hicks, and he showed them where to place their hands to give Davitt a smooth roll onto the stretcher.

"I've inserted an oropharyngeal airway so we can move him," Bobbie told Hicks. Davitt couldn't choke on his own vomit now. The airway device blocked off the opening of the esophagus, going straight into his trachea.

"BP on the low side," Hicks said, deflating the cuff. "His pulse is still weak."

"Okay, let's move, on three," Bobbie said.

"Over here," Yoon directed when they arrived at the medical center. "Doctor Henry's team is using the theatre for Joy's surgery."

Bobbie scrubbed in, glad Joy had the facilities of the theatre and relieved that it was too small to share. She'd rather not see her little sister being cut into, opened up, rather not listen to the rasp of the ventilator at Joy's every breath, the beep of each heartbeat. Bobbie put any more thoughts of her sister lying under the scalpel out of her head. She focused on Davitt, working quickly to set up intravenous access while Hicks applied an oxygen mask. Davitt's color didn't worsen, but Bobbie would have like to have seen it improve.

"Let's elevate his head. Can we set this bed at a thirty-degree angle?" Bobbie asked, stepping back and raising her gloved hands.

A medical aide typed on the intepanel on the wall near the bed. With a squeaky hiss, the bed adjusted, elevating Davitt's head above his heart.

"We need hypertonic saline IV." Bobbie flicked her fingers to activate her ONIV but realized with an icy flush that she was on her own for this one. "Let's have anti-seizure drugs on hand. Bring whatever you have. If there's any edema, we'll need drugs for that too."

"Edema?' the aide asked.

"Swelling of the brain. Too soon to tell, but we need to be prepared," Bobbie said. "Sedatives will work too. Go quick. The guy in the pharmacy will help you."

With wordless efficiency, Hicks set up the portable 3D-imaging scanner. Bobbie stared at the images of Davitt's head and neck on the intepanel. Jumbled and confusing to begin with, Bobbie pushed away her impatience as she orientated her eye to the medium.

Concentrate... concentrate.

Bobbie began to make sense of the images.

"Cervical spine intact, no fractures. I see a compound depressed fracture on the occipital with cerebrospinal fluid leakage," Bobbie said. "There's bone pressing in on the brain here." She pointed to the screen.

"That will require surgery." Hicks' tone was neutral, but when Bobbie looked up and caught his eye, she could tell he was thinking the same thing she was.

We're geri-a-fucking-tricians.

"Yes." Bobbie sounded more confident than she felt. "At least waiting for the theatre will give us time to prep." Henry would be too exhausted to help them, and he was an obstetrician, not a brain surgeon, nor even a general surgeon. It was up to them.

Christ almighty, Bobbie hoped they had a damn good library. Without ONIV, they'd have to research the procedure the old-fashioned way – digital copy.

"Sure," Hicks said, scanning the intepanel where Davitt's vital signs were on display. "He's stable for now. The delay will give us time to see how the brain swells – if it does."

"Edema may not happen," Bobbie said. "But yes, that depressed fracture needs to be fixed."

Bobbie and Hicks spent the next two hours poring over medical directories and textbooks, figuring out the details of the procedure they'd need to use for Davitt's surgery.

"I've had more surgery time than you. I should lead," Bobbie said.

For a second, Hicks looked as though he might object; then he nodded. "You're sure?" he asked.

"Certain." Bobbie tried to absorb as much information as she could, telling herself she could do this, but she found herself unnerved. If they couldn't save Davitt, or if he were brain-damaged, who would develop the anti-nanobots?

Henry appeared at the door.

Bobbie sprang to her feet. "How is she?"

"Joy is in recovery now." Henry looked tired and sad.

Bobbie took a step in that direction.

"She's asleep," Henry said gently, putting a hand on Bobbie's shoulder. "Let her sleep for now. She has a lot to face when she awakens."

Bobbie went cold inside. "Why? What do you mean?"

"We had to remove her ovaries, as well as the uterus, so Joy will never have her own genetic offspring. If she'd kept her ovaries, Joy could have used a surrogate uterus." Henry squeezed Bobbie's shoulder. "I'm sorry. Those deformed zygotic cells were everywhere. We were lucky they hadn't spread to another organ system."

"Did you preserve tissue samples?" Bobbie asked.

Henry raised an eyebrow and nodded.

"I'll go talk to Jimmy," Hicks said.

"No," Bobbie said. "I'll do it. I need a break to let the prep sink in. Don't worry, I'll be quick. We still have an hour before we can get Davitt into surgery." Her shoulders drooped, suddenly weak.

"What is it?" Hicks asked, ducking down to look her in the face.

"I wanted to be there for Joy waking up," Bobbie said, brushing away her disappointment. "But now, I'll be operating on Davitt."

* * *

Jimmy's agitation filled the tiny cell; he paced and blustered, protesting his innocence, repeating it again to Mo, who stood guard at the door.

"Shut up and listen to me," Bobbie shouted, drawing level with the cell door and facing him down, shocking him into silence.

"Joy just had a very serious operation." Bobbie lowered her voice, though she knew Mo would overhear her. "She lost the baby. It never formed properly."

Jimmy kept his eyes down, his silence reverberating around Bobbie.

"She won't be able to have children," Bobbie added.

Jimmy's mouth warped to the side as he gnawed his lips. "That's another thing Davitt has to answer for!" he spat.

"He might not be answering for anything after what you did," Bobbie said, wondering how Jimmy had the gall to sidestep any responsibility.

"Stop acting so fucking pious," Jimmy hissed. "You wanted me to do it."

"What are you talking about?" Bobbie asked, stepping back from the fury etched on Jimmy's face.

"You told me you wanted him dead," Jimmy said, his eyes open wide. "I was going to fix it. I did it for the greater good, to protect Joy, you, humanity– it's justice! You should be electing me for mayor of this shithole or, at the very least, giving me a medal for bravery."

"Are you – serious?" Bobbie nearly said crazy. Of course he was crazy! Her stomach lifted at the memory of the crunch of the hammer connecting with Davitt's head.

"He was trying to escape. Mo had left us alone. As mayor, I'd sack his ass." Jimmy cast a glance in Mo's direction.

Bobbie followed his gaze. Mo lowered his eyes, his cheeks flaming.

"Escape to where?" Bobbie asked. Davitt had been sedated on the way here. He couldn't know which direction to fly, never mind dodge the dangerous dust storms of the Central Valley.

"How can you defend him now?" Jimmy raged. "After what he did to my Gloria? I can't get it out of my head, how she died. You know, you were there."

Bobbie caught her breath. She was there alright – she'd tasered Granny, killed her.

Jimmy stopped pacing and glared at Bobbie, saying, "Doesn't it haunt you? How can you not care anymore? How could you just let him get back to work, business as normal? How could you trust him? He's an evil bastard. Violent, sneaky..."

Bobbie stared back at Jimmy while he raved some more, circling through the same grievances.

She cut him off. "Stop!"

"What if he had escaped? How would I live with myself?" Jimmy's orange stare bore into Bobbie.

"How could he escape?" she asked.

This delusional Jimmy would justify his actions in his own twisted mind no matter what Bobbie said. Why was she giving him airtime?

"There are no guards at the hoverport," Jimmy said. "It would be easy for him to steal a craft."

"Jacob is setting up guard duty at the hoverport now." Bobbie needed to wrap this conversation up and leave, but Jimmy's arguments sucked her in.

"Did I just hear the sound of gates slamming and horses' hooves?" Jimmy said.

Bobbie kept her voice cool despite the pulse she felt in her neck. "I just came to let you know how Joy was doing. She's in recovery now."

"Right, thanks for letting me know," Jimmy said, suddenly cordial again.

"That's it? That's all you can say?" Bobbie asked.

"Well, if you let me out of here, I could go talk to her myself."

"No chance!"

"And Davitt, what's his prognosis?" Jimmy asked.

"None of your damn business." Bobbie reckoned that Jimmy had already figured out that if Davitt died, their hopes of stopping rejuvenation would die with him. Without Davitt, it would take years to develop an anti-nanobot, and by then, the world would be overrun by psychopaths capable of this and worse. Bobbie thought again of Granny spearing Justin with the garden fork and swallowed hard.

"You're going to have to operate, aren't you?" Jimmy's voice broke through her gruesome thoughts. "I don't fancy his chances. No offense, but with you, a crumblies' doctor, doing brain surgery..."

Bobbie moved to the cell door without answering him.

"Well, look on the bright side," Jimmy snorted derisively. "At least it's not rocket science."

Bobbie stormed out, slamming the door behind her before she gave in to the temptation to taser the fucker herself.

CHAPTER 16

"They're clearing up the operating theatre now," Hicks said when Bobbie met him at the medical center. "We'll be able to take Davitt in and start his surgery soon. We've had a chance to monitor him. He's stable."

"And Joy?" Bobbie asked, opening up an intepanel on the desk in front of them with details of procedures on surgery for skull fractures.

"Still sleeping, but stable. Your dad's with her at the moment."

Bobbie nodded and took Hicks' hand. "Jimmy's gone too far."

Hicks massaged her palm with his thumb. "We have to be certain before we can, you know..."

Bobbie knew, alright. Granny's distorted face, muscles melting beneath skin, flashed through her thoughts. She pushed the image away and said, "Jimmy didn't want Davitt making those anti-nanobots."

"It wasn't self-defense, it was self-preservation. But let's not get ahead of ourselves here," Hicks said. "We can't tase Jimmy yet – we need his tissue samples."

"Yeah," Bobbie said. "But ethically, we can't force him to cooperate."

"We have to," Hicks said. "We can't stay here forever. At some point, we'll be heading back out into Belus Land, and we'll need answers."

"I need us to be aware of what it is we're doing." Bobbie stretched out her shoulders and neck. "It's a bit rich – us blasting Davitt for experimenting on folk without their consent, then doing the same thing."

"This is different. Taking a few samples won't hurt Jimmy," Hicks said.

Bobbie thought of Jimmy, the dear old man who was sweet on Granny. He had been such a gentleman. He'd always worn his tweed coat over his sensorfabric. That had made her smile; the unnecessary garment had worked against the sensorfabric technology, but he'd worn it anyway – until the nanobots had infected him.

"The affair with Joy, the attack – none of it is his fault," Bobbie said. "He's acting under the influence of the nanobots."

"All the more reason," Hicks said, "to try to dismantle them."

"Technically, Jimmy's not of sound mind, so we're not treating him the same way that Davitt treated Granny." Bobbie needed to rationalize these thoughts out loud to see if they sounded right – or at least, less wrong.

She sat on the nearby stool. "We do have nanobots from Joy's tissue. We can certainly culture those. We can ask her permission, and I think she'd give it, though it would be better to see how the nanobots are behaving in senescent cells like Jimmy's. But it's something."

"Feel any better now you've worked that out?" Hicks said with a half-smile. He leaned against Bobbie, wrapped his arms around her waist, and gave her a squeeze.

"Not really." Bobbie laid her head on Hicks' shoulder, soothed by his presence. She rested there a moment, then motioned to the intepanel. "Let's go over the procedure for Davitt's surgery once more. It's nearly time."

* * *

Bobbie doubted she would ever perform another procedure that would wring her out like this one had. She'd drawn on every resource, reached deep into her skill bank, and was confident she'd done a damn fine job with what she had. But would it be enough to save Davitt?

Tremors hit her limbs as she surveyed the aftermath of the surgery. Bloody swabs, black and gelatinous, piled into a tray awaiting disposal. Yoon cleaned and sterilized the forceps Bobbie had used to reposition pieces of bone. Bobbie stared at her quaking fingers. An hour ago, she had been cool-headed and focused on the task. Now, Davitt's surgery haunted Bobbie in a series of vivid replays.

Davitt's shaved head was smooth beneath her sani-skin-covered fingertips, his glossy black curls gone; the subcutaneous follicles left behind had lent a blue tinge to his scalp. Bobbie saw the ragged edges where the skin had split under the force of the hammer.

She still could hear Hicks' gentle voice saying, "You've got this," as she'd braced herself for the first incision.

The fragments of Davitt's skull had been like a broken egg beneath her forceps. The stench of burning flesh as Bobbie cut Davitt's skin with the electric cautery would take forever to wash out of her memory. In the background, the click-click-woosh of Davitt's breathing, helped by a machine, had simultaneously lulled and unnerved her.

Bobbie had the fine-tuned manipulation required to pull pieces of Davitt's skull out of his brain, had understood and followed the procedure on the intepanel, had exchanged instructions with Hicks, and had taken a slight deviation from the plan as a blood vessel bled more than they'd anticipated. Together Bobbie and Hicks had stopped the bleeding, reset the skull, and sewn the tattered edges of Davitt's scalp together like a bad piece of patchwork.

All they could do was wait. Davitt might never function normally again, might never talk; never walk; never see, or might never wake up.

Bobbie knew she would wake – abruptly – in the dark of the night, seeing the pink brain tissue quivering under the broken skull, with that feeling of anxiety gnawing at her guts – Did I do it right? Could I have done it better?

"You did a great job," Hicks said, as though reading her mind. He handed her a cup with warm beige liquid in it. "Drink up."

Liquid slopped up the side of the cup but didn't spill. Bobbie took a sip – sweetened tea.

"I don't take sugar," she said, irritated.

"This time you do," Hicks said. "You need it. Keep the old blood sugars up. And we both need to rest."

"After I see Joy," Bobbie said. "Then I'll sleep." The tea tasted good, but not as good as the sense that she was being taken care of. Bobbie looked at Hicks, caught his eye, and smiled. "Thanks," she said softly.

* * *

Most of the in-patients were women. The one nearest Joy was heavily pregnant. Bobbie's heart clenched with her sister's loss. It would be hard for Joy, seeing all these expectant mothers after learning she'd never join their ranks.

"Let's set up a screen, please?" Bobbie said to the young man mopping the floor. She settled into a seat near Joy, allowing her eyes to grow heavy and welcoming the deepening of her breathing and the sensation of letting go. Disturbing visuals crammed into Bobbie's psyche, woozy images that dissipated into nonsensical confetti. The pictures merged and flowed with the hushed whistle of her breath.

Something touched Bobbie's hand, jerking her along an intense silver thread to consciousness, leaving her dizzy. Bobbie sat up suddenly. "What? What? What is it?"

"Sorry," Joy said in a hoarse whisper.

Bobbie looked at the hand that rested on hers, and her brain clicked into gear. "How are you feeling?"

"Sore," Joy said, rubbing her throat.

"The endotracheal tube will have grazed your throat." Bobbie flipped her hand around to grasp Joy's.

"I'm thirsty," Joy croaked.

Bobbie brought a cup of water to Joy's lips. "Here. Do you need pain relief?"

Joy winced as she sat forward to take a sip. "No, I can handle it. What did the doc say?"

"The good news is, he's confident he removed all the growths," Bobbie said, trying to inject brightness into her voice, but it rang hollow. "Do we have your permission to use the tissue we took during surgery for our research, to clone more cells infected with nanobots?"

"Of course. Anything you need. And the bad news?" Joy added in a small voice.

Bobbie looked away from her sister's sad, dark eyes, and pushed away the thought that Joy had been reckless. All those years, Bobbie had scolded her about her wild behavior, times when Joy had disappeared for weeks on end, yet this was the worst trouble Joy had landed herself in, right under Bobbie's nose.

"You won't be able to have children," Bobbie said. "They had to remove your ovaries."

"I see."

"I'm sorry." Bobbie had nothing better to say. Her heart constricted, but she managed not to cry.

Joy's mouth tucked in, and she blinked hard, staring up at the ceiling. She let out a long shuddering sigh before squeezing Bobbie's hand. "Where's Jimmy?" she whispered.

Again, Bobbie felt that familiar rush of irritation. Why couldn't Joy have been more careful?

Yet, of all the messages Bobbie had to deliver, she would have given anything to pass over this one. Bad news about medical conditions was one thing, but how could Bobbie tell her sister that the man Joy loved, whom she had unwittingly sacrificed so much for, had tried to murder someone?

"Joy, I want to you remember something really important," Bobbie began.

Joy's hand tightened on Bobbie's.

Bobbie pressed on. "Jimmy's not himself. Like the way Granny wasn't herself after she got younger."

"I know, but Davitt said the next phase of rejuvenation was better," Joy said, the hope in her voice shredding Bobbie. "Maybe he's okay. I've not seen him be like Granny was."

Bobbie held up her hand. "Joy, you have to face–"

"No! I know what you're going to say." Joy tried to sit up, winced, and sank back into the pillows. "You're going to tell me that love is blind. God! Such a cliché." She turned from Bobbie.

"I wasn't going to say that," Bobbie said. "Believe me, I wish that was my argument, but..." Bobbie reached for Joy's hand, stopped, then stroked Joy's hair lightly with the back of her fingers. "There's no easy way to tell you this. Jimmy attacked Davitt and injured him so badly that Davitt nearly died. Hicks and I have just finished operating on Davitt's skull. On his skull," Bobbie repeated. "We're not trained to do that, and he may never recover, and if he doesn't, we'll blame ourselves." Bobbie pinched the bridge of her nose and squeezed her eyes shut.

"Je-sus," Joy said on a long exhale. "Why?"

"Does it matter why? Jimmy smashed the back of Davitt's skull with a hammer. Jimmy claims Davitt was trying to escape, but we witnessed the end of the fight. We know he was lying." Bobbie watched her words land heavily on Joy, each one another lead brick of upset and distress.

Joy lay wrapped in stunned silence. Tiny beads of sweat popped on her brow, giving a sheen to her creamy skin. Her eyes, wide open in a thousand-mile stare, landed somewhere beyond the walls.

Bobbie touched her shoulder. Joy hauled her gaze back to the here and now. Though they didn't drop, Bobbie saw Joy's tears. They reflected the lights from the ward, amassed and quivered as if trying to extinguish the last sparks of her faith in Jimmy. Bobbie looked closer. Of course, that wasn't a spark, couldn't possibly be a spark, but...

Bobbie pulled the penlight from her pocket and checked again. Joy's usually black-brown eyes glinted in the penlight. Joy blinked and pulled away.

"Hold still," Bobbie said, her heartbeat skittering.

Joy froze.

Bobbie saw it again – a flash of orange pigment in Joy's iris.

A surge of fear made Bobbie lightheaded. Joy was young. The nanobots weren't supposed to manifest in her tissues, according to Davitt. But now...

Bobbie studied her sister's face. A slightly darker patch of skin just nestled in the hollow of her cheekbone: the beginnings of a mole, Bobbie now saw. A gasp stuck in her lungs as Bobbie fought to keep her face calm and her gaze steady, but it didn't fool Joy.

"What?" Joy said slowly as worry creased her brow.

"Joy, you know how you bypassed the Succor Tech biosensors?" Bobbie said.

"Ah-huh."

"Does that mean you still have your medulla sensor, or not?"

"I still have it." Joy wriggled in the bed, winced, and lay still again.

"I see," Bobbie said, patting Joy's hand. A medulla would make things tricky. Bobbie could have shocked Joy with a taser to destroy the nanobots before they got any further, but now she ran the risk of blowing up the medulla sensor used by Belus Corp to monitor the body chemistry of every able-bodied citizen to keep them in peak physical health. That same sensor, under a surge of electrical current, would be like a tiny bomb in the base of Joy's brain. Of course, not all settings on a taser delivered a big enough charge to blow the medulla sensor. Bobbie knew that tasers were used in the PARC, but only under the strictest of conditions. The only tasers Bobbie had access to had been tampered with, and she couldn't trust them to deliver a small enough current.

"What's this got to do with anything?" Joy asked. "Oh, my God!" She clamped a hand over her mouth as Bobbie watched the realization dawn in her eyes. "You have to shock me? Are my eyes orange? Show me." She struggled to sit up and gasped in pain.

"Lie still," Bobbie said and handed her a mirror from the utensil tray on the on the bedside locker. "Your eyes are still brown. But there are specks of orange."

"Oh, God. Oh, God!" Joy opened her eyes wide, peering as close to the mirror as she could.

"We'll figure this out," Bobbie said, trying to hide her own frazzled thoughts from Joy as much as possible.

"You have to operate, take out the medulla sensor, then tase me," Joy said.

Not more brain surgery.

"It's a huge risk." There was no way Bobbie was prepared to open up Joy's brain; she had to figure out something better. But what?

"I don't care." Joy clutched Bobbie's arm. "You have to – unless there's another option."

"We'll look at all the options," Bobbie said, her mind churning. "I promise, but right now, you need to rest. It's late." Bobbie heard the click of the timer on the IV, delivering Joy's next dose of pain relief and antibiotics. "Your meds will help you sleep. I need to talk to Hicks about this." Bobbie leaned in and brushed Joy's forehead with dry lips. "We'll figure out the best way forward. By the time you wake up, we'll have a plan."

Joy nodded as her eyes drifted shut – a welcome escape, Bobbie reckoned.

Desperate for a solution, Bobbie wanted to act now – go to the lab, get to work, formulate a plan – but the day's events had left her exhausted and wrung out. Her body felt so heavy Bobbie could barely walk, and her head spun. Instead of going to the lab, Bobbie made her way to her quarters.

Hicks was already there, in bed and fast asleep. In the dim light, Bobbie sat on the edge of the bed and studied the curve of his eyelashes resting on smooth skin, his lips slightly parted – portals to the ebb and flow of his breath. The warmth from Hicks' body reached Bobbie's skin, and she could no longer resist the urge to wrap herself around him, soak in his strength. She eased herself down to lie facing his back, snaked her hands around his waist, and clutched him to her. Hicks stretched in her arms, his muscles pulling taut beneath Bobbie's touch.

"Hello, you," Hicks said with a drowsy smile. "How's Joy?"

Bobbie hesitated, not wanting to spoil the moment, nor burden him with the news that the nanobots were now fully active and affecting Joy's systems. But she hesitated a moment too long. Hicks always could read her brain waves.

"What's wrong?" Hicks sat up abruptly, shaking off the inertia of sleepiness. "Tell me."

Bobbie told him. He listened with complete attention; his fatigue banished by the hour of sleep he'd managed to grab.

"We have to figure out how to give Joy a shock big enough to fry the nanobots, but not blow her medulla sensor," Bobbie said.

Hicks pulled a face. "Taser?"

Bobbie shuddered. "I tasered Granny."

"And Granny died, but that was only because the nanobots were the only thing holding her together by then. Joy's different. They don't have the same impact yet."

"What if the current is too strong? I'm worried it'll blow the medulla sensor the way it did with Detective Cross."

"But that taser was tampered with," Hicks said.

"Perhaps. I don't know if the tasers here are safe. We need to figure out how much current the medulla sensor can take before it blows. We need to set up some tests." But Bobbie didn't know how much they had to test out any plan they came up with. How fast did the nanobots multiply? At what point would it be too late to use the electric and end up damaging Joy's cellular structure? She wanted to scream with frustration at not knowing the answers.

"What about defibrillation?" Hicks said. "We know it doesn't blow the sensors in our patients. Would that do it?"

"It might, but we'd risk giving her cardiac arrest or an irregular heart rhythm, or damage the cardiac muscle." Bobbie rubbed her temples. "But if it destroys the nanobots, it's safer than removing her medulla sensor."

"We have no way of asking Davitt, with him still unconscious." Hicks massaged Bobbie's shoulders, making her groan.

"What a choice," Bobbie said wearily. "Which do we risk damaging? Joy's heart or her brain?"

CHAPTER 17

Bobbie sat on one of the glassy-smooth boulders a little way from the mouth of the caves. The morning sun cast black shadows into the ripples and folds of the steep valley sides. Light flashed and sparked mini-rainbows from the odd crystal where the interior of the tunnels lay exposed from the landslide. When she'd first arrived, Bobbie missed Ireland's continuous theatre of clouds, longed for respite from the sun's glare, and loathed the dry, sucking quality of the air. But this devastated landscape had grown on her.

Bobbie had slept fitfully after her conversation with Joy about how to kill the nanobots in Joy's system. Tired but unable to sleep, Bobbie had gotten up and come outside to find a spot to sit quietly, calm her mind, and try to think straight.

"It's breathtaking," Slade said from behind.

Bobbie jumped and turned to face her.

"I didn't mean to startle you," Slade said. "It's beautiful, isn't it?"

"I never thought of it like that." Bobbie lied, unwilling to view anything through the same lens as Slade. Using the smooth rock beneath her palm to steady her, Bobbie squinted as she looked up at Slade's silhouette, outlined in the glow of the morning sun. "I was just taking a few moments with my coffee," she said, holding up an empty cup.

Go away.

"This place must have been beautiful before the Melters." Slade moved around to perch herself on the rock beside Bobbie. She folded her arms and looked across the valley. Bobbie shifted away from her but followed Slade's gaze up the steep rocky sides.

"Did you know that they used to have a waterfall of fire from up there?" Slade pointed to the jagged ridge. "Glacier Point."

"A waterfall of fire?" Bobbie couldn't imagine it. Did Slade mean a flow of lava? The rock formations didn't support that.

"Nearly two hundred years ago, early settlers came to vacation here. They camped up there and lit a fire each night, then kicked the burning embers over the edge."

"It must have been quite the spectacle," Bobbie said, her frosty wariness of Slade thawed by the wonder her story inspired. "Weren't they afraid of forest fires? Jimmy said this place was full of trees, before."

Slade shrugged. "I don't know. Maybe there weren't any trees below the peak. Maybe they'd already been cleared. I don't think those early settlers cared. The Europeans displaced and annihilated the first peoples. This valley was the scene of gruesome bloodshed – a culture wiped out. It was criminal, just criminal. It's ironic that a stray hit from the Melters topped off its devastation."

"I didn't know that," Bobbie said, relaxing the muscles in her shoulders, not quite sure where Slade was going with this. "It had a reputation as a haven of natural beauty when I was a child."

"It depends on whose account of history you read," Slade said. "Or believe." She let that sit for a few seconds. "That's why what we do next is so important." She turned and fixed Bobbie with a stern look. "I need your answer now. Will you come with us to Switzerland?"

"Jesus, is that all you can think about? Davitt almost died, and Joy–" Bobbie stopped. How much had Joy told anyone of her condition? Bobbie wrung her fingers through each other.

Slade smiled. "I spoke with Joy."

How the hell could Slade smile at a time like this?

Seemingly oblivious to Bobbie's rancor, Slade continued, "She was surprised to learn who Ori was. Thought she might be in trouble for trapping me in the elevator that time."

Bobbie sensed the power that Slade must have felt at that moment and resented her playing super-spy. Was this just a game to her?

Slade's tone changed. "Considering what's happened, we have more reason to move forward as quickly as possible. We have to protect people from this. What would have happened if we hadn't known what to look for with Joy? We need those anti-nanobots yesterday. What's your prognosis on Davitt?"

"It's too soon to tell," Bobbie said. "If he wakes up, and I mean if, he may not be able to talk or remember anything. If he does, his mobility might be impacted, and if it isn't, I can't see him being able to travel in three months' time, even if we did have answers by then."

"We have to go to Switzerland now – without Davitt. We have to move to stop rejuvenation right away," Slade said. "I've arranged an emergency meeting of the board."

"Right now?" Bobbie lifted her hands palm-up. "I've no way to make the anti-nanobots."

"You have to warn the medical board." Slade held Bobbie's gaze, but used one hand to push Bobbie's hands onto a bundle in her lap.

"Can't you just tell them? Why am I necessary?" Bobbie asked, pulling her hands out from under Slade's.

"You're the expert witness. You have the medical credentials. I can get hold of your old records, the psychologist's reports you had compiled on the rejunevees' mental states, but it has to come from one of their own," Slade said, lifting one thigh and clasping her hands around her knee.

"I'm a wanted person in Belus Land. What happens after the conference? How will you guarantee my safety?" Bobbie stood up and faced Slade.

Slade leaned back lazily against the rock, still eye-level with Bobbie, and said calmly, "We will do whatever we have to."

"I have to stay here," Bobbie said, her voice loud. "Davitt needs my care, and so does Joy."

Slade set her foot back on the ground. "You're saying no?"

"I'm saying it's impossible right now. We've had a major setback here," Bobbie said, biting back her anger. "I can go over Davitt's data and try to cobble together the information to make the anti-nanobots, but I'm a geriatrician, dammit, not a nanobiologist, or a brain surgeon or a heart specialist." She realized she was shouting. "I have a sister to worry about." She turned away from Slade and headed back to the caves, but Slade overtook her, blocking Bobbie's way.

"I'm sorry you feel that way, Bobbie," Slade said, as Jacob and Mo emerged from the nearest cave and strode towards them.

Bobbie looked from Slade to Mo and Jacob. "What's going on?"

Mo and Jacob lined up on either side of Bobbie.

Slade, standing in front of Bobbie, cleared her throat and said, "I'm detaining you for refusing to co-operate, and for conspiracy in the attempted murder of Davitt Ellis–"

"That's ridiculous! Get your hands off me!" Bobbie snatched her arm from Jacob's grasp. "I treated Davitt. I saved him," Bobbie said, jabbing a finger at Slade.

Slade stepped to the side, and Jacob filled the space in front of Bobbie, his face set rigid. "Jimmy said he was acting on your instructions," Jacob said.

"What?" Anger shot through Bobbie.

Jacob caught hold of her arm again and squeezed hard above her elbow.

"You're hurting me!" Bobbie gasped.

"Stop!" Slade commanded, and Jacob let go. "Jacob, please step back."

Jacob threw Bobbie a dark look, but backed away.

Bobbie rubbed her arm, trying frantically to make sense of the situation. Somewhere within the bubble of her anger, Bobbie knew she had to comply, had to set the record straight, but she also realized with a fizz of panic that she was at Slade's mercy. This was Slade's camp, her kingdom, and Slade made the rules. Even so, it was incredible that Slade would take the word of a crazed sociopath over Bobbie.

"Where is my father?" Bobbie asked, her voice strong, confident.

"He's with Joy," Slade said. "But he'll join us for the hearing."

"Hearing?" Bobbie said as indignation flared white-hot. "Are you kidding me? You believe Jimmy?"

"The sooner we get the facts straight, the better." Slade looked levelly at Bobbie. "Wouldn't you agree?"

"The fact is I'm innocent," Bobbie said. "This is ridiculous!"

"Just agree to come with me to Switzerland, Bobbie, and we can discuss the rest," Slade said, her expression unreadable.

"You're blackmailing me?" Bobbie said, her heart slamming in her chest.

Slade turned her back and made to walk off.

"You bitch!" Bobbie balled her fists and lunged for Slade, grabbing for her shoulder.

Mo sprang between his mother and Bobbie.

Too late, Bobbie pivoted. A stinging sensation bit just under her shoulder blade. Bobbie's body stiffened like a board. She tried to move, tried to fight it, tried to gain control, but couldn't.

Bobbie tried screaming, "Enough, enough!" but the cry stayed trapped in her chest. As soon as Mo turned the gun off, Bobbie heard her voice hack out, "Fuck! Fuck!"

Still cognizant, Bobbie's muscles turned to jelly, and she collapsed in a heap. Rocks dug unto her back. She saw the blue sky above her, felt the rush of dry air into her lungs. Bobbie was alive. The current hadn't blown up her medulla sensor.

Bobbie's mind zoomed in on the area at the back of her skull. She didn't have the coordination to raise a hand to see if the area was tender or felt hot, but she didn't have to. The back of her head was one of the few places that didn't sing with pain. Her medulla sensor, used by Belus Corp to monitor her biochemistry, didn't seem to be affected in a way that harmed her. Perhaps the sensor was damaged, maybe to never work again. Fat lot Bobbie cared about that. Belus had used those sensors to control, making sure the good little citizens were in perfect fitness to perform their duties.

Bobbie tried again to lift her hand to the nape of her neck but couldn't get her muscles to work. She lay still, eyes closed, dazed, her mind racing.

Slade's voice hissed somewhere above her: "Mo, I'm fine. Put that away."

Mo whispered, but Bobbie still heard, "I wasn't going to risk letting her–"

"Just get her to her feet." The exasperation in Slade's tone surprised Bobbie. Hadn't Slade won, again, by beating Bobbie into submission – why was the woman so annoyed, so fucking hard to please, Bobbie wondered.

Slade was trying to coerce Bobbie, bully her, but needed her – alive. Slade wouldn't risk blowing up Bobbie's medulla sensor by tasing her, so Slade must know the setting on that taser was safe, that it would only stun and not blow up the medulla sensor and kill the victim. But Slade had tased Bobbie, all the same, and was using brute force to get her to do as she was told.

Bobbie considered playing unconscious, letting her limbs fall leaden, making it harder for them to move her, then realized she didn't need to fake it.

Mo handed the taser to Slade and helped Jacob lift Bobbie, grabbing her under the other arm. The weight of her body hurt where the men pulled at her arms. So much for making Jacob and Mo carry her – it only added to the pain in her stricken muscles. Bobbie groaned and tried to talk, only managing garbled words.

As they dragged Bobbie towards the cave door, her muscles began to fire, complying with her commands to walk. She managed a feeble stagger, so the men didn't pull so hard on her arms.

By the time they reached the jail cell, Bobbie was back in control, though her heart felt like it was bursting. She followed the instructions this time. With pain lingering in every muscle, Bobbie sure as hell didn't want to invite another zap.

They sat her down in a cell similar to the one Davitt had been held in, and then they left, slamming the door. The noise echoed through the cavernous ceilings.

Loneliness swooped in, but Bobbie was too angry and disgusted to cry. The bed smelled of urine. A potty in the corner, though empty, didn't look like it had gotten more than a quick rinse after its last use. Every muscle burned under her skin, but not as hot as Bobbie's rage. How dare they tase her? They could have killed her.

Bobbie revisited the horror of finding Detective Cross dead in her apartment: the staring eyes, the deep bruising at the nape of her neck. Another ally gone. That taser had been tampered with to deliver a fatal current. It may even have been enough to kill without the added help from blowing up the obligatory sensor in Cross's brainstem.

Bobbie had taken that taser and later used it on Granny, to lethal effect.

But normal tasers, ones that hadn't been damaged, had a range of settings. Could the same current Slade used on Bobbie destroy Joy's nanobots? Joy, though weak after the surgery, might withstand a shock like that if given some time to mend and, Bobbie thought ruefully, some pain relief. The idea gave Bobbie enough hope to lift her spirits. She stood up on shaky legs. Feeling a hundred years old, stiff, and weakened, Bobbie reached the door and banged on it.

"Slade!" Bobbie yelled.

Nothing.

She thumped her fists against the door again. "Slade!"

Bobbie held her breath and listened.

Nothing.

How long would Slade hold her in this cell? How long could she hold Bobbie? Once Hicks woke up, he'd come looking for her. Would they tase him too?

Bobbie hammered the door. "Let me outta here."

Still no sound.

Hicks had no more authority than Bobbie had, but her father was important here. Was Luke on Bobbie's side? He'd traded the best years of Bobbie's life, of being with her, for the Candels, for this cause he'd found. Would Luke save her now?

Bobbie found it impossible to gauge time. Seconds could as easily have taken hours to pass. She tried to lie on the cot, but it stank of vomit and alcohol. She tried pacing, but her limbs still wobbled. Sitting on the edge of the cot was the best compromise, until Bobbie's agitation got the better of her. She stood up and hammered on the door again and again.

A commotion at the end of the tunnel bounced a melee of voices up the tunnel.

One voice stood out – her father's, urgent and in control.

A clatter of keys hit the floor, and an angry voice rose behind that.

Hicks!

"You idiot! Hurry the fuck up, Jacob, or you'll feel my boot up your arse," Hicks yelled.

That made Bobbie grin. Hicks rarely lost his cool, but when he did, it was unstoppable – like a volcanic eruption. Trembling with relief, Bobbie sat back down on the stinking bed.

The door opened. Hicks ran to Bobbie, scooping her into his arms. For a flurry of seconds, Bobbie didn't need another thing for the rest of her life except to be with Hicks. She buried her face into the softness of his neck and breathed him in.

"Are you okay?" Hicks asked, his voice a warm hum in her ear.

"Yes," Bobbie said. "They tased me."

"Fuckers!"

"I know, but listen," Bobbie pulled back to look into Hicks' worried gray eyes. "It hurt like hell, but it didn't kill me – obviously. It might be what we need to do for Joy."

"Okay," Hicks said, and looked around the cell. "This is what you're thinking about? In this shit hole?"

"No. Yes. No." Bobbie started to laugh, and the inappropriateness fueled it further.

"You're quite mad." Hicks pulled her to him in another bear hug. "Let's get out of here."

"I can't believe Slade put me in here," Bobbie said, her laughter drying up.

"Bobbie," her father said from the doorway. "Are you alright?"

"Yes. No thanks to Slade and her goons." Bobbie held onto Hicks' arm as they left the cells and walked down the tunnel towards fresh air.

Slade stepped into the tunnel and blocked their exit. "Jimmy made serious accusations against you."

"And you believed him?" Luke said, his nostrils flaring.

"Bobbie, do you deny that at Helen Lake you said that your grandmother died because of Davitt and that he should be dead too?" Slade asked.

Caught off guard, Bobbie searched her memory for the incident, the words, the sentiment, while she protested. "What? No! I mean, I didn't mean it. I might have said something like that in the heat of an argument. Jesus Christ!" She buried her fingers in the hair at the crown of her head and panted into the space framed by her elbows and forearms. Could Jimmy really think she meant that? Was she somehow to blame for what he did?

"At the cliff top," Slade continued smoothly, "you told Jimmy to throw Davitt over the cliff."

"I did not!" Bobbie roared, flinging her arms wide. Then she remembered Jimmy threatening to throw Davitt over the cliff, and she had made a dig at Davitt about letting Jimmy or helping him or something like that. What had she said? Bobbie searched for the memory. Jimmy had remembered, but Jimmy was a sociopath, and as such, he'd twist the truth and manipulate anyone he could – even Slade, who was up for a bit of exploitation of her own.

"Oh God," Bobbie groaned. "You seriously think I meant it? We were under extreme stress, and Davitt was being an arse. Dad, you know I wouldn't condone murder."

"Look, Bobbie," Slade said, pointing a finger. "I flat-out don't trust you. You're refusing to help us. This whole 'I'm a doctor; therefore, I'm a humanitarian' shit doesn't wash with me. You're in this for your own ends. Unless something directly affects you, you don't give a flying fuck about anyone else."

"That's bullshit," Bobbie said. "I gave up my life to be here."

"You gave up your life for your grandmother," Slade said.

"No, it wasn't like that." A claxon roared in Bobbie's head. Was Slade right? Was Bobbie really a *fuck you, Jack, I'm okay* gal? She was doing her best, but her best for what end?

Bobbie stood speechless, her mind whirring as Slade went on, "What if others get pregnant like Joy did? The doctors won't know what to look for; they could die. As long as you are here, you are under lock and key."

"You can't do that!" Hicks said, stepping forward.

"I can." Slade gave Hicks the stink eye. "And I can have you locked up too."

"Alright! Alright. I'll go, fuck you," Bobbie yelled, holding up her hands. She knew she had to, and not just because Slade was bullying her into it. Slade was right. If Bobbie could stop the spread of rejuvenation, she had to give it a try, though the whole plan scared the shit out of her. This was about more than Bobbie's family, but she had to make sure she gave them the best chance too. "But please, first let me treat Joy with the taser you used on me, to destroy her nanobots."

"You have a day," Slade said.

"A week," Bobbie countered. "I'd like to run a couple of tests on sample medulla sensors to be completely sure she won't be harmed. And Joy needs recovery time."

"Consider yourself the test. You've got two days." Slade's black eyes glittered. "The pain relief she's on now will help."

Bobbie chewed her lip. "Four – she needs time for the wound glue to bind. I don't want her wound to open as the muscles spasm."

"Fine. Early morning departure, though. To beat the dust storms."

Bobbie swallowed hard and nodded.

"I'm going, too." Hicks took Bobbie's hand and squeezed tight.

"There's only room from three." Luke stared him down. "Slade, Bobbie, and me."

"Use a bigger vehicle," Hicks said, with an edge to his voice.

"We can't wait that long. There's one hovercar in the bay, and we're preparing it for departure," Slade said. "There's no more due to arrive until a week from now –"

"Then why not –" Bobbie began, but she knew the answer as she spoke.

Slade stared her down. "We can't put this off any longer."

"Whoa," Hicks said. "Luke, really, you're willing to send your own daughter into God knows what danger?"

"I'm not sending her anywhere. I'll be protecting her," Luke said.

"We haven't discussed that," Slade said. "Mo or Jacob may go instead."

"We don't need to discuss this. I'm going, Ori." Luke faced Slade again. "Go be useful somewhere."

Slade stood for a second, then shook her head, muttering, "Fine, have it your way." She nodded at Mo, and together they strode off. Bobbie watched them, allowing herself to savor Slade's defeat – albeit a small one.

"I'm sorry she did this to you, Bobbie," Luke said quietly. "She really needs you; we need you. Without your help, rejuvenation will spread faster."

"I get it, Dad, really I do." Although Bobbie sounded measured, she fumed on the inside. He should be protecting her, but he had let Slade tase and blackmail her. Luke was her fucking father! But then again, he had always chosen his damn cause over Bobbie. Why would he change now? Don't think about it, Bobbie told herself as she said aloud, "And at least we now know we can try taser therapy on Joy." She looked her father in the eye, keeping a tight rein on her tone, but heard emotion leak into her words as she said, "More to the point, Dad, how do you trust Slade enough to go to Switzerland with her after that little episode? I know she'll get us there, but what about getting us out?"

CHAPTER 18

"Do it," Joy said. "Today. Now! My eyes are more and more orange."

Joy sat on the examination table, swinging her feet, the innocent, childlike gesture tugging at Bobbie. The little side room they were in was private, away from the general medical ward, which seemed to be bursting with pregnant women and mewling newborns. Bobbie could hardly bear it and could only imagine how hard it must be for Joy. Hollowed cheeks and dark smudges below Joy's eyes told of the strain she was under.

Bobbie cast her eye over Joy's vitals on the intepanel beside the bed. "I'm afraid of opening your wound. When the current hits, your muscles will spasm."

Joy winced. "Worst case, you glue me up again." She looked at herself in a hand mirror. "That spot developed into a mole overnight, Bobbie. I'm scared." She looked at Bobbie with eyes that glittered with more orange flecks by the hour. "Let's get this over with."

Joy was brave. Rash too, Bobbie thought, and far from sentimental. Joy hadn't mentioned Jimmy again: no mooning around after a lost love, no discussion of her infertility.

"Talking won't change anything," Joy had said when Bobbie had offered an ear.

Bobbie lifted the taser. Arcs of blue light fizzled between the prongs.

Joy took one look and shrank back. "Wait," she said. "What about my ONIV?"

Bobbie lowered her taser, puzzled that Joy's stoicism vanished at the thought of losing her ONIV.

"We don't know," Bobbie said slowly. "When the taser is used in Belus Land, it's used on people in the PARC who have broken the law. They wouldn't have access to ONIV. I don't have any information on how the shock affects their ONIV when they're re-introduced to society– "

"If they're re-introduced to society." A muscle twitched in Joy's jaw.

"You could insert a new one," Bobbie said. "When you go back to Belus Land. You don't need one here anyway – we're offline."

"No!" Joy looked around wildly. "No, I can't! It won't be the same."

ONIVs were bio-mechanically integrated into an individual's nervous systems. Bobbie remembered how easily Joy had adapted to her ONIV as a child and had subsequently hacked her own system when she was a young adult. It would take years for Joy to program a new one as robust as the one she had grown up with.

Joy continued, "The AI component in this one would be lost. I'd have the same capacity as a child."

"Can't we take one from an adult who has... who no longer needs theirs?" Bobbie didn't want to say it, but there were a few corpses buried at the compound who would have ONIVs. "There would be less catching up to do."

"Wouldn't work. The new generation ONIVs have bio-components that grow with the host. My body would reject it. The first-gen ONIV didn't have that, but they're so limited and hard to find. I couldn't carry out my function within the Candels," Joy said. "I use my upgraded ONIV to infiltrate and disrupt Belus Corp. Without that, I'm useless."

"Joy, we have no time to work around your ONIV," Bobbie said. "The more your cells rely on the nanobots to support them, the more cellular damage you risk when they're destroyed. Every hour, every minute, increases that risk. There's more than your ONIV in jeopardy. You'll catch up. I know you will."

"Please, just give me a little more time to figure it out," Joy pleaded. "Can't you take it out and reinsert it?"

"That's a really difficult procedure. I've never done it. I'd need time to research. Please, Joy, you can't risk waiting that long, you said so yourself only moments ago," Bobbie said, trying to hide her concern that perhaps Joy's stalling wasn't due to fear of losing her ONIV, but rather that the nanobots had already altered her psyche – Joy's flip-flop in the decision wasn't like her. Bobbie's old annoyances with Joy also bubbled to the surface. Was this just Joy being overdramatic, or was there really an issue? Bobbie kept up her persuasion: "And besides, your ONIV will probably be okay. We've tested medulla sensors with this current for the past two days, and they were fine, remember? We've no way to test the functionality of the ONIV here, but it will probably be fine too. Five minutes ago, you were for killing the nanobots."

Bobbie was terrified of the nanobots' effect on Joy's brain. Granny's personality had reverted to true type as soon as the nanobots had stopped working, but it was such a brief interlude; it hadn't given Bobbie a lot of data. There was no telling what, if any, repercussions there would be if the nanobots had already crossed Joy's blood-brain barrier.

Joy swallowed, paled, then nodded. "My only purpose is to undermine Belus Corp, and the only way I can do that effectively is by using my ONIV, my specially-built

ONIV, to hack into Belus systems and manipulate them. You have to promise me you'll do everything you can to avoid damaging my ONIV. Bobbie, promise?"

"Of course. I'll be shooting in your lower body." Bobbie took both Joy's hands in hers. They felt fragile, bones wrapped in skin. Bobbie needed to dismantle the nanobots now – their effects strengthened by the hour. There was no putting it off. But where the hell was Hicks? He was supposed to meet Bobbie here half an hour ago. At times like this, the ONIV would have been great: a quick blink to ask him, "Where are you?"

Instead, Bobbie said to Joy, "The electric shock will get rid of the nanobots, and it won't blow your medulla sensor. You'll live, and you'll still be you. Not a psychopath."

"A life without living," Joy said with a bitter edge.

"What do you mean?" Bobbie asked.

"Sure, I'll be alive, but what use will I be to anyone?" said Joy, hunching her shoulders. "A hacker who can't hack, it's like a fish that can't swim. Pointless."

"Don't say that." Bobbie pulled her into a hug, but Joy didn't soften into her embrace. Bobbie pulled back and took her sister's face in her hands. "You are brilliant, inventive, and committed. You'll find a way to swim. You always do. As long as you are alive, you have options, potential."

Both of Joy's eyes were fully orange now, the nanobots amassing at exponential speed. Bobbie reckoned the more they multiplied, the faster they could reproduce, like bacteria. "I can't wait for Hicks. I have to do this right now." Bobbie went to the door and spotted Henry working on an intepanel further down the ward. Henry looked up, and Bobbie beckoned him over.

Frowning, Henry approached. "Is Joy okay?"

"Not really," Bobbie said. "I have to shock her right away. Can you assist?"

"What do we need to do?" Henry moved into the room and closed the door behind him. "Hello, Joy."

Joy nodded but didn't speak.

"Joy," Bobbie said, "I'll give you a sedative and something to temporarily paralyze your muscles to avoid any violent contractions and reduce the risk of opening your stitches."

"But shouldn't we administer a short-acting anesthetic, like you would for electroconvulsive therapy?" Henry said.

"Ideally, yes, but we haven't time," Bobbie said. "For that, she'd need to fast for seven hours and be intubated. For ICT, the shock needs to be administered for a longer period... minutes. With the taser, she only needs a few seconds." Bobbie tucked Joy's hair back from her forehead. "It will be quick, I promise."

"Do it," Joy said. "Just... get it over with."

"That a girl." Bobbie kissed her sister's forehead, her heart dragging at the idea of the pain Joy was going to experience. Bobbie placed the medication patch on Joy's skin at the base of her neck, and watched the black of Joy's pupils pushing out against the now vibrant orange pupils. Joy's eyelids closed. One last look at the intepanel told Bobbie that Joy's heart rate and oxygen saturation level were normal.

She wished Hicks was with her. Where the hell was he? If there had been a medical emergency, she'd have known about it. How could he have forgotten something as important as this?

Bobbie raised her arm, took a breath, and shot the taser into Joy's thigh.

Joy gasped. Her body twitched. Her orange eyes shot open, lost focus, and slid closed. The graph of the heart-output on the intepanel juddered from rhythmical peaks and troughs into a jagged, irregular line as the shock rocketed through Joy's heart muscle.

"I'm sorry," Bobbie said. "It's over now."

But the line on the screen stayed stuck in an even serrated pattern, showing Joy's heart rate caught in ventricular fibrillation.

"Fuck! Cardiac arrest. Paddles." Bobbie ripped the gown from Joy's chest and snatched the paddles from Henry. "Clear."

Bobbie applied the paddles to Joy's chest. Joy's body arched, then slumped.

The intepanel graphic registered the electric shock, but the numbers told Bobbie that Joy's cardiac rhythm was still disturbed. The lower chambers only quivered, preventing the heart from pumping any blood. The erratic line on the screen filled Bobbie with terror.

I'm Doctor Chan, and this is not my sister!

"Again." Bobbie placed the paddles. "Clear."

Joy arched, and her fingers twitched. The short-term paralysis drug was wearing off. Bobbie couldn't risk giving a sedative. It wouldn't help Joy's heart function, especially with the heart's electrical activity so disordered.

No change in output, and now Joy's lips had blue hues.

"Joy," Bobbie cried. "Joy, try, dammit!"

Focus, Doctor Chan.

"Henry, epinephrine," Bobbie said.

"Here." Henry held up a jet of the drug.

"After the next charge."

"Got it."

"Clear."

Joy's body convulsed again. The output on the screen still showed Joy's heart fluttering.

"Now. Henry," Bobbie said.

The jet hissed against Joy's skin.

The graph peaked. The display stuttered. A glowing line spidered across the screen. To Bobbie's relief, it fell into a normal rhythm.

Joy's eyelids flickered but stayed closed. Her lips reddened.

"Joy," Bobbie said, pulling her gown to cover her up again. Bobbie lifted Joy's hand and rubbed it between her own. "Joy, can you hear me?"

Joy made a soft sound like a kitten mewing. The mole on her face changed from a dark brown to a red-blue, a bruise.

Fear chilled Bobbie. Again, she saw Granny's face as the nanobots broke down her cells, subcutaneous bleeding turning her skin purple. Had Joy been relying more heavily on the nanobots than Bobbie had realized? Was Joy going to hemorrhage internally like Granny had? Bobbie swallowed her fear, clenched her jaw, took a deep breath. She searched Joy's skin for more evidence of bruising.

Bobbie fought the urge to yank Joy's eyelids open. "Can you open your eyes?"

Joy's face screwed up, but she kept her eyelids shut. "Is it over?" she whispered.

"Yes. Please open your eyes for me so I can check you over." The bruise where the mole had been hadn't grown much more. Perhaps the nanobots had only been present there because they'd needed to follow the DNA blueprint and were supporting the presence of the mole. Without them, the cells that made up the mole had just disintegrated.

"Sleepy," Joy said.

"I know. I'll let you sleep as long as you want in a moment. Just look at me for one second first." Bobbie recognized that Joy's fatigue was due to the widespread cellular damage throughout her body; hopefully, low-level, no more than an immune reaction would cause. Rest and time should set her to rights... if Bobbie had destroyed the nanobots.

Joy's eyelids fluttered, and she dragged them open.

Two pools of chocolate brown stared at Bobbie.

"We did it." Bobbie hugged Joy, but Joy stayed stiff and unresponsive. Bobbie backed off, fighting for composure against the wave of emotion breaking over her.

"You used those on me?" Joy stared at the paddles Henry was packing away.

"You need to sleep now," Bobbie said. "You gave us a bad scare there."

"Wait!" Joy propped herself up on her elbows. "You tased me and used the paddles?"

"We had to. You would have died," Bobbie said.

Joy flopped back and stared at the ceiling. Her chin dimpled as she bit down on her lower lip. She took a deep breath without looking at Bobbie, saying in a tone-dead voice, "There's no way my ONIV will have survived that amount of electrical stimulation. You may as well have let me die."

"Don't say that," Bobbie said, rubbing Joy's hand, not knowing what else to say.

CHAPTER 19

Heat-shimmered air rose at the far end of the valley. Bobbie shielded her eyes against the mid-afternoon sun and scanned the bulbous rock formations that housed the camp. Where should she begin her search for Hicks? She'd checked their quarters, the lab, and the medical room. No sign of him. He might be in the gardens. It wasn't like him to lose track of time, but perhaps he'd misunderstood the arrangements. Without ONIV, you had to make a plan and stick to it. They weren't used to that.

Hicks had a farming background. Maybe he'd succumbed to the pull of the land? Bobbie liked the idea of Hicks growing crops, imagined his back bent over a shovel, his muscles gleaming as he lifted clods of earth. She pictured them homesteading, with children and a dog, like an old late-twentieth-century movie, bathed in buttery light, skipping through wheat fields. Bobbie let the mental image softened her agitation towards Hicks at letting her down, at making her worry about his whereabouts.

Her father appeared at the door of a nearby cave and waved to Bobbie.

She answered with a wave and walked towards Luke, asking, "Have you seen Hicks?"

The sun made Luke's hair gleam blue-black, reminding Bobbie of Joy's. Bobbie twisted a strand of her own copper mop around one finger.

"Haven't seen him. Walk with me?" Luke said, his dark eyes crinkled in a warm smile. "I'm going to the hoverport to prepare for our trip."

"Do you mind if we walk by the gardens?" Bobbie asked, falling into step beside Luke. If Hicks wasn't there – of course he'd be there – the hoverport was as good a place as any to continue her search.

"Yes, I could do with some sunshine. I'm feeling cooped up," Luke said. Their feet crunched on the grit, creating a puff of dust in their wake. "You did a great job with Joy. You saved her life, you know."

"The procedure nearly killed her first." Bobbie shivered despite the heat.

"But it had to be done," Luke said.

Walking, talking, spending time with her father still felt surreal, as if Bobbie were in a vivid dream. She wanted to take his hand like she had as a little girl, when her legs were short and she'd had to trot alongside him to keep up. But a chasm had developed in his absence, exacerbated by the lingering sense that Luke had chosen Joy over Bobbie. Her head told Bobbie he'd done the right thing all those years ago. She understood why Luke hadn't contacted her, not trusted her, but it still stung deep in her heart, leaving an itch Bobbie couldn't quite get at.

Luke and Bobbie came upon the first of the gardens, rich with the smell of tomato vines. Glossy fruit weighed down the stems in a range of colors from green to mouthwatering red.

There was no-one at this end of the raised beds, and Bobbie couldn't tell if there was anyone further along, as the pole-beans formed a natural fence to the next section. She'd have to wind in and out between the beds the whole way down to find Hicks. Bobbie still had a couple of hours before she was needed back in the medical center, and a walk in the gardens with her father was as nice a way to while away the time as any.

They rounded the corner, and the low vegetation of the potato-beds opened up their view. Leafy plants grew knee-high in neat drills. The order of it soothed Bobbie. Still no sign of Hicks. Off in the distance, a gardening teacher showed six youngsters how to weed. The kids ranged in age from about eight to thirteen.

"Dad, what will Joy do if she can't access her ONIV?" Bobbie said, moving on to the next garden section. She couldn't bear the thought of never being a doctor again, and Bobbie imagined Joy was feeling a similar dread at losing her career.

"She'll adapt," Luke said. "We've all had to. What you young folk don't realize is that as we age, we change. When I was young, I craved the adrenaline rush," he said.

"Like Joy always was – is?" Bobbie said. Before this, before Joy was broken...

"Yes. But in my forties, things changed. I developed an appreciation for a slower life. I achieved contentment. So did your mother. Then the war ripped that away from us. I discovered skills I never knew I had. Your mother and I both appreciated those years before the war, even losing Gracie the way we did. Because of Gracie, maybe. Your mother hung on to that contentment after the war. She was stronger than me."

"How do you know?" The conversation sparked aches in the tender areas of Bobbie's memory; she was keen to air those, and maybe exorcise some ghosts in the process. But it still stung.

"We kept in touch. She sent blinks – they weren't intimate, the whole colony gets to see everything sent in." Luke's face took on a faraway look, as though he could see back to that era.

"Can I read them? Are they saved?" Bobbie asked.

"Of course. I play them over and over –" Luke refocused his gaze on Bobbie and said in a gravelly voice, "She was the love of my life."

"...And Hang?" Bobbie didn't want to cause Luke pain, but the question had popped out unbidden.

Luke's face closed in.

"You don't have to tell me," Bobbie said, not sure that she really wanted to open that can of worms. The sense of betrayal bloomed again, blood-red petals unfurling into dark crevices where she'd shoved her hurt, and evoking angst Bobbie feared would spiral beyond her control. She closed her eyes and inhaled, counted to three, and exhaled. A sprinkler burst to life in the bed beside her, the smell of dampened earth rising around them. Bobbie inhaled again deeply, letting the fragrance soothe her.

"No, I know, but I think Hang's mother..." Luke pursed his lips for a beat. "Sue... she always knew that your mother came first. I did love Sue, but in a different way. If I'd been less focused on the cause, perhaps she'd still be here. I blame myself for Sue's death, and it's been the hardest burden I've ever had to bear."

Bobbie thought of the years she'd spent with Davitt, giving him a lesser love, never fully committing to him because her heart lay with Hicks. If Davitt had died in the hammer attack, would she have felt guilty? Bobbie couldn't be certain, but her father's pain felt tangible to her.

"Perhaps we'd suffer less guilt if we expected less of ourselves, Dad," she said.

"But then we'd achieve less too, right?"

"What we expect of ourselves doesn't necessarily match what we deliver," Bobbie said.

Bobbie had taken a couple of steps before she realized he'd stopped. She turned back to him.

Luke smiled and placed his hand on her shoulder. The warmth from it filled her, comforted her.

"Daughter, when did you get to be so wise?" Luke pulled her into a hug, and Bobbie gave in to the embrace, breathed in his scent – home, love, comfort.

"I love you, Dad," Bobbie said.

"I love you too, and I'm so damn proud of you. Always have been," Luke said.

His words were balm to Bobbie. "We'll get through this," she said. "We'll get Joy through this too. Hang as well," Bobbie added. "I'm glad we have him."

"Me too." Luke let her go and tweaked her chin, just as he used to when she was a little girl. "Now, come help me get this hovercraft sorted out, then I'll take you for dinner. No Kitty's Kitchen here, though."

"Oh my God, I'd forgotten about that place," Bobbie said, keeping pace with Luke. Most Friday evenings when she was a little girl, Dad took Gracie, Bobbie, and their mum out to dinner at Kitty's Kitchen, a local restaurant at the bottom of Market Street. Sean, the owner, would greet them by name. Bobbie always had the same thing.

"What I wouldn't give for that chicken lasagna and salad. I can't remember the last time I had anything that good." Bobbie licked her lips at the memory.

"Oh, I hear ya," Luke said, grinning.

As they rounded the corner, Bobbie could see there was only one craft in the hanger. It was an older model, the Lilium F1-EZ, lozenge-shaped, with stubby wings and a ducktail – large enough to carry three passengers, with a cargo area of four cubic meters – the perfect craft for loading up with supplies in Belus Land.

"Slow day today," Bobbie said.

"Yup, but we're expecting some of the smaller vessels back this evening," Luke said. "We don't like to have everyone gone or here at the same time."

Luke halted abruptly and put his arm out, stopping Bobbie. About half a dozen people had dropped what they were doing and were now shouting and running towards the hovercraft.

Three shots rang out.

Adrenaline fired through Bobbie as she ducked. People ran for cover. The taillights on the F1–EZ blazed on.

"Stay here." Luke pushed Bobbie under the cover of a stack of crates and ran towards the F1–EZ.

Bobbie tried to follow him. "Dad, no!"

Another volley of shots rang out. Bobbie pulled back, trembling.

Luke ran a dozen paces to a metal locker. He flung open the door and grabbed a laser rifle from within. Using the open door as cover, he dropped to one knee and aimed at the hovercraft.

A man nearby spun, clipped by a shot from the craft, and dropped to the ground. Crouched low, Bobbie ran to him on shaking legs.

Two armed women, lying behind boxes near Luke, fired at the hovercraft.

Blood spurted from the injured man's thigh. Bobbie clamped her hand over the wound. If the bullet hit the femoral artery, he would bleed to death in minutes. Bobbie pressed down.

The man yelped.

"I have to apply pressure to stop the bleeding," Bobbie said. "I'm a doctor. Just try to stay calm."

The man met her gaze with wild pain-filled eyes. He looked down at his wound. Hot sticky blood oozed up between Bobbie's fingers. His eyes slid back in his head, and he went limp. Bobbie could feel blood still pulsing. She couldn't let go, but they were both out in the open. She curled her legs under her, making her body as small as possible as she plugged the man's wound with her hand.

More yelling, more shots. The hovercraft's engine roared into take-off mode.

Bobbie looked up as the craft swung around, staring in through the front floor-to-roof windscreen.

Jimmy sat at the helm, hands moving over the console. Jacob sat in the chair beside him, pointing a gun out the side window.

Bobbie did a double-take as her rage flared at Jimmy.

How was Jacob there with Jimmy? Jacob, who had rescued them from the cliff, Mo's best friend – why was Slade's son's best friend helping Jimmy escape? Was he working for Belus? What did it say about Mo, about Slade? Bitch! What did this mean for the colony?

Jacob looked back, distracted by something. He tried to pull the gun back in through the window, but it snagged on the frame.

The craft was gaining height, so from where she sat, Bobbie only saw hands bound at the wrists hook around Jacob's neck, and his feet lift. High energy beams randomly shot from his weapon, zinging above the engine's thrum into the hangar, hitting the floor, ceiling, and walls – Jacob's finger on the trigger, his other hand trying to defend himself. Jacob let go of the gun. It tumbled from the window as he swung around and grabbed his assailant and pulled him bodily forward over his own head. Jacob's attacker landed on his back in the space between the front of the chair and the windscreen.

Horrified, Bobby recognized the third man in the hovercraft.

"It's Hicks. Hold your fire!" Bobbie screamed at the people in the hangar emerging from their own cover. The wounded man had passed out, but still, she couldn't let go. "Dad, look."

Everyone stared as Jimmy fought to keep the craft under control. Jacob wrestled with Hicks in the confined space beside him.

Bobbie couldn't breathe.

Jacob, gaining the advantage due to Hicks' bound wrists, sat astride him and punched Hicks in the head. The momentum of the blow turned Hicks' face to look out through the windscreen.

"NO!" Bobbie cried, her heartbeat thrashing in her ears.

Hicks, his face bloodied and swollen, lay beneath Jacob, his eyes open, panting. Hicks kicked out, knocked Jacob against Jimmy, and the hovercraft dropped to almost ground level.

But Jimmy recovered control and swooped the craft low over the ground, burning people below with the jets. The craft gained height with a whirr and hovered three meters from where Bobbie was frozen to her casualty.

She was close enough to see Hicks' face. Bobbie lip-read him shouting her name, the anguish in his eyes shredding her heart. She had to tear her eyes away and duck, anticipating the blast of the engines coming closer. Bobbie felt the burn of the heat along her extended arms. The man beneath her hands groaned. At the last second, the craft veered away and took off, in a fading throb.

"Help, I need help over here," Bobbie yelled. She had to help Hicks, but he was gone, leaving her petrified in a torment of helplessness.

People ran along the ground, shooting blasts that fell short of the shrinking speck of the hovercraft.

"Put your hand here, keep the pressure on. He still has a pulse," Bobbie directed the hangar staff. She longed to run after the hovercraft, but that would be useless now. She gasped for breath as futility stabbed her. Medics were with her, easing her hands from the shot man, asking what they could do. Robotically, Bobbie carried out the handoff. "Get him down to the medical center right now. Henry's there. I'll be right down." Bobbie stood up and swung around. "Dad?"

"Right here," Luke said, helping a woman crouched beside him to her feet.

"I saw Hicks. Jimmy and Jacob have him tied up in the hovercraft. They've beaten him." Panic laced with fear seared Bobbie so badly she nearly doubled over. "We have to go after them."

"We can't," Luke said. "There's no more vehicles, and none due in for hours." He ran to the radio control station, shouting, "Get Slade down here now," to a stunned-looking mechanic.

Stress bubbled up from Bobbie's chest, singeing her throat and pounding into her head. She couldn't bear to lose Hicks. But there were patients to attend to – Bobbie was needed in the medical center immediately.

"I have to find him, Dad." Bobbie ran a few steps in the direction the hovercraft had gone in, then stopped, whirled to face Luke, and thrust out her blood-covered hands. "Do something!"

"I promise you," Luke said, working quickly with dials and switches. "We'll find him. There are several crafts due to arrive in the next few hours. I'm radioing them now to tell them to be on the alert to intercept. Jacob has to go via San Francisco – it's the only way out. They'll catch them there." He turned, feeding instructions into a microphone.

"And if they don't?" Bobbie asked, frazzled.

Luke gave her a dark look.

"If Hicks is not back as soon as that transport arrives," Bobbie said, "I'm on the first craft out."

She didn't wait for the answer. There was only one answer. But first, she had to be a doctor.

CHAPTER 20

It had taken minutes to transfer the injured man to the medical wing, but how far had Hicks traveled from Bobbie during that time? Her heartbeat pounded in her head. Bobbie had to push thoughts of Hicks out of her brain, or she'd be useless to everyone, including Hicks. Inhaling deeply, she forced herself to calm down and focus on the needs of the patient in front of her.

"Give the patient another unit of syntho-blood, and pain relief as needed for the first twenty-four hours," Bobbie told Yoon as she sewed the punctured skin. The man would live. Bobbie had saved his leg.

Bobbie's willpower wavered, letting her thoughts slide back to Hicks. Where had they taken him? And why take him at all? Hicks knew as much as Jimmy. If Jacob was bringing Jimmy to Belus to be debriefed, Hicks had little else to offer. What value was Hicks to Belus? Maybe Hicks had come across them trying to leave, but Jacob and Jimmy could have just killed him and run. The thought made Bobbie sick. Perhaps Jimmy still had a shred of decency buried deep down. Bobbie thought of Granny fully rejuvenated, raving mad. A look had flashed in Granny's eyes once when Bobbie had mentioned Gracie: something brief, something registering Granny's humanity. Maybe Jimmy was still in there, the old Jimmy. Perhaps he hadn't the stomach for murdering his friend.

Bobbie's terror visited her afresh, when she replayed the moment she saw Hicks, Jacob and Jimmy in the hovercraft. She remembered screaming at the people in the hangar not to shoot. Of course – Hicks had been their human shield. The people on the ground could have brought down the craft but having Hicks on board had caused confusion and reluctance to shoot – enough to help Jimmy and Jacob get away. But Christ Almighty, what would happen when Hicks could no longer contribute? Bobbie had to get him back, but how?

Bobbie had never felt so utterly alone and helpless. Through every trauma she'd ever suffered, she'd had Hicks to lean on.

"Henry can manage from here." Bobbie peeled the sani-skin off her hands and left the medical wing.

Her father's office door was ajar.

Slade was already there.

Bobbie braced herself for the argument – Slade would probably not want her tearing off to find Hicks. Slade would want Bobbie to go straight to the medical board.

"Slade, Dad," Bobbie said as she entered without knocking. "Once we find Hicks, I'll present our findings, but we have to go now."

"Agreed," Slade said.

Bobbie was stunned. No argument?

"We're leaving in an hour," Slade said, closing an intescreen on the desk in front of her.

"An hour?" said Bobbie. "What if Jacob contacts Belus by then?"

"I've disabled the comms from their craft. Unfortunately, that makes it harder for us to track them," Slade said. "Still, it gives us a chance to catch up with them."

"Can't they just blink as soon as they're away from here?" asked Bobbie.

"Joy is working on masking their signals permanently as we speak."

"But Joy's just had surgery, she shouldn't be—"

"It's all hands on deck, Bobbie. If word gets out, Fox will call down an airstrike on this place. Joy can recuperate in front of a computer or not at all."

That took Bobbie's breath away. She looked to her father, but Luke stared at the ground, avoiding eye contact, his face drawn and troubled.

An icy prickle spread up Bobbie's back and crawled across her scalp. She tried to remember her geography lessons. The nearest fully-functioning city she knew of was Whitehorse in Canada. It would take the hovercraft approximately ten hours to get there. After that, Jacob and Jimmy would be able to contact Belus one way or another, if that's what they chose to do.

"But how will we find them?" asked Bobbie, panic tightening her chest.

"We have contingencies in motion," said Slade, rising. "And evacuation plans are commencing, just in case."

"Contingencies?" Bobbie asked, wishing she'd been able to see what Slade had been reading on the intepanel.

"As of now, we're on Delta Protocol," Slade said.

"Jesus." Luke looked away, still unable to meet Bobbie's eyes.

"Dad, what does that mean?" Bobbie asked, more scared than before.

"I can't go with you, but I'll be–" Luke began.

Slade shot a warning look at Luke. "There are several aspects to Delta Protocol, and the first is that everyone is on a strictly need-to-know basis."

Luke swallowed. Tiny muscles under his skin quivered where his lower jaw met his ear.

"What are you talking about?" Bobbie asked. "Why isn't Dad coming?" Maybe he was needed here to evacuate the base? She ignored the splinter of resentment as her father chose the cause over her yet again.

"You need to put your trust in us now," Slade said, placing her hands on the desk and leaning towards Bobbie. "Have we let you down yet? Though you nearly fucked up our plans on several occasions, didn't we get you to the research center, and away from it? We're a team, and we're only as strong as our weakest component. This morning we discovered that was Jacob. Now buck up and follow orders, girl. Don't be the next weak link."

Bobbie itched to tell Slade to fuck off, but she bit her tongue. Hicks was nothing to Slade, and Bobbie needed to keep Slade sweet to get help.

"Jacob will have his orders, or perhaps Jimmy wants Hicks as a peace offering for Fox. You were both the 'ones that got away' from her. From what I've heard, her ego is pretty dented, and that bitch has an ego." Luke glanced at Bobbie. "It's likely that Belus wants to interrogate Hicks."

The thought made Bobbie's stomach drop. "Which PARC will they take him to?"

Luke and Slade exchanged a look.

"If she's going to help get him back, she needs to know some of this," Luke said, tipping his head towards Bobbie. "And you can still maintain Delta Protocol."

"What the fuck is Delta –" Bobbie began.

"It's simple." Slade cut her off. "I'll ask Fox."

Bobbie stared at her, stunned.

"It's okay. Jacob knows me as Ori but doesn't know what I do out in Belus Land, though Jimmy will soon set him straight."

"And you're sure that Lisette knows nothing about your involvement with the..." Bobbie stopped. What was the group at Yosemite? Rebels? Underground? It sounded so quaint and turn of the century.

"The Candels, Bobbie. We're rebelling. Or revolting... if you prefer." Slade turned back to Bobbie, a ghost of a smile twitching her lips. "But we're damn good at operating under the radar... it's how we got our name."

"So you say, but how exactly will we find Hicks?" Bobbie's thoughts were a jumble – if only she could think straight.

"I'll tell you when you need to know," Slade said. "So stop asking."

"For God's sake." Bobbie slammed her fist on the countertop. An intescreen spluttered open on the wall above, then flashed an error message. "We're on the same side here!"

"Calm down, Bobbie," Luke said.

Bobbie swung to face him. The blue light from the error screen made the hollows in his cheeks look greyer, his eyes sunken, his face older and frailer. She reined in her anger.

"I have my reasons, and it's how we do things. It's safer for everyone. But I can tell you this; I can get to Fox before they can by throwing some security issues in their way, snarl things up for them." Slade's lips curled. "I'm good at that."

"I'll bet you are," Bobbie said, swallowing the sour taste in her mouth with difficulty.

* * *

Bobbie found her sister in the comms center annexed to the hangar. Joy sat hunched over the panel, the only color in her pale skin provided by the flickering hues from the screen.

"You should be lying down," Bobbie said, touching Joy's shoulder.

"It's all hands-on, and I–I have to–" Joy burst into tears.

"You're exhausted." Bobbie wrapped her arms around Joy's neck, but Joy pulled away.

"You don't understand," Joy whispered. "Delta Protocol. I have to manage, try –" She buried her hands in her face, then clenched her hands into fists and knuckled the tears away from her eyes.

"Tell me, please. What the hell is this fucking Delta Protocol?" Bobbie sat down in the chair beside Joy, reached out, and covered Joy's hands; their trembling struck a blade of fear deep through Bobbie's anxiety. "Tell me quickly, Joy. I have to leave now to find Hicks. I was just coming to say goodbye."

"Jesus," Joy swallowed. "We have these protocols for a reason, Bobbie. We need to obey them."

"Look, aren't I part of the team now? Tell me what Delta Protocol is – something about it is scaring you, and that makes it my business too."

"I can tell you that there are four parts to it. The first part is, everything is strictly on a need-to-know basis, so by telling you the rest, I would be breaking the protocol." Joy turned her face from Bobbie's and stared at the screen. The light reflected in the moisture of her eyes, making them glisten, reminding Bobbie of the orange flecks she'd seen in Joy's eyes before the electric shock.

"Joy, I do need to know." Bobbie squeezed Joy's hand. "I understand why Slade doesn't trust me, or anyone for that matter, but Joy, it's me, your big sis. You know you can trust me."

"I know."

"Then tell me."

"In broad strokes." Joy set her jaw and seemed to disappear inside herself before giving her head a shake. "The second part is, we have to split up the leadership. That's why Dad can't go with you."

"I get that." Bobbie was disappointed her father wasn't coming, but relieved that she wasn't going to put him in danger.

"The third –" Joy dropped to a whisper that Bobbie strained to hear. "The third and fourth parts involve stopping the traitor and killing him."

"The traitor being Jacob, right?" Fear gripped Bobbie tighter as Joy's chin wobbled.

Joy swallowed hard, fighting for composure. "Yes, he is, but in this case, it means I have to contact our other outposts and alert them to be on the lookout for the hovercraft and direct them to shoot it down on sight."

"Shit!" Bobbie said. "Slade is fucking ruthless."

"She has to be."

"But why would they go to one of those places anyway?" Bobbie wondered how many other camps there were.

"They won't. That's not the problem," Joy said, her eyes filling up again. "To implement the fourth part..." Joy drew in a wavering breath, then continued, "I have to send a coded message from Ori to Belus Corps that will alert them to the hovercraft. I'm telling them that there are dangerous underground rebels on board and that they are to be shot down on sight."

"No!" Bobbie pulled back from Joy. "No, you can't. They won't stand a chance. Hicks will be..."

She couldn't say the words.

Joy grabbed Bobbie's hands and pulled her close. "Do you think I want to? Hicks is like a brother to me, and Jimmy –" Joy chewed her lip. Her hands slipped away from Bobbie's as Joy wrapped her arms around her torso. Joy looked tiny.

"You still love him?" Bobbie said. Sadness trickled through her anxiety like malignant syrup.

Joy shrugged, and Bobbie recognized the look on her sister's face – pulling down the hatch, giving nothing away.

Joy looked back at her screen as she said, "The one sliver of hope we have is that Jacob knows this place so well, he'll know that Delta Protocol would have been set in place as soon as he left."

"Are you sure?"

Joy didn't answer.

"Joy?"

Joy shook her head. "Look, Ori's not a monster. She is trying to save Hicks. But if they get to Belus first, if they aren't shot down, what do you think will happen to Hicks?" She stopped and stared, wide-eyed.

The room tipped, grayed. Bobbie let go of Joy's hands and gripped the desk in front of her. Bobbie's vision settled despite her racing pulse.

Joy didn't seem to notice Bobbie's discomfort, and went on. "Delta Protocol is horrible, but it buys Ori time. Jacob knows he can't go straight to Belus. He knows he must land and find a new craft, one that's fully fueled. He can't call ahead. I've stopped the hovercraft's comms, and their blinks are plugged."

Bobbie sat mute, trying to process what she had learned, trying to breathe past the pain in her chest, trying not to break into shards. Her fingertips hurt. Bobbie released her grip on the edge of the desk and flexed her fingers. She didn't look down as she felt Joy's hands clasp hers.

Joy squeezed Bobbie's hands gently. "Jacob is smart. He won't let them get shot down. I'm sorry, perhaps I shouldn't have told you."

"You did the right thing." Bobbie pulled Joy to her in a hug and whispered, "Thank you. It's good to see the bigger picture. I hope you're right about Jacob." Bobbie put her hands to her face and squeezed her temples.

"You have a job to do, Bobbie," Joy said. "Get Hicks, and trust Ori. She knows what she's doing."

"I hope so." Bobbie fought down her anger at Slade for putting Hicks in such danger. The protection of the camp, stopping rejuvenation, exposing Belus Corps came first. Bobbie needed to knuckle down and get the conference done, convince the medical world to work with them against rejuvenation. Okay, Bobbie decided, concentrate on what she could do right now – Hicks would want them to stop rejuvenation. Bobbie had to trust that Slade was doing all she could.

* * *

From outside, the hovercraft looked like every other utility-type lozenge that floated through the skies of Belus Land. Inside, the three front seats faced forward, but the ones in the second row were reduced to two and set up facing each other across a desk. The intepanel set into the desk glowed in the ready-to-use state. Bobbie sat and touched the panel. Half of it opened in a screen. She recognized a series of icons – her patients' notes – the patients who had undergone rejuvenation alongside Granny.

Two men with tools worked on the third and last row of seats, unscrewing them from the floor and opening up space.

"More room for supplies," one of the men explained as Bobbie stared.

Missing Hicks filled every corner of her being. Bobbie missed having him to bounce her ideas off, missed the quiet comfort of his solidity beside her, and missed feeling that everything would be okay, though she wondered if she'd ever really felt that way. She couldn't concentrate on anything.

"Working already?" Slade climbed up into the craft and settled herself in the chair across the desk from Bobbie. "Good, let's not waste time."

"How much does the medical board know already?" Bobbie asked, shelving her distaste for Slade and opening her files.

"Nothing." Slade clicked open her own set of files. Bobbie tried to read them, but they seemed to be encrypted. Slade probably had the key in her ONIV. That woman had every angle covered. Perhaps Joy was right.

"How can they know nothing?" Bobbie asked. "I've already spoken to them about it, less than three months ago. When we first noticed the symptoms. When you wouldn't allow me to treat Aayushi Dhawan and investigate further."

"There's been a staff reshuffle," Slade said, seemingly ignoring Bobbie's dig. "You'll have to begin with outlining the symptoms, and then go on to the side effects."

"Straightforward enough. Let me compile the report." Bobbie sighed, selecting tables of data and useful graphics. "Let me know if you'd add anything."

Bobbie was so engrossed in her work that she hardly noticed that Mo had climbed in, settled in a front-row seat, and started the engines. It wasn't until the hovercraft lifted, making her stomach lurch, that Bobbie realized they were underway. Slade didn't look up; her fingers worked the screen, her eyes keen and intelligent, processing the information Bobbie fed her.

"That looks comprehensive," Slade said after a while, flicking through the presentation as it began to take shape. "It's concise and clear."

"But we need to highlight the role Belus Corps has had." Bobbie opened a file with a picture of Davitt. "I can link the male DNA to Davitt–"

The hovercraft swung to the left, throwing Bobbie hard against her seatbelt. Her chair spun away from the desk. She'd forgotten to set the brake on the swivel mechanism.

"Sorry," Mo called from the front console. "That sand fiend was a bit close for me."

As Bobbie got her feet under her and swiveled the chair back to the desk, she saw the Central Valley, with its terrifying forest of swirling dust storms. Mo had set course for a corridor that seemed clear, for now, but Bobbie knew full well that these monsters moved erratically. The hovercraft might be flung to the desert floor or tossed to the heavens at any second.

"Everyone okay?" Mo asked, shouting over his shoulder but giving his full attention to the way ahead.

"I'm okay," Bobbie answered, heart thumping.

"At least you were strapped in," Slade said in a muffled voice, pushing back off the desk and firmly into her seat. Holding a bloodied sleeve to her nose, Slade lifted her head. "Nothing serious, but it fucking hurts." She took her arm away. Blood edged her nostrils.

"Let me see," Bobbie said.

"I'm fine," Slade said. "I don't want you unbuckling to get the first aid kit. You can sort me out when we get over the ocean."

"Okay. Well, I was about to say," Bobbie said, using the diversion of work to calm her stomach and divert her attention from being jostled and bumped, "I was able to determine that the DNA came from Davitt when I noticed many of the rejuvenees had a feature on their earlobe just like he has." She zoomed in on the image of his earlobe to show a little nick out of the pinna. "He later admitted that he spliced the DNA blueprint used by the nanobots from three DNA samples. One was his, but he doesn't know where the other two came from. Another was badly deteriorated, a poorly frozen sample, he thinks."

"That's odd," Slade said. "We've been able to cryogenically freeze cells for a long time now. You'd expect that whoever was behind this would use good samples."

"Agreed. Now, the third sample is female. Have a look at this." Bobbie had photos of the six female rejuvenees arranged in three rows. The top row showed the women in their elderly state, distinct individuals. The middle row had only three pictures – these were the original photos from when they were younger, each woman very different in features from the next.

Bobbie pointed to the bottom row. "These are the women after they rejuvenated. Watch." She pulled the pictures across and lined up the eyes, superimposing the features. "They look the same. Each one has a mole in the same place."

The hovercraft dropped about two meters, and Bobbie grabbed the edge of the table for support. Slade rode out the motion, staring at the image.

"Uncanny," Slade whispered.

"I suggest we run a facial recognition program," Bobbie said.

Slade's fingers flitted over the screen. "On it."

The engines ratcheted into a high-pitched whine. Bobbie felt the g-force immobilize her as they climbed. Out through the front window, Bobbie saw the blue of the sky, and for that she was grateful. The craft leveled off. Below, a cluster of a dozen storms swirled about two stories high, big enough to wipe them out but small enough to climb over.

"Seems like the giants are taking a rest today," said Mo, looking back and catching her eye. "But these little buggers make it choppy."

The hovercraft jolted and shook. Bobbie meditated – breathe in, two, three, and out, two, three. It did little to calm either her nerves or her stomach.

"Holy shit," Slade said.

"Sorry, Mum," Mo said.

"No, that's not it. Bobbie, look." Slade slid the facial recognition panel over to Bobbie's workspace.

"Seventy percent Lisette Fox." Bobbie stared at the composite face beside the face of Lisette Fox, looking old and weathered compared to the rejuvenated composite face, the orange eyes adding an ethereal spark to the merged countenance. "In statistical terms, it's high, but it still leaves room for doubt. I'd be happier if Fox had a mole too.

It's odd that the Rejuvenees each have one, and she doesn't, nor does Davitt. Unless it came from the third donor."

"Perhaps one of these will help." Slade opened a picture album in the space between them.

"Oh yes, that really looks like a solid match." Bobbie pointed at a picture of Lisette Fox with a handsome man and Slade in their early twenties, standing beside what looked like a sperm whale washed up on the banks of the Seine in Paris.

"Is that the Notre Dame Cathedral in the background?" Bobbie peered closer at the picture. "How did a whale get so far upriver?" Not that it mattered, but Bobbie found herself intrigued.

Slade laughed a deep throaty laugh. "It's a fake whale," she said. "But we wondered the same as you when we came upon it on our walk. It was a stunt to highlight the problems of whales beaching themselves. Before we had bigger things to worry about."

"And who's the man with you?" Bobbie pointed to the guy in the picture.

"That's my brother, Gustav." Bobbie heard the sadness as Slade continued, "He and Lisette were in love. They lived and worked together until the war. Something in Lisette broke when the war came, and he disappeared." The last word splintered and stuck in Slade's throat.

"I'm sorry." Bobbie knew grief. Though surprised at Slade showing her tender underbelly, Bobbie understood how the death of a sibling took its toll in unexpected ways. It had made Bobbie waste years of love by not letting anyone close to her. Had Slade's grief hardened her into the soldier she was now?

"The worst part was, we never got a chance to say goodbye. He just vanished into the war. Lisette said she woke up one morning and he was gone. I could never understand why. He always told me he'd never fight, that he was a scientist and a pacifist and not cut out for soldiering – evidently," Slade added with a bitter laugh, "since he was pretty crap at it and got himself killed, right at the start of it too."

The man didn't bear much resemblance to his sister, but Bobbie felt like she knew his face. Maybe because his features looked like Slade's – broad forehead, high cheekbones – though he had tousled blond hair where Slade's hair was dark. Gustav had a handsome face and a kind smile. He definitely reminded Bobbie of someone, but she couldn't place him. Before she could figure it out, Slade had moved on.

"Here's the one I was really looking for," Slade said, and slid it in front of Bobbie: a close-up of Slade and Lisette, fresh-faced teenagers in their school uniforms, holding an award between them.

Bobbie studied it in silence.

Slade said, "We won the regional science shield for the school."

Bobbie felt a rush of triumph. "There." She pointed at a mole on Lisette's face, in exactly the same position as the moles had been on Granny and Joy's faces.

"Lisette always hated that mole," Slade mused. "I'd completely forgotten about her mole, it's been so long since I saw her with it. She had it removed in her late teens. Claimed it was to stop it being cancerous, but I always suspected it was vanity. Run the facial recognition again, younger face, with mole."

They waited.

The screen flashed up eighty-seven percent.

"Much better," said Bobbie.

Slade punched her fist into the palm of her hand. "We've got her now."

"I'd say this is strong evidence that Fox set up the whole project to further her own anti-aging goal." Bobbie looked up. They were over the ocean now, the smell of the sea bringing a strange rush of comfort. They were out of the desert, past the dust devils.

"Perhaps there's a bigger plan afoot. I'm more of the opinion that she's building a slave trade. She's already used narcotics to control them; maybe she's working with the Melters. She could trade them. This virus has infected thousands of people," Slade said. "Maybe more. My sources are a week out of date. We're not sure how virulent the virus is."

Even thinking about Lisette Fox working with the Melters brought Bobbie out in a cold sweat.

"We've no evidence for any interaction with the Melters," Bobbie said. "As soon as you mention that to the medical board, they'll think you're crazy, paranoid. I don't know." She sighed. "It just feels too far-fetched."

"More far-fetched than centenarians looking like thirty-year-olds?" Slade straightened up and arched her back in a stretch.

"We can see that. It's right there in front of us. Bring up the Melters, and we start to sound hysterical," Bobbie said. "I'd go with her own interest in staying young, because that's what she's actually accomplished. A nanobot that will take her DNA and keep it young. She's come up against some problems – the small matter of insanity – but she's a good scientist. Unethical, but thorough. The bigger her sample size, the more data she can collect, the better her product will be."

"I agree. Perhaps down the line, it might be applied to others," Slade said, "But so far there's little evidence to suggest that she cares about mass production of a version that's tailored to the individual." Slade tapped her fingertip and thumb together.

"You're blinking?" Bobbie asked with a begrudged rush of excitement. She'd like to reconnect, to look up anything she wanted, to plug back into the world. "Can I?"

"Yes, I am, and no, you can't. It would give away your presence. Belus has painted you as a fanatical lunatic, an outlaw on the run, but you won't be seen like this after a rational discussion face-to-face with the board at the Swiss facility." Slade rotated first one shoulder, then the other.

"Right," Bobbie said sourly. "So why don't we just use teleconference with the board?"

"No," Slade said. "You have to meet in person so they can't accuse me of tampering with the stream."

"But the medical board," Bobbie said, clicking off her seatbelt and reaching for the medical kit. "If they turn me in, how can I help you with Hicks?"

"It's up to you to win them over, Bobbie," Slade said, tipping her head back and letting Bobbie examine her nose. "Start with Doctor Aziz – if you win her over, the rest will follow. What doctor would support rejuvenation if they knew and believed the truth?"

"Is she new to the board?" Bobbie hadn't met this doctor, hadn't even heard of her.

"Yes. I've heard rumors of some reshuffling of board members, but I'm not sure about my source. Unfortunately, I'll have to wait to get the updates by blink when we arrive. Bottom line, these doctors are the place to start, and Aziz may be less closed-minded than the rest."

"I hope she has the influence you think she has. The last time I spoke to the board, they didn't believe me." Bobbie hunkered in front of Slade to examine her bloodied nose. "Back when I wanted more time to examine the patients, like Granny."

"Because I was working against you, undercover," Slade said.

Bobbie waited for the apology, but it didn't arrive. Slade was so self-assured she was doing the right thing that Bobbie envied her. Bobbie's confidence was in shreds.

"Not broken," Bobbie said, giving Slade a wipe for the blood around her nostrils before moving back to her seat.

"Didn't think so," Slade said, "but thanks." She paused, then said, "After today, my cover is busted. My role will change within the Candels, and yours will become more important. You'll be a witness for what is truly going on. Bobbie, you should also know this; your blinks are disabled for another reason. Joy has hooked our system into your ONIV using Foureyes. It will activate once we get to Belus Land. Everything you see will be sent back to her console and will be stored, ready to broadcast."

"I'd better behave myself then," Bobbie said with a heavy heart. "The world is watching."

"Will be watching," Slade said. "When we figure out the Holy Grail."

"Holy Grail?" Bobbie wished Slade wouldn't talk in riddles.

"Belus controls what goes out on the media. If we could crack that, we'd be able to educate the masses," Slade answered.

"If we can't get the broadcast out, what's the point?" Bobbie asked.

"We can send it out person-to-person through blinks," Slade said. "It's slow, and people often dismiss news sent this way as crank messages and phishing. But it's the best we can do, for now. With the medical board backing us, we have more credibility. It's all up to you, Bobbie." Slade gave a thin smile.

Bobbie swallowed back the swell of nausea. Was she ready for this responsibility? She wasn't sure if she could pull it off, but one thing Bobbie knew for sure: she was the authority on the side effects of Rejuvenation. It didn't take confidence to lay those facts out before the medical board.

Outside, steamy afternoon clouds built up over the ocean, brilliant white against azure blue as far as Bobbie could see. Warm damp air settled against Bobbie's skin like a welcome embrace after the tight, arid air in Yosemite.

"Alright. I get it. I have everything I need to say to the board. Sooner it's done, the sooner we can find Hicks." Bobbie looked back over the report file. "Let's go over it again, you can ask me questions you think they might ask. This has to be word perfect."

Facts might be facts, but would the board believe Bobbie? Her heart pounded and sweat trickled down her spine. Would she be able to convince them?

CHAPTER 21

The room in Geneva had twelve chairs around an oval intepanel table, and off-white walls, floor, and ceiling, the same as the 3D-presence conference room Bobbie had often used in the Buckets. Being here helped her compartmentalize, the way she used to at work when her mother was dying. Bobbie's worry for Hicks was a smothering fog that she had managed to squeeze into a dark corner, at least for now.

This time, the 3D projectors were off, and the seats were filled with live bodies. Each doctor's name appeared on the intedesk in front of them. Twelve of the top doctors in the world had gathered to hear Bobbie speak. They didn't look up as Bobbie and Slade entered. Some of them chatted, but most stared off into space with the unfocused eyes of a blink reader.

Bobbie took the opportunity to seek out familiar faces and names, but she didn't recognize any of them. Her old tutor had been on the old board, had supported Bobbie. What had happened to the doctors she'd spoken to a couple of months ago, when she'd first realized something was up? This was one hell of a *reshuffle*. Dread sucked at what was left of Bobbie's confidence.

Bobbie turned to Slade and asked under her breath, "Where's Doctor Coughlin?"

Slade held her gaze, her lips pressed tight, and gave her head a quick shake.

Fear soured Bobbie's stomach. "Doctor Jarret, and Avignon, and the others?"

Slade bit her lip and slowly shook her head.

"Without anybody noticing?" Bobbie whispered.

"Fox controls the media. She decided it wasn't newsworthy," Slade answered as she smiled a greeting around the room. "My blinks are only getting caught up now. Christ almighty!"

"What?" Bobbie's chest constricted. Jarret had been the chair of the European medical board based in Zurich. Bobbie had to assume these new people were puppets of Belus Corp. Would they listen?

"I'm on it, Bobbie, but it might get nasty..." Slade's eyes had that 'busy blinking' look.

Oh, to be connected, instead of this frustration. Bobbie waited for Slade to finish reading her blink feed. She didn't have to wait long.

"We have half an hour," Slade said. "Then we have to leave."

"I thought we had more time–"

"Sorry – things are moving more swiftly than I thought." Slade clapped her hands, two sharp beats, and the room stilled. The doctors turned their attention to Bobbie and Slade. Some of them looked irritated, busy; others looked curious, and a few threw worried glances at their colleagues.

"You're that doctor the info-reports talked about," Doctor Prosser said, and peered closer before tapping her fingers together as her gaze shifted focus. "The one whose grandmother killed those people at the research center."

"What?" Bobbie asked, horrified. Granny had killed one person, and the only other people who knew were Hicks and Joy. "What are you talking about?"

"Serial killer, the report said – and you helped her escape." Doctor Prosser touched the screen, and the info-report appeared.

"Seven bodies were found stabbed through the eyes with dining forks. The doctors on site determined the time of death to be approximately four a.m.," the reporter said calmly into the screen. Behind him, rows of bodies with sheets draped over them were lined up on gurneys.

"That's a lie! They were alive at eight that morning. Granny and I barely escaped with our lives. I was shot in the process!" Bobbie said, trying to reign in the frantic pitch of her voice.

"I can verify Doctor Chan's story," Slade said. Fingers flicking, her gaze drifted.

Behind the reporter, the intepanel screen showed a wide-angled shot of the building's roof. "Another three were thrown off the rooftop as Doctor Chan fled with her grandmother, Gloria Joyce, who is said to have developed unusual strength as a result of the experimental anti-aging therapy Chan had been working on..."

"No. No – it's lies." Bobbie wanted to scream, but that wasn't going to fix anything.

"... along with Doctor Ellis, who left with them that evening."

Murmuring broke out amongst the medical board.

Slade put her hand up and waited for a lull to fall.

"This is a cover-up." Slade tapped her fingertips. "I have video footage to prove this report is false."

"The suspect's whereabouts are as yet unknown–" The screen froze.

Several of the doctors stood. One, a doctor named Coolidge, made it as far as the door.

"Don't leave," Slade said. "Your very presence here has compromised you. Belus can make up anything they like about any of you. They can broadcast it, fill the info-reports with whatever they want. Then they can make you disappear. Think about it, Doctor Coolidge."

The doctor at the door turned back towards Slade. "What do you mean?"

"What happened to your predecessor?" Slade asked slowly.

"I–I... it's not... There were rumors, but ..." Color drained from Coolidge's face.

"Exactly," Slade said. "But you weren't sure if they were true, because you knew Doctor Coughlin, and you knew he didn't overindulge in alcohol. I'll tell you what happened – he became inconvenient. You thought something was off. You might have been more curious about your promotions, if you hadn't already known, deep down, that Belus pulled strings." Slade held them in place with a solid stare.

"How dare you?" Coolidge said. "I worked damn hard for this position. As did my colleagues." She waved a hand in the air.

"Damn right," Doctor Franco said, standing.

Several doctors sat in silence, their gaze glued to the floor, but others pushed back their chairs. Sweat dampened Bobbie's back. She held her breath, her eyes on Slade.

"You won't leave," Slade said. "I'll block your ONIV until you sit down and listen. And if that's not enough to keep you here, I'm certain I can find some damning reports on each and everyone's professional practice that might make it to the news. As you can see, it doesn't have to be true – it just has to be out there."

Coolidge sat back down. The others mumbled but followed her example.

Bobbie breathed again.

"You've just ruined our careers," said Franco.

"We're giving you the chance to save humanity. Or are your careers more important?" Slade asked.

Silence.

"I thought so," Slade said. "Watch this before you judge Doctor Chan."

The image flickered and was replaced by footage of twelve rejuvenees with glowing orange eyes standing in a semi-circle around Bobbie and Hicks, their backs against a set of elevators.

"That's us at the research center, begging the rejuvenees to come with us," Bobbie said. "They were being held against their will. We were trying to free them."

"Note the time stamp – eight forty-five am," Slade said. "On the same day after these people were supposed to be dead with forks in their eyes. Jesus Christ, forks? Who the hell thought that crap up?"

Bobbie winced inwardly, sure there was a message there about what Granny had done. What would it matter anyway if word got out about what Granny had truly done, now that the world thought she was a mass murderer and Bobbie her accomplice? The injustice of it nearly unraveled Bobbie. She fought the swell of emotion burning her throat, fought to keep herself together. There was too much to lose. Bobbie ground her teeth and forced herself to concentrate.

The footage showed Bobbie, Hicks, Granny, Davitt, and Joy as they entered the lift. The screen split – one half following Bobbie's group, while the other stayed on the rejuvenees in the lab.

Slade said, "You'll notice that the time stamp stays the same as we follow both feeds."

As Bobbie watched footage of her desperate attempt to save Granny and flee from the labs, she burned with ferocious hatred. For years, she'd been defending Fox, but that bitch had kidnapped her grandmother, turned her into a psycho, and framed her for mass murder. Bobbie must see justice served.

"It's clear," Bobbie said through gritted teeth, "that when we left the research center, the other subjects were alive. We are innocent."

Slade added, "There's a copy of this, and cross-references with the identification of the people in the videos, with your reports. Blinking to you as we speak." She put her hands on her hips. "Now, can we please get on with this? Time is short."

"What is this about, Doctor Slade?" Doctor Franco said.

Doctor Kali, the woman sitting beside Franco, stared out over the tops of everyone's heads, a frown gouging her brow. Her fingers tapped, possibly constructing a blink conversation – summoning Belus guards right now, perhaps?

"Please." Slade raised an arm. "Let Doctor Chan explain what's been happening. Then you decide." She turned to Bobbie and mouthed, "Ten minutes."

Bobbie licked her lips, her mouth suddenly dry, and swallowed. "I did not develop this – we had to coerce this information out of Doctor Ellis." Bobbie worked the intedesk, showing images from Davitt's research, his data tables, and a description of how the nanobots shored up the age-damaged DNA in the rejuvenees cells, then outlined the disastrous effect the nanobots had on their brain chemistry.

"These side effects... have they found any treatment?" Doctor Kali asked.

"Not yet," Bobbie said. "So far, the only way Belus has been able to control their behavior is by using narcotics."

"I find that hard to believe," said a woman, Doctor Aziz, sitting at Bobbie's right hand.

"I've seen it," Bobbie said. "They kept my grandmother at that facility on the west coast of Ireland and hooked her and the rest of my patients intravenously. They became dependent on the drugs. Addicted."

Silence slammed the room once more. No-one moved.

Bobbie plunged into the vacuum with the details of her report. To her relief, the doctors seemed suitably horrified when Bobbie explained that Davitt had packaged the nanobots into a virus that acted as a delivery system, and that this was what Lisette Fox had unleashed in her public launch of rejuvenation.

"So, to clarify," Coolidge said. "The virus does nothing on its own. It's only a vector for the nanobots?"

"Exactly," Bobbie said.

"And the nanobots are what makes people rejuvenate, not the virus?"

"Yes," Bobbie said. "I know you can see the possibilities of an anti-aging solution, but please believe me when I tell you that this technology is far from ready to be used. Belus needs to stop releasing the virus and attempt to reverse rejuvenation's effects before more people get infected. Rejuvenated people become sociopaths."

The psychologist's reports on Granny and her cohort appeared on the intedesk, including pictures of the aftermath of an arson attack and another horrible image of a dismembered cat.

"These people's minds are so affected that they think nothing of rape, murder, arson. I've seen it all." Bobbie closed her eyes for a second but couldn't blot out the image of a garden fork in a man's guts. Bobbie gave her listeners a moment to flick through the images, grateful that the murder Granny had committed wasn't part of the evidence file.

"You're saying your grandmother is a serial killer," Doctor Franco said.

"No, my grandmother is dead," Bobbie said. "What I'm saying is that any one of these rejuvenated patients could be a serial killer."

She took a deep breath. "But that's not the worst of it. The fate of humankind is at risk. Women of childbearing age are at risk." Bobbie brought up Joy's files with the name redacted and explained what had happened. "At worst," she concluded, "it will kill young women; at best, leave them infertile. We also don't know if a rejuvenee's sperm might spread nanobots and cause an infestation without fertilization taking place. If we don't stop rejuvenation, we will reach a point where we cannot, as a species, naturally reproduce." Bobbie stopped, brought up images of the tumors that had grown in Joy's uterus, and scanned the faces looking up at her.

No-one blinked or fidgeted.

"Lisette Fox has been behind this project from the first unwilling victims harvested for trials on a scale not witnessed since the last century." Bobbie brought up the before and after pictures of the female rejuvenees, merged the pictures like they had in the van, and then overlaid the picture of a young Lisette Fox.

Shuffling and murmuring erupted in pockets around the room.

Bobbie raised her voice. "Fox is personally involved, and each and every one of us is at risk."

She let that settle.

The doctors looked at each other. Some broke into muted conversations with the person next to them. Some seemed angry; others shook their heads in disbelief, warding off the truth.

"Have you conducted a DNA test yet?" asked a squat doctor from the far end of the table – Doctor Moreno, according to his nameplate. Sweat gleamed on his forehead. He reminded Bobbie of a toad.

"No, not yet," Bobbie said. "But the evidence is striking. Facial recognition programs give an eighty-seven percent match."

"That's a high correlation, but there is room for error," Moreno said.

"I know, and that's why I urge you to demand a DNA sample from Fox," Bobbie said.

Alarm wafted like a bad smell through the room. If the last board had been disbanded so easily, so swiftly, what hope had these newcomers? But if they had no clout, why the hell had Slade decided to fight from this corner?

"Last time I looked, Lisette had no such mole," Moreno said. Sweat dampened the neck of his tunic.

"She had one when she was young." Slade pulled up the image of Lisette Fox and herself at the Science fair. "She had it removed," she said to the group as a lull dropped over them.

"But she couldn't remove it from her DNA," Bobbie said. "The same DNA she gave to Doctor Ellis to work on."

"She's trying to help humanity," Doctor Kali said. "Fox is one of the good guys. She beat the Melters, for heaven's sakes! She saved the whole damn human race."

"Perhaps, but her ethics are questionable, to say the least," Moreno grumbled.

Bobbie listened to the doctors' debate, trying to gauge if she was winning them over.

"Many advances in science involved questionable ethics. Look at Jenner – he infected a child with cowpox and then with smallpox," Doctor Kali said.

A chorus of protest erupted around the table.

"That's ridiculous! You can't compare medical practice now with what went on four hundred years ago."

"And he was criticized at the time!"

"But look where his actions took us, the lives he saved."

"Same with stem research, and IVF. Where would we be if we'd been too concerned with ethics?"

"More to the point, imagine how far on we'd be if we had ignored the ethical questions with those technologies sooner," Doctor Kali shot back. "Fox is doing this for medical advancement–"

"Actually, I think Lisette is trying to create a cure for her own aging," Bobbie cut in. She threw a look at Slade, who had opened her mouth. The last thing Bobbie wanted was the *Melter theory* muddying the waters.

Slade said nothing.

"What evidence do you have?" Doctor Kali asked.

"Think about how you'd go about developing a genetic treatment. You'd source the most healthy gene sequence you could and insert it into the patient, right?" Bobbie looked around the group.

The doctors nodded and muttered agreement.

Bobbie continued, "Human genome sequencing is quick and reliable. We can now determine the gene sequences for so many cures that our problem now is people living too long."

More murmurs of agreement.

"But Fox used only two sources of DNA. Doctor Ellis donated his DNA when he saw how deteriorated the male sample was. Fox was willing to use damaged DNA to build the blueprint." Bobbie could almost see realization igniting in the eyes of her listeners. She turned to Doctor Kali and asked, "Would you use damaged DNA to build a template? Would you use your own by itself, if you were one hundred percent certain it was not flawed? Do you think Fox is certain that she alone is not a carrier for some recessive harmful gene mutation?"

"I agree," Doctor Kali said. "She should have perfected the blueprint, but maybe she was afraid of opposition."

"Oh, come on, Doctor Kali. We're entering into humanity's ultimate ethical game here. Who would oppose properly-conducted research into the development of a blueprint for a perfect set of DNA?" Doctor Prosser asked.

"I would!"

"Me."

"Me too!"

"Of course you would!" Bobbie took the reins again. "Think about it – one DNA blueprint for humanity. Think about what we'd lose." Bobbie scanned the room, taking in the blonde hair of Prosser next to the ebony-skinned Kali; Coolidge with her tight curls and freckles sprinkled beneath blue eyes; Franco tall and gangly beside squat Moreno. Bobbie's hand went to her own hair, gleaming bronze and gold as she wrapped the end of a strand around her finger.

"But according to Doctor Ellis' notes, this was only phase one. Phase two would have the nanobots adapt to each individual's DNA," Doctor Kali said, her eyes unfocused as she read directly from the texts Slade had blinked to them.

"I personally believe, along with Slade" – Bobbie looked at Slade, who nodded – "that the only person who benefits from this is Fox. At the very least, she's proven herself to be reckless and unethical, with no regard for human life. She's willing to risk humanity's future. She's using the general population as her private Petri dish. These are the actions of a megalomaniac, and we have to stop her."

"But how?" Coolidge asked. "We're just doctors."

"Take a united front," Slade said, standing beside Bobbie. "I know your careers have been fast-tracked."

Moreno stood abruptly. "What are you inferring?"

"How dare you," Kali said.

"You are in no position to moralize," Slade said. "You know it too – some of you may know why." She looked at Coolidge, who turned her head away.

Bobbie sensed a tide of shame that sent a flush through the cheeks of many of those gathered. Some dropped their eyes. Franco stuck his chin out and pressed his lips together but didn't make eye contact with anyone. The doctors shuffled about and cleared their throats, but no-one spoke.

Slade leaned forward, placing her palms on the desk, elbows locked, and peered into the faces of those at the table. "Tell everyone you know what you've learned today. Fox has the media tied up, but if you have any resources in that industry, now is the time to utilize them. Broadcast from your ONIV. Pay attention to this new wave of rejuvenees, the ones Fox presented in the media briefing last week. There are over a hundred, and God knows how many more are infected. You'll see that what we're saying is true." Slade straightened up. "We need your support to stop this."

"But we'll be silenced, or sent to the PARC," Franco said in a hoarse whisper.

"Not if we stick together," Prosser said.

Slade's face darkened as she said, "You know what I am. You know what power and influence I wield... I will protect you."

"Like you protected Coughlin?" Franco hissed.

Slade threw him a daggered glare.

"We have limited choices here," Aziz said. "I suggest we review the facts and then decide."

Slade smiled. "I'll blink you the recording of Doctor Chan's statement, witnessed by you today. Stand by that statement. I have people in place to help you. I have operatives working on finding and freeing the old board, the people you replaced."

A murmur rippled around the table.

Slade caught Bobbie's eye and slid her gaze to her hand, fingers spread – five minutes left.

Bobbie's pulse rocketed. She held up her hand. "Listen to us," Bobbie urged. "It's time to take your stand. Believe me, your futures, your lives, and the lives of those you love are at risk, whichever path you choose from the moment you leave this room. Spread the word. Stop rejuvenation before it causes untold damage to the able-bodied, too. Make the right choice. Choose to stand against Fox's immoral leadership."

"If the evidence of what you say pans out, you have my support," Aziz said. "Anyone else?"

The doctors looked at each other, shifting uncomfortably.

Slade turned to Bobbie and mouthed, "Well done," before saying aloud, "We need to leave, now."

Slade strode out of the room, leaving those behind swallowed by silence.

"Thank you," Bobbie said before following Slade. She pulled level with Slade's stride. "Do you think they'll stick together?"

"I hope so."

"Now can we focus on Hicks? We have to find him."

They turned the corner to face a battalion of six armed men, with Lisette Fox at the rear.

"Ah, Lisette, perfect timing, as usual," Slade said.

Terror stole Bobbie's voice. She stepped back, but Slade had slipped behind her, blocking her escape.

"I promised you I'd find the Little Renegade." Slade raised a hand and punched a hypodermic needle into Bobbie's arm.

A sharp pain registered through her panic. Utter confusion morphed to betrayal. Bobbie lunged at Slade – but only in her brain. Nerve signals urging her arms to move, to slam her fists into Slade's treacherous face, failed to reach Bobbie's muscles. As everything faded to black, Bobbie heard Lisette say, "Darling, an injection? How quaint!"

CHAPTER 22

Light flashed in Bobbie's head. She had no idea where she was, but her vision coalesced around a figure. Granny – young, perfect, reaching out, palms up, fingers wiggling, come, come. Bobbie yearned to touch her.

"Am I dead?" Bobbie asked. Surges of nausea convinced her otherwise. "Where are we?" Everything blurred, except Granny's lips – they curled into a cruel smile.

Bobbie squeezed her eyes closed. When she opened them, she was in Granny's apartment. Granny sat in her favorite chair, youthful and vibrant, looking out the window over the seabed. Bodies drifted down. Each bloated corpse stared at Bobbie with orange eyes.

Bobbie tried to speak. Her mouth framed words, but none came.

Granny's face rippled, the skin wrinkling like crepe paper, and Granny shrank into the chair until all that remained was a parched gray skin.

A screech of agony blistered Bobbie's ears. The rawness in her throat signaled that Bobbie was the one screaming. Pain lashed every limb; every cell – wet, hot, like petrol on fire.

A voice spoke, tinny and distant. "The treatment is not working... pain relief... truth... interference."

Bobbie could only make out a collection of nonsense sounds and words. The pain receded. Warmth spread through her shoulders and neck. For a second, Bobbie fought the urge to drift off but gave in, floating, light as a feather, wafting, wafting...

She stood on a clifftop. Waves pounded the rocks below in time with the blood pumping through her head. Wind pulled at her hair, flicking the orange ends.

A white horse rode over the waves towards Bobbie, its rider flat to its back, her arms hugging its neck. The horse leaped to shore and pulled up beside Bobbie. The rider was thirteen-year-old Gracie, unaffected by progeria, her skin radiant with youth, her black hair thick and glossy, wind-tossed behind her in a parody of the horse's mane and tail. She looked like a female version of Hang. Both shared their father's black eyes, but Gracie had more of her mother's features, the thin nose and narrow chin.

Bobbie's heart swelled. This was her twin as Bobbie had never experienced her, as Gracie should have been.

"Come away with me," Gracie said, her voice filled with the wind as she reached out a hand.

Bobbie stretched to take Gracie's hand. When they connected, Bobbie felt a chill. She pulled back. Gracie snatched at Bobbie's withdrawing hand and held tight, looking down at Bobbie with a dark-lidded gaze. Gracie's eyes flashed, her mouth a grimace. Locks of her black hair fell away, draping over the horse's back, over Bobbie, a suffocating blanket of silky hair paralyzing Bobbie with horror.

Gracie shrank. Wizened and frail, she crumbled, still clutching Bobbie's hand.

"No," Bobbie howled. "I'm sorry! I couldn't do anything. I didn't know what to do." Bobbie heard herself now as she sank into swirls of gray that cleared to show Yosemite Valley, bombs raining down, bodies strewn everywhere.

Bobbie could only watch from the cliff. Beside her, Joy was kicking fire embers over the edge, the flames snatching at her legs, catching hold, and climbing up to her torso. Then Bobbie saw that Joy cradled a misshapen baby – an ear growing where its nose should be, flailing too many limbs, five legs with feet hosting too many toes. The flame licked around the baby, but Joy didn't seem to notice the fire burning her skin away. Instead, Joy's eyes glowed orange as she screamed, "Give me your ONIV!"

Hicks appeared from the mist. Bobbie would be okay. She had Hicks. Bobbie reached for him, but found her limbs frozen as a hammer plunged from above and embedded in his skull. Blood pumped in all directions.

"I'm sorry," Bobbie screamed, not sure what she was sorry about other than she'd failed, miserably failed them.

"Shush." The distant voice came closer. "We're adjusting your treatment."

Bobbie felt sticky. Dampness permeated her body. She forced her eyes open – or were they already open? A cloud obscured her vision as if her ONIV had malfunctioned, but Bobbie wasn't connected to ONIV. She could barely move – her limbs heavy, laden, stuck down.

Her breath stuttered in the mouthpiece between her teeth – a respirator. Bobbie was looking through a mask into a vat of suspension gel. Her heart rattled in her chest as terror gripped her tighter. She was in the PARC, undergoing full immersion treatment.

Bobbie had trained here, delivered these "treatments" to "patients" for behavior modification, and had used the suspension gel to deliver psychoactive medication by absorption through the skin's surface. When Bobbie came out of the tank, she'd be unable to resist interrogation. The chemicals wouldn't flush from her body tissues for days. She'd witnessed patients suffer pain, hallucinations, and disorientation – now she was experiencing it.

After Bobbie's interrogation, when Belus no longer needed her, would the doctors lobotomize her? Or just kill her? One thing was certain. Belus would never let Bobbie go; that much was clear.

A spongy hum kicked in, and gravity weighed her down. Bobbie's feet connected with the floor. Muscles engaged, balanced, worked to keep her upright. The tank was emptying. Her nerves uncoiled the closer she got to her release.

Bobbie would end up telling Belus Corp everything she knew; she wouldn't be able to stop herself. What did she know? Bobbie knew that snake, Slade, had handed her over. It was likely Belus also had Hicks. Loss drenched her fear. Without him, what was the point of anything in a world that had gone to shit? Why would Bobbie want to go on, even if they let her go? But there was Joy, Hang and her dad – she still had them if, and it was a huge if, she didn't hand them to Belus Corp on a plate, though Slade had probably beaten her to the post on that score. So why did they need to interrogate Bobbie? Why would Slade stop at handing her over? Luke, Joy, Hang were probably captured too. And what about the rest of the camp? Had she heard they'd been bombed, or had she dreamt that?

Gurgles issued at Bobbie's feet – the last of the gel sucking through the drain. There was no telling how much psychoactive truth serum, or PaTS, her body had absorbed, but delivered this way, PaTS effects would be strong and long. Bobbie's skin goosebumped as a deluge of water hit her head. The doctors washed the gel off to reduce the risk of their own contamination. She closed her eyes and mouth. Bobbie knew the water was also laced with PaTS. Anything to enhance its effects.

Christ, how had Bobbie justified these procedures? How could she change anyone's mind about Belus when she had lived with this and knew this? It had taken extreme circumstances to become aware of the evil backbone of Belus. Those doctors Bobbie had spoken with might never see things the way she now did. Had Bobbie lost the battle against rejuvenation? She was a prisoner, vanished now in the system. As good as buried.

Shower finished, the door of her chamber opened, and a nurse stood ready, eyes respectfully averted, carrying a set of clothes.

"Thank you," Bobbie muttered as she accepted the clothes.

The nurse put her hands on the small of her back and stretched. Her belly pushed out her tunic in a full dome.

Bobbie finished dressing and turned to the nurse.

The woman's eyes flashed orange.

Bobbie felt sick. "How far along are you?" she asked.

The nurse rubbed her tummy. "Only three months. I'm big, eh?"

"When's your scan?" Bobbie said, sweating as she worked on not letting her mouth tumble out everything her brain was screaming. Who's the father? How long have you known him? He's a rejuvenee. You're infected with nanobots. You'll die if you don't get help.

Perhaps the nurse read Bobbie's thoughts; she looked alarmed. Bobbie thought she hadn't said anything aloud, but with the drugs in her system, it was hard to be sure.

"The scans are at four months now, for unregistered pregnancies. The shortages – you know," the nurse said, leading Bobbie past a row of empty chambers.

"Slow day," Bobbie blurted.

"Pardon?"

"No other patients? Never mind... Just me? The other chambers –" Bobbie wished she could shut herself up.

"You'll feel better after your treatment. It will help to calm you, especially after a nice chat to get to the bottom of what's troubling you." The nurse smiled kindly, but the orange flecks unnerved Bobbie.

"You're not pregnant," Bobbie said in a hoarse whisper. "If you don't get help soon, you'll die."

The woman looked at her with wide eyes.

"I'm a doctor. You have to believe me," Bobbie said.

The nurse flicked a glance over Bobbie's shoulder towards the room of vats. Of course the nurse believed her. Bobbie had just bathed in truth serum.

"I did my training in the PARC in Wales," Bobbie said. "I know how this goes, and you know I can't lie. You need to get scanned as soon as possible."

"Stop talking, please." Fear rattled in the nurse's features.

"And you need to be tased." Bobbie couldn't control her own thoughts and words. "This wasn't how I'd have liked to approach this, but you'll hand me over at any minute to the interrogation team, and you'll be gone. There won't be anyone to help you. You'll die. Horribly."

With glassy eyes, the nurse put her finger to the touchpad. The door slid open.

"Listen," Bobbie hissed. "I know that the father of your baby is a rejuvenee. And he forced himself upon you, didn't he?"

"Shut up!" the nurse said fiercely. "Move on."

Bobbie felt the nurse's hand on the small of her back as she moved into the therapy room.

"She's ready to talk," the nurse said. She averted her eyes and backed out of the room, leaving Bobbie alone.

The therapy room looked innocuous, just like the room Bobbie used back at The Buckets to examine her patients – intepaneled walls and a thinly padded examination table. But Bobbie knew that beyond the intepanels sat three observers. In a world riddled with digital manipulation, all recording for evidence needed authentication.

Bobbie glared at the intewalls. "Do I know you? Did you train with me?" She jammed her face against the panel. "Are any of you on the medical board? That new phony board that usurped the good doctors Fox got rid of? She can get rid of you too, you know. What happened to them? Can't you see through Fox's bullshit?" Bobbie flopped onto her back, slid down the wall, and sat on the floor with her head in her hands. Her wet hair felt cold where it stuck to her bare forearms. "Look what it took to clear my mind of the institutionalized brainwashing," she muttered to herself, then lifted her head and shouted, "What hope is there?"

"Good morning," a clear high-toned voice, digital but somehow female, spoke. "State your name."

"What's in a name?" Bobbie said. "I mean, you know who I am. Why would I be here if you didn't?"

"State your name."

"I – um." Bobbie searched for the words. "Fuck! What is my name? It's on the tip of my tongue. Oh God, I can't think straight." She tunneled inwards, trying to stop the words as they fought their way out of her mouth. "You know my name. You know it." The urge to please the pleasant voice pummeled her.

"Is your name Doctor Bobbie Chan?" the voice asked.

"Yes, yes! I'm a doctor." Bobbie flooded with relief.

"State your name."

"I'm a doctor," Bobbie repeated, wild with frustration. "My name is–" Christ Almighty! It was gone again. "Christ Almighty." She was pretty sure that wasn't her name. "I'm a doctor. Doctor... Oh shit." Nope, that wasn't it either.

Sweat ran down Bobbie's back. The urge to speak, to tell the digital voice what was in her head, was overwhelming, but the right words wouldn't come.

"You have to help the nurse. She's sick." Bobbie panted with the effort of these statements. "Nanobots everywhere. You have to tase her, that will get them, the electric current, that is."

"Doctor Bobbie Chan, where have you been for the past month?"

"Yes, I'm a doctor. Yes." Bobbie wanted to tell the voice about the camp, how dry and hot it was, that her father was alive, that Slade was a sly underhanded bitch. There were holes in her memory, and no logic to what she remembered. She knew she shouldn't, but Bobbie needed to tell them. "It will release this buildup of pressure in my head. I'll feel better once I've told you. Let me focus." Bobbie slammed the palm of her hand against the side of her head, whacking it off the intepanels. "My mother died. In the Buckets in Belfast. She had cancer. But now you're in danger too. All of us. Please listen to me."

Emotion throbbed through Bobbie with every word. Her voice cracked. She stood up and ran to one wall. She pressed her hands and face against it. "Fox has released Rejuvenation on the population, but it's making everyone insane."

"Where have you been for the past month?"

"In caves." Bobbie clamped her hands over her mouth, turned her back to the intewall, and slowly slipped down to sit huddled on the floor. Her arms shook as she squeezed her knees to her chest and rocked. Everything Bobbie knew was going to spill out of her.

"Where are these caves?" the voice asked.

Bobbie didn't know, couldn't remember, but the urge to tell them, to get the right answer, was so strong she heard herself groan in frustration.

"Leave me alone," Bobbie screamed. "I can't remember! You did it wrong. The PaTS are screwed up. I don't know." She curled into a ball. Something was dreadfully wrong with her. "Could I have been infected with nanobots too? Am I going insane?"

"Take a deep breath. Think back. Can you describe something you saw?" The voice was calm, melodic.

"Dust," Bobbie said. Fractured images of something familiar flickered in her memory, making her catch her breath. No, no, I don't want to remember, must not remember – I'll give them away. Give who away?

"Focus on the flow of your breath, in," the voice said, "and out."

Bobbie was hyperventilating.

"Let the words out, let it flow," the voice soothed.

"Use me." Bobbie said the words without any comprehension of them. Whatever was blocking her memories was wearing off. Fragments of images steadied from shimmering to solid. She saw domes and tunnels. "Use me," Bobbie repeated. "Wait, tell me something real. It's just my confusion. I need to find my bearings. I've seen this before... You've mixed up the dosage."

Bobbie had seen patients go through this before. She could not lie, but she could play for time, distract herself, give herself space to think of something other than... "Youse se me." Her speech slurred as Bobbie batted back the words, struggled against the powerful drug-driven urge to tell.

"Where am I?" Bobbie screamed. "I'm confused. Help me. Show me where I am."

Three walls of the room changed to show a cityscape. Bobbie was high up, looking down on a huge wide river. To her right, a barge of mist floated along the lowest widest section of water, swirling around two square gothic towers.

"Notre Dame Cathedral. Am I in Paris? Yes! There's the Eiffel Tower," Bobbie said, swinging around. A sky seethed in billowing white and gray clouds swallowed the tower's higher reaches. Below her, the streets were full of gondolas and hovercrafts. "Those Parisians are clever bastards. They adapted to the decades-long flooding of their beloved city in style. We're at the top of the Montparnasse Tower! I worked in this PARC facility as a student doctor. Fox must have transferred me from the medical conference in Geneva. I remember talking to the doctors, and that bitch Slade injecting me."

Too much was coming back. Bobbie had to do something to stop herself from telling them everything. She had to get out onto that terrace.

"It's not enough," Bobbie said. "These are just pictures. If I'm really in the Paris PARC, open the door to the terrace. Let me see for myself. You know I need the reality adjustment. Remember Protocol 18. You don't want a repeat of the Lavelle case."

How did Bobbie remember that when she couldn't remember what happened a week ago? The Lavelle case was a good reference, though. The staff at the PARC in Wales had mis-administered the drugs, and the subject's hallucinations had escalated so violently that she had smashed her head off the wall with such force that it killed her. It was later established that the use of intepanels failed to ground the patients in reality and added to their disorientation. Patients need to be taken outside, to feel the air on their faces, to touch the brickwork, to hear the noises.

In the PARC, each of the interview rooms had access to an outdoor area with a view for that purpose. The Paris PARC had a terrace. Bobbie had walked along it many times as a student. The PARC let patients out on it with strict regulations, handcuffing the patients and using a leash, tying people up like dogs, but allowing them outside.

Bobbie had to get her head straight now, while making the doctors think she was losing it. She had to stop herself from talking because she knew too much, and it was stacking up in her brain, waiting to be told.

Hugging her arms around her torso, Bobbie rocked and moaned.

"Get off me," Bobbie screamed, and pretended to push away imaginary beings. Crazy elbowed its way easily into her head. She gave in, dancing and spinning, singing snatches of long-forgotten songs, painfully out of tune. Head back, laughing maniacally, Bobbie took a run at the wall, closed her eyes for impact. It hurt. Blood gushed from her nose and ran into her mouth, metallic and salty. Bobbie rubbed her hair across her face, pretending to love the feeling of it sticking to her skin.

"Doctor Chan, Protocol 18 has been activated." The calm voice sounded out of place in Bobbie's manic ears.

An intepanel slid back, and the nurse stood for a second in the doorway, leash in hand, looking at Bobbie as if not sure how to proceed.

"Bring her to the terrace," the voice said. "Five minutes."

Bobbie struggled to her feet as the nurse steadied her. The orange coloration in the nurse's eyes was intensifying.

"You need help," Bobbie whispered in the nurse's ear as she held out her hands.

"So do you," the nurse replied so softly that Bobbie wasn't sure she heard her correctly. The cuffs were loose, and the nurse hadn't attached the leash to them.

Bobbie's limbs still felt wobbly. The nurse kept the pace slower than Bobbie needed. She pulled forward and felt the nurse's hand pull on her arm as they walked through the door. The leash jangled against the door frame but remained in the nurse's hands, unattached to the cuffs. From a distance, it might look like Bobbie was hooked up to it.

"Steady there," the nurse said, but wouldn't make eye contact with Bobbie. The nurse seemed to be reading a blink, and for a moment, Bobbie was incensed at how unprofessional the woman was. Why would she be professional at this stage? Bobbie was a rat in a cage, with nothing more to do than talk. It was definitely over for her father and Joy – and those children the camp had saved – for nothing now, if Bobbie talked. Without Hicks, Bobbie had nothing left anyway.

They were out on the terrace. Wind tore at Bobbie's clothes and whipped her hair across her face. The skin above her lips tightened as the blood dried. The breeze felt fresh, full of life. Life. Bobbie pushed the idea away. It was too late for that. The hand on her arm loosened its grip. Bobbie snatched her arm away.

"Wait," the nurse said. "Not yet!"

With both hands, Bobbie pushed the woman against the door. The nurse stumbled back, off balance, arms swinging.

Bobbie turned and ran the short distance to the wall along the edge of the terrace. She grabbed the rail along the top and hauled herself up onto the wall, teetering two hundred meters above the city of Paris.

Don't think about it. You have to protect them.

Bobbie swung her legs over the rail. Blood tickled her upper lip – her nose might be broken, but that didn't matter. She eased herself over the edge and hung there, watching her blood drip out of sight. Bobbie's primordial drive to survive kept her hands welded to the bar, and her toes jammed into a crack in the concrete.

But there was no other way out.

Bobbie had to let go.

CHAPTER 23

Bobbie hung two hundred feet above the ground, buffeted by wind laden with the smell of stagnant water from the river below her. The clatter of traffic and music from an advertisement board jangled around her. Bobbie would never survive that drop, and she was glad: better dead than incarcerated in the PARC.

"Let go," Bobbie whispered, but her muscles wouldn't obey. Her toes stayed jammed against a rim where the bricks met. The metal rail was thin enough that her fingers reached all the way around. Her nails bit into the base of her palms. Sweat lubricated Bobbie's hands, making them slide, pinching folds of her palm against the metal rail. Again, she willed herself to let go, but she couldn't. As her toes lost purchase, Bobbie's shoulders took her weight. Hands grabbed Bobbie's forearms. Bobbie looked up into the orange eyes of the nurse.

"She's coming," the nurse yelled above the screech of the wind, her eyes searching the skies behind Bobbie. "Hold on a bit longer. She'll be here."

Bobbie twisted her head and saw a hovercraft coming at them– a basic utility craft with a cockpit and a cargo bay. Bobbie had seen these being loaded up with cranes, but where? A loading dock somewhere... Her memory fog wafted, patchy and confusing, but cleared fast as the adrenaline in her system burnt out the last of the chemical's effects. The transparent dome covering the cockpit gave Bobbie a clear view of the pilot.

Joy!

Bobbie's heart lifted. Joy was alive, and if she'd survived, perhaps so had her dad and everyone else she had left behind.

Joy maneuvered the craft into position fifty meters below. Too far down. The fall to the hovercraft, if Bobbie didn't miss her target, could still kill her if she let go. One gust of wind could slam Joy into the building. Bobbie prayed her sister's piloting skills were up to the task. The hatch to the cargo bay slowly opened as the craft rose. If Bobbie could just hold on a bit longer, she could drop right into it.

The nurse's hold loosened. Bobbie gripped the rail harder, her feet scrambling against the concrete, but cramps wracked her hands. Her grip on the rail slid. Joy was about ten meters below her and rising. Was that close enough?

The nurse's hands ripped away from Bobbie's arm, and two men bent over the railing. They grabbed for Bobbie. Pushing off with her feet, Bobbie let go of the rail and pulled her arms out of their reach.

Bobbie dropped like a sack of wet sand.

Her gut rose to meet her mouth with the first lurching, falling sensation. A scream tore from her lungs. Her arms and legs flailed as her body fought to keep upright. Her back slammed into something hard, knocking the wind from her lungs. The world froze as Bobbie struggled to drag in a breath. Pain stabbed into her ribs. She was no longer falling but moving up into the clouds. Head, arms, legs seemed okay, but every inhale sent a blaze of agony from her ribs.

Cautiously Bobbie moved her head. She lay on a mattress, its corners curled where it was too big for the cargo area of Joy's hovercraft. Had they been expecting her to jump? Or was Joy living in this vehicle? Confusion wafted through Bobbie. She clawed at her mental clouds, struggling to extract some sense, but gave up as pain burrowed through.

"You okay?" Joy shouted over the whirr of the engine.

"Yeah," Bobbie wheezed. Despite her euphoria, Bobbie groaned at the pain in her side and moved gingerly onto all fours.

"What? Bobbie, are you okay?" Joy swung her head around but quickly turned, facing forward.

Bobbie winced as she dragged in a draught of air. "I'm okay."

"What the hell were you doing?" Joy roared from the controls.

Bobbie crawled forward to the cockpit, the agony in her ribs a burst of bright colors in her head. She wanted to wrap her arms around Joy, to hug her tight, but time and a cracked rib limited Bobbie to a brief pat on Joy's shoulder.

"Jesus! You're covered in blood," Joy said as Bobbie climbed into the seat beside her.

Slowly, Bobbie touched her nostrils. They felt tacky. Blood from her nose covered her fingers.

"Eugh," Joy said and threw Bobbie a cloth pulled from under her seat.

Bobbie held it up between her finger and thumb. It was wrinkled and a bit crusty.

"It's clean," Joy said. "I haven't used it yet. Hold on."

Joy accelerated. The G-force pushed Bobbie backward, making breathing agony.

Joy's mouth set in a line, eyes alert and focused, but her body was relaxed and comfortable. She gave the controls her complete attention. They zoomed through the sky faster than Bobbie had ever traveled. The exhilaration recharged her system, leaving her less frightened by her patchy memory, her decision to kill herself, and nearly falling to her death. The force of accelerating eased off as they settled into a constant speed.

"What are you doing here?" Bobbie said, despite being delighted to see Joy and relieved to know she was still alive and not caught up in an airstrike. "You can barely walk!"

"I'm sitting down."

"You're putting your life in danger."

"We're all in danger. Right now, you're the number one asset to save."

"Number one asset, my arse!"

"You, big sis, have lit a fuse." Joy beamed.

"What are you talking about?"

"Whatever you said to those doctors has sparked a huge backlash."

"Jesus. How long have I been in the PARC?"

"A week," Joy said.

"That long!" Bobbie could barely believe it – it had felt like only a few hours to her muddled mind, and yet those dreams...

Joy was still talking, "Doctor Franco managed to broadcast everything you said through ONIV, and people are listening. You're a hero, Bobbie!"

"Franco? Wow – he seemed like one of the hardest to convince." Bobbie's thoughts swirled.

"Well, you did it," Joy said. "Belus is doing what it does best: spin and containment. But a lot of people believed the medical board. Civilians are out on the streets, protesting, rioting, and Belus is pushing back – damn hard, too," she said. "They've killed people."

"Oh God," Bobbie groaned as the craft turned, and the seatbelts dug into her side. "Fox still has too much power. We need to convince people within Belus, too."

"I've been at this for years – it'll happen," Joy said. "This might just be the first wave of a series of waves set in motion. We've started to get the message to people, but it will take time."

"We don't have time," Bobbie said, looking at Joy's pale face and sunken eyes – beautiful brown eyes without a trace of orange. She reached across and touched Joy's cheek. Her temperature seemed normal, so no infection, but Joy's pallor could be from bleeding. The front of Joy's tunic was clean, giving no immediate evidence of any problem. Bobbie would have to wait until they were somewhere safe before she could do a full examination. How could they hope to control and treat a global release of nanobots? The very idea was overwhelming.

"You need rest," Bobbie said.

"I couldn't leave Hicks here anymore than you could," Joy said.

"Wait," Bobbie said. "You found him?"

"We did."

"Where is he?" Bobbie asked, flooding with relief.

"Dad's picking him up from the other side of the building as we speak."

"He was in the PARC? Can I talk to him?"

"Sure, but comms are a little patchy. Don't worry, we'll be back at the new base in no time."

"New base?" Bobbie still couldn't remember where the old base was. Use me.

Yosemite! Had she told the interrogators? Would Belus figure it out?

"We had to clear out of Yosemite once that sneaky piece of shit Jacob got away," Joy said, pressing her fingers to her ear. She frowned and tapped her ear.

"What about your ONIV?" Bobbie asked.

"I don't know yet. I haven't had a chance to try it – I don't want to risk further damage to it by turning it on without testing it in safe mode in a controlled environment. I'm communicating with Dad through the comms on the craft." Joy pulled back her hair and showed Bobbie the bud nestled in her ear. Joy tapped it again and turned to look out the window, away from Bobbie.

"The nurse," Bobbie said. "We need to rescue her. Her baby, it's like your –" Joy needed no reminders, and Bobbie battled back the words. She looked back where'd they come from, but the Montparnasse skyscraper and the Eiffel Tower already looked small on the horizon.

"Slade's on it," Joy said.

"No! Slade's the one who put me in there," Bobbie said. "We can't trust her, Joy."

"Trust me. For once in your life, please."

"But she handed me over to Fox! The bitch double-crossed me, all of us."

"No, that was the plan," Joy said.

"What?"

"She injected nano-trackers into your bloodstream," Joy said. "Between that and the live feed from your ONIV, we knew exactly where you were at every moment. Slade knew they'd bring you to the same place for interrogation as Hicks."

"Nano-trackers! How long are they active for?" Bobbie asked, horrified that she might never be able to hide from Slade again.

"About a week. They're pretty robust. And she wasn't taking any chances, so she gave you a pretty hefty dose."

"And I couldn't know the plan, because she knew I'd talk if the drugs took hold." Bobbie put her face in her hands. "Christ!"

"Slade also put some kind of memory blocker into the sedative along with the nano-tracker. She didn't know how effective they'd be, but she wanted to give you a fighting chance against the interrogators. She risked being taken herself. It was a close call. Jacob was in debriefing as she handed you over. She only just escaped." Joy looked from the controls into the skies ahead and directed her voice into the control panel: "Normal traffic, no sign of a patrol yet."

"Christ, Joy, I thought I was going insane!" Bobbie wasn't sure if she felt relieved. Her disorientation had been terrifying. "What about the medical board? Are they safe?"

"We've had to provide a safe haven for them until they get themselves organized," Joy said. "Fox is pissed. She has no medical board, and the civic council is starting to ask awkward questions. We have her on the hop."

"It won't be enough," Bobbie said. "Fox's too powerful. She controls the media completely. She can make people believe whatever she wants to."

"She's never been challenged like this before. That's a good start," Joy said.

"Did they interrogate Hicks?" Bobbie couldn't wait to see him.

Joy touched her earpiece again. "It's clear. We're at maximum speed, four hundred knots, heading west. We'll be over the south coast of Ireland in twenty minutes." Joy listened intently to something in her earpiece. She frowned. "Please repeat."

She held her fingers to the earpiece and lowered her head. "Say again."

She turned to Bobbie and said, "It's Dad. The message is patchy, but they have to ditch on Mont Saint Michel."

"Where's that?"

"It's an island off the coast of France. Their craft took a hit, and the battery was damaged. They're low on power. We'll have to swing back and pick them up."

"Will they get there okay?" Bobbie asked. Her broken rib flared as her breathing sped up.

"Dad said they have enough power to get them to the island, but not across the channel." Joy turned her attention back to the console. "Dad, what are your coordinates right now?" She tapped the screen. "Dad?"

"What's wrong?" Adrenaline coursed through Bobbie.

"Dad, do you copy?" Joy turned to Bobbie, her face bleak. "He might have turned off the comms to conserve power. Let me see if I can get through to Slade." Joy worked the screen with one hand, touching the other to her earpiece. Wide-eyed, Joy shook her head slowly. "Maybe the problem is on this end. I can't get Slade either."

"Could they both have been ..." Bobbie couldn't say the words. "I could try my ONIV."

"It won't work. It's been redirected to store live footage back at base."

"Then they'll see this and come help, won't they?" Bobbie said.

"Yes, but they won't get here in time," Joy said.

"Shit," Bobbie said. "Let's just go to the island and find them." A line of blue winked on the horizon beneath a bank of low cloud.

"But if they didn't make it to the island..."

"We have to locate their hovercraft," Bobbie said, terrified at the idea of her dad and Hicks sinking into the ocean.

"I need my ONIV," Joy said.

"But you just said... Is it safe?"

"I only need a few seconds to get the coordinates, ten max. There's a chance I can get in and send them to display on the console and get out again before I do any damage. If it works at all, that is. Console, go to auto." Joy sat back in her seat. Her eyes took on a trance-like gaze, fingertips fluttering together. She frowned, concentrating; then her expression melted into a soft smile. "I'm in," she said. A window opened on the dash in front of her, and a map appeared. A tiny flag pinged into view.

Bobbie whistled a loud exhalation.

"They made it to the island," Joy said.

"Thank God," Bobbie said, panting.

"Shit! Shit! Shit!" Joy's face scrunched up in concentration.

"What?"

"I can't close it." Joy's fingers tapped frantically. "It's trying to open every blink I've missed while it's been shut down. It shouldn't do that." Beads of sweat popped on her forehead. Her zoned-out eyes beat from side to side. "Dammit," she hissed. "No. No. No. Please no! Fuck!" She slammed her hand to her forehead and bent forward, groaning.

"Joy! Talk to me," Bobbie said, frightened.

Joy straightened up in her seat, her face deathly white. "It's gone," she whispered. "My ONIV. It's fried." She swiped a tear from her cheek, her face set in a grim expression.

Bobbie reached for Joy's hand. "We'll figure out the ONIV later," she said.

"There's nothing to figure out. It's gone."

Her desolation tore at Bobbie's heart.

"Maybe so," Bobbie said. "But right now, we're in the middle of a mission. We have the coordinates. Let's get Dad and Hicks and get our asses to that new base."

Joy hauled in a breath. "That's the island. It's covered in cloud, but we should be coming to it any minute." She took the controls back from the autopilot.

Bobbie welcomed the deceleration. There was something comforting about the shift in the pitch of the engine noise. It was the sound of arrival, getting home.

The visibility closed in as they descended through the cloud layer, and the disorientation that Bobbie had experienced in the PARC hit her again, making her heart pound. The craft made an arcing turn, and for a panicked moment, Bobbie couldn't tell which way was up. They dropped below the cloud and the island appeared, a steep cone covered in ancient buildings. There were no natural features visible. Waves slapped against stone walls, punctuated in places by deeply-recessed windows. Most of the town was flooded. Barnacles, mussels, seaweed, and algae competed for space, encrusting the walls, showing the tidal zones. Only the abbey, built on the peak of the rocky island, remained seaweed- and seashell-free, above the high tide. Bobbie couldn't tell if the tide was coming in or going out, but she figured it was at the halfway mark.

On one side, the wall had broken down. Waves slopped against the base of the wall, tugging at fronds of seaweed. Three hovercrafts sat in a courtyard area at the top of steep stone steps that led down into a maze of streets.

"Whose are they?" Bobbie asked

"That's Dad's, see the damage?" Joy pointed to the one that had a panel missing and wires and tubing hanging from the craft. "That's Slade's. I'm guessing she tried to share some power with him." Two thick cables ran from the power socket of Slade's craft to the socket of Luke's.

"Where is everyone? Who was in the third craft?" Bobbie asked.

"I'm guessing that's why no-one answered." Joy leaned into the turn as she lined up for her approach. "Room for a little one," she muttered. The engines kicked up a notch as she maneuvered into her approach.

"Look!" Bobbie pointed at two figures running through a street below. "It's Dad. But where's Hicks?" Her heart hammered.

As Luke reached the narrow stone steps, he looked up. One side of his face was swollen from forehead to lips, his eye barely open in the bruised, turgid flesh.

"Dad!" Bobbie cried out, pressed against the window, and waved.

Luke grabbed the iron handrail and began a labored climb up the steep steps.

A wooden door to a church at the far end of the street flung open. The pregnant nurse who'd helped Bobbie at the PARC appeared and lumbered towards Luke, impeded by her heavy belly and skidding on slimy heaps of brown seaweed covering the path. Blood ran down her arm from a wound on her shoulder. Luke turned back to help her.

The nurse looked back as Slade limped from the doorway, armed with a laser gun.

Bobbie screamed a warning, but the people on the ground couldn't hear it. The hovercraft was nearly above the courtyard. Joy had to slow down to land safely.

The nurse reached Luke at the bottom of the steps. He shoved her forward to climb up, looked back, spotted Slade, and ran towards her.

Slade raised her weapon.

"No!" Bobbie screamed again, so hard she felt her vocal cords strain. Despite the shards of pain in her ribs, Bobbie twisted and strained against her seatbelt to keep her father and Slade in her line of sight as the hovercraft flew over them.

Six armed men poured out the church door after Slade. She pivoted towards them, dropped to one knee, fired.

Shock registered on the men's faces before they slumped to the ground, eviscerated. Those behind cowered and dropped, either wounded or using their comrades' bodies as cover.

Shots blazed along the street in streaks of neon green. Joy swerved, slamming Bobbie against her seatbelt. Pain exploded in her side. Her ribs were definitely cracked now. Bobbie panted through her agony.

"Sorry, tight spot," Joy said, and lowered the craft to land between the others and the wall of the courtyard. Joy shut down the engines.

Bobbie snapped off her belt and jumped out, gasping with the pain. The high-pitched whine of laser fire in the street below cut across the thrum of the hovercraft. Bobbie spun, scanning the ruins, trying to locate the narrow steps.

An archway led from their courtyard into the ruined abbey, where most of the beams were missing and the roof gone. Bobbie ran into the abbey, searching for the top of the steps. Rotting wooden benches lay strewn over a floor of broken tiles. Cavernous fireplaces dotted along crumbling walls. A crab skittered into a hole at the back of a fireplace to Bobbie's left.

The nurse's head appeared above rubble at a low doorway in the crumbling wall. She hauled herself over the debris and landed in a heap.

"Bobbie!" the nurse cried.

"Quick." Bobbie grabbed the nurse under the shoulder and hoisted her to her feet, squealing through her own pain. Bobbie caught her breath, then asked, "What's your name?"

"Janet."

"I owe you my life. Thanks." The skimpy word didn't cover it.

Bobbie dragged Janet through the archway and into the courtyard to the hovercraft, tripping over rocks and squelching through mounds of seaweed. "Get in," she shouted.

Janet pulled herself into the hovercraft with one hand. The thumb on her other hand jutted out at an unnatural angle.

"Stay there. I have to get Dad," Bobbie said.

The cockpit was empty. Bobbie whipped her head around. Joy was running to the archway.

"Get into the pilot seat and be ready to take off – I'll be back with Dad and Hicks," Bobbie called to her.

Joy nodded, her face dark with fear, and ran back to the hovercraft.

Bobbie could still hear the whizz of the laser fight. Fear churned her stomach. Where was Hicks?

Crouching over, she ran back through the abbey, to within a few feet of the stairs Janet had come up. Bobbie dropped to her knees, lowered herself gingerly to lie on her stomach, and concentrated on her breathing – dragging in air despite the agony. Sweat dripped down her forehead and stung her eyes. Bobbie listened.

The shooting had stopped.

Waves pounded the walls outside, a rhythmic swoosh and rattle. Wind moaned through the gaps in the walls, but other than the eternal voice of nature, there was silence.

Bobbie could hardly bear to look over the broken section of the wall, afraid she'd see her father and Hicks dead on the street below.

If the gunmen were still advancing, Bobbie would make an easy target. Her heartbeat pounded in her ears as she cocked her head. She heard nothing other than the purr of the hovercraft engine.

Bobbie crawled forward on her belly and peeked over the edge.

A pile of bodies lay at one end. There was no sign of her father, Hicks, or Slade. Bobbie couldn't see the bottom of the steps without leaning over more. She scooted back from the edge and pushed herself up into a crouched position.

The rasp of feet on stone, the iron bar attached to the wall flexed in its mount – someone was climbing.

Bobbie cast around for a weapon and found none. She balled her hand into a fist, tensed her arm muscles, and waited.

CHAPTER 24

Luke appeared at the top of the steps, winded, bloodied, but on his feet. Bobbie ran to him and helped him over the rubble.

"You're okay?" she asked.

Luke nodded, panting.

Bobbie looked past his shoulder. "Where's Hicks?"

Luke shook his head, his face tortured.

Bobbie felt sucked underwater. "Is he –" She had no air. She heaved without drawing a breath.

Her father grabbed her by the shoulders, her face close to his. "He's alive, but we had to leave him behind. The rescue failed. There were too many of them. I'm sorry."

Bobbie's legs buckled.

"We have to get Slade and get out of here – they'll send more." Luke pulled Bobbie to her feet. "We're no good to Hicks dead."

The wind howled. Waves thundered against the island, pounded in her head.

"Bobbie!" Luke slapped her.

Bobbie surfaced, gasping at the sting.

"Move," Luke yelled in her face.

"'Kay," Bobbie managed to say between the gulps of breath that stabbed her side. She welcomed the pain, welcomed how it pierced her numbness.

Get through this. Get Hicks back.

Luke nodded back down onto the street. "Wait here, Slade needs help." He left.

Heart thudding, Bobbie leaned over the rubble and looked down the stone steps. Water flooded into the streets. Slade stood waist-deep. She had one hand clamped over her upper arm. Blood washed between her fingers. Her face was parchment pale. Slade panted as she leaned against the wall at the bottom of the steps. Judging by the blood soaked into her clothes, she had lost a substantial amount. Even if she had the strength to pull herself up the twenty steps using the iron handrail, it didn't look like Slade would make it to the top before passing out.

Bobbie squinted, trying to pierce the gloom of the doorway at the end of the street beyond the floating bodies of the six people Slade had shot. What a waste of life – of all their lives.

Hicks sitting by her side on a blanket in a sunny meadow. Children running. A dog barking. Dandelion seeds floating, glowing in sunbeams.

"Bobbie!" Luke reached the top of the stairs, propping Slade up in his arms. He staggered, steadied himself. His soaked clothes stuck to his skin. "Quick, help me get her into the hovercraft."

Bobbie took part of Slade's weight as they ran for the hovercraft. Janet, the nurse from the PARC, already had the medical kit open as she worked on gluing her own wounds. Bobbie helped Luke set Slade into the hovercraft. Winded, Luke bent double to catch his breath. Slade met Bobbie's gaze, confident dark eyes in a waxy face. "We'll do everything we can to get him back. I promise."

No!

"I'm sorry for putting you through hell for nothing."

No!

"I fucked up."

Bobbie pressed her lips together, but the feeling of being underwater, of drowning, returned. Slade had nothing to apologize for, and they both knew it. Slade was a soldier. Her actions against Bobbie had been calculated and weighed for the benefit of the Candels, but for Bobbie, the hatred lingered. If it wasn't for her father, might Bobbie walk away, leave Slade to whatever demons Belus Corps would release upon her?

Slade slumped against the back of the passenger seat. The muscle on the injured upper arm, shorn to the bone, gaped. Bobbie, standing at the doorway, leaned in and grabbed Slade's good arm to steady her. Luke hurried around the other side of the craft and climbed in and took a seat beside Joy.

"Fuck!" Slade spat, as Bobbie closed over the wound in one quick movement.

"We'll get this cleaned out under anesthesia," Bobbie said. Wound glue wasn't going to work. Bobbie wound a bandage around Slade's arm as Slade hissed and swore. As much as resentment slithered in Bobbie's guts for Slade, she took no pleasure from Slade's pain.

"You'll have to keep the pressure on to stop the bleeding," Bobbie said to Janet.

"Give me a sec. I'll come around to your side." Janet passed the medical kit over and backed out of the far door to the cargo hold.

Slade nodded; eyes squeezed shut with pain.

"Hurry," Joy said, not taking her eyes off the screens on the control's console. "We've got hovercrafts approaching."

"How long have we got?" Bobbie asked Joy before shouting across the inside of the craft, hoping her voice would carry, "Janet, quick."

"Tide's coming in," Luke said, peering out the front windscreen as a wave crashed on the other side of the wall, flinging sea spray across the windscreen.

Bobbie leaned in the hovercraft door to check on Slade, but her head yanked back, her hair caught on something. An arm went around her neck, and Bobbie felt a stinging sensation on her throat below her earlobe.

Bobbie caught the familiar musky scent of old Jimmy and felt the solid muscle of a rejuvenated body firm and warm against her back. Fear blazed in her chest. She tore at the arm around her throat.

He gave her a vicious shake, and she froze. Her broken ribs throbbed.

"No one move," Jimmy's voice boomed in her ear. "Or I'll cut her throat too."

He twisted Bobbie around so she could see the body lying at the back of the hovercraft.

"No!" Bobbie choked back a sob.

Janet stared blankly into nothingness. Blood soaked from a line across her neck into her tunic, spreading a gruesome halo on the ground around her head and pregnancy-swollen torso.

"That a girl, Bobbie. I just came here for Joy. I don't need to kill you, do I?" Jimmy would kill Bobbie if he felt like it. She felt her insides go loose and watery. Only a matter of hours ago, she had been prepared to die, but now she wanted desperately to live. Terrified, she stopped moving.

Bobbie clenched her teeth. "No."

"Oh dear God, Jimmy," Joy hissed, climbing down from the van, her eyes huge as she stared at where Janet lay. "What have you done?"

"Just a token of my love, darling." Jimmy chuckled deep in his chest. Bobbie felt it rumble through his ribs into her back, where he held her tight against him.

Bobbie mouthed, "Stay back," to Joy.

With her gaze fixed on Jimmy, Joy slowly stepped around Janet's body. Her hand moved to her belly, where Bobbie had stitched her up.

"I'll go with you. Don't hurt her, Jimmy," Joy said softly.

Luke skidded to a stop as he rounded the back of the hovercraft.

"You bastard!" Luke raised his gun.

Bobbie stifled a cry as the pressure increased to a biting sting below her ear. Warmth trickled down her neck.

"Put the gun down. I'll slit her throat if you don't hand over what's mine," Jimmy said with a calm tone that sent prickles crawling over Bobbie's scalp.

Luke aimed his gun in Jimmy's direction.

Jimmy tightened his grip on Bobbie's neck and tucked his body behind hers. Bobbie squirmed, trying to give her father a chance to shoot, but Jimmy's hold on her neck constricted more.

"The gun, Luke. Now. Or you're another daughter down." Jimmy shook Bobbie by the hair and tightened his grip around her neck.

Bobbie's vision swam as she watched Luke set the gun at his feet.

"Kick it away," Jimmy said.

"You hurt either of them, you're a dead man." Luke straightened up to his full height.

Bobbie's gasps made a strange sucking noise.

"Be gentle with her, Jimmy," Joy said, approaching as if Jimmy were a wild horse. "I'll come with you." She slipped through the space between the craft and the wall. "Let Bobbie go."

"No!" Bobbie coughed. "Don't go with him."

"I have to," Joy said. "Jimmy, not so tight." Joy stroked Jimmy's forearm, locked around Bobbie's throat. Bobbie felt the tension in his muscle leak away. She focused on Joy's fingers, inches from her face.

"You'll come with me?" Jimmy asked, loosening his grip.

"No," Bobbie said, gulping air. "Take me."

"Now why would I do that?" Jimmy asked, his silky tone giving Bobbie gooseflesh. "It's easier to kill you."

"The Jimmy I know wouldn't do that," Bobbie croaked.

"I'm so much more than the Jimmy you knew," he sneered.

"Don't play with her, darling." Joy's voice stayed mellow. "Of course you wouldn't do that."

Bobbie searched her sister's face. Joy's eyes were dark and expressionless as they stared back at her.

"Bobbie, switch with Joy," Slade said, standing propped against the hovercraft, her face gray, her voice hoarse.

"No!" Bobbie said. "I can't let her go with this lunatic!"

"You're the asset, Bobbie," Slade said. A warning flashed in her eyes. "Jimmy wants her."

"Ab-so-lutely! You're nothing to me," Jimmy crooned, his breath sickeningly warm in Bobbie's ear.

"We were friends once. Almost family," Bobbie said.

"Looks like I'll be inserting myself into your family again very soon." Jimmy chuckled again.

Bobbie wanted to vomit.

Joy remained expressionless, but her fingers worked their way up Jimmy's arm and out of Bobbie's sight. "You know I lost the baby?" she said gently.

"I know. I'll make it up to you, Joy. I'll make you forever young, and we'll be immortal," Jimmy said.

"And crazy!" Bobbie gritted her teeth. "Your nanobots almost killed her. If you infect her again, she'll develop those nano tumors again. And they will kill her, then neither of us have her." This bastard had abducted Hicks too, but Bobbie couldn't put that into words.

"Oh, don't go all King Solomon on me, Bobbie," Jimmy said.

"What the fuck are you on about?" Bobbie snapped.

A wave breached the wall. Water slopped around their feet and swirled around the landing pads of the hovercrafts.

"Oh dear," Jimmy said, sounding for a moment exactly like Old Jimmy. He sighed heavily in Bobbie's ear, his breath humid on her skin. "Best hurry up. The saltwater will wreak havoc with the landing gear. But not to worry about Joy, I'll take care of her."

"If you loved her, you'd–" Luke began.

"I'm going, Dad." Joy gave Jimmy a smile that didn't reach her eyes. Her eyebrows pinched, and her chin wobbled as she held back tears. Her hair fell forward as she added, "I have to go with him. I love him and he loves me."

The sideways glance and the minute flaring of Joy's nostrils told Bobbie that Joy was lying. It would keep Bobbie safe in this moment, but they both knew Jimmy would kill Joy when he got tired of her. Joy had seen what Granny had done to her lover. Joy knew exactly what she was doing, and it tore Bobbie to pieces. As much as Bobbie wanted to protect Joy, others needed Bobbie herself.

Slade might die without Bobbie's medical attention.

Bobbie had to free Hicks.

The medical board needed her expertise.

Davitt, if he survived, needed her assistance. And if he didn't survive, Bobbie would be more essential in the fight against Rejuvenation.

And Belus guards were minutes away...

Bobbie had the sensation of rising through water, of her head breaking through the surface into sparkling air.

Her father had given up everyone he'd loved to fight Belus, because he had seen the gross cruelty they were capable of. Slade had worked undercover against Belus all her adult life because she had lifted the veil masking their injustices. Joy had joined as a foot-soldier in her teens. If Bobbie ignored her role in the fight, she'd be throwing away everything they'd fought for and lost up to this point. Did she have what it would take to fight this fight?

What if Bobbie needed her sister? Her needs didn't matter. In the bigger picture, neither did Joy's. Nor Hicks.'

The cause had to come first.

Another wave crashed over the wall, soaking them with white spray.

Bobbie swallowed her rising grief and looked Joy in the eye. "I understand."

Joy gave her a sad smile. Bobbie couldn't haul her gaze away, drinking in every feature of her sister as Joy stepped forward. Joy was smart and strong. She would escape Jimmy. Bobbie had to believe that.

Jimmy's grip softened, but he didn't let go of Bobbie until he had Joy by the arm.

Luke took a step towards the gun.

"Back off." Slade's voice was husky with pain. "That's an order."

A mask fell over Luke's features. His eyes were the only indication of the effort he put into controlling his urge to fight for his daughters. He stepped back.

"Sorry, my darling, this is just a precaution." Jimmy pulled Joy in close to his body and, in the same movement, shoved Bobbie away, transferring the knife to Joy's throat.

Bobbie fell to her knees in the cold seawater. "Wait!"

Jimmy gave an exaggerated sigh. "What now?"

"This belongs to Joy." Bobbie dragged herself to her feet and fished the rag she'd used to mop up her bloody nose from her pocket. She balled up the bloodstained rag and handed it to Joy.

"You've always given me more than you had to." Joy locked eyes with her sister. Joy understood the significance of the blood on the rag. Bobbie would do everything to find her.

"Very sweet, now let's go!" Jimmy said. "Belus are coming in hot from the east. I'm going to go southwest. I suggest you lot go anyway, but those two. They won't know who to follow. You follow me – I kill her." He looked sideways at Joy. "Sorry, darling. Needs must."

Joy swallowed. Tears shivered in her eyes.

"Take care of her. She needs... recovery time," Bobbie said through gritted teeth.

"I know," Jimmy said. "I love her. I won't hurt her if I do have to kill her."

His orange eyes glinted cold and cruel.

"Bobbie, Luke, let's go," Slade said.

A laser shot zapped through the air.

Bobbie spun around.

Three men and a woman dressed in navy tunic and trousers – Belus security uniforms – stood at the gap in the wall, heavily armed. For a second, Bobbie thought it was Lisette Fox. And was that Davitt with her? Christ almighty! Wait, no. That man wasn't Davitt, though he looked like him, while another was blond like Jimmy, both much younger.

They had the cloned features and orange eyes of rejuvenees. The woman still had her weapon in the air. Her lip curled into a cruel smile as she tipped the barrel down and said, "Next shot cuts through flesh. Belus says they want a chat with you lot. I reckon you can chat plenty without your legs."

Bobbie nearly cried out in despair. They were too late and too wounded to fight. If Belus were recruiting rejuvenees as soldiers, how many people had the nanobots contaminated? Lisette Fox had won. They would be questioned at the PARC for every last bit of info they could give; then they would die, quietly, so that no one would ever know.

Sick with dread, Bobbie stood glued to the spot.

"Whose orders are you working under?" Slade asked. Bobbie could see she was working hard to command authority, but Slade, weak as wet paper, struggled to stay on her feet.

"Not yours, that's for damn sure." The female guard stepped down into the courtyard. Seawater came up over her boots, but the guard ignored the cold water soaking up her trouser legs. The men followed her and sloshed through the ankle-deep water towards Bobbie's group.

"Take them," Jimmy said. "But you can let me go. I'm one of you."

"Leave the girl," a guard said.

"No," Jimmy said. "You don't need her. These three have the details you need. This one" – he nodded at Bobbie – "is their key asset."

Slade sank to her knees. Water soaked up to her thighs. "I can tell you anything you need to know. Let them go." Despite Slade looking so broken and pathetic, Bobbie admired the woman's guts.

"What a hero," the female guard sneered. "Not gonna happen like that. You're not the boss anymore, Slade. You're all coming with us."

"But–" Jimmy began.

"Move!"

Jimmy pulled Joy around, shielding his body from the guns before him. Joy yelped and stumbled, but he held her tight as he scuttled back, stepping up onto a low wall. Joy cried out in pain as Jimmy dragged her with him.

"Please, stop hurting her," Bobbie cried, but Jimmy ignored her.

"Let them go," the small guard said in a bored tone. "We'll kill them some other day. Come on. My feet are cold."

"No," the woman said. She tilted her head toward Jimmy and Joy. "Lee, go get them. We have warrants for each of them and bonuses to collect."

From where she stood, Bobbie saw the battery light on their hovercraft blink from red to green, recharged by the solar panel while they'd been parked. Three strides to Bobbie's left, Luke's hovercraft had its battery-charge cable still sticking up out of its casing, not fully retracted. A charging cable ran from Slade's craft directly into the front of Luke's. Had they been jump-starting Luke's hovercraft? Electricity. If there was enough charge, it would save them.

Bobbie's heart thumped wildly. She had one chance. If she missed, or if the cable wouldn't come loose, she'd be shot dead – but she'd be better off dead than going back to the PARC.

One of the guards sloshed towards Joy. Jimmy held her against him on top of the low wall. The leader lowered her gun and used it to point the way. "Walk. Before you need to be carried."

All eyes were on the trio.

Bobbie flung herself towards the cable.

A shot thundered.

The bullet whizzed past, so close it tugged at Bobbie's hair.

Bobbie yanked the cable loose as she splashed onto the flooded floor of the courtyard. Slade screamed. A jolt fired through Bobbie as the battery discharged into the seawater. Her limbs contracted, stiffening her body. Her muscles relaxed. Bobbie struggled to her hands and knees, her cracked ribs screaming. The release was quick. Was it long enough? What about Slade? She was barely holding on already.

"Bobbie!" called Luke. "Bobbie!"

"I'm okay." Bobbie pushed up with her arms, quivering from the shock, and struggled to her feet, splashing and stumbling as her muscles regained coordination. "You okay, Dad?"

"Yep!" Luke was halfway to the guards, who stood like waxen dummies, their faces frozen in stunned bewilderment.

The guards' weapons dropped from their grasps, and they sank to their knees, trembling. Their expressions seemed to slide from their faces, loose-lipped and slack-jawed. Bobbie wasn't sure what was happening to them. Granny's reaction to the taser had been much more immediate.

Luke reached the first gun, fished it from the water, and held it to a guard's head.

He swung the gun between Jimmy and the guards. "You're coming with us now."

All four guards began to shake, the rigors spreading through them violently until their entire bodies convulsed with seizures.

Luke stepped back in revulsion. Bobbie had seen this before, but her father hadn't.

"Fuck me pink!" Jimmy said, mesmerized with horror. He gawked at the water slapping against the wall he and Joy stood on.

Bobbie hurried to Slade, who had slumped onto her side in the rising water. Her breathing was clear, her pulse weak. Slade moaned and looked around at the guards. She screwed up her face, turned away, but turned back as though unable to resist staring despite her revulsion.

The guards shook themselves to pieces. Their tissue disintegrated – their muscles unable to hold bones and organs in position, tendons unable to join limbs, blood vessels unable to contain blood – they crumbled like sandcastles in the tide, leaving nothing but four piles of flaccid flesh.

"Good God," muttered Slade.

A clatter of feet on stone drew Bobbie's attention to Jimmy and Joy.

Jimmy dragged Joy along the top of the wall. He looked at the water with wild eyes, missed his step, and went forward onto one knee. To break his fall, he let go of Joy and dropped the knife. It skittered off the wall and into the water in the courtyard below.

Joy kicked Jimmy hard in the gut. He grunted and folded forward. The momentum of the kick forced Joy backward to land in the water.

Joy came up clasping the knife, and plunged it into Jimmy's back. Shock paralyzed Bobbie.

"For my baby!" Joy clenched her teeth, pulled the knife out, and sank it to the hilt again. "For my fertility." Blood squirted out in pulses, splattering across Joy's face, arms and torso. She sank the blade again. "And for my ONIV!"

Air wheezed and rattled through the holes in Jimmy's back. "Joy..." he rasped. Air hissed out in one long whoosh.

Joy stood over Jimmy's body and spat on his corpse. "Immortal, my ass."

Bobbie regained use of her limbs and ran to Joy's side, took the knife from her, and folded Joy into a hug. Joy stood wooden, unyielding.

"It's over now," Bobbie whispered into her ear. A lie. Thanks to Jimmy, Joy had lost her ONIV, would never have children, and now she'd have the memory of killing Jimmy forever. Bobbie led Joy toward the hovercraft door.

Luke stared at the mess of bodies that had once been guards. They bobbed gently in thigh-deep water, rising and falling with the ocean swell like a parody of breathing.

Bobbie turned toward the lump that had been the woman in charge. The woman's legs had crumbled in a pile beneath her torso. She had slumped against a pile of rocks so that her torso remained eerily upright and out of the water. Her head hung at an unnatural angle to the side. The few remaining wisps of her hair writhed in the sea breeze. Strands of tendon stretched at the neck. Sinew had snapped like overplayed guitar strings. The head lolled, black sockets ogling eternity, slack lips revealing clenched teeth.

It reminded Bobbie of a snowman she'd made as a child. After one day, its head had rolled off its body and across the lawn. Gracie had laughed so much she'd had an asthma attack.

"Her ONIV," said Bobbie, pointing. "It's linked into the Belus network. We can use it to find out where Hicks is."

CHAPTER 25

"She's dead now. The ONIV will have signed off," Joy said. She looked at Bobbie, her expression bland and distant. "It will initiate the deceased person's Data Privacy Protocol, and all data will be wiped. Another dead ONIV."

Slade shuffled forward to join Bobbie, Joy, and Luke as they peered at the corpse.

"I wonder how long ago she was first implanted with an ONIV?" Slade said.

"What difference would it make?" Bobbie said.

"If she's an ultra-elder, she may have received one of the first ONIVs." Luke nudged the corpse with his foot. The smell of mushy flesh made Bobbie gag.

"Jesus, do you have to do that?" Bobbie edged back, pressing the back of her hand to her nose. "The first ONIVs... Didn't they have internal data storage? Like a local cache of data?"

"I thought they removed those chips when they upgraded to the ones that upload straight to the net?" Luke said.

"Only for people who requested it. Far easier to whack in a new one beside the old one." The effort of talking seemed to weigh Slade down. "I'm pretty sure I saw her before her recruitment." Slade leaned on Bobbie, her hands cold.

Despite her injury and blood loss, Slade fought to stay alert, though she looked to Bobbie like she might drop at any moment. They were wasting too much time; Bobbie had to move things along, but an idea took shape in her head.

"Could the old one could still be recording, be connected?" Bobbie asked.

"In theory, yes." Slade wobbled.

Bobbie put her arm around her waist. "Dad, take her back to the hovercraft." Bobbie guided Slade to her father. "Joy, quick, help me with this." Her stomach churned. This was not going to be pleasant.

"Even if you got the old ONIV, it needs to be implanted in someone's..." Joy stopped, her eyes widened, and she leaned forward. "Yes! That's it." Joy waded into the water and bent over the corpse.

"No! No way!" Luke splashed through the water to Bobbie, having helped Slade to the hovercraft a few yards away. "It's configured for her. We don't know what it would do to Joy."

Bobbie hugged her father. "We've lost, Dad. Don't you see? Fox has an army of rejuvenees. Hicks is missing. We need to know what she's planning."

"We need to go. Now!" said Slade from the hovercraft. "There are hovercrafts approaching from the south, and we're going to be completely underwater soon."

The rise of the tide had slowed. Bobbie reckoned it might be close to turning, but Slade was right about approaching crafts. Bobbie didn't want to be around when they arrived. "Dad, we've no time to debate this."

Bobbie took Jimmy's knife and strode to the corpse. In one swipe, she'd removed the rejuvenee's head. Bobbie's stomach flipped. She dry-heaved.

"Can we take them all?" Joy asked, ripping the tunic off the torso and fashioning it into a sack.

"No time." The sickening stench clawed at Bobbie's nostrils. "She's the leader, so she'll have more information than the others anyway."

"Bobbie, Joy, I can't let you..." Luke began.

"We're taking it. Let's go," Bobbie said. "Before any more Belus agents arrive. Argue about it later." Bobbie swept a look at Slade, sitting in the doorway of the hovercraft. Slade's hand was turning blue. "And we need to hurry if we're going to save Slade's arm."

Nurse Janet's body floated face-down in the water, two meters away.

"We can't leave her here," Bobbie said. Sadness for the brave woman who'd saved her life caught her off-guard. Maybe Janet's pregnancy wasn't like Joy's had been. Maybe Janet's baby had been viable.

Luke scooped up Janet's body and carried her to the hovercraft. Bobbie helped Luke gently lay her at the back of the cargo area, and climbed in beside her.

Joy stowed the severed head, then stepped down into water that swirled around her thighs and grabbed for another rejuvenee's body, spinning in the current carried towards her.

"No!" Pain tore through her torso as Bobbie reached for Joy and missed.

"I've got it. Just one more," Joy yelled over her shoulder. The body jerked as Joy's hold counteracted the pull of the current. For a second Joy seemed able to pull against the tide, but another body whacked her legs from behind and swiped her feet out from beneath her. Joy disappeared beneath the water as Bobbie lunged again. No luck.

Bobbie jumped into the water, but held on to the hovercraft with one hand and grappled in the water with the other. Rushing water sucked at her feet. Bobbie felt tangled hair, hopefully not a dead body or seaweed, and pulled up in one sharp movement, ignoring her pounding heart and the stab from her ribs. Joy's head popped out of the water, her eyes wide, coughing, her hands clawing at Bobbie's arm. Joy's feet gained traction below her. She dove toward Bobbie and clutched her sister to her.

"I've got you." Bobbie hauled Joy up the steps into the hovercraft with her and lay on the ground beside her sister, looking up into her father's stricken eyes.

"What the hell were you thinking, Joy?" Luke said.

Bobbie recognized his anger from her childhood, and it felt like the only normal thing that had happened in a long time.

"Sorry. No time." Joy recovered, scrambled to her feet, and jumped in behind the controls, leaving Bobbie on the floor of the hovercraft. Luke, speeding through a take-off checklist, joined Joy at the controls seconds later.

Rolling onto her side and getting to all fours, Bobbie welcomed the humming throb of the engines firing up as she crawled to a storage box in the back of the hovervan and found cargo-wrap to cover Janet's body. Bobbie gasped and grunted with pain at every movement, but at least she was alive. Janet's body wrapped, exhaustion hit Bobbie proper. She made her way back to her seat on all fours, not trusting herself to stand.

Bobbie caught her breath at the thought of Hicks. What was Belus doing to him? Bobbie revisited that sense of sinking through deep water. How could she float without Hicks?

She let her mind slide back to a better time – a moment in the sun: Hicks, twelve years old, pushing Gracie's chair at speed along the seafront at Portstewart. The wind tugging their hair sideways, stealing their laughter, and tossing it to the waves.

Bobbie had loved Hicks even then.

The hovercraft rose, and the ruins below slid out of view.

Heavy-limbed, Bobbie turned in her seat and crouched. Half-walking, half-pulling herself along the seats, she made her way to the passenger seats behind Joy to check on Slade. Her pulse was weak, but Slade was cognizant.

"You should be strapped in," Slade hissed through gritted teeth. Pain etched deep into her face, and her eyes rolled beneath drooping lids.

Bobbie adjusted Slade's seatback, elevating her feet. Blood oozed through the bandage around Slade's shoulder.

"She needs a transfusion," Bobbie said. "Where's the base?" She pulled a plastic medical case from the cargo area before strapping herself into the seat beside Slade's.

"One second." Luke's eyes zoned out for a few seconds, then refocused. "There, I've stopped your blink transmission. Best to play it safe until we get to Norway."

"Norway?" Bobbie asked, confused. "That's where the base is? Why? There's such a large population there. How can you have a secret base there?"

"The fjords are mazes," Luke said. "Not all of them have been mapped since the sea levels rose." The engines whirred, and the craft lifted.

"The medical case has a saline drip kit," Bobbie said, rummaging through the plastic case and assembling the kit. She pulled out a packet and read the label with a small but brief surge of welcome relief. "There's enough syntho-blood here to keep Slade alive for a few hours, but we need to get her to a proper medical center. Does the base have that?"

"It does," Luke said. "Just keep her alive until we get there."

Another wave of fatigue washed over Bobbie. Their team members were either beaten or broken – or left behind.

Swim to the surface, Bobbie, I don't like it down here. Bobbie shook Hicks' voice from her head. Beside her, Slade's eyes closed. Her breaths lengthened. Sleep wouldn't do her any harm, but Slade needed that transfusion.

"Won't be needing this now," Joy said, handing a bloody rag to Bobbie.

"I'm not sure it would have worked," Bobbie said.

"It would have," Luke said from the controls. "Good thinking, Bobbie. The signal from the nano-trackers is weak, but they still would have sent enough data for us to find her."

"One less item on my to-do list, li'l sis." Bobbie patted Joy's shoulder.

Take the victories, Hicks always told her.

As the craft rose higher, Bobbie watched the sea engulf the tiny island. The tide of rejuvenees was rising too. Would the Candels sink beneath it?

Bobbie struck out for the surface, rising up on hope and bobbing into the fresh air of a positive mind. Bobbie would find Hicks, somehow. Together they could fix rejuvenation. Together they could bring down Lisette Fox. Once they were back together, Bobbie and Hicks would have a fighting chance to stay afloat.

THE END

ABOUT THE AUTHOR

BYDDI LEE, A NATIVE OF ARMAGH, County Armagh, Northern Ireland, wrote Rejuvenation, a speculative fiction trilogy, after having published flash fiction, short stories and her novel, *March to November.*

Byddi co-founded and manages Flash Fiction Armagh which was shortlisted as Best Regular Spoken Word Night in the Saboteur Awards[1]. She co-edits *The Bramley – An Anthology of Flash Fiction Armagh* with two other members of the Armagh Theatre Group. Byddi wrote *IMPACT – Armagh's Train Disaster* which was staged for the anniversary of the tragedy in June 2019 in the Abbey Lane Theatre in Armagh.

In October 2019, Byddi received an Arts Council for Northern Ireland (ACNI) grant for her writing.

---

[1] Sabotage Reviews provides dynamic commentary and reviews with focus on independent, small-budget literature; poetry pamphlets, short stories and live performance.

WORKS BY THE AUTHOR

NOVELS

THE REJUVENATION TRILOGY
Rejuvenation, book 1
Rejuvenation, book 2
Rejuvenation, book 3

March To November

PLAYS

IMPACT – Armagh's Train Disaster

Printed in Great Britain
by Amazon

78584699R00123